IGCSE 0523 & IBDP Chinese B SL

FUTURE Coursebook 2

展望

吳星華
編著

掃描二維碼或登錄網站 www.jpchinese.org/future2 聆聽錄音、下載參考答案。

Scan the QR code or log in to listen to the recording, and download the reference answer.

Preface

前言

《展望》是一套為有一定中文基礎的學習者編寫的國際中文教材，主要適合學習 IGCSE 中文作為第二語言（0523）和 IBDP 中文 B 普通課程（SL）的學生使用。

本套教材共兩冊，旨在通過對相關主題和語言文本的學習，培養學生的語言能力、概念性理解能力，加強學生對中華文化的認識和對多元文化的理解。通過學習本書，發展學生的接受技能、表達技能和互動交流技能。

Future is a set of international Chinese coursebooks written for learners with a certain Chinese foundation. It is chiefly applicable for students who are learning IGCSE Chinese as a Second Language (0523) and IBDP Chinese B Standard Level (SL) courses.

The set of coursebooks includes two volumes, aiming at enhancing language skills, conceptual understanding, and strengthening students' perception of Chinese culture and multi-culture through the study of related topics and texts. Moreover, students' receptive skills, expression skills and communication skills will be developed by studying the series of books.

教材特色 Coursebook Features

學習目標

明確每課聽、説、讀、寫的具體學習目標，全面培養四項技能。

Clarify the specific goals of listening, speaking, reading and writing in each lesson, then cultivate them comprehensively.

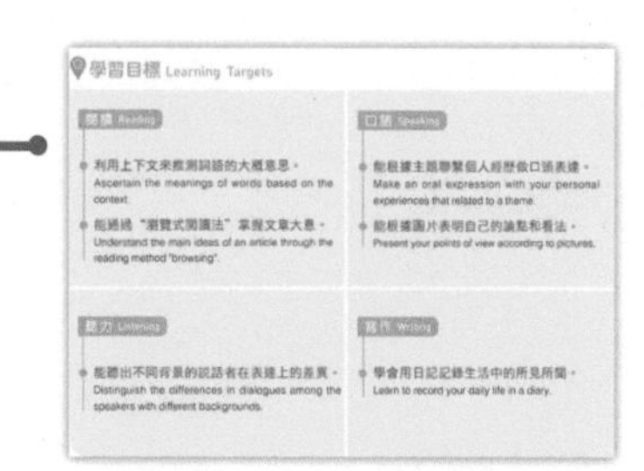

課文

緊扣 IGCSE 0523 和 IBDP 中文 B 的新大綱，題材豐富，體裁多樣。

Texts are closely aligned with the latest test syllabus of IGCSE 0523 and IBDP Chinese B courses with various perspectives and text types.

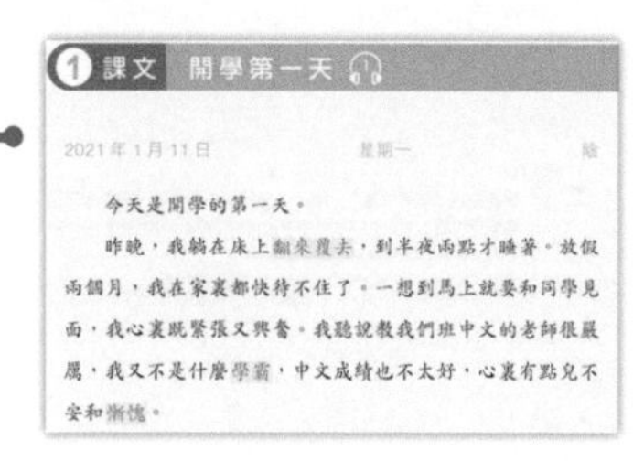

生詞短語

選取了使用頻率高、交際性強的詞語，符合學生的實際需要。

Vacabulary selected is high frequently used and practical communicative which meets students' needs.

Culture Point

1. 在中國，為了讓學生保持身體健康，保護視力，避免近視，大多學校每天都要做早操和眼保健操。
In China, students in most school need to do morning exercises and eye exercises every day. These are for keeping health and protecting their eyes from bad eyesight and nearsightedness.
2. 語言具有地域性特點，特定的語言存在著差異，不同地區叫法不一樣。如：
Languages contain regional traits. There are differences in a specific language, and the name of it can differ in regions. For example:

文化提示

選取典型的中國文化現象加以說明，加強學生對中華文化的感知與理解。

Explain the typical phenomena of Chinese culture to reinforce the students' perception and understanding on Chinese culture.

課文理解 Reading Comprehensions

① 為什麼"我"還沒開學，心裏就既緊張又興奮？
② 到了學校為什麼"我"的心情又變好了？
③ 為什麼大家都說新學期校園生活會十分忙碌？
④ "我"最害怕的事情是什麼？

課文理解

針對課文內容提出相應的問題，考察學生對課文的理解程度。

Inspect students' comprehension level of the text by asking students the corresponding questions.

概念與拓展理解 Concepts and Further Understanding

概念與拓展理解

結合課文，基於概念提出拓展問題，培養學生的概念性理解能力。

Students are able to learn conceptual comprehension skills by answering the extended questions based on the concepts in the text.

語法重點 Key Points of Grammar

語法重點

重視語法，對語法點進行了細緻的講解。

Detailed explanations on grammar points are included.

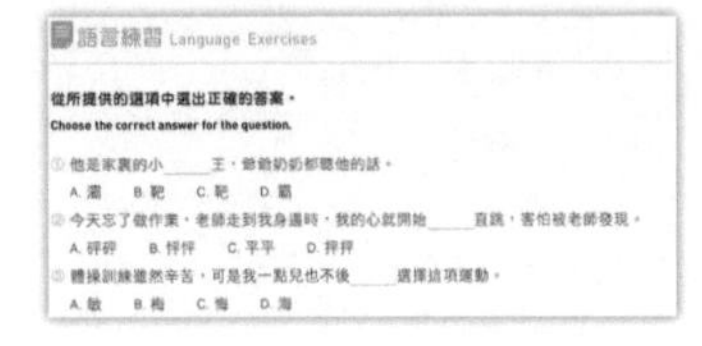

語言練習 Language Exercises

語言練習

設計了豐富的語言練習，以鞏固所學內容，考察學生對語言知識的掌握情況。

A variety of language exercises are designed to reinforce what students have learned, and inspect how much they have learned.

口語訓練 Speaking Tasks

口語訓練

提供 IGCSE 0523 和 IBDP 中文 B SL 考試的口語材料和口試技巧，培養學生在特定語境下互動交流的能力。

Oral presentation materials and skills related to IGCSE 0523 and IBDP Chinese B SL are provided to help students improve the ability on interaction and communication in particular contexts.

閱讀訓練

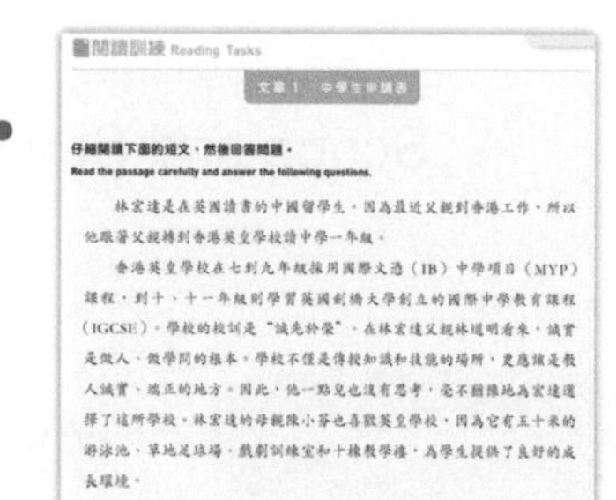

提供 IGCSE 0523 和 IBDP 中文 B SL 考試的閱讀材料、練習題目和閱讀技巧，培養學生理解不同類型文本的能力。

Reading materials, exercises, and skills related to IGCSE 0523 and IBDP Chinese B SL are provided to cultivate students' abilities to comprehend different types of texts.

聽力訓練

提供 IGCSE 0523 和 IBDP 中文 B SL 考試的聽力材料、練習題目和聽力技巧，培養學生的中文聆聽能力。

Listening materials, exercises, and skills related to IGCSE 0523 and IBDP Chinese B SL are provided to cultivate students' listening ability.

寫作訓練

覆蓋 IGCSE 0523 和 IBDP 中文 B SL 考試的所有寫作文本格式，提供寫作技巧，指導學生針對不同的目的進行寫作。結合不同的文本類型、語體和語氣，培養學生的概念性理解能力。

In accordance with all the writing formats of the IGCSE 0523 and IBDP Chinese B SL, the coursebooks contain the skills and techniques to guide students to write articles on various themes. By combining different types of text, styles, and tones, students will improve their conceptual understanding abilities.

錄音及參考答案

掃描二維碼或登錄網站 www.jpchinese.org/future2 聆聽錄音、下載參考答案。

Scan the QR code or log in to listen to the recording, and download the reference answer.

Contents 目錄

Scope and Sequence

單元	課	章節	內容	語言點	技巧	寫作法	文體	文化
Unit 1 My Personal World 個人世界	Lesson 1 Community life 社區生活	課文一	感謝義工 P8	被動句		如何敘述一件事	信件	飲食文化、尊敬老人
		課文二	年輕的志工 P14	能願動詞				
		閱讀理解一	資助感謝信 P20		提問法			
		閱讀理解二	《如常》紀錄片分享會 P22		如何閱讀廣告			
		聽力一	義工周小麗 P24					
		聽力二	傳承 P25		如何聽對話和對白			
		口語訓練			在口頭及書面表達中使用成語			
	Lesson 2 Customs and Traditions 風俗與傳統	課文一	各地慶祝春節 P30	轉折關係複句		如何寫好新聞報道	新聞報道	中國的傳統節日
		課文二	年輕人應該重視對傳統節日的慶祝 P36	選擇關係複句				
		閱讀理解一	李子柒為何火遍全球 P44		如何抓住新聞的主要內容			
		閱讀理解二	蔡志忠漫畫 P46		連句成段，理解段落意思			
		聽力一	中國民俗 P48		提高聽力心理素質			
		聽力二	年輕茶藝師 P49		遇到聽不懂的字詞怎麼辦			
		口語訓練			如何介紹節日			
	Lesson 3 Lifestyle 生活方式	課文一	營養早餐指南 P54	遞進關係複句		指南的重點	指南	中國人的早餐文化、菊花、傘、筷子
		課文二	日常生活禮儀 P60	順承關係複句				
		閱讀理解一	疫情改變了我們的生活方式 P67		準確把握文章的寫作目的			
		閱讀理解二	青少年厭食問題的口頭報告 P70		分清主次，概括段落大意			
		聽力一	2020 新生活方式 P73					
		聽力二	如何養成健康的網絡生活方式 P73		如何應對事實細節題和聽力填空題			
		口語訓練			如何讓口頭表達更真實			

Scope and Sequence

單元	課	章節	內容	語言點	技巧	寫作法	文體	文化
Unit 2 Our World 我們的世界	Lesson 4 Science and Technology 科學與技術	課文一	看《嫦娥五號直播》有感 P81	因果關係複句		如何寫好評論	評論	四大發明、嫦娥奔月、中國高鐵
		課文二	科技改變生活 P89	假設關係複句				
		閱讀理解一	第六屆智能城市博覽會 P95		尋讀法			
		閱讀理解二	人類最糟糕的發明 P98		關鍵點的劃注			
		聽力一	基因編輯 P101		如何猜詞語			
		聽力二	對話鍾南山 P102		如何讀題			
		口語訓練			如何描述事物			
	Lesson 5 Arts 藝術	課文一	學習音樂有利於學生發展 P107	介詞		如何確定立場	辯論	中國民樂、京劇
		課文二	京劇學習指南 P115	副詞				
		閱讀理解一	新加坡藝術 P122		發揮想象力，理解句子的意思			
		閱讀理解二	在線少兒美術課程 P125					
		聽力一	美的感受 P127		如何應對填寫詞語的題型			
		聽力二	藝術人生 P128					
		口語訓練			欲揚先抑			
	Lesson 6 Education and Future Career Plans 教育與未來職業規劃	課文一	申請大學獎學金 P133	目的關係複句		如何在個人陳述中說明自己的優缺點	個人陳述	孔子、北京師範大學、中國四大名著、秦始皇陵兵馬俑
		課文二	VR 教學體驗 P140	結果補語				
		閱讀理解一	2 1 世紀的學生需要哪些能力 P147		積累詞語和句子			
		閱讀理解二	維護校園秩序指南 P149					
		聽力一	混合式學習方式 P152		圈畫關鍵詞			
		聽力二	素養教育 P153					
		口語訓練			如何介紹職業規劃			

單元	課	章節	內容	語言點	技巧	寫作法	文體	文化
Unit 3 The World Around Us 同一個世界	Lesson 7 Globalization 全球化	課文一	全球化對傳統文化影響的口頭報告 P160	數詞		如何寫好口頭報告	口頭報告	麵條、尊老愛幼
		課文二	防範恐怖襲擊指南 P166	承接關係複句				
		閱讀理解一	舌尖上的世界 P173		簡單提取信息			
		閱讀理解二	關於疫情全球化的思考 P176					
		聽力一	全球化 P178					
		聽力二	全球化是世界衝突的根源 P179		搶讀預測			
		口語訓練			如何做口頭報告			
	Lesson 8 The Environment 環境	課文一	保護地球 從我做起 P183	讓步關係複句		如何寫小冊子 / 宣傳冊 / 傳單	小冊子 / 宣傳冊 / 傳單	勤儉節約、公德心
		課文二	一次性口罩對生態環境的影響 P190	感歎句				
		閱讀理解一	地球遭到破壞的四大現象 P196		從說明文中準確獲取信息			
		閱讀理解二	全球變暖的十大危害 P199					
		聽力一	後天 P201					
		聽力二	光污染 P201		學會做筆記			
		口語訓練			如何回答體驗類的問題			
	Lesson 9 Recycling Resource and Renewable Energy 回收資源與可再生能源	課文一	創建綠色校園 P206	祈使句		如何寫提案	提案	天人合一、木材水運、水磨
		課文二	開發可再生能源 P212	可能補語				
		閱讀理解一	各國節水方法 P219					
		閱讀理解二	快時尚破壞生態環境 P221		如何找近義詞			
		聽力一	為地球發聲 P224					
		聽力二	新加坡垃圾島 P225		培養即時複述的習慣			
		口語訓練			如何回答觀點類的問題			

My Personal World
個人世界

Unit

Lesson 1

Community Life
社區生活

Lesson 2

Customs and Traditions
風俗與傳統

Lesson 3

Lifestyle
生活方式

Lesson

1 Community Life

社 區 生 活

導 入 Introduction

“社區”是相互有聯繫、有某些共同特徵的人群共同居住的一定的區域。社區成員之間的聯繫紐帶是共同的語言、風俗和文化，由此產生團結和歸屬感。每個社區都有共同的活動場所或活動中心。生活在社區的每一個年輕人要認識到集體生活的重要性，互幫互助，為改善社區環境盡一份力。

A "community" could be defined as a certain area where people get connected with each other and have some common characteristics. The ties linking the community members are common languages, customs and cultures, resulting in a common sense of union and belonging. Every community has a common activity venue or activity center. Every young person living in the community should understand the importance of living in a community. People should help each other and contribute to improve the community environment.

學習目標 Learning Targets

閱讀 Reading

- 能通過“提問法”掌握文章大意。
  Grasp the general idea of the article through the Questioning Method.

口語 Speaking

- 能在口頭及書面表達中使用成語，增強語言的表現力和感染力。
  Use idioms in speaking and writing to enhance the expressiveness and appeal of Chinese language.

聽力 Listening

- 能聽懂對話和獨白。
  Understand the conversation and monologue.

寫作 Writing

- 學會敘述一件事。
  Learn to narrate a story in detail.

生詞短語

biān jí
編 輯 editor

yì qíng
疫 情 epidemic

shè qū
社 區 community

xīn guān fèi yán
新 冠 肺 炎 covid-19

Wǔ hàn
武 漢 the capital of Hubei Province

zhào gù
照 顧 take care of

bài nián
拜 年 wish happy new year

gū dān
孤 單 lonely

gǎn shòu
感 受 feel

wēn nuǎn
溫 暖 warmth

zhàn shèng
戰 勝 overcome

xìn xīn
信 心 confidence

liáng tǐ wēn
量 體 溫 take temperature

dǎ sǎo wèi shēng
打 掃 衛 生 clean up

yě shēng dòng wù
野 生 動 物 wild animals

guān huái
關 懷 care

gǔ lì
鼓 勵 encourage

1 課文 感謝義工

尊敬的編輯：

您好！我是香港沙田居民。最近在《香港日報》上讀到一些疫情期間發生的故事，我覺得很感動。因此，我也想跟您說說我的經歷，希望更多的人看到在社區發生的好人好事。

2019 年新冠肺炎疫情發生後，由於我那段時間去過武漢，大家怕我把肺炎傳給其他人，所以我就被要求待在家裏，哪裏也不能去。我妻子很早就去世了，我也沒有孩子，所以自己一個人住，沒人照顧我。社區義工了解了我的情況以後，就輪流給我送飯菜，解決我的生活困難。這次新冠肺炎疫情剛好發生在春節期間，飛機、火車、汽車都停了，人們無法出門，各自待在家裏。親戚朋友也不能上門，大家都改用微信拜年，沒有人可以說話，這讓我覺得更孤單了。還好，義工經常給我打電話，關心我的生活。他們有空的時候，也買一些禮物送到我家門口。雖然只能遠遠地看著他們，但這些都讓我感受到了家的溫暖，也讓我對香港戰勝疫情充滿信心。後來，香港疫情好一些了，義工們就親自上門，幫我量體溫，打掃衛生，還教我如何預防新冠肺炎，比如要經常洗手，多喝水，不吃野生動物等等。這次因疫情而待在家裏的經歷，讓我感受到了社區義工帶來的家人般的關懷，如果沒有他們，我不知道如何度過這些隔離的日子。

新冠肺炎疫情雖然很嚴重，但是在社區義工的關心和照顧下，我仍感到非常幸福。再次感謝社區義工對我生活上的細心照顧。希望編輯能把我的故事分享給大家，鼓勵大家互相幫助，一起渡過這次難關！

此致

敬禮！

李大雙

2020年5月2日

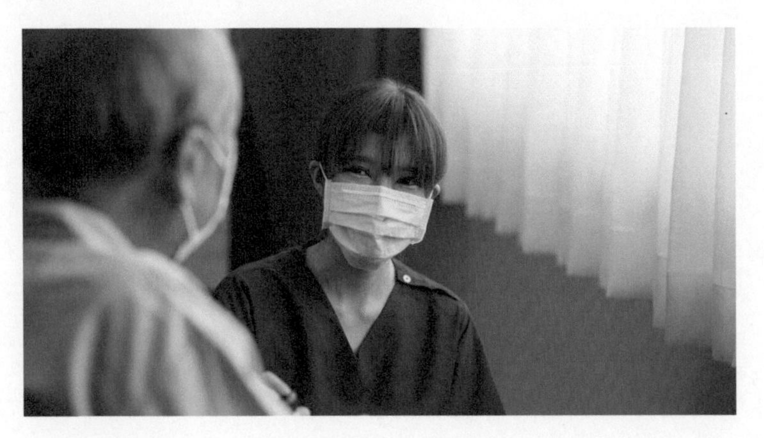

Culture Point

飲食文化 Food Culture

中國人有"藥補不如食補"的說法，人們希望通過食補達到強健身體的目的。在有些人的觀點中，越是稀有或奇怪的食材往往越具有神奇的藥效。但這種觀點卻害了很多野生動物。在科技高度發達的今天，我們應該以科學的眼光看待事物。現在的中醫也基本都是使用草藥，以動物入藥的極少。食用野生動物是人類無知的表現。

Chinese people believe that "Diet cures more than doctors". People hope to strengthen their body through food. Some people believe that very rare or strange materials for cooking always have magical effects. But this view has harmed many wild animals. Nowadays, we have highly developed technology and we should look at things from a scientific perspective. Even the traditional Chinese medicine is herbal based these days and very few animals are used as Chinese medicine. The existence of the market of wild animals as food is people's ignorance.

語法重點 Key Points of Grammar

被動句 Passive Sentences

① "被"字句用於表示被動的含義，主語通常是謂語動詞的受事，由"被"引出動作的發出者。

The word "被" is commonly used in passive sentences. The subject is usually the object of the verb. The executor of the action usually appears after "被" in the sentence.

E.g.
- 我被老師罵了。I was scolded by the teacher.
- 我被媽媽痛打了一頓。I was beaten up by my mother.

② 在口語中，也常用“讓”“叫”“給”來代替“被”。
In spoken language, we can use “讓” “叫” or “給” to replace “被”.

E.g.
- 這張紙叫小孩弄髒了。The paper was soiled by the child.
- 森林讓火燒光了。The forest was burned down by fire.

③ 有時候句子中雖然沒有“被”“讓”“叫”“給”等詞，但有意義上的被動。
Some sentences don't have “被” “讓” “叫” “給”, but they are passive sentences in the actual meaning.

E.g.
- 衣服弄髒了。The clothes are soiled.
- 作業做完了。The homework is done.

課文理解 Reading Comprehensions

① 李大雙為什麼要寫這封信？

② 李大雙為什麼被要求待在家裏？

③ 義工為李大雙做了哪些事情？

④ 為什麼李大雙對戰勝新冠肺炎疫情充滿信心？

⑤ 義工教李大雙如何預防新冠肺炎？

概念與拓展理解 Concepts and Further Understanding

① 課文一的寫作對象是誰？Who is the target audience in Text 1?

② 課文一的語氣是親切、自然還是尊敬的？為什麼？
Is the tone of Text 1 kind, natural or respectful? Why?

③ 如果寫作對象改成李大雙的朋友，寫信的方式還一樣嗎？
If the target audience is changed to a friend of Li Dashuang, will the way of writing the letter still be the same?

④ 如果沒有義工的關心，李大雙能渡過這次難關嗎？為什麼？
Without the care of volunteers, can Li Dashuang survive this difficult time? Why?

⑤ 義工為什麼要幫助李大雙？社區的作用是什麼？
Why do volunteers help Li Dashuang? What is the role of a community?

語言練習 Language Exercises

在方塊裏填字，使內框與外框的字組成詞語。

Fill in the inner boxes to make compound words with the words in outer box.

①

受	流	恩
好	□	冒
情	想	覺

②

習	體	度
保	□	和
柔	馨	暖

③

用	封	心
書	□	賴
箱	息	任

④

海	開	口
過	□	鍵
懷	注	心

從所提供的選項中選出正確的答案。Choose the correct answer for the question.

⑤ 日本女孩花澤靜香刻苦學習中文，就是為了有一天能到中國當義工______顧大熊貓。

A. 昭　B. 召　C. 照　D. 招

⑥ 到今天下午為止，總共有兩千五百人得了新冠______炎。

A. 肝　B. 肥　C. 市　D. 肺

⑦ 法國新冠肺炎疫情發生後，當地華人______區取消了很多春節活動。

A. 社　B. 設　C. 土　D. 址

⑧ 新加坡機場對所有外國旅客都要進行______體溫檢查。

A. 旦　B. 量　C. 兩　D. 裏

⑨ 大年初一，我們全家都要去爺爺奶奶家______年。

A. 拜　B. 掰　C. 百　D. 邦

⑩ 家裏安安靜靜的，一個人也沒有，我有點兒______單。

A. 呱　B. 瓜　C. 孤　D. 狐

選出與下列劃線詞語意思相同的選項。

Choose the synonyms of the underlined words below.

⑪ 冬天裏喝一杯熱茶，讓人覺得很暖和。 ☐

A. 溫暖　B. 開心　C. 溫柔　D. 關懷

⑫ 大家要對戰勝疾病有信心，不要相信虛假信息。 ☐

A. 打敗　B. 戰鬥　C. 經歷　D. 渡過

選擇正確的詞語填空。Fill in the blanks with the right words.

武漢　感謝　感受　疫情　關懷　飲食　野生動物　信心　編輯

⑬ 這次去越南旅行，媽媽再三叮囑我要注意____________衛生。

⑭ 2020 年年初，在____________發生的新冠肺炎疫情引起了全世界的關注。

⑮ 冬天到了哈爾濱，你就可以____________到“冰天雪地”。

⑯ 認為吃____________後身體就會變強壯的想法是錯誤的。

⑰ 在新冠肺炎____________期間，多數人都戴口罩出門。

⑱ 要做成一件事，首先必須要有____________。

⑲ 對於大家的幫助，我發自內心地表示____________。

⑳ 這本書很好，我想寫一封感謝信給這本書的____________。

㉑ 春節到了，獨居老人更需要我們的____________。

把下面的把字句變成被動句。

Rewrite the following sentences into passive sentences.

㉒ 小偷把我的錢搶走了。

㉓ 我把錢包落在的士（出租車 / 德士）上了。

㉔ 弟弟把我的自行車（腳踏車）弄丟了。

㉕ 我把爸爸的眼鏡摔壞了。

㉖ 妹妹把可樂都喝光了。

課堂活動 Class Activities

找詞語遊戲 Word Hunting Game

把學生分成 A、B 兩組。A 組同學面向白板坐，B 組同學背對白板。A 組選出一位同學，從課文一生詞表中選出一個詞語寫在白板上，例如：病毒。A 組的其他任意一個同學想一個包含詞語"病毒"的句子，然後講出來給大家聽，但是詞語"病毒"必須用"什麼"來代替，例如：最近，大家都很擔心受到"什麼"的傳染？B 組同學必須在 10 秒鐘內回答出"什麼"代表的詞語：病毒。每組猜 10 個詞，猜對一個得一分，得分多的組獲勝。裁判可以由老師來擔任。

Devide students into 2 groups which are named Group A and Group B. Students of Group A face the whiteboard to sit while Group B back to the whiteboard. One student from Group A writes a word chosen from the Text 1 vocabulary list on whiteboard. For example, 病毒. Any other student from Group A makes a sentence using " 病毒 " and speak out to class. But he / she must replace the word " 病毒 " with the word " 什麼 ". For example: Recently, people worry about what they might be affected by. Students from Group B must find out the word " 病毒 " from the vocabulary list for which the word " 什麼 " represents within 10 seconds. Each group answers 10 questions. One mark for each correct answer. Group with the higher final mark wins. Teacher may act as a judge.

口語訓練 Speaking Tasks

第一部分 **根據主題"社區生活"，做 2–3 分鐘的口頭表達。做口頭表達之前，先根據提示寫大綱。**

Make a 2-3 minutes oral presentation on the theme "community life". Before you start, use the form below to make an outline.

大綱 Outline	內容 Content
觀點 Perspectives	
事例 Examples	
名人名言 Famous quotes / 熟語 Idioms	
經歷 Experiences	
總結 Summary	

Tips

在口頭及書面表達中使用成語，能增強語言的表現力和感染力。成語是漢民族長期使用的定型化的短語，數量繁多，歷史悠久，運用廣泛，具有語言凝練、音韻和諧的特點。

The use of idioms in oral and written forms will enhance the expressiveness and appeal of the language. Idioms are fixed phrases used for a long time by the Han people in their language. They are numerous, historic and widely used. Idioms are condensed language and have harmonious phonology.

第二部分 **回答下面的問題。Answer the following questions.**

① 你參加過哪些社區活動？　② 你認為參加社區活動重要嗎？為什麼？

③ 你認為社區開展什麼活動會比較受歡迎？　④ 籌辦社區活動應該注意什麼？

⑤ 有些人認為社區活動對老年人比較有用，對青少年沒有什麼好處，你怎麼看？

生詞短語

zhì gōng
志工 volunteer

bāng dào máng
幫倒忙
do a disservice

má fan
麻煩 trouble

běn néng
本能 instinct

xīn lǐ sù zhì
心理素質
psychological quality

chǔ jìng
處境 situation

péi bàn
陪伴 accompany

huāng zhāng
慌張 panic

shī kòng
失控 out of control

shāng hài
傷害 hurt

xīn líng
心靈 soul

cuò zhé
挫折 failure

máng mù
盲目 blindness

2 課文 年輕的志工

——訪問志工薛小紅

很多年輕人受到志工的鼓勵和影響，也加入了他們的行列。今天，我們很高興請來了台灣最年輕的志工薛小紅（以下簡稱"薛"），她雖然才十五歲，但是參與志工行動快五年了。下面請她來和我們談談對做志工的看法。

記 小紅，你好！你能先給大家介紹一下志工是做什麼的嗎？

薛 志工是自願付出自己的時間去幫助他人的人。我的看法是：做志工是在不幫倒忙的情況下給對方提供幫助，帶來快樂。這聽起來簡單，做起來卻不容易。你的出現如果給對方造成麻煩就不好了。

記 你為什麼這麼小就開始做志工呢？

薛 我媽媽也是志工。最初是因為家裏沒人照看我，媽媽就帶著我一起做志工。後來是因為本能，我覺得做志工就是自己想做，而不是為了什麼而做。另外，通過做志工，我也得到了很多快樂，所以我喜歡做志工。

記 那麼，你認為年輕人做志工要具備什麼條件呢？

薛 首先，我認為年輕人要有較好的心理素質。因為我們照顧的對象大多處境不好，他們有時心情也很差，你要想清楚你是否能接受。特別是我們年輕人的經驗不多，有時候很難應對。大多數時間志工都是在陪伴對方，這個過程中可能會出現各種各樣的問題，不慌張、不失控是做志工必須具備的基本條件。

記 年輕人做志工要注意什麼？

薛 就是要堅持。有些年輕志工一開始給對方很多關懷和愛心，可是沒過多久就突然不做了，這反而會給對方帶來很大傷害。

記 那你能對想做志工的年輕朋友說點兒什麼嗎？

薛 我想跟大家說，做志工是一件很平常的事，不要覺得做志工多麼偉大。其實，我們得到的遠比我們付出的多，比如心靈的成長、能平靜對待挫折等等。

記 是的，愛心不需要盲目，需要做足夠的準備，並用平常心對待。感謝你接受我們的採訪！

Culture Point

中華民族歷來就有助人為樂、扶貧濟困的傳統美德。到老人院做志工是對傳統美德的繼承與實踐。俗話說，"老吾老，以及人之老"，意思是孝敬和自己沒有血緣關係的老人，就像孝敬自己的長輩一樣。做志工就是弘揚中華民族敬老、愛老、助老的傳統美德。

The Chinese nation has the traditional virtues of helping others and helping the poor. Volunteering in a nursing home is the inheritance and practice of traditional virtues. As the saying goes, "love others' elderly as you would love your own." To be a volunteer is to promote the traditional virtues of the Chinese nation of respecting, loving and helping the elderly.

語法重點 Key Points of Grammar

能願動詞 Modal Verbs

能願動詞又叫助動詞，"想""會""能""要""可以"等放在動詞前面表示意願、能力或可能。

Modal verbs such as "想""會""能""要""可以" are used before verbs to show will, capability or possibility.

Structure 主語 + 想 / 會 / 能 / 要 / 可以 + 動詞 + 賓語 + 其他成分

Subject + 想 / 會 / 能 / 要 / 可以 + Verb + Object + Other elements

E.g.
- 我想去中國。I want to go to China.
- 我會講四種語言。I can speak four languages.
- 我能寫漢字。I can write Chinese characters.
- 我要出去。I am going out.
- 我可以說中文。I can speak Chinese.

注意 Notes

能願動詞的否定式，需要把“不”加在“想”“會”“能”“要”“可以”的前面。

The negative forms of these modal verbs are formed with “不” before them.

Structure 主語 + 不 + 想 / 會 / 能 / 要 / 可以 + 動詞 + 賓語 + 其他成分

Subject + 不 + 想 / 會 / 能 / 要 / 可以 + Verb + Object + Other elements

E.g. ● 我不想去中國。I don't want to go to China.

課文理解 Reading Comprehensions

① 什麼是志工？

② “幫倒忙”是什麼意思？

③ 通過做志工，薛小紅得到了什麼？

④ 做志工必須具備的基本條件是什麼？

⑤ 年輕人做志工需要注意什麼？

 概念與拓展理解 Concepts and Further Understanding

① 課文二屬於什麼文體？ What is the text type of Text 2?

② 志工、義工和志願者的意思都一樣嗎？

Are the meanings of 志工, 義工 and 志願者 all the same?

③ 課文二的寫作目的是什麼？ What is the writing purpose of Text 2?

④ 做志工可以要求來回的路費和午餐嗎？
Should volunteers ask for transport expenses and free lunches?

⑤ 採訪的語氣是正式的還是非正式的？為什麼？
Should the tone of the interview be formal or informal? Why?

語言練習 Language Exercises

把下面的詞語組成正確的詞組。Connect the corresponding words below to form a correct phrase.

① 社區	麻煩	② 傷害	挫折
鼓勵	學習	面對	相信
招惹	志工	盲目	身心

從生詞表裏找出與下列詞語意思相同或相近的詞。
Find words with the same or similar meanings as the following words in the vocabulary list.

③ 放縱＿＿＿＿＿＿ ④ 焦急＿＿＿＿＿＿ ⑤ 跟從＿＿＿＿＿＿

從生詞表裏找出與下列詞語意思相反的詞。
Find words with the opposite meanings to the following words in the vocabulary list.

⑥ 壓制＿＿＿＿＿＿ ⑦ 自覺＿＿＿＿＿＿ ⑧ 順利＿＿＿＿＿＿

選擇正確的詞語填空。Fill in the blanks with the right words.

幫倒忙　麻煩　本能　志工　心理素質　傷害　心靈

⑨ ＿＿＿＿＿一救出流浪狗，就趕緊將它送到了醫院。
⑩ 優美的大自然可以淨化人的＿＿＿＿＿。
⑪ 我們不要做＿＿＿＿＿他人的事情，要有同理心。

⑫ 她的__________很好，每次上台演講都不慌張。

⑬ 出生不久的小鴨子第一次下水就會游泳，因為這是它的__________。

⑭ 這件事我自己可以辦，就不__________你了。

⑮ 新冠肺炎疫情已經很嚴重了，媒體不應該__________，發佈不實信息。

判斷句子正誤，並訂正。Read the following sentences and correct the mistake if there is any.

⑯ 你要不吃飯。

⑰ 週末你想去不打乒乓球？

⑱ 我要去圖書館買東西。

⑲ 小明很厲害，他邊看電視邊做作業可以。

⑳ 我現在能不去國外旅行，因為新冠肺炎疫情還很嚴重。

課堂活動 Class Activities

社區居委會地圖 Community Center Map

你熟悉你所居住的社區居委會嗎？你認為好的居委會應該有哪些設施？請在下面的方框裏簡要畫出居委會的各種設施，向同學們介紹每個設施的功能，並解釋這些設施為什麼對提高居民的生活質量有幫助。

Are you familiar with your neighborhood committee center? What facilities do you think a good neighborhood committee center should have? In the box below, please briefly draw the various facilities of the neighborhood committee, introduce the function of each facility to the class and explain why these facilities are helpful to improve the life quality of the residents.

E.g.

- 乒乓球館：老年人可以在這裏打球，鍛煉身體。

  Table tennis room: the elderly can play table tennis and do exercise here.

口語訓練 Speaking Tasks

第一部分 **根據圖片，做 3-4 分鐘的口頭表達。做口頭表達之前，先根據提示寫大綱。**

Make a 3-4 minutes oral presentation based on the picture. Before you start, use the form below to make an outline.

大綱 Outline	內容 Content
圖片內容 Information of the picture	
圖片主題 + 文化 Theme of the picture and culture	
提出觀點 Make your points	
延伸個人經歷 Relate to personal experiences	
名人名言 Famous quotes / 熟語 Idioms	
總結 Summary	

第二部分 **回答下面的問題。Answer the following questions.**

① 你做過哪些義工？

② 為什麼要做義工？

③ 做義工的感受是什麼？

④ 你認為做義工是否可以收錢？

⑤ 如果你所在的社區還沒有開展義工活動，你將如何讓你的社區變得更好、更有活力？

技能訓練 Skill Tasks

閱讀訓練 Reading Tasks

文章 1 資助感謝信

仔細閱讀下面的短文，然後回答問題。

Read the passage carefully and answer the following questions.

尊敬的工會領導、叔叔、阿姨：

你們好！我叫徐大東，17 歲，2004 年 12 月 11 日在中國出生，現在加入了新加坡國籍，就讀於新加坡光明中學；我的弟弟叫徐小東，11 歲，在金文小學讀書。開學已經快兩個月了，在讀書的這些日子裏，我和弟弟一直很慶幸能得到工會提供的助學金，如果沒有工會提供的幫助，我和弟弟就沒有學校可以上。在這裏，我代表我的家人，向你們表示感謝！

我的父親徐衛東是新加坡的一名地鐵司機，我的母親張小英沒有上班，前不久還因為車禍失去了雙腿，現在在家休養，每個月需要去醫院做一次檢查。父親是我們家裏唯一工作的人，由於母親看病需要花很多錢，所以，家裏沒有剩餘的錢繼續供我和弟弟上學讀書。我曾經想放棄讀書，出去打工賺錢，幫助父親撐起這個家，減輕父親的負擔，讓弟弟可以完成學業。但這個想法遭到父親的強烈反對，他覺得讀書是最好的出路，不可以讓我失去未來。

就在最困難的時候，工會的領導、叔叔、阿姨們親自到我們家了解我們的生活條件和學習情況。回到工會後，馬上幫我和弟弟申請了“助學金”，還和工會其他叔叔阿姨一起，定期到我們家送我母親去醫院做健康檢查。

工會領導和叔叔阿姨們這樣的關愛，令我們感受到了家庭般的溫暖。正是在工會這個大家庭裏，我們學到了什麼是社會的“正能量”以及工會團結互助的精神。今後我將努力學習，爭取考上新加坡國立大學，將來可以去新加坡交通部工作，奉獻自己。我會以工會的叔叔阿姨為榜樣，傳承你們的愛心，幫助需要幫助的人！

此致

敬禮！

徐大東

2021 年 5 月 1 日

假設你是徐大東，根據以上短文，填寫助學登記表。

If you were Xu Dadong, fill in the registration form according to information from the passage.

助學登記表

① 姓名：	② 年齡：	③ 出生年月：
④ 出生地：	⑤ 國籍：	⑥ 就讀學校：
⑦ 父親：	⑧ 職業：	
⑨ 母親：	⑩ 職業：	
⑪ 兄弟姐妹：	⑫ 年齡：	⑬ 就讀學校：
⑭ 報考大學：		
⑮ 申請助學金的理由：		
⑯ 畢業後打算：		

Tips

提問法 Questioning

在閱讀過程中，學會用提問法來理解文章的整體結構，有助於了解文章的大意。

Asking questions while reading helps you to understand the overall structure of the article and catch the main idea of the article.

例如，文章 1 可以按照“作者為什麼要寫這封信”“事情是怎麼發生和發展的”“最後結局怎麼樣”這種提問法，把文章的整個思路梳理出來。

For example, you can sort out the main idea of passage 1 by asking questions like:

· Why did the author write this letter?

· How does the matter happen and be developed?

· What is the ending of the story?

請根據文章 1 填寫下表。Fill in the table below according to passage 1.

作者為什麼要寫這封信？	
事情是如何發生的？	
事情是如何發展的？	
最後結局怎麼樣？	

文章 2 《如常》紀錄片分享會

④ 分享者

作家蔣勳

他說：「你看到一個人受苦，你覺得不忍，那個是最了不起的資源。」

① ★ 《如常》紀錄片，海外首映！★

台灣團隊花費一年半時間製作，整理 7,000 多分鐘的紀錄影像，最後剪成 72 分鐘的影片成品。

② 紀錄了獨居老人、失去父母的少年、生病仍堅持做志工的中年人、跟生命戰鬥的人等多組人物故事，真實展現偏遠農村資源短缺、人口外流、留守兒童、隔代教育等社會問題……了解“志工人群”的關懷行動，傳達“付出不求回報”的信念，用生命陪伴生命的感人過程。

《如常》紀錄片，海外首映！新加坡專場！

③ 《如常》紀錄片分享會

【–7–】 2021 年 3 月 19 日（星期五）

【–8–】 3:30pm – 7:00pm

【–9–】 青年中心

【–10–】 只限六歲或以上者入場。

改編自：https://www.tzuchi.org.sg/news-and-stories/local-news/20191019/

根據 ❶、❷，選出最接近左邊詞語的解釋。把答案寫在橫線上。

According to ❶,❷, choose the correct definitions and write the answers on the lines.

① "紀錄片" ________ A. 第一次播放。

② "首映" ________ B. 記下要錄的片子。

③ "製作" ________ C. 長期一個人住。

④ "獨居" ________ D. 首次反映出真實情況。

⑤ "志工" ________ E. 以真實生活為創作的寫實影像。

F. 獨立。

G. 有志氣的工人。

H. 用原材料做成各種不同的作品。

I. 自願付出時間去服務社會的人。

根據 ❶、❷，選出五個正確的敘述，把答案寫在橫線上。

According to ❶,❷, choose five true statements and write the answers on the lines.

文中提到關於《如常》紀錄片的情況包括：

⑥ ________ A. 花了 18 個月製作。

________ B. 花了 7000 多分鐘製作。

________ C. 紀錄獨居老人的生活。

________ D. 展現單親家庭問題。

________ E. 展現人口流動問題。

F. 展現家庭教育問題。

G. 傳達志工奉獻精神。

H. 在新加坡製作。

根據 ❸，從下面提供的詞彙中，選出合適的詞填空。

According to ❸, choose an appropriate word from the list that completes each gap in the following text.

⑦ [–7–] ________ A. 年齡

⑧ [–8–] ________ B. 時間

⑨ [–9–] ________ C. 歲數

⑩ [–10–] ________ D. 地址

E. 入場

F. 日期

G. 地點

根據 ④，劃線的詞語指的是誰 / 什麼？從文本中找出詞語答題。

According to ④, to whom or to what do the underline words refer? Use words in the passage to answer.

⑪ 他說……

⑫ 那個是最了不起的資源……

選擇正確的答案。Choose the correct answer.

⑬ 這是________。

A. 一篇日記　B. 一張宣傳單　C. 一封書信　D. 一篇訪談稿

> **Tips**
>
> **如何閱讀廣告？**
>
> **How to read advertisements?**
>
> 首先，了解是誰寫的廣告；其次，知道廣告的目標人群和廣告的目的；最後，不要忽略細節，尤其注意特殊說明部分。一旦掌握了閱讀廣告的技巧，就可以全面理解廣告內容，並有針對性地快速答題。
>
> Firstly, be clear about who made the advertisements. Secondly, understand the target audience and purposes of the advertisements. Finally, don't ignore the details, especially pay attention to the special instructions. Once you have mastered the skills of reading advertisements, you will be able to understand the content of the advertisements as much as you could and answer the questions quickly.

聽力訓練 Listening Tasks

一、《義工周小麗》

你將聽到一位社區義工講述如何幫助社區居民的錄音。你將聽到兩遍，請根據聽到的信息改正每句話裏劃線的詞語。把答案寫在括號裏。

You will hear a volunteer telling the story of how she helped community residents. This audio clip will be played twice, please correct the underlined words in each sentence based on the information you heard. Write the answers in brackets.

請先閱讀一下問題。Please read the questions first.

例：周小麗今年四十三歲。
　　周小麗今年（四十五）歲。

① 周小麗每天到社區做至少 10 個小時的義工。
　　周小麗每天到社區做至少（__________）的義工。

② 每個得到過周小麗幫助的人，都對她的行為不以為然。
　　每個得到過周小麗幫助的人，都對她的行為（__________）。

③ 周小麗認為將知識教給別人是幫助社區的最基本的方法。
　　周小麗認為將知識教給別人是幫助社區的最（__________）的方法。

④ 在新冠肺炎疫情期間，周小麗幫助社區組織發放食物活動。
　　在新冠肺炎疫情期間，周小麗幫助社區組織（__________）活動。

⑤ 在社區做義工，周小麗覺得很疲憊。

在社區做義工，周小麗覺得很 (__________)。

⑥ 社區空間的改變影響了大家的生活質量。

社區空間的改變 (__________) 了大家的生活質量。

⑦ 社區管理者忽視了周小麗的建議。

社區管理者 (__________) 了周小麗的建議。

⑧ 周小麗所在的社區被評為香港最乾淨的社區。

周小麗所在的社區被評為香港最 (__________) 的社區。

二、《傳承》 4

你即將聽到第二個聽力片段，在聽力片段二播放之前，你將有四分鐘的時間先閱讀題目。聽力片段將播放兩次，聽力片段結束後，你將有兩分鐘的時間來檢查你的答案。請用中文回答問題。

You are going to hear the second audio clip. You have 4 minutes to read the questions before it starts. The audio clip will be played twice. After it ends, you have 2 minutes to check the answers. Please answer the questions in Chinese.

根據第二個聽力片段，回答問題 ①-⑩ 。Answer the questions ①-⑩ according to the second audio clip.

根據第二個聽力片段的內容，從 A，B，C 中，選出一個正確的答案，把答案寫在橫線上。

According to the second audio clip, choose the right answer for the questions. Write the answers on the lines.

① 這個節目播放於________。

A. 大年三十　B. 除夕　C. 大年初一

② 紀錄片的名字叫________。

A.《傳承》　B.《慈濟如常》　C.《陳瑞凰》

③ 紀錄片主要講述了________的故事。

A. 貧苦家庭的小孩　B. 孤苦老人　C. 以上都是

請在正確的選項裏打勾（✓）。Tick (✓) the correct options.

這是誰的觀點？	老人	陳瑞凰	老人和陳瑞凰
④ 要親身經歷才懂什麼是苦難。	____	____	____
⑤ 生活再寂寞也要忍耐。	____	____	____
⑥ 多活一天多賺一天。	____	____	____
⑦ 感激志工對自己的幫助。	____	____	____
⑧ 要把志工精神傳承下去。	____	____	____

回答下面的問題。Answer the following questions.

⑨ 紀錄片提出的關鍵問題是什麼？

⑩ 阿嬤沒去看醫生的原因是什麼？至少列出兩個。

Tips

如何聽對話和對白？
How to listen to dialogues?

聆聽對話的時候，第一遍要以平常心去聽，千萬不要為沒有聽懂其中一兩個生詞而著急，以至於影響後面信息的獲取。另外，要學會邊聽邊記錄一些重要信息，例如數字、年份、地點以及人物關係等，這樣做的目的是為第二次聽錄音時提供依據，對第一次聽到的信息進行檢查，查缺補漏，並根據試題做出正確的選擇。

When listening to a dialogue, keep an easy mind when the audio is played for the first time. Don't be panic because of one or two new vocabularies you don't understand. This will affect the acquisition of information in the later part of the audio. In addition, learn to write down some important information while listening, such as numbers, year, location, people's relationships, etc. This is to provide support for the second time listening to verify the information in the audio; catch some missing information and make the right choice based on the questions.

寫作訓練：給編輯的信 Writing Tasks: Reader's Letters

熱身

● **根據課文一，討論給編輯的信的格式是什麼。According to Text 1, discuss the format of the reader's letters.**

你認為應該如何寫好這封信？How do you think to write a proper reader's letter?

格式 參考課文一

標題

尊敬的編輯：

□□開頭：問候語 + 自我介紹 + 寫信目的

□□正文：事件發生的背景 / 發展 / 結局

□□結尾：對編輯的期待

□□此致

敬禮！

姓名

X 年 X 月 X 日

練習一

假設你是陳天，最近一家報紙正在討論是否應該將動物園遷出市區。對此主題，你所在社區居民舉辦了一場討論會，他們請你給該報寫一封信，反映大家討論的結果。

Tips

文體：給編輯的信

Text Type: Reader's Letter

給編輯的一封信是個人寫給報社編輯的一封信，主要針對最近在報紙上的文章或者主題，或者身邊發生的事向編輯表達自己的看法，語氣要正式。

A reader's letter is a letter written by an individual to the editor of a newspaper. It mainly expresses the writer's views to the editor on the recent articles or topics in the newspaper, or what happened around him/her. The tone should be formal.

以下是一些別人的觀點，你可以參考，也可以提出自己的意見。但必須明確表示傾向。字數：250–300 個漢字。

動物園遊客太多，導致交通堵塞，而且郊區環境對動物比較好。

動物已經習慣自己的生活環境，搬遷容易造成動物大量死亡。

Tips

如何敘述一件事？

How to describe an incident?

儘量圍繞"寫信目的"進行敘述，清楚說明自己的觀點或者說明事件是如何發生、發展的，並說明事件結局，結尾要再次表達自己的觀點和看法。

Focus on "the purpose of writing" and narrate the incident. Clearly state your point of view or explain how the incident occurred and developed, and address the outcome of the incident. Express your opinions again at the end of your writing.

練習二

政府決定在社區建立老人院，方便家人陪伴和照顧老人。但是住在社區的年輕人對此表示反對，大家聚在社區一起討論這件事，並決定讓你代表大家給報社寫一封信，向報社說明討論結果。選用合適的文本類型完成寫作。字數：300–480 個漢字。

演講稿	給編輯的信	博客

Lesson 2

Customs and Traditions
風俗與傳統

導入 Introduction

“百里不同風，千里不同俗”，反映了風俗會因地而異的特點。隨著社會的變遷，原有風俗中不合時宜的部分，也會隨著時代的變化而改變。中國人向來有“天下一家”的觀念，慶祝傳統節日有利於加強親人們之間的溝通與情感的共鳴，增強身份認同感。語言習得有助於更深入地了解當地飲食習慣和食物在傳統文化及其慶祝活動中的作用。

"Local customs vary over even small geographical distances", and this reflects the characteristics that customs will vary from place to place. As the society changes, the outdated parts of the original customs will also change with the times. The Chinese have always had the concept of "All the people under the sky are of one family". Celebration of traditional festivals is conducive to strengthen the communication and emotional resonance between relatives and enhance the recognition of identity. Language acquisition contributes to a deeper understanding of eating habits and the role of food in cultural celebrations and traditions.

學習目標 Learning Targets

閱讀 Reading

- 學會抓住新聞的主要內容。
  Learn to grasp the main content of the news.
- 能通過連接句子的方法理解段意。
  Use the method of connecting sentences to understand paragraph meaning.

口語 Speaking

- 學會介紹節日，説明節日的由來。
  Learn to introduce festivals and explain the origins of them.

聽力 Listening

- 提高做聽力題時的心理素質。
  Learn to improve the mental quality while listening.

寫作 Writing

- 學會寫新聞報道。
  Learn to write news reports.

1 課文 各地慶祝春節

2022 年 2 月 17 日　　程小芳報道

春節是中國人最重要的節日。同樣是慶祝春節，全國各地的慶祝方式卻不一樣。不過，不同特色的慶祝活動都體現了喜慶的氣氛和年的熱鬧。

北京人認為不逛廟會就不算過年。在廟會上，人們會看到精彩的舞龍、舞獅表演，還可以品嚐到各式各樣的地方小吃。遊客在逛廟會的時候最喜歡買風車。隨風而轉的風車代表一帆風順，轉個不停象徵著新年的好運不斷。風車不僅是工藝品，更是北京春節廟會的文化標誌之一。

在江西，有新年吃魚、掛乾魚的習俗。大家用竹子編出不同形狀的魚掛在門口，祝願生活幸福，年年有餘。有遊客表示："這麼大的魚，我還是第一次看到，真高興！跟魚沾點兒喜氣！"

"踩街"是福建傳統的春節節目。儘管這個活動已經有一百多年歷史了，它仍然是當下人們最喜歡的春節活動之一。演員裝扮成戲劇中的人物，走上街頭，跟著音樂節奏跳

生詞短語

- xǐ qìng 喜慶 joyous
- qì fēn 氣氛 ambience
- guàng miào huì 逛廟會 go to the temple fair
- pǐn cháng 品嚐 taste
- fēng chē 風車 windmill
- yī fān fēng shùn 一帆風順 smooth sailing
- xiàng zhēng 象徵 symbolize
- gōng yì pǐn 工藝品 handicraft
- biāo zhì 標誌 sign
- nián nián yǒu yú 年年有餘 with something left over every year
- zhān 沾 receive favors
- xǐ qì 喜氣 happiness
- cǎi jiē 踩街 walking on stilts
- fú jiàn 福建 Fujian Province
- jié mù 節目 program
- huó dòng 活動 activity
- niǔ yāng ge 扭秧歌 Yangko dances
- nián wèi 年味 Spring Festival atmosphere
- chuán chéng 傳承 inherit

舞。這些有趣的表演吸引了許多人停下腳步觀看。

在東北，大家最喜歡看扭秧歌。它原來是農民在田裏幹活時的一種舞蹈，現在卻成為不可缺少的群眾休閒娛樂活動。有觀眾表示：“每年春節我都會專門回來扭秧歌，感覺喜慶、紅火，非常有年味。希望我們的生活就像秧歌一樣，越來越好！”

春節期間，中國各地都會舉行豐富多彩的活動，在慶祝新年的同時，不但體現了地方風俗特色，也傳承了中華傳統文化。

Culture Points

春節 Chinese Spring Festival

春節是中國的農曆新年，在正月初一。在中國的傳統節日中，這是一個最重要、最熱鬧的節日。春節的前一天叫“除夕”。除夕之夜，是家人團聚的時刻，大家圍坐在一起，吃一頓豐盛的年夜飯。通常人們會邊聊天邊看電視節目，一直到天亮，這叫做守歲。過了除夕就是大年初一，人們就要走親戚，看朋友，互相拜年。拜年時要説一些祝願幸福、健康的吉祥話。這是春節的重要習俗。另外，放鞭炮和吃餃子也是春節很重要的兩個元素。

The first day of the first lunar month in China is the Chinese Spring Festival. Among all the traditional Chinese festivals, this is the most important and the most bustling one. New Year's Eve is the time for a happy reunion of all the family members. People sit around the table to have a sumptuous New Year's Eve dinner. Normally, people will chat and watch TV programs until dawn. This is called "shousui". From the first day of the lunar year, people start visiting relatives and friends to greet each other. Auspicious words of happiness and health are essential when greeting others. This is a very important custom for the Spring Festival. Firecrackers and dumplings are the other two important elements of the celebration.

語法重點 Key Points of Grammar

轉折關係複句 Adversative Complex Sentence

後一個分句與前個分句的意思相反或相對，或部分相反。

The meaning of the latter clause is opposite or relative to the previous clause, or partly opposite.

常用關聯詞 Common Conjunctive Words

雖然……但是 / 可是……；儘管……可是 / 還是……；……然而 / 卻……

... but / however... ; although / even though / even if... but / however...; ... but / however...

E.g.

- 雖然天氣很冷，但是我們都像往常一樣去游泳。
  Although it was very cold, we all went swimming as usual.
- 儘管考了 99 分，他還是不高興。
  Even though scoring 99 points in the test, he was still unhappy.
- 我有很多話要說，一時卻說不出來。
  There is much to say, but I can't speak out even a word.

課文理解 Reading Comprehensions

① 北京人過年為什麼要逛廟會？

② 江西人過年時為什麼要在門口掛魚？

③ "踩街" 在福建流行多久了？

④ 東北人過年時為什麼要扭秧歌？

⑤ 中國各地用不同的方式慶祝春節有什麼好處？

概念與拓展理解 Concepts and Further Understanding

① 為什麼要慶祝傳統節日？ Why do we celebrate traditional festivals?

② 傳統節日的慶祝方式為什麼隨著時間的流逝卻沒有改變？
Why has the traditional way of celebrating festivals not changed over time?

③ 慶祝活動在多大程度上反映了文化價值？
To what extent does the celebration reflect cultural values?

④ 這些慶祝活動如何使具有相似文化背景的人們更加團結在一起？
How do these celebrations bring people with similar culture backgrounds together more closely?

⑤ 隨著全球化進程的加快，我們看到各地的民俗文化受到威脅，這會給傳統知識和文化多樣性帶來哪些負面影響？
With the increasing global awareness, there are threats to folk cultural activities everywhere. What negative effects will it bring on the traditional knowledge and cultural diversity?

語言練習 Language Exercises

從所提供的選項中選出正確的答案。Choose the correct answer for the question.

① 毛毛的手被火燒到了，這幾天，他的手不能________水。

A. 佔　B. 站　C. 粘　D. 沾

② 公園裏的小草不能亂________。

A. 踩　B. 採　C. 彩　D. 睬

③ 慶祝中秋節有助於________承中華傳統文化。

A. 專　B. 傳　C. 轉　D. 磚

④ 心情不好的時候，我就喜歡________街。

A. 逛　B. 狂　C. 踩　D. 走

⑤ 我奶奶每天晚上都去公園________秧歌。

A. 丑　B. 妞　C. 紐　D. 扭

選出與下列劃線詞語意思相同的選項。Choose the synonyms of the underlined words below.

⑥ 春節到了，家家戶戶貼對聯，到處都是歡樂的氣氛。　☐

A. 喜歡　B. 喜慶　C. 喜愛　D. 慶祝

⑦ 明天你就要出國留學了，祝你一帆風順。 ☐

A. 一隻船在行駛 B. 勝利歸來 C. 順風行駛 D. 一切順利

選擇正確的詞語填空。Fill in the blanks with the right words.

風車 品嚐 象徵 藝術品 標誌 氣氛 年年有餘 喜氣 福建 年味

⑧ 吳老師上課喜歡帶大家做遊戲，課堂________很活躍。

⑨ 台灣的對面就是位於中國大陸東南部的________。

⑩ 週末我們打算去美食街________各地美食。

⑪ 開車要注意看路上安全行駛的________。

⑫ 龍是古代中國最高權力的________。

⑬ 中國人吃年夜飯的時候，一定要有魚，代表________。

⑭ 過年在家時，只要貼上春聯，掛上燈籠，再放個鞭炮，________就更濃了。

⑮ 美術館裏有很多價值連城的精美________。

⑯ 逛廟會的時候，每個小孩手裏都會拿著一個________，希望新的一年更加順利、快樂、幸福、健康。

⑰ 過年了，公園裏張燈結彩，________洋洋。

填入正確的關聯詞。Fill in the blanks with appropriate correlative conjunctions.

⑱ ____________天色已晚，但是老師仍然在教室裏備課。

⑲ 儘管我跟他說了對不起，____________他就是不原諒我。

⑳ 這間屋子很大，我____________看不到陽光。

㉑ 這次比賽他沒有拿到第一名，____________他並不灰心。

課堂活動 Class Activities

找一找 Lost and Found Games

老師在 PPT 上呈現 10 個左右的生詞。將學生分成兩組。讓 A、B 兩組學生同時記憶生詞。一分鐘後，學生閉上眼睛，老師在 PPT 上刪除或增加生詞。學生睜開眼睛，A、B 兩組搶答哪個生詞刪除或增加了。重複以上步驟，回答更快且正確率更高的小組獲勝。

The teacher presents about 10 new words on the PPT. Divide students into Group A and Group B. Students from both groups are to memorize the new words at the same time. One minute later, students are to close their eyes and the teacher deletes or adds more new words on the PPT. Students open eyes. Students from both groups need to quickly answer the changes of the word list. Repeat these steps and the group from which the students answer faster and with more correct answers wins.

口語訓練 Speaking Tasks

第一部分 **根據主題"風俗與傳統"，選擇一個傳統節日，做2-3分鐘的口頭表達。做口頭表達之前，先根據提示寫大綱。**

Choose a festival, make a 2-3 minutes oral presentation on the theme "customs and traditions". Before you start, use the form below to make an outline.

大綱 Outline	內容 Content
觀點 Perspectives	
事例 Examples	
名人名言 Famous quotes / 熟語 Idioms	
經歷 Experiences	
總結 Summary	

第二部分 **回答下面的問題。Answer the following questions.**

① 春節和聖誕節，你更喜歡慶祝哪一個節日，為什麼？

② 有些年輕的華人不願意慶祝中國傳統節日，更願意慶祝西方節日，對此你有什麼看法？

③ 你的學校是如何慶祝春節的？

④ 在你的國家，華人慶祝春節的方式和在中國有什麼不同嗎？

⑤ 在你的國家，有什麼傳統節日？你們怎麼慶祝？

Tips

如何介紹節日？

How to introduce a festival?

可以先說明節日的日期和由來，再運用舉例子的方法，簡要介紹一到兩個具有代表性的慶祝方式和節日習俗。如果能加上與節日相關的故事或傳說，你的口頭表達就會更加精彩。最後建議說說自己的經歷，再點出這個節日的意義。

You can first explain the date and origin of the festival. Then use the examples to briefly introduce one or two representative ways of celebration and festival customs. If you can add stories or legends related to the festival, your oral expression will be even more attractive. Finally, you'd better talk about your own experience and point out the meaning of this festival.

2 課文 年輕人應該重視對傳統節日的慶祝 6

尊敬的主席、評委，對方辯友：

大家好！我是高一（5）班的潘小安。今天辯論的主題是“年輕人是否應該重視對傳統節日的慶祝”。作為正方，我方認為“年輕人應該重視對傳統節日的慶祝”，以下是我方的理由：

首先，根據調查，80%的年輕人喜歡慶祝“外來節日”是因為他們覺得外來節日比較時髦。在他們看來，傳統節日沒有外來節日熱鬧、有趣。所以他們只關注萬聖節的南瓜，情人節的玫瑰，聖誕節的老人，忽視了農曆新年的舞龍、舞獅，端午節的龍舟，中秋節的燈籠。大家應該知道，傳統節日是民族文化的重要組成部分，沒有了這些傳統慶祝活動，我們將失去自己的文化特色，甚至丟失我們自己的信仰。

其次，每個傳統節日背後都有其不同的意義。例如，中國人過春節，體現了一家人嚮往和平、健康、快樂的生活願望；中秋節吃月餅，表達了遠在他鄉的人對家鄉的思念；元宵節吃湯圓，是希望萬事如意，家庭圓圓滿滿；端午節吃粽子，是為了紀念偉大的愛國詩人屈原。這些節日所代表的意義及飲食文化是任何一個外來節日都無法取代的。對方辯友，難道你們能否認這個事實嗎？

最後，我想告訴對方辯友，中國傳統節日體現的是愛國、愛家、自強不息的傳統文化精神。例如春節回家、清明節掃

生詞短語

píng wěi 評委 judge
biàn yǒu 辯友 debater
biàn lùn 辯論 debate
zhǔ tí 主題 theme
diào chá 調查 investigate
shí máo 時髦 fashionable
wàn shèng jié 萬聖節 Halloween
méi gui 玫瑰 rose
shèng dàn jié 聖誕節 Christmas
hū shì 忽視 ignore
duān wǔ jié 端午節 Dragon Boat Festival
xìn yǎng 信仰 faith
yuàn wàng 願望 wish
jì niàn 紀念 commemorate
qū yuán 屈原 Quyuan
zì qiáng bù xī 自強不息 exert oneself constantly
qīng míng jié 清明節 Qingming Festival
sǎo mù 掃墓 sweep a grave
rèn tóng gǎn 認同感 sense of identity
zhī yuán 支援 support
níng jù lì 凝聚力 cohesion

墓、端午節紀念屈原的傳統習俗能夠喚起人們對親人、家庭、故鄉、祖國的情感，喚起人們對文化的認同感。“一人有難，八方支援”“百善孝為先”等俗語就是傳統節日強大文化凝聚力的體現。正是因為有這些文化精神的存在，傳統節日及習俗經過幾千年後還能流傳到今天，這體現出了傳統節日強大的文化生命力。

綜上所述，我方再次強調“年輕人應該重視對傳統節日的慶祝”。我們應該停止盲目追求和崇拜外來文化。如果我們輕視自己的傳統文化，那麼我們將失去屬於自己的文化特色。中華傳統文化需要我們年輕人來傳承，我們應該從自身做起，加強對傳統文化的宣傳，保護、弘揚華人的傳統文化。

謝謝各位！

改編自：https://www.sohu.com/a/284313192_804689

生詞短語

qiáng diào
強 調 emphasize

chóng bài
崇 拜 adore

qīng shì
輕 視 despise

hóng yáng
弘 揚 carry forward

Culture Points

元宵節 The Lantern Festival

農曆正月十五，是中國傳統的元宵節。這天晚上，人們會聚在一起看花燈，猜燈謎，吃湯圓，希望家人團圓、和睦、幸福，生活圓圓滿滿。

The 15th day of the first lunar month is the Chinese traditional Lantern Festival. As night falls, people go in crowds to enjoy colorful lanterns, guess the riddles and eat glutinous rice dumplings at that time. This is to wish that family members will remain united, harmonious, happy and satisfied.

清明節 The Qingming Festival

清明節通常在農曆三月。在這一天，人們有掃墓和踏青插柳的習俗。中國人有敬老的傳統，對去世的先人更是緬懷和崇敬。因此，每到清明節這天，家家戶戶都要去祭掃祖先的墳墓，除雜草，添新土，上香，擺上食物和紙錢，表示對祖先的思念和敬意。

The Qingming Festival falls in the third lunar month or around. On this day, people have the custom of sweeping the graves for their ancestors, taking an outing in the countryside and wearing a willow twig on their head. The Chinese have the tradition to respect the aged, to cherish the memory of their forefathers and to respect them. Thus, when the day comes, every family will go to the countryside to hold a memorial ceremony at their ancestors' tombs. People get rid of any weeds growing around the tomb, add new earth, burn incense and offer food and paper coins to show their remembrance and respect for their ancestors.

端午節 The Dragon Boat Festival

農曆五月初五，是中國傳統的端午節。在這一天，人們要吃粽子，賽龍舟，來紀念中國古代偉大的愛國詩人屈原。

The fifth day of the fifth lunar month is the Chinese traditional Dragon Boat Festival. On that day, people eat zongzi (Pyramid-shaped dumplings made of glutinous rice wrapped in bamboo or reed leaves) and hold dragon-boat races to commemorate the great patriotic poet Qu Yuan in ancient China.

中秋節 The Mid-Autumn Festival

農曆八月十五，是中國傳統的中秋節。在這一天，人們有賞月和吃月餅的習俗。按照傳統習慣，中國人在賞月時，還要擺出瓜果和月餅等食品，一邊賞月一邊品嚐。月餅是圓的，象徵著團圓。這時，遠離家鄉的人也會仰望明月，表達對故鄉和親人的思念。

The 15th day of the eighth lunar month is the Chinese traditional Mid-Autumn Festival. On that day, the Chinese have the customs of admiring the moon and eating moon cakes. According to the traditional customs, the Chinese people enjoy fruits and moon cakes while admiring the moon. As the moon is round, it symbolizes reunion. At that time, the people far away from their hometown will also look up at the moon and miss their hometown and families.

語法重點 Key Points of Grammar

選擇關係複句 Alternative Complex Sentence

幾個分句分別敘述的幾件事或幾種情況不能同時並存，需要在其中選擇一件或一種。

The clauses state different things that are alternatives, and only one of them is chosen.

選擇關係也叫取捨關係，包括確定選擇和不定選擇兩類。

Alternative relationship is also called selective relationship which includes determinate selection and indeterminate selection.

① 確定選擇：表示兩種情況中，只有一種更合適，且已經做出了取捨。

Determinate selection: It means that out of the two situations, only one is more appropriate and the choice has been made.

a. 前取後捨：寧可……也不……　Accept first part and reject second part: would rather...than...

E.g. ● 小凱寧可上學遲到，也不願意花錢打的士。

Xiao Kai would rather be late for school than spending money to take a taxi.

b. 前捨後取：與其……不如……　Reject first part, accept second part: instead of

E.g. ● 與其在家閒著沒事幹，不如去老人院做義工。

Instead of doing nothing at home, it is better to volunteer in a nursing home.

② 不定選擇：表示前後兩種情況都有可能出現，但不會同時存在。

Indeterminate selection: It means that the two situations are both possible, but not present at the same time.

a. 亟待取捨：表示對兩種或兩種以上情況哪種會出現而產生的疑問，內心還存有一種取捨的疑慮。如：是……還是……？

Urgent choice: It means that there are doubts about which of two or more situations will occur, and there is still a kind of doubt about the choice. Such as: Is it...or...?

E.g. ● 這次考試為什麼沒考好？是因為粗心，還是因為沒有認真複習？

Why didn't you get a good grade this time? Was it because you were careless or you didn't review the content carefully?

b. 無須取捨：表示對兩種或兩種以上情況，無論哪種會出現都在意料之中，沒有必要取捨。如：不是……就是……；或是……或是……；要麼……要麼……

No need to choose: It means that it is expected that two or more situations will occur, and there is no need to choose. Such as: either...or...; ...or...

E.g. ● 他一放學，不是去踢足球，就是去打籃球，沒辦法安靜一會兒。
He is not a quiet person and either goes to play football or basketball after school.

課文理解 Reading Comprehensions

① 為什麼年輕人喜歡慶祝外來節日？

② 不同的中國傳統節日都有哪些慶祝活動？

③ 傳統節日背後有哪些不同的意義？請舉例說明。

④ 中國傳統節日體現了什麼文化精神？

⑤ 為什麼要重視對傳統節日的慶祝？

概念與拓展理解 Concepts and Further Understanding

① 在傳統節日的慶祝活動中我們會吃什麼食物？我們為什麼要吃這些食物？
What foods do we eat on special celebrations? Why do we eat these specific foods?

② 哪些飲食傳統背後有烹飪故事或歷史？請舉例說明。
Which food traditions have culinary story or history behind them? Please give an example.

③ 不同社區的飲食文化有何不同？
How is food culture different in different communities?

④ 食物喜好在當代社會中能在多大程度上反映一個人的文化背景？
How far does food reflect one's cultural background in contemporary society?

---

⑤ 食物是一種用於理解社會關係、家庭、血統和文化象徵意義的媒介嗎？
Is food a medium for the understanding of social relationships, family, kinship and cultural symbolism?

語言練習 Language Exercises

把下面的詞語組成正確的詞組。Connect the corresponding words below to form a correct phrase.

① 崇拜	願望	② 失去	重點
調查	研究	強調	健康
實現	明星	忽視	信仰

從生詞表裏找出與下列詞語意思相同或相近的詞。

Find words with the same or similar meanings as the following words in the vocabulary list.

③ 幫助________ ④ 小看________ ⑤ 爭論________

從生詞表裏找出與下列詞語意思相反的詞。

Find words with the opposite meanings to the following words in the vocabulary list.

⑥ 過時________ ⑦ 漠視________ ⑧ 遺忘________

選擇正確的詞語填空。Fill in the blanks with the right words.

評委　辯友　主題　萬聖節　玫瑰　聖誕節　端午節
信仰　掃墓　清明節　屈原　認同感　凝聚力

⑨ 每年________，我們都會在爺爺的墳墓前擺放鮮花，寄託我們無限的哀思。
⑩ 慶祝傳統文化節日是增強國人文化________的重要手段。
⑪ 遇到困難的時候，大家應該互幫互助，這樣才能增強社區的________。
⑫ 這次比賽，她的琵琶彈得很好，獲得了________的一致好評。

⑬ ＿＿＿＿＿是中國古代偉大的愛國詩人，＿＿＿＿＿是紀念他的節日。

⑭ ＿＿＿＿＿給了我力量，幫助我渡過了這次難關。

⑮ 如何保護環境是這次會議的＿＿＿＿＿。

⑯ ＿＿＿＿＿當天，孩子們會打扮成各種人物去每家每戶敲門。

⑰ 清明＿＿＿＿＿不單單是一種祭祀活動，更是中華文明優良傳統的體現。

⑱ ＿＿＿＿＿象徵著純潔的愛情，也是和平、友誼、勇氣的化身。

⑲ 現在的一些年輕人看著別人過＿＿＿＿＿自己也趕時髦，但如果真讓他說說為什麼有聖誕樹，他卻不知道。

⑳ 面對對方＿＿＿＿＿的提問，他不慌不忙地回答，贏得了全場觀眾的掌聲。

填入正確的關聯詞。Fill in the blanks with appropriate correlative conjunctions.

㉑ 小亮住在蒙古，一放學＿＿＿＿＿放羊，＿＿＿＿＿騎馬。

㉒ 我＿＿＿＿＿考試不及格，＿＿＿＿＿偷看別人的考卷。

㉓ 你每天怎麼上學？＿＿＿＿＿走路＿＿＿＿＿坐公車？

㉔ ＿＿＿＿＿求別人幫助自己做作業，＿＿＿＿＿靠自己完成。

課堂活動 Class Activities

搶寶座遊戲 Game of Thrones

老師給學生每人發五張詞卡。這些詞卡的內容可以重複。學生要在 1 分鐘內記住自己手裏的詞卡，要會讀，會寫，還要理解意思。老師讓學生圍成一個圓圈，在圓圈中間擺一張椅子。學生按順時針一直走動。老師說出一個詞語，有這個詞卡的學生開始搶寶座。搶到寶座的人，必須到黑板前寫出這個詞，並說出意思，如果不會寫或說不出意思，則不算。而都會的同學把字卡交給老師。誰手裏的字卡最早交完，誰就贏。

The teacher issues five word cards to each student. These word cards can be repeated. Students would be given 1 minute to memorize the word cards in their hands. They must be able to read, write, and understand the meaning. The teacher asks the students to form a circle and place a chair in the middle of the circle. Students keep moving clockwise. The teacher says a word, and the students with the word card begin to grab the throne. Those who grab the throne must go to the blackboard to write the word and say the meaning. If they can't write it or say the meaning, the grabbing is invalid. Students who answer correctly hand the card to the teacher. Whoever has no card left in his hand at the earliest will win.

口語訓練 Speaking Tasks

第一部分 **根據圖片，做 3–4 分鐘的口頭表達。做口頭表達之前，先根據提示寫大綱。**

Make a 3-4 minutes oral presentation based on the picture. Before you start, use the form below to make an outline.

大綱 Outline	內容 Content
圖片內容 Information of the picture	
圖片主題 + 文化 Theme of the picture and culture	
提出觀點 Make your points	
延伸個人經歷 Relate to personal experiences	
名人名言 Famous quotes / 熟語 Idioms	
總結 Summary	

第二部分 **回答下面的問題。Answer the following questions.**

① 你們家會過端午節嗎？怎麼過節？

② 年輕人覺得粽子不好吃，也不喜歡過端午節，你怎麼看？

③ 除了端午節背後屈原的歷史故事，你還知道哪些傳統節日背後的故事？

④ 中國傳統節日一般都有特定的食物，你最喜歡哪一種？為什麼？

⑤ 現在賽龍舟已經不僅僅是端午節特有的活動，還發展成了一項體育比賽，你怎麼看待這件事？

技能訓練 Skill Tasks

閱讀訓練 Reading Tasks

文章 1 李子柒為何火遍全球

仔細閱讀下面的短文，然後回答問題。

Read the passage carefully and answer the following questions.

2020 年 12 月 11 日　　四川日報報道

2019 年，四川姑娘李子柒在社交平台“抖音”發佈了和鄉村生活、傳統美食、傳統文化等內容相關的視頻。全網播放量近 5 億，點讚數超過 60 萬，粉絲量達到 3000 多萬，李子柒在國內外成為了網紅。她為何能火遍全球呢？

在她的視頻中，人們能看到用黃豆釀造醬油、手工造紙、染布等傳統手藝，也能讀到田園生活背後的溫情。這些都滿足了現代都市人對田園生活的嚮往，也打開了西方世界了解中國文化的一個窗口。在她的視頻裏，雖然沒有直接用語言去誇中國的好，卻講好了中國文化，講好了中國故事。她只是很安靜地在那裏幹著農活，偶爾跟奶奶說幾句四川方言，但卻促使世界各地的人開始了解有趣的中國傳統文化，並喜歡上中國人的勤奮和聰明。不得不說，她用平常心做出了一個國際文化傳播的奇跡。

除了宣傳四川美食及傳統文化，李子柒的視頻也改變了年輕人對中國傳統文化的態度。很多國外年輕網友表達了對她生活的喜愛，他們也很想去中國旅遊，品嚐中國獨特的美食，還想和中國人一起慶祝中國的傳統節日。李子柒跟上了時代的腳步，利用互聯網向世界展示了中國農村生活的美和中國傳統文化的博大精深。李子柒是文化自信的代表，是文化傳播的榜樣。

我們正在通過不同的方式讓世界了解全面、真實、立體的中國。比如 600 歲“網紅”——故宮讓文物活了起來，讓世界感受到了中國文化的生命力與創新力；在雲南的妹子，通過拍攝自己生產的雲南美食為世界送去“雲南的味道”；在博物館當導遊的“網紅大爺”，通過網絡講述中國市民生活的巨大變化……

在互聯網時代，文化傳播和交流更加多樣化。我們需要更多的“李子柒”，需要更多有品質、有溫度的好故事，讓更多的人通過網絡讀懂中國文化、愛上中國文化。

改編自：https://baijiahao.baidu.com/s?id=1652662991360515301&wfr=spider&for=pc

根據以上短文，回答下面的問題。

Based on the passage above, answer the following questions.

① 李子柒的視頻主要內容是什麼？

② 都市人為什麼喜歡李子柒的視頻？

③ 為什麼世界各地的人都喜歡李子柒的視頻？

④ 除了宣傳傳統文化，李子柒的視頻對年輕人還有什麼影響？

⑤ 國外年輕網友看了李子柒的視頻後，有什麼想法？至少舉一個例子。

⑥ 為什麼説李子柒是文化傳播的榜樣？

⑦ 600 歲的故宮是如何讓世界感受到中國文化的生命力與創新力的？

⑧ 雲南的妹子是如何讓世界品嚐“雲南的味道”的？

⑨ 在博物館當導遊的大爺，是如何成為網紅的？

⑩ 為什麼我們需要更多的“李子柒”？

Tips

如何抓住新聞的主要內容？

How to grasp the main idea of the news?

新聞通常會把最重要的內容寫在第一段，也就是導語。然後每一段寫一個事實。通常，報道者只是客觀記錄這些事實，不發表自己的評論和意見。

News usually writes the most important content in the first paragraph, which is the introduction. Then write a fact for each paragraph. Usually these facts are only objective records, and reporters do not publish their own comments and opinions.

導語是新聞的第一段，通常用“五何法”（何時、何地、何人、何事、何故）來敘述新聞事件的主要內容。

The introduction is the first paragraph of the news. It usually uses the “5W” method (when, where, who, what, and why) to describe the main content of a news event.

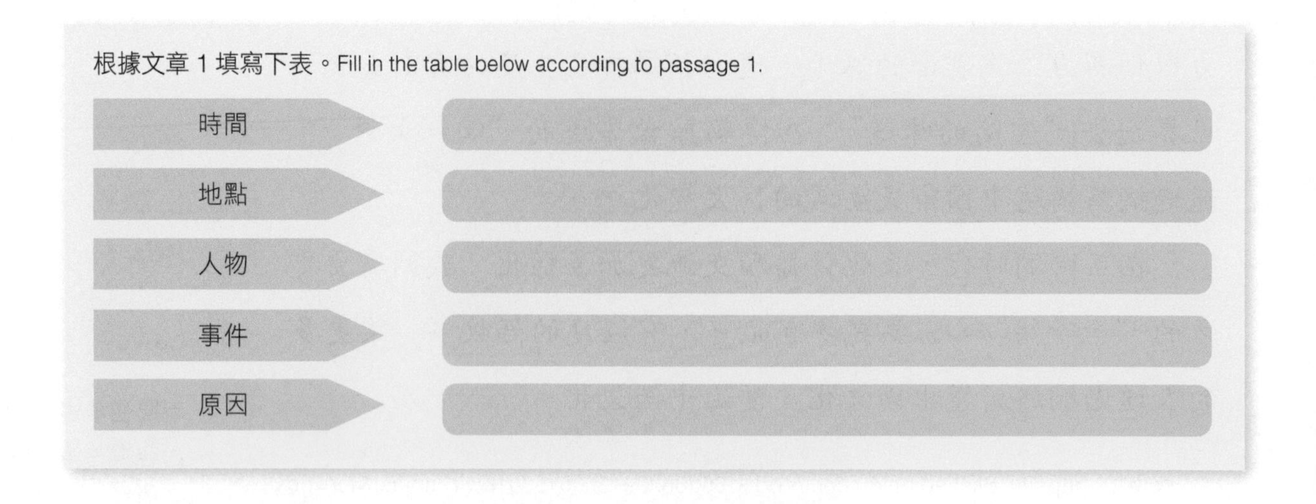

根據文章 1 填寫下表。Fill in the table below according to passage 1.

時間	
地點	
人物	
事件	
原因	

文章 2 蔡志忠漫畫

❶ 【–1–】

蔡志忠漫畫系列《老子說》《莊子說》全 2 冊中英文對照版

¥ 78.60

★ 現代出版社

★ 運費：杭州—北京 包郵

★ 累計評價：49

★ 送淘寶積分：39

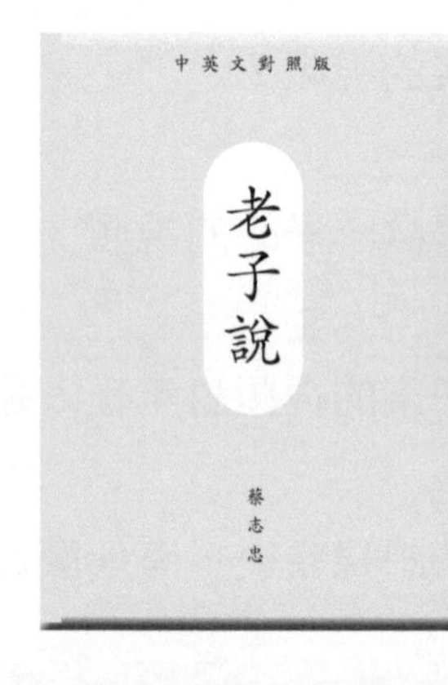

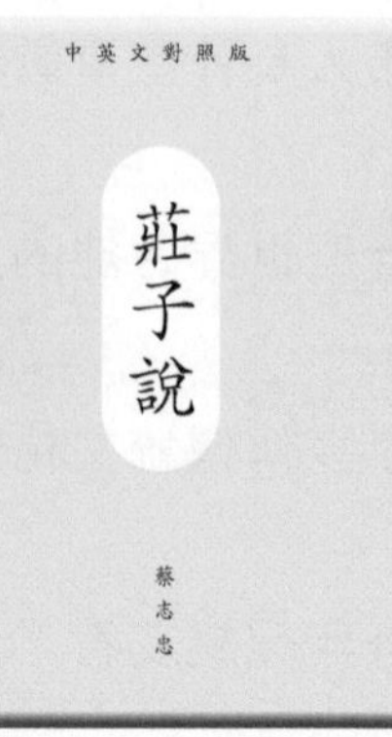

品質優選 閱讀放心 正版保證

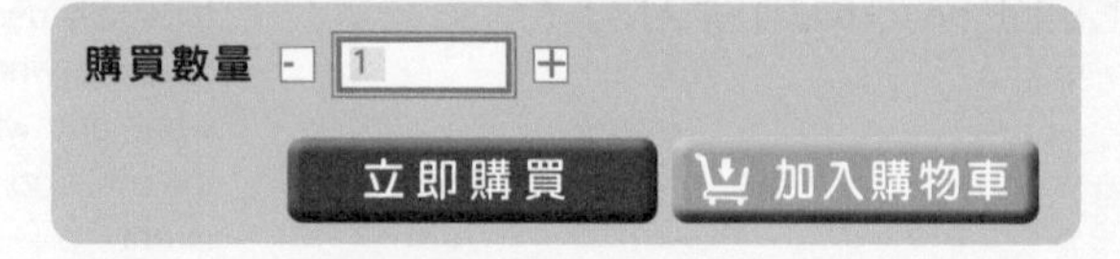

❷ 【–2–】

中國早期思想家的著作，一直影響著中國文化和社會的方方面面，從教育到藝術，從政治、戰爭到日常禮節等。漫畫家蔡志忠一直致力於用他獨特的方法——跨越了語言和文化的漫畫——將這些古代經典著作的智慧帶入現代人的生活。現在文化表達方式越來越豐富了，而蔡志忠的漫畫是世界性的，因為東方哲學、中國哲學是具有普遍價值的，提倡人與自然的和諧，與他人的和諧以及與自己內心的和諧。經蔡志忠改編的作品為海外了解中國文化打開了一個窗口。

❸ 【–3–】

本套書包括蔡志忠漫畫中國思想、漫畫中國傳統文化經典。採用中英文對照的方式，用精煉的文字講出中國傳統儒家精神（人與人的和諧）、道家精神（人與自然的和諧）。對讀者來說，國學、英文、漫畫，看一本書就有三大收穫！

風趣生動的漫畫　通俗易懂的文字　消除文化隔膜　**語言文化交流**

改編自：https://detail.tmall.com/item.htm?spm=a230r.1.14.41. 5ae27ec69fDDBu&id=614132399403&ns=1&abbucket=14

根據文章 2，選出最適合的段落標題，把答案寫在橫線上。

According to passage 2, choose the appropriate titles and write the answers on the lines.

① [–1–] ________　A. 蔡志忠
② [–2–] ________　B. 蔡志忠漫畫
③ [–3–] ________　C. 主要內容
D. 圖書特色
E. 背景介紹
F. 語言文化

根據文章 2，選出五個正確的敘述，把答案寫在橫線上。

According to passage 2, choose five true statements and write the answers on the lines.

關於《蔡志忠漫畫》，正確的是：

④ ________　A. 漫畫由三聯書店出版。

Tips

連句成段，理解段落意思

Understand every sentence to summarize the meaning of a whole paragraph

這個方法就是要先弄清段落中每句話的意思，然後歸納出自然段的段意。這也是讀懂整篇文章的重要基礎。

This method is to first clarify the meaning of each sentence in the paragraph, and then summarize the meaning of the natural paragraph. This is also the important basis for reading the entire article.

例如：第三段總共有三句話。第一句直接告訴我們這套書包括蔡志忠哪些漫畫主題。第二句話介紹這套書的特色。第三句話講購買這套書的收穫。把這三句話的意思連起來，可以看出這三句話都在講這套圖書的特別之處。

For example: There are three sentences in the third paragraph. The first sentence directly tells us the themes of Tsai Chih-chung's comic books. The second sentence introduces the characteristics of this set of books. The third sentence talks about what reader can get from reading this set of books. Joining these three sentences together, you can see that these three sentences are talking about the special features of this set of books.

________ B. 買這套書可以免費寄到北京。
________ C. 買這套書要花費 78.6 港幣。
________ D. 至少有 49 人買了這套書。
________ E. 道家思想強調人與自然的和諧相處。
F. 這套書有英文翻譯。
G. 蔡志忠的作品只適合中國人閱讀。
H. 蔡志忠漫畫裏文字比較少。

根據 ❷，找出最合適的詞語完成下面的句子。

According to ❷, complete the sentences with the most suitable words.

⑤ 中國社會的各個方面一直受到中國早期思想家著作的________。
⑥ 蔡志忠將古代經典著作帶入現代人生活的方法很________。
⑦ 外國人可以通過蔡志忠的作品來了解________。
⑧ 蔡志忠的作品是外國人了解中國的一個________。

根據 ❸，劃線的詞語指的是誰 / 什麼？從文本中找出詞語答題。

According to ❸, to whom or to what do the underlined words refer? Use words in the text to answer.

⑨ 本套書包括……

____

⑩ 看一本書就有三大收穫……

____

聽力訓練 Listening Tasks

一、《中國民俗》

你將聽到六段錄音，每段錄音兩遍。請在相應的橫線上回答問題 ① 至 ⑥。回答應簡短扼要。每段錄音後會有停頓，請在停頓期間閱讀問題。

You will hear 6 recordings, and each audio will be played twice. Answer the questions ①-⑥ with short answers. There will be a pause after each recording is played. Please read the questions during the pause.

① 為什麼要設立教師節？

② 重陽節又叫什麼節日？

③ "毛毛" 是什麼意思？

④ 很多國家在春節期間發行什麼來表達對中國新年的祝福？

⑤ "抓週兒" 在什麼時候進行？

⑥ "烤乳豬" 是哪個菜系裏最有名的菜？

二、《年輕茶藝師》 8

你即將聽到第二個聽力片段，在聽力片段二播放之前，你將有四分鐘的時間先閱讀題目。聽力片段將播放兩次，聽力片段結束後你將有兩分鐘的時間來檢查你的答案。請用中文回答問題。

You are going to hear the second audio clip. You have 4 minutes to read the questions before it starts. The audio clip will be played twice. After it ends, you have 2 minutes to check the answers. Please answer the questions in Chinese.

根據第二個聽力片段，回答問題 ①-⑨ 。

Answer the questions ①-⑨ according to the second audio clip.

根據第二個聽力片段的內容，從 A，B，C 中，選出一個正確的答案，把答案寫在橫線上。

According to the second audio clip, choose the right answer for the questions. Write the answers on the lines.

① 今天的節目叫________。

A. 感動中國　　B. 感受中國　　C. 年輕茶藝師

Tips

提高聽力心理素質

Improve the mental quality while listening

在做聽力的時候，不要遇到不懂的詞語或句子就慌。其實很多聽力只考察簡單的詞彙，其他那些複雜的詞語或句子只是起到干擾考生答題的作用。時刻記住保持鎮定，不要慌張。不自信只會使情況更糟糕。

When doing listening, don't be panic when you hear a word or sentence you don't understand. In fact, many listening sessions only examine simple vocabulary. Some complicated sentence patterns or words are only to interfer the test takers' answer. Always remember to stay calm and don't be panic. Being not confident will only make the situation worse.

例如第 6 題，四大菜系中，"淮揚菜" 大家可能都不熟悉，可是不要因為聽不懂淮揚菜，覺得很難，心裏就慌了，導致聽不進去後面的內容。實際上，題目是在考察 "烤乳豬" 和 "廣東菜" 的關係，其他信息聽不懂也沒有關係。

For example, most of students may not be familiar with the Huaiyang cuisine in question 6. Students shouldn't be panic when they found they don't understand what Huaiyang cuisine is. This will affect the acquisition of the information in the later part of the audio. In fact, this question is to test the students' understanding of the relationship between Roast suckling pig and Cantonese cuisine. It doesn't matter if you don't understand other information.

Tips

遇到聽不懂的字詞怎麼辦？

What should you do if you don't understand the words you're listening to?

在聆聽的過程中要有技巧，遇到一時不能理解的字詞，不要停下來思索，而要堅持繼續聽，以防錯過更多有效信息。同時，可以在聽到會的詞語後，先寫出該詞的偏旁部首或拼音字母，提醒自己，在完全聽完後，再逐個補全。這樣可以很好地避免因為錯過一個詞語而錯過後面的內容。

In the process of listening, you must have skills, that is, when you encounter a word that you can't understand for a while, don't stop to think, but keep listening to prevent you from missing more effective information. At the same time, you can first write the radicals or pinyin letters of the word after you hear the meaning, remind yourself that you can complete it one by one after you have heard it completely. This kind of listening skill can avoid missing a word and missing the following content.

② 神農發現喝了茶後，人會變得很________。

A. 想睡　　B. 安靜　　C. 精神

③ 年輕人每天喝奶茶，每人平均喝________。

A. 半杯　　B. 一杯　　C. 兩杯

填空題，每個空格最多填三個詞語。

Fill in the blanks, three words for each blank at maximum.

年輕人覺得泡茶很麻煩，喝奶茶更方便。其實，茶的表現形式很【-4-】，包含深厚的歷史文化。年輕人對茶的印象很【-5-】，所以要引導他們親近【-6-】，了解茶葉有趣的一面，才能讓他們喜歡喝茶。因此，我決定在上海開一間【-7-】。

④ [-4-] ____________　　⑤ [-5-] ____________

⑥ [-6-] ____________　　⑦ [-7-] ____________

回答下面的問題。Answer the following questions.

⑧ 茶給中國人的生活帶來什麼好處？請舉出一例。

____

⑨ 茶有哪些不同的呈現形式？請舉出一例。

____

寫作訓練：新聞報道 Writing Tasks: News Report

熱身

- **根據課文一，討論新聞報道的格式是什麼。**

According to Text 1, discuss the format of a news report.

● 如何寫好新聞報道？How to write a news report?

Tips

文體：新聞報道

Text Type: News Report

新聞報道是對最新發生的事件進行的報道。

News report involves the reporting of the information regarding latest events in society.

格式 **參考課文一**

標題

X 年 X 月 X 日　XX 報道

□□導語：新聞事件的時間、地點、人物等

□□主體：具體介紹各項事實 / 新聞事件的經過

□□結語：總結

練習一

你的學校正在舉辦中國新年慶祝活動。你是校報記者，請寫一篇新聞報道。

字數：100–120 個漢字。

新聞報道必須包括以下內容：

- 活動的時間、地點和參加人員
- 活動的內容
- 同學們對這次活動的看法

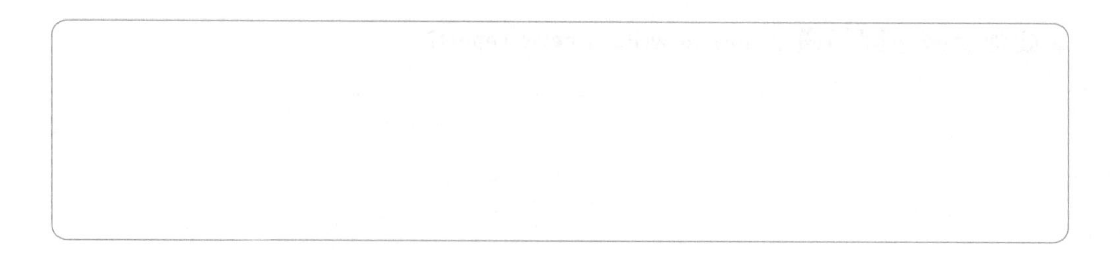

練習二

你所在的社區正在舉辦中秋節活動，吸引了很多老人和小孩子來參加。你是校報記者，請報道這次活動的經過，並採訪社區居民對這次活動的看法。選用合適的文本類型完成寫作。字數：300–480 個漢字。

新聞報道	給編輯的信	博客

Tips

事實性新聞一般根據讀者對事件的關心程度或者是事件的重大程度，按照先後順序進行報道。新聞通常由導語、主體和結語三部分組成。

Factual news is reported in order according to the degree of readers' concern or the importance of the event. News is usually composed of three parts: introduction, main body and conclusion.

導語：利用"五何法"（何時、何地、何人、何事、何故）來交代新聞事實。

Introduction: use the "5W" method (when, where, who, what, and why) to explain news facts.

主體：對導語進行具體擴展。

Main body: expand the lead part, and specifically introduce the report part of the lead.

結語：總結全文。

Conclusion: summarize the full text.

Lesson 3 Lifestyle

生活方式

導入 Introduction

生活方式是指人們長期受一定社會文化、經濟、風俗、家庭影響而形成的一系列的生活習慣、制度和意識。隨著科技的發展和互聯網的普及，現代人的生活節奏變得越來越快，從而產生了很多的“現代病”。如何在緊張、忙碌的生活中保持健康？我們需要一起探索健康的生活方式。

Life style refers to a series of life habits, life systems and life consciousness formed by people under the influence of certain social culture, economy, customs and family for a long time. With the development of science and technology and popularization of Internet, the pace of life of modern people has become faster and faster, resulting many “modern diseases”. How to stay healthy in the hectic modern life? We need to explore healthy lifestyles together.

學習目標 Learning Targets

閱讀 Reading

- 能夠準確把握文章的寫作目的，並能分清主次，概括段落大意。
Learn to accurately grasp the writing purpose of the articles, distinguish and summarize the main idea of the paragraph.

口語 Speaking

- 學會在口頭陳述中讓自己的表達更加真實。
Learn to make your own expressions more truthful in oral statements.

聽力 Listening

- 學會用聽力材料中的細節信息完成填空題。
Learn to use the detailed information in the materials to complete the fill-in-the-blank questions.

寫作 Writing

- 學會寫好指南。
Learn to write a guide.

生詞短語

yíng yǎng
營養 nutrition

xī hóng shì
西紅柿 tomato

jī dàn
雞蛋 egg

zhǐ nán
指南 guide

cái liào
材料 ingredient

tiáo liào
調料 seasoning

yán
鹽 salt

bái táng
白糖 white sugar

bù zhòu
步驟 steps

qiē
切 cut

dǎ sǎn
打散 beat

guō
鍋 pot

níng gù
凝固 solidify

fānchǎo
翻炒 stir

ruǎn
軟 soft

shǎo xǔ
少許 a little bit

shāo jiāo
燒焦 burned

áo
熬 stew

dào
道 dish (a measure word)

cài yáo
菜餚 cuisine

1 課文 營養早餐指南 9

俗話說，“早餐要吃好，午餐要吃飽，晚餐要吃少。”每天吃營養早餐對身體健康非常重要。那麼，應該如何做出美味可口又健康的營養早餐呢？希望這份《西紅柿炒雞蛋營養早餐指南》能幫助你解決問題。

一、材料

1. 雞蛋兩個

2. 西紅柿兩個

二、調料

1. 鹽

2. 白糖

三、步驟

1. 把西紅柿洗乾淨。

2. 把西紅柿切成小塊兒。

3. 在碗裏打兩個雞蛋，加入鹽後打散。

4. 開小火，往鍋裏倒油。油熱後把蛋液倒入鍋中，蛋液凝固後，輕輕翻炒，關火，把雞蛋盛出備用。

5. 往鍋裏重新倒油，油熱後倒入西紅柿，翻炒。

6. 西紅柿變軟後，倒入提前炒好的雞蛋，加少許鹽和白糖，輕輕翻炒。

7. 關火，將西紅柿炒雞蛋倒入盤中。

四、注意事項

1. 不要放太多鹽和白糖。

2. 不要加水，西紅柿變軟後會出很多汁。

3. 火不要開太大，否則會燒焦，要用小火把西紅柿的汁液慢慢熬出來。

4. 注意用火安全。

西紅柿炒雞蛋是中國的一道家常菜餚，不但做法簡單，而且營養很豐富。這道菜不光顏色好看，還很美味可口，早餐可以配粥一起吃。希望這份指南可以幫助大家做出美味的菜品。培養健康的生活方式，從營養早餐開始！

美食營養中心

2022 年 3 月 15 日

改編自：https://www.meishij.net/zuofa/xihongshichaojidan_21.html

Culture Point

中國人的早餐文化
Chinese Breakfast Culture

中國人向來很重視早餐，這份一日之初的食物可以帶給我們一天中第一次的滿足和慰藉。在中國很多地方都有“過早”的習慣。早餐可以說是一種文化載體，一種飲食代表著一種文化，而一種文化又是一個地方、一個群體的聯繫紐帶。比如，廣州的早餐叫“歎茶”，“歎”是廣州方言，含有“品味”和“享受”之意。一份報紙，三五親友，幾籠點心，一壺清茶，就度過一整個上午。“歎茶”已經成為了廣東人生活的重要標誌。

Chinese people have always valued breakfast. Breakfast represents the first satisfaction and comfort that brought to Chinese at the beginning of the day. There is the custom of “eating breakfast” in many regions of China. Breakfast is a cultural carrier. A specific food represents a specific culture. And this culture also connect the people of the region. For example, breakfast in Guangzhou is called “歎茶”. “歎” is the Guangzhou dialect which means “taste” and “enjoy”. Newspaper, friends and relatives, snacks and tea are the great companions of Cantonese in the morning of the day. “歎茶” has become the key element of Cantonese life.

語法重點 Key Points of Grammar

遞進關係複句 Progressive Complex Sentence

由兩個有遞進關係的分句組成，後一個分句比前一個分句更進一層。

Consisting of two clauses with a progressive relationship. The latter clause is one level higher than the previous clause.

常用關聯詞 Common Conjunctive Words

Structure 不但……而且……；不僅……而且 / 還……；除了……還……；不光……還 / 也……

not only... but also... ; not only... but also...; except (besides) ... ; not only... but also...

E.g.
- 參加體操訓練，不僅可以鍛煉身體，而且可以交新朋友。Taking part in gymnastics training can not only build up your body, but also make new friends.
- 這個暑假，我除了讀書，還游了泳。Besides reading, I also went swimming during the summer holiday.
- 陶老師不光是我的老師，也是我的朋友。Ms Tao is not only my teacher but also my friend.

課文理解 Reading Comprehensions

① 課文一是關於什麼的指南？

② 為什麼每天早餐要吃好？

③ 為什麼炒菜的時候不要加水？

④ 炒菜的時候，為什麼火不能開太大？

⑤ 為什麼西紅柿炒雞蛋是家常菜餚？

概念與拓展理解 Concepts and Further Understanding

① 我們如何選擇要吃的東西？How do we choose what we are going to eat?

② 我們居住的地方如何影響我們對食物的選擇？How does where we live influence our food choices?

③ 我們的家庭背景如何影響我們對飲食的選擇？How does our family background affect what we choose to eat?

④ 廣告活動如何影響人們對食物的選擇？How do advertisements affect our selections of food?

⑤ 人工合成的食品可以經常吃嗎？Is it ok to eat synthetic foods often?

語言練習 Language Exercises

從所提供的選項中選出正確的答案。Choose the correct answer for the question.

① 西紅________不但能夠炒著吃，也能生吃，營養非常豐富。

A. 市　B. 柿　C. 飾　D. 式

② 每年過生日，奶奶都會給我煮幾個紅皮雞________。

A. 但　B. 胥　C. 旦　D. 蛋

③ 火藥、________南針、印刷術和造紙術是中國古代的四大發明。

A. 指　B. 支　C. 只　D. 旨

④ 中藥很苦，加點白________會好一些。

A. 唐　B. 塘　C. 糖　D. 搪

⑤ 魚燒________了，味道很苦。

A. 樵　B. 蕉　C. 焦　D. 礁

⑥ 我不喜歡這________菜，請換其他的菜吧。

A. 道　B. 首　C. 到　D. 隨

⑦ 她的頭髮又長又黑又________，真好看。

A. 欠　B. 軟　C. 暖　D. 亂

⑧ 媽媽每天早上都會煮一________粥。

A. 蝸　B. 禍　C. 窩　D. 鍋

⑨ 我不小心________到了手，血一直流。

A. 刀　B. 七　C. 切　D. 土

選出與下列劃線詞語意思相同的選項。Choose the synonyms of the underlined words below.

⑩ 往湯裏加一點兒鹽，這樣才會好喝。　☐

A. 許多　B. 大量　C. 很多　D. 少許

根據意思寫詞語。Write words according to the meanings.

⑪ 用於做成成品的東西。________________

⑫ 從食物中獲取有用的東西。________________

⑬ 製作食品時需要添加的佐料。________________

⑭ 把整片的物體分開。________________

填入正確的關聯詞。Fill in the blanks with appropriate correlative conjunctions.

⑮ 壯壯____________會唱歌，也會彈鋼琴。

⑯ 媽媽每天____________上班，還要做很多家務。

⑰ 新手機____________好用，而且很漂亮。

⑱ 暑假期間，李想____________在敬老院做義工，還給留守兒童補習英語。

課堂活動 Class Activities

大胃口 Big Appetite

將學生分成 A、B 兩組。每組學生按照 1-11 號編號。組員圍圈而坐，第一個人開始說"我今天吃了一碗粥"，第二位接著說"我今天吃了一碗粥，兩個雞蛋"，第三位則說"我今天吃了一碗粥，兩個雞蛋，三個西紅柿"。……第十號同學的句子是"我今天吃了一碗粥，兩個雞蛋，三個西紅柿，四塊豬肉，五片餅乾，六塊巧克力，七根油條，八個橘子，九個蘋果，喝了十杯水"。第十一位同學把第十位同學說的話寫在黑板上。（等第十位同學說完，才能上去寫。）A 組寫完，再進行 B 組。兩組互相核對。哪一組寫得最多、最準確，哪一組就贏。

Divide students into Group A and Group B. Students in each group are numbered according to numbers 1-11. The group members sit in a circle. One student starts to say "I ate a bowl of porridge today". The second goes on to say "I ate a bowl of porridge and two eggs today", and the third goes "I ate a bowl of porridge , two eggs and three tomatoes today." The 10th student's sentence is "I ate a bowl of porridge, two eggs, three tomatoes, four pieces of pork, five biscuits, six pieces of chocolate, seven fried dough sticks, eight oranges, nine apples and drank ten glasses of water today". The 11th student writes on the blackboard what the 10th student said. (Only wait for the 10th classmate to finish before writing.) After Group A finishes writing, Group B starts to write. After that, the two groups check each other's writings. The group with the most and accurate writings wins.

Tips

如何讓口頭表達更真實？

How to make your verbal expressions more real?

在做口頭表達時，聯繫自己或者他人的經歷，能讓你的口頭表達更加真實和生動。講述個人經歷的時候一定要是自己印象深刻的事件，而不是捏造的，這樣才能使你的口頭表達更加可信。

During oral presentation, if you can relate to your own or other people's experiences, your verbal expressions can be more real and vivid. When telling your personal experiences, you must choose the most impressive event, not fabricated, so as to make your verbal expressions more credible.

除此之外，還可以根據自己的經驗，發表對主題的看法，並提出建議，這會讓你的口頭表達更加有深度。

In addition, you can also express your views on the subject and make suggestions based on your own experience to make your oral presentation more in-depth.

口語訓練 Speaking Tasks

第一部分　根據主題“生活方式”，選擇一種生活方式，做 2-3 分鐘的口頭表達。做口頭表達之前，先根據提示寫大綱。

Choose a lifestyle, make a 2-3 minutes oral presentation on the theme "lifestyle". Before you start, use the form below to make an outline.

大綱 Outline	內容 Content
觀點 Perspectives	
事例 Examples	
名人名言 Famous quotes / 熟語 Idioms	
經歷 Experiences	
總結 Summary	

第二部分　回答下面的問題。Answer the following questions.

① 現在人們的生活條件好了，生活觀念也發生了變化。年輕人不崇尚節儉的生活方式，你有什麼看法？

② 你的家庭對你現在的生活方式有影響嗎？

③ 你的生活方式和父母的生活方式有哪些不同？為什麼？

④ 健康的生活方式有哪些？

⑤ 年輕人有哪些不健康的生活方式？應如何改善？

2 課文 日常生活禮儀 10

生詞短語

rì cháng shēng huó
日常生活 daily life

xiāng chǔ
相處 get along with

lǐ yí
禮儀 etiquette

jiè shào
介紹 introduce

cháng shí
常識
general knowledge

dǎ zhāo hu
打招呼 greeting

jiē dài
接待 receive

dà máng
大忙 big favor

bài fǎng
拜訪 visit

jù cān
聚餐 dine together

fǒu zé
否則 otherwise

jié hūn
結婚 get married

sòng bié
送別 send off

xīn yì
心意 mind

xiào hua
笑話 joke

jiāo wǎng
交往 associate

在日常生活中，為了能夠與他人更好地相處，我們必須懂得日常生活禮儀。下面為大家介紹一些日常生活禮儀常識，希望可以幫助大家！

一、打招呼

打招呼是一種禮貌的行為。如果你碰到一個認識的人，比如鄰居，那麼就應該打個招呼，這是最基本的禮儀。當我們和朋友出行，見到了另外一個朋友時，我們還要很有禮貌地互相介紹。介紹的時候應該先介紹朋友，然後再介紹自己，這也是一種禮貌。

二、喝茶

當今社會，用茶來接待客人是人們日常社交中最普遍的生活禮儀。所以，懂得喝茶禮儀是很重要的。給客人倒茶時，不要倒得太滿；而客人則要用雙手接過茶杯，並點頭表示感謝。這不僅是對客人、朋友的尊重，也能體現自己的修養。

三、表示感謝

如果別人幫助了你，你就應該跟對方說聲“謝謝”。如果別人幫了你大忙，你還可以帶上禮物去拜訪他，這是向別人表示感謝的一種方式。

四、用餐

聚餐的時候，不要一坐下來就開始吃飯。應該要等長輩先拿起筷子，你再拿起筷子。也不要搶在別人面前動筷子，否則別人會覺得你很沒有禮貌。

五、贈送禮物

每逢節日、結婚、生日、送別親友時，中國人都要送點兒禮物來表達自己的心意。送禮的時候要注意一些中國的傳統習俗，不要鬧出“送菊花給老師”“送傘給朋友”的笑話。所以我們要多看一些禮儀方面的書，特別是一些介紹傳統習俗的書。

中國素有“禮儀之邦”的美稱，禮儀的重點是尊重人。我們在與人交往時要禮貌待人、尊重他人，這樣才能贏得他人的尊重。日常生活的禮儀十分重要，它既是個人修養的外在表現，也是建立良好人際關係的基礎。

日常禮儀中心

2022 年 4 月 15 日

改編自：http://www.ruiwen.com/liyichangshi/1119223.html

Culture Point

菊花 Chrysanthemum

菊花雖然是常見的花卉，但很少有人會拿菊花送人。那麼，送菊花代表什麼意思呢？不同顏色的菊花有著不同的花語，不能隨意送人，比如白菊花雖然美麗，但是它卻代表著崇敬嚴肅，一般用來悼念已去世的人，如果送人的話容易引起誤會。

Although chrysanthemum is a common flower, few people give it to others. What does it mean to send chrysanthemum? Different colors of chrysanthemum have different meanings, so you can't give it away freely. For example, although white chrysanthemum is beautiful, it represents reverence and solemnity, and is generally used to mourn the deceased. Giving it away freely may cause misunderstanding.

傘 Umbrella

朋友之間送傘是不恰當的，因為中文裏"傘"的諧音是"散"，如果送了傘就是想要分開的意思。

It is not good to send umbrellas between friends, because the homophony of umbrella is separation. If they send an umbrella, it means they want to separate.

筷子 Chopsticks

筷子是中國古代的發明，是中國人的主要餐具。筷子文化在中國源遠流長，是中國飲食文化的一部分。中國人使用筷子有一些禁忌，比如：

Chopsticks are an invention by ancient Chinese people. Chopsticks are the main tableware of the Chinese people. The chopsticks culture in China has a long history and is part of Chinese food culture. Chinese people have some taboos when using chopsticks, such as:

1. 不要用筷子敲擊鍋碗瓢盆，因為在過去只有乞討者才會用筷子敲碗，以此來吸引別人的注意。

   Don't knock pots and pans with chopsticks. Because only beggars knock bowls with chopsticks to attract the attention of others in the past.

2. 不能把筷子在菜盤裏揮來揮去，上下亂翻，找自己想吃的東西，這樣的做法很不禮貌。

   It is impolite to flip chopsticks up and down in the dishes to look for one's favourite food.

3. 不要拿著筷子隨便亂指。這是一種缺乏修養、極其不禮貌的行為。這如同用食指指別人，有指責對方的意思。

   Don't use chopsticks to point others. It shows a lack of cultivation and is considered as an extremely impolite behavior. Similar as pointing others with index finger, it means blaming others on the table.

4. 不要把筷子豎直插到飯碗中。因為民間的傳統是為已故亡靈上香時才這樣做，如果把一副筷子插入飯碗中央，好像是在詛咒一起用餐的人，這種行為是決不被接受的。

   Do not stick the chopsticks upright on the rice bowl. Because according to the Chinese folk traditions, people do this only when they offering incense to the souls of the dead. If you stick a pair of chopsticks into the middle of a bowl of rice, it could be interpreted as cursing the people who are dining together with you. This behavior is definitely not accepted by Chinese.

語法重點 Key Points of Grammar

順承關係複句　Successive Complex Sentence

表示連續發生的事情或動作，彼此順序不能變動。

Indicates events or actions that occur continuously, and their order cannot be changed.

① 先……再 / 然後……：表示動作的先後順序，一般用於還沒有發生的事情。

Firstly..., then...: To indicate the sequence of actions, generally used for things that haven't happened yet.

E.g. ● 今天我們會先學生詞，再玩兒遊戲。Today we will learn the vocabulary first, and then play the games.

② 一……就……：表示兩個動作緊接著發生。

once..., ...: To indicate that two actions occur immediately.

E.g. ● 毛毛一下課，就去足球場踢足球了。Once the lesson ended, Maomao went to the field to play football.

課文理解 Reading Comprehensions

① 什麼時候需要打招呼？

② 日常社交中接待客人最普遍的禮儀是什麼？

③ 如何表示對別人的感謝？

④ 大家一起吃飯的時候，為什麼要先等長輩拿起筷子？

⑤ 為什麼不可以送菊花給老師？

概念與拓展理解 Concepts and Further Understanding

① 人類用什麼方法將傳統生活方式延續下來？
What methods do humans use to continue the traditional life styles?

② 為什麼有些傳統的生活方式傳承下來了，有些卻消失了？
Why some traditional lifestyles have been passed down, but some have disappeared?

③ 家庭背景如何影響我們的生活方式？
How does family background affect our lifestyles?

④ 儀式和習俗在傳統生活方式的構成方面具有什麼特殊作用？
What are the special roles of rituals and customs in the composition of traditional lifestyles?

⑤ 科學的發展對我們的生活方式造成了哪些影響？
How has the development of science affected our lifestyle?

語言練習 Language Exercises

把下面的詞語組成正確的詞組。Connect the corresponding words below to form a correct phrase.

① 日常	常識	② 接待	聚餐
基本	生活	傳統	禮儀
送別	親人	同學	客人

從生詞表裏找出與下列詞語意思相同或相近的詞。

Find words with the same or similar meanings as the following words in the vocabulary list.

③ 看望______ ④ 不然______ ⑤ 想法______

從生詞表裏找出與下列詞語意思相反的詞。

Find words with the opposite meanings to the following words in the vocabulary list.

⑥ 迎接__________ ⑦ 不理睬__________ ⑧ 分手__________

選擇正確的詞語填空。Fill in the blanks with the right words.

笑話　相處　介紹　交往　結婚

⑨ 韓老師上課很會講__________，我們都很喜歡她。

⑩ 爸爸媽媽__________二十多年了，我從來沒看過他們吵架。

⑪ 校長向我們__________了新來的老師。

⑫ 人際__________很重要，你要學會和周圍的人做朋友。

⑬ 鄰居之間要互相幫助，和睦__________。

填入正確的關聯詞。Fill in the blanks with appropriate correlative conjunctions.

⑭ 老師__________下課__________找我談話。

⑮ 媽媽回家以後一般都會__________煮飯，__________洗衣服。

課堂活動 Class Activities

聽寫大比拼 Dictation Competition

學生分成 A、B 兩組。每組學生按照 1-10 號編號。A、B 組的 1 號站到黑板前準備好。老師説出詞語。A、B 組的 1 號學生在黑板上寫出詞語。A 組的 2 號學生上台改 B 組學生寫的詞語，B 組的 2 號學生上台改 A 組學生寫的詞語。對的打 √，錯的打 ×，並訂正。以此類推。老師最後給兩組評分。哪一組分數高則哪一組贏。

Divide students into Group A and Group B. Students in each group are numbered according to numbers 1-10. The No.1 students of Group A and B get ready in front of the blackboard. The teacher says the words. The No.1 students from Group A and B write the words on the blackboard. The No. 2 student in Group A comes to the stage to correct the words written by students of Group B, and the No. 2 student in Group B comes to the stage to correct the words written by students of Group A. If the words are right, tick √; if they are wrong, cross ×, and write out the correct words. Repeat the steps. The teacher finally grades the two groups. The group with the higher score wins.

口語訓練 Speaking Tasks

第一部分 **根據圖片，做 3–4 分鐘的口頭表達。做口頭表達之前，先根據提示寫大綱。**

Make a 3-4 minutes oral presentation based on the picture. Before you start, use the form below to make an outline.

大綱 Outline	內容 Content
圖片內容 Information of the picture	
圖片主題 + 文化 Theme of the picture and culture	
提出觀點 Make your points	
延伸個人經歷 Relate to personal experiences	
名人名言 Famous quotes / 熟語 Idioms	
總結 Summary	

第二部分 **回答下面的問題。Answer the following questions.**

① 為什麼現在很多人都喜歡上網購物？

② 上網購物有什麼不好的地方嗎？

③ 有人認為手機短信改變了我們的交流方式，你同意嗎？

④ 無所不在的智能手機、平板電腦和遊戲機讓現代年輕人久坐不動，越來越胖。你有什麼辦法讓年輕人少看手機、多做運動？

⑤ 科技在給人們的生活帶來方便的同時，也帶來了不好的影響。你能舉一些例子嗎？

技能訓練 Skill Tasks

閱讀訓練 Reading Tasks

文章 1 疫情改變了我們的生活方式

仔細閱讀下面的短文，然後回答問題。

Read the passage carefully and answer the following questions.

各位老師、同學：

大家好！2020 年的疫情，對我們是一場重大的考驗，也給我們上了一堂深刻而生動的生活課。今天我想跟大家談談疫情是如何改變我們的生活方式的。

首先，疫情讓我們養成良好的生活習慣。

調查報告顯示，受疫情影響，98.06% 的深圳市民已經養成外出回家後立即洗手的習慣。另外，以前大家聚餐，共吃一盤菜，這是生活中最常見的飲食習慣。但現在，為了避免病毒傳播，九成上海受訪者外出就餐會使用公筷、公勺或分餐。疫情在一定程度上改變了我們傳統的就餐方式，防止“病從口入”。

其次，疫情讓家庭生活變得更和睦。

疫情期間，大家只能在家開火做飯。80% 的香港市民認為一家人一起研究如何做菜，大大提高了家庭生活質量。除此之外，在這段與家人相聚的時光裏，大家一起鍛煉、一起讀書、一起遊戲，家庭氛圍越來越好。北京青年報調查顯示，71.9% 的青年和父母有了更多共同的愛好。大家開始回歸健康的生活方式，拉近了家人之間的距離。

最後，疫情讓我們以“讀”攻毒，知識水平也提高了。

宅家期間，省去上班通勤時間，大家有更多的時間投入到高質量的閱讀和學習中。50% 的廣州學生認為在家上網學習更好，還能以更舒服的方式閱讀。閱讀為正處於恐懼、緊張狀態的人們點亮“精神燈塔”。在一份關於《因為疫情待在家中的你們每天都在幹什麼》的調查問卷中，超過六成的四川人回答稱“看書”。此外，在居家隔離的日子裏，大家只要動一動手指，就可以開啟一場虛擬藝術之旅，給心靈“排毒”。杭州很多博物館、藝術表演中心等利用 5G、VR 等技術手段開直播，讓網民猶如身臨其境一般觀看展覽、欣賞表演。

疫情打亂了生活的節奏，也改變了我們的生活方式。分餐制、勤洗手、多鍛煉⋯⋯這些健康的行為習慣，值得我們長期堅持下去。經過這次疫情，大家都意識到健康的生活方式可以讓我們的生活更美好。希望大家以這次疫情為契機，把健康的生活方式堅持下去。

改編自：https://www.meipian.cn/2upa2o21

根據以上短文把下列詞語和句子配對。

Match the sentences with the words according to the short passage above.

例：深圳市民 ___D___

① 上海市民 ______

② 香港市民 ______

③ 北京青年 ______

④ 廣州學生 ______

⑤ 四川人 ______

⑥ 杭州人 ______

A. 外出就餐要使用公筷。

B. 能像在現場觀看一樣看演出、展覽。

C. 疫情期間大多在家看書。

D. 養成了外出回家立即洗手的習慣。

E. 出門看演出。

F. 家庭生活質量提高了。

G. 可以通過閱讀提高智商。

H. 能更舒服地閱讀了。

I. 和家人有了更多共同的愛好。

根據短文填空。Fill in the blanks with the given words.

例：疫情 對 我們 是一場重大 考驗 。

實驗　我們　對　考驗

⑦ 疫情期間，大家________ ________ ________，家庭氛圍更和睦了。

一起　活動　做　一定

⑧ ________在家上班，大家________更多時間在家________。

有　舒服　閱讀　因為

根據短文回答下面的問題。Answer the following question based on the passage above.

⑨ 這篇文章的寫作目的是什麼？

____

Tips

準確把握文章的寫作目的 Grasp the Purpose of Writing Articles Accurately

閱讀一篇文章，僅僅做到概括主要內容是不夠的。了解了文章的主要內容後，我們還需要進一步把握文章的寫作目的，這樣才算是真正讀懂了一篇文章。文章的寫作目的由文本內容體現。所以在閱讀文章時，首先要通讀全文，了解文章的體裁和主要內容，然後再通過內容去把握文章的寫作目的。

When you read an article, it is not enough to just summarize the main content. After scanning the main content of the article, we also need to grasp the purpose of writing the article, so as to truly understand an article. The writing purpose of the article is revealed by the content of the text. Therefore, when reading the article, you must first read the full text, understand the genre and the main content of the article, and then grasp the purpose of the article according to the content.

例如，通過閱讀，我們知道文章一首先提出疫情改變了我們的生活方式，然後從三個方面舉例說明疫情如何改變了我們的生活方式，並使大家開始意識到健康的生活習慣讓我們的生活更美好。所以作者的寫作目的是希望大家以這次疫情為契機，把健康的生活習慣堅持下去。本文的寫作目的在文末直接點了出來。

For example, through reading, we know that the first article pointed out that the epidemic has changed our way of life, and then gave three examples of how the epidemic has changed our way of life, which makes people began to realize that healthy lifestyles make our lives better. Therefore, the author's final writing purpose is to hope that everyone will take this epidemic as a chance and stick to healthy living habits. The purpose of writing this article is directly pointed out at the end of the article.

文章 2 青少年厭食問題的口頭報告

尊敬的校長、各位老師：

大家好！我是學生會主席何小良。今天我將在這裏向各位做關於青少年厭食問題的口頭報告，希望能引起大家的注意。

一、【–1–】

❶ 隨著青春期的臨近，青少年的身心健康問題引起了人們的重視。學生會此次開展調查的目的是通過對青少年厭食症的了解，更好地幫助他們調節心情、注意飲食均衡，從而提高學習效率、改善身心健康。

二、【–2–】

❷ 我們用不記名的方式，通過電話採訪、發送電子郵件、訪問等方式對全校 1200 名學生進行了調查。

三、【–3–】

❸ 調查顯示：約有 10% 的學生得了厭食症，而且大部分都是女生。

四、【–4–】

❹ 造成學生得厭食症的主要原因有兩個。一是有的學生想要保持苗條的身材而節食；二是一些學生因心情不好拒絕飲食，時間長了就會產生厭食的問題。

五、【–5–】

❺ 從上述調查結果來看，很多學生因厭食症而無法專心學習，我們認為應該及早發現、及早治療，才可有效減少厭食症對青少年身心健康的傷害。我們建議青少年保持平和的心態，接受自己的狀態，並努力地去做出改變。在體重正常的狀況下，不要使用斷食、節食等不健康的方式來減肥。老師和同學要多關心患上厭食症的學生，多和他們聊天。家長也可以

和孩子談談心，讓孩子把學校裏或者生活上一些不開心的事情說出來，再教他們怎麼去面對和解決問題，以避免學生因受負面情緒影響而厭食。

謝謝大家！

改編自：https://jingyan.baidu.com/article/fb48e8bee747b96e622e14ad.html

根據文章 2，選出最適合的段落標題，把答案寫在橫線上。

According to passage 2, choose the appropriate titles and write the answers on the lines.

① [–1–] ________ A. 調查分析
② [–2–] ________ B. 調查方法
③ [–3–] ________ C. 建議
④ [–4–] ________ D. 調查結果
⑤ [–5–] ________ E. 調查對象
F. 調查目的

根據文章 2，選出最接近左邊詞語的解釋。把答案寫在橫線上。

According to passage 2, choose the correct definitions and write the answers on the lines.

⑥ 報告 ________ A. 呈現
⑦ 調節 ________ B. 報道
⑧ 顯示 ________ C. 安排
⑨ 拒絕 ________ D. 中斷
⑩ 傷害 ________ E. 調整
F. 據説
G. 破壞
H. 講述
I. 傷心

根據 ❺，回答下面的問題。Answer the following question according to ❺.

⑪ 青少年自己應如何面對厭食症？

a. ____________________

b. ____________________

c. ____________________

根據文章 2，選出五個正確的敘述。把答案寫在橫線上。

According to passage 2, choose five true statements and write the answers on the lines.

關於青少年厭食的口頭報告中提到：

⑫ ________ A. 厭食症跟心情有關係。

________ B. 得厭食症的青少年大部分是男生。

________ C. 想要保持好身材而節食，是造成厭食的主要原因之一。

________ D. 學生會通過面對面的形式採訪得厭食症的青少年。

________ E. 得了厭食症，學生就無法專心讀書。

F. 有些學生會通過斷食來減肥。

G. 在學校大概有 15% 的學生得厭食症。

H. 老師和同學要多關心得厭食症的學生。

選出正確的答案。Choose the correct answer.

⑬ 這是一篇 ______ 。

A. 調查報告　B. 口頭報告　C. 演講稿　D. 評論

Tips

分清主次，概括段落大意　Distinguish the main idea of the general paragraph

段落是通向全篇的橋樑，只有準確概括段落大意，才能抓住文章的重點，從而把握文章。分清主次、概括段落大意是深入理解課文的重要途徑之一，也是進行分析、概括、綜合為主的邏輯思維訓練的一種重要方法。

Paragraphs are the bridge to the whole article. Only by accurately summarizing the main idea of the paragraph, can we grasp the main point of the article. It is one of the important ways to understand the text in depth. It is also an important logical thinking training method based on analyzing, summarizing and synthesizing.

因此，在閱讀時要對段落中的每一句話通過分析、比較，分清哪些是主要的，哪些是次要的，抓住段落中與全文主要意思有密切關係的內容，取主捨次，然後運用簡練、準確的語言進行概括表達。

Therefore, when reading each sentence in the paragraph, it is necessary to analyze, compare, and distinguish which is the main and which is the secondary by analyzing and comparing each sentence. Grasp the content in the paragraph that is closely related to the main idea of the full text, and focus on the main points. Then make general expression concisely and accurately.

例如第 ❶ 段，一共講了三句話，三層意思。第一層講青少年身心健康問題引起人們的重視；第二層講調查的目的；第三層講治療厭食症的好處。通過這三層，我們發現第一層和第三層都是圍繞第二層來寫的。所以，第一、三層是次要內容，第二層就是主要內容。

For example, in paragraph ❶, there are three sentences with three meanings in total. The first layer talks about teenagers' physical and mental health issues that arouse people's attention. The second layer investigates the purpose. The third layer treats the benefits of anorexia. Through these three layers, we find that the first and the third layers are written around the second layer. Therefore, the first and the third levels are the secondary content, and the second level is the main content.

聽力訓練 Listening Tasks

一、《2020 新生活方式》

你將聽到六段錄音，每段錄音兩遍。請在相應的橫線上回答問題 ①–⑥。回答應簡短扼要。每段錄音後會有停頓，請在停頓期間閱讀問題。

You will hear 6 recordings, and each audio will be played twice. Answer the questions ①-⑥ with short answers. There will be a pause after each recording is played. Please read the questions during the pause.

① 2020 年生活方式最明顯的改變是什麼？

____

② 這家飯館沒有什麼菜？

____

③ 今天直播的推薦產品是什麼？

____

④ 疫情期間，人們開始用什麼樣的方式旅行？

____

⑤ 上網課有什麼好處？

____

⑥ 疫情讓很多人意識到什麼？

____

二、《如何養成健康的網絡生活方式？》

你即將聽到第二個聽力片段，在聽力片段二播放之前，你將有四分鐘的時間先閱讀題目。聽力片段將播放兩次，聽力片段結束後你將有兩分鐘的時間來檢查你的答案。請用中文回答問題。

You are going to hear the second audio clip. You have 4 minutes to read the questions before it starts. The audio clip will be played twice. After it ends, you have 2 mintes to check the answers. Please answer the questions in Chinese.

根據第二個聽力片段，回答問題 ①-⑨ 。

Answer the question ①-⑨, according to the second audio clip.

Tips

如何應對事實細節題？How to deal with questions for facts and details?

短文式聽力提問題型之一是細節把握題，主要考查的細節包括具體時間、地點、主要人物、事件、各類數字等，問題一般為：六何法（何時、何地、何事、為何、何人、如何）。這種題型要求考生聽到文中出現時間、數字時一定要特別敏感，及時做好筆記；文中一旦出現以因果連詞（如：因為、由於等）和轉折連詞（如：但是、雖然、可是等）引導的句子，要格外留心，這些地方往往就是考點。

One of the short essay listening questioning methods is providing facts and details. The main details include specific time, place, main characters, events, various numbers, etc. The general question includes: 5W+1H (when, where, what, why , who and how). This type of question requires candidates to be particularly sensitive when hearing the time and numbers appearing in the text and to take notes in time; you should pay attention to those casual conjunctions (such as because, due to, etc.) and transitional conjunctions (such as but, although, etc.), because the sentences with those words are usually the keypoints.

根據第二個聽力片段的內容，從 A，B，C 中，選出一個正確的答案，把答案寫在橫線上。

According to the second audio clip, choose the right answer for the questions. Write the answers on the lines.

① 王小燕是______。

A. 主播　　B. 網絡健康專家　　C. 身心健康專家

② 學生的眼睛變壞的原因是______。

A. 被媽媽發現　　B. 每天晚上不睡覺　　C. 關著燈打遊戲

③ 熬夜打遊戲的結果不包括______。

A. 和媽媽關係不好

B. 上課沒精神

C. 學習效率低

填空題，每個空格最多填三個詞語。Fill in the blanks, three words for each blank at maximum.

如果家長不同意給學生買電腦，學生可以到【-4-】去上網。學生也可以和家長【-5-】一下上網的好處。例如，學生可以在網上查找參考資料，【-6-】最新的知識。學生還可以通過網絡【-7-】自己平時需要的學習工具和生活用品，既省時又省力。

④ [-4-] ______________________________

⑤ [-5-] ______________________________

⑥ [-6-] ______________________________

⑦ [-7-] ______________________________

回答下面的問題。Answer the following questions.

⑧ 網絡聊天工具有哪些？請舉出一例。

⑨ 網絡詐騙包括哪些？請舉出一例。

如何應對聽力填空題？

How to deal with fill-in-the-blank questions in listening?

1. 先看短文，預測聽寫內容
   Read the essay first and predict the content of the dictation.

   聽力填空題通常是一個完整的片段，大概在 100-200 個字左右。一共聽兩遍。考生可利用聽正文前的空隙，先看一遍這個片段，了解大概的內容。通常在片段開頭會出現主題句，比如聽力二樣本裏第一句話就是 "關於網絡的好處……"。考生不要漏掉這個重要的句子，因為它有助於你了解主要內容，這樣你就不會慌張，影響正常水平的發揮了。

   The text for listening fill-in-the-blank questions is usually a complete fragment with about 100-200 words. Candidates can listen to it twice. Candidates can take advantage of the gap before listening to the text to read the short essay first, so as to understand the general content, which is usually written at the beginning of the fragment. For example, the first sentence in the second listening sample is: The benefits of the Internet... Candidates should not miss this important sentence, because it helps you understand the main content, so that you will not be panic and your normal level of performance will not be affected.

2. 使用速記方法，從文中找出答案
   Use shorthand methods to find answers from the text.

   學生們在聽寫時，往往記下了聽寫的第一個詞，而後面的不是記不住就是來不及寫。針對這一問題，平時就要練習使用速記方法，迅速記下聽到的每個詞語，不漏掉任何內容。此外，還出現另一種現象，就是學生聽懂了詞意，但不會寫詞語。對於這種情況，考生除了平時要多掌握詞彙，考試中還可以從上下文查找，看是否有幫助指示的地方。

   When students are dictating, they often memorize the first word of the dictation, but for the rest they are either unable to remember or too late to write. To solve this problem, students should practice using shorthand methods at ordinary times, quickly jot down every word you hear, and do not miss anything. In addition, it occurs that students can understand the meaning of words but don't know how to write. In this situation, candidates should learn more vocabulary. During the test, they can look for clues from the context given.

Tips

文體：指南

Text Type: Guide

指南是為人們提供指導性資料的文體，用於介紹事物的性能、特點、作用、注意事項等。

A guide is a style of writing that is instructive in nature, and is used to introduce the performance, characteristics, functions, precautions, etc. of things.

寫作訓練：指南 Writing Tasks: Guide

熱身

- **根據課文一，討論指南的格式是什麼。**

  According to Text 1, discuss the format of a guide.

- **如何寫好指南？How to write a guide?**

格式 參考課文一

標題

□□開頭：介紹目的 / 產品簡介

□□正文：分段介紹 / 列點介紹

□□結尾：總結全文 + 表達希望

XXX

XX 年 X 月 X 日

練習

為了慶祝中國春節，老師讓大家做一種中國傳統食品，比如水餃、湯圓、月餅等。請選擇一種食品，向大家介紹如何製作這種美食。選用合適的文本類型完成寫作。字數：300–480 個漢字。

新聞報道	演講稿	指南

Tips

指南的重點 The Focus of A Guide

指南的標題要一目了然，一看就知道內容是什麼，才會吸引受眾往下看。開頭可以使用一些反問句、設問句來引起讀者的注意。注意指南是正式文稿，不要寫自己的看法和感想。

The title should be clear at a glance, and you can know what the content is at a glance, so that it will attract the target audience to continue to read. At the beginning, you can use some rhetorical questions to communicate with readers. Please note that the guide is a formal manuscript, do not write your own opinions and thoughts.

Our World
我們的世界

Unit

Lesson 4

Science and Technology
科學與技術

Lesson 5

Arts
藝術

Lesson 6

Education and Future Career Plans
教育與未來職業計劃

Lesson 4

Science and Technology

科學與技術

導入 Introduction

科學與技術的革新改變了我們的生活方式。從馬車到飛機，從油燈到節能燈，從遠在天邊的語音聊天到近在眼前的視頻聊天，從古老的四大發明到嫦娥五號飛天計劃，從李時珍的《本草綱目》到新冠疫苗的研發，從線下購物到網絡購物，科技每時每刻都在發展和創新，讓人們的生活越來越美好。但科技有時可能也讓我們的生活變得更糟糕：網絡讓年輕人誤入歧途，也遺忘了中華民族的美德；真假新聞讓我們難以辨別。作為年輕人，我們應該永遠保持探索世界的好奇心，爭取做具有科學態度、追求真理的新時代青年。

The development of science and technology has changed our lifestyles. Technology brings us a lot convenience: from horse-drawn carriages to airplanes, from oil lamps to energy-saving lamps, from voice call to real time video call, from the four great ancient inventions to the Chang'e 5 space project, from Li Shizhen's *Compendium of Materia Medica* to the development of COVID-19 vaccines, from offline shopping to online shopping. Technology is developing and innovating all the time, making people's life better and better. But it seems that technology sometimes also brings our life negative impacts. Some online information will lead teenagers astray and makes them forget the virtues of the Chinese nation. There is also fake news online which often mislead our view. As a teenager, we should always maintain a curiosity of exploration and striving for the best with an attitude of being scientific and pursuing truth.

學習目標 Learning Targets

閱讀 Reading

- 學會使用尋讀法，快速準確找出信息。
  Learn to use the searching method to find out information quickly and accurately.

口語 Speaking

- 學會用擬人手法讓説明的事物更加清晰、具體，更有趣味。
  Learn to use anthropomorphism to introduce issue/objects more clearly, specifically and in a more interesting manner.

聽力 Listening

- 學會在做改錯題時，劃出關鍵詞。
  Learn to draw out the key words in the question when solving the correction questions.
- 學會在聽力考試前抓緊時間讀題。
  Learn to read the questions before the listening audio being played.

寫作 Writing

- 學會如何寫好評論。
  Learn to write a review.

1 課文　看《嫦娥五號直播》有感 13

陳小珍

今天，從新聞直播中看到關於嫦娥五號成功返回地面的消息後，我激動萬分。這是中國首次實現收集月球樣本返回地球，標誌著中國的科技事業取得重大進步，每一位華人都為此感到驕傲和自豪！

主持人主要介紹了從嫦娥一號到五號執行的不同任務，讓觀眾了解了中國探月工程的每一步。在新聞直播中，還發生了一件趣事，一隻小動物從嫦娥五號返回器旁邊跑過，成功吸引了廣大網友的注意。這讓本次新聞直播一下子變得生動起來，大家都說是嫦娥把月亮上的兔子帶回家了，讓兔子也來地球玩一玩。

這次直播讓我印象最深刻的，是主持人的解說。因為和其他主持人不同，他能用簡單的語言介紹嫦娥五號的構成和工作過程，利用形象生動的比喻以及簡單的科學道理進行講解，所以這次直播大家都觀看得很輕鬆。這樣一來，原本很難理解的探月工程就變得十分接地氣，這對普及民眾的科學知識很重要。主持人講解的不僅是一堂生動的探月知識課，還是一堂豐富的科技創新課。

嫦娥五號的成功返回，讓我們離

生詞短語

- xīn wén 新聞 news
- zhí bō 直播 live broadcasting
- cháng'é 嫦娥 Chang'e
- fǎn huí 返回 return
- jī dòng wàn fēn 激動萬分 greatly excited
- zhǔ chí rén 主持人 host
- tàn yuè gōng chéng 探月工程 lunar exploration program
- wǎng yǒu 網友 netizen
- jiě shuō 解說 explain
- gòu chéng 構成 constitution
- guò chéng 過程 process
- bǐ yù 比喻 analogy
- dào lǐ 道理 reason
- qīng sōng 輕鬆 relaxed
- jiē dì qì 接地氣 grounded
- pǔ jí 普及 popularize
- yǔ zhòu 宇宙 universe
- tàn suǒ 探索 explore
- guǎng kuò 廣闊 broad
- chuán bō zhě 傳播者 communicator
- jiě shì 解釋 explain
- gāo shēn 高深 profound
- tuī dòng 推動 promote
- yì wù 義務 obligation

宇宙又近了一步。人類對科學的研究、對宇宙的探索是廣闊的。這次直播在科技與大眾之間架起了一座橋，讓每一個人都能更好地了解科學知識！我從小就對科技新聞感興趣，主持人的精彩解說，讓我明白了科技傳播者的重要性，也堅定了我想成為主持人的決心。希望在不久的將來，我也能作為一名主持人，用年輕人的語言以及他們易於接受的方式，去解釋一些高深的科技詞語。只有多用大家熟悉的語言來解釋科技，科技才能被更多的人所認識，才能真正走進我們的生活。

從中國古代的四大發明到現代的嫦娥五號，一次次的創新都讓人們體會到科技對人類美好生活所起的巨大推動作用。既然科技發展是國家強大的基礎，那麼普及科學知識就變得更加重要，也是我們年輕人應該承擔的責任和義務。我們應該像新聞直播的主持人那樣，為普及科學知識盡自己的一份力！

Culture Point

中國古代的四大發明 Four Great Inventions of Ancient China

中國是世界文明古國之一。古代中國的科技非常發達，勤勞智慧的中國人為世界貢獻了許多發明創造，其中最有名的是指南針、造紙術、印刷術和火藥，被稱作“中國古代的四大發明”。

China is one of the ancient civilizations in the world. The science technology in ancient China was advanced in the world. Chinese is industrious and wise that contributed to the world a great number of inventions and creations such as the compass, papermaking, printing and gunpowder, which are known as Four Great Inventions of Ancient China.

嫦娥奔月 Chang'e Flying to the Moon

傳説嫦娥本是后羿的妻子。后羿射下九個太陽後，西王母給了他不老仙藥，但后羿不捨得吃，就交給妻子保管。后羿的一個弟子想要吃仙藥，有一天趁后羿不在，就逼嫦娥交出仙藥，嫦娥沒有辦法只好自己吞下仙藥，向天上飛去。當日正是八月十五，月亮又大又亮，嫦娥就只好住在月亮上了。后羿思念妻子，於是擺上月餅、茶和水果等，等著嫦娥從月亮飛回家，夫妻團聚。中國科學家藉助這個家喻戶曉的美麗傳説，把探月計劃比喻成嫦娥奔月，既符合中國文化，又能傳播科技知識。

Legend has it that Chang'e is Houyi's wife. Queen Mother of the West gave Houyi one elixir of life as a reward of his shotting off the nine extra suns for people. Houyi was reluctant to take it alone so he gave it to his wife Chang'e for safekeeping. One of Houyi's disciple wanted to obtain the elixir and forced Chang'e to hand over to him one day when Houyi was not around. Chang'e had no choice but to swallow the elixir and flew into the sky. That day was August 15 in Chinese lunar calendar and the moon was big and bright. Chang'e stopped on the moon and lived there since then. Houyi missed his wife, so he put out moon cakes, tea and other fruits, waiting for Chang'e to fly back to reunite. This is an well-known and beautiful ancient Chinese legend. Chinese scientists compare the moon exploration project to Chang'e flying to the moon, which not only conforms to Chinese culture but also spreads the knowledge of science and technology.

語法重點 Key Points of Grammar

因果關係複句

Causal Complex Sentence

由兩個有因果關係的分句組成，分句之間是原因和結果的關係。

It consists of two clauses with a casual relationship. Relationship between the clauses is cause and effect.

常用關聯詞

Common Conjunctive Words

因為……，所以……；既然……就……；由於……；因此……

because of…; since/now that…; due to…; therefore…

E.g.

- 因為疫情嚴重，所以大家都被要求待在家裏。
  Because of the seriousness of the epidemic, everyone was required to stay at home.
- 既然生病了，就不要去上學。
  Since you are sick, don't go to school.
- 由於一直上網打遊戲，毛毛的眼睛近視了。
  Because of playing online games very often, Maomao's eyes became short-sighted.
- 可可從小失去了父母，因此很早就學會了獨立。
  Keke lost her parents when she was a child, therefore she learned to be independent at an early age.

課文理解 Reading Comprehensions

① "我"為什麼很激動？

② 新聞直播的內容是什麼？

③ 直播時發生了什麼有趣的事？

④ 讓“我”印象最深刻的是什麼？

⑤ 為什麼用大眾熟悉的語言解釋科技很重要？

概念與拓展理解 Concepts and Further Understanding

① 語言如何幫助人類分享科技知識？
How does language help humans share scientific and technological knowledge?

② 有影響力的個人可以用什麼樣的方式對科學發展做出貢獻？
In what ways do the influential individuals contribute to the development of science?

③ 科學的發展是否會隨著時代、文化或傳統的變遷而變化？
Will the development of science change with the changes of the times, cultures or traditions?

④ 不同國家之間科學的競爭是否會妨礙知識的傳播？
Will scientific competition among different countries hinder the spreading of knowledge?

⑤ 科學研究是否應該遵守倫理的約束？
Should scientific research comply with ethical constraints?

語言練習 Language Exercises

在方塊裏填字，使內框與外框的字組成詞語。

Fill in the outer boxes to make compound words with the word in the inner box.

①

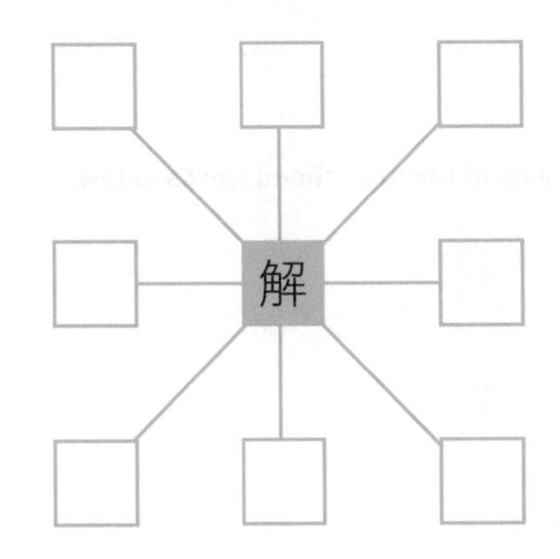

②

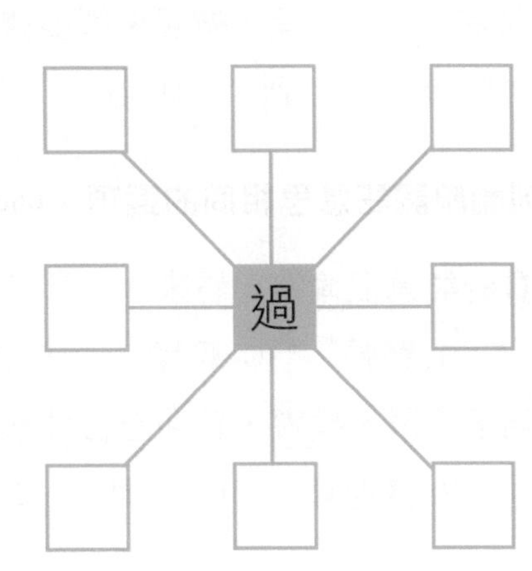

③

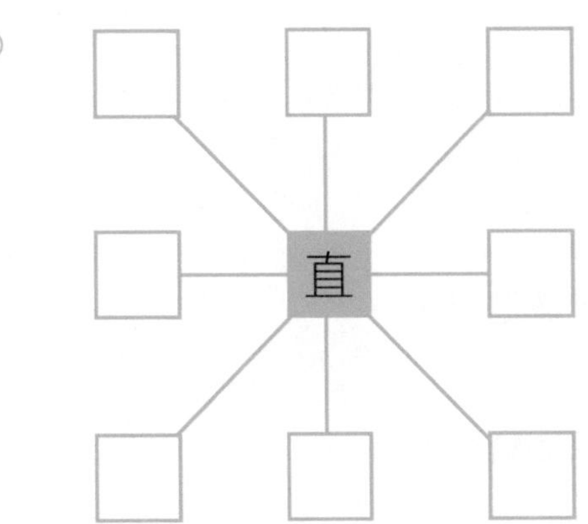

④

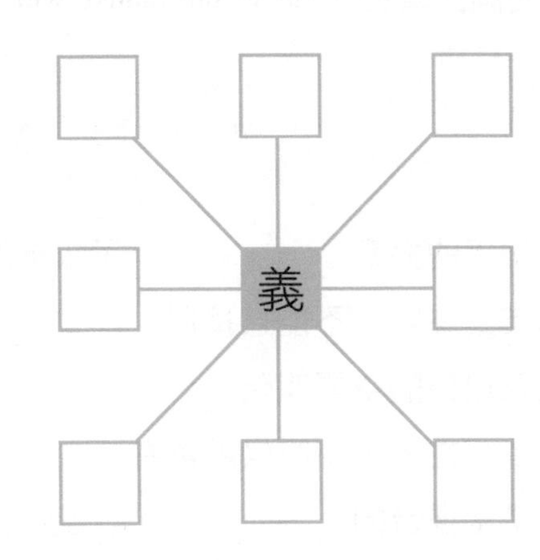

從所提供的選項中選出正確的答案。Choose the correct answer to the question.

⑤ 我每天晚上都邊看________聞邊吃飯。

A. 辛　B. 親　C. 心　D. 新

⑥ 一聽到媽媽生病的消息，她馬上就坐飛機________回新加坡。

A. 反　B. 返　C. 飯　D. 泛

⑦ 李明一看到劍橋大學的錄取通知書，就________動得跳了起來。

A. 激　B. 邀　C. 傲　D. 敖

⑧ 他的理想是將來成為一名生物科學家，________索生命的奧秘。

A. 深　B. 琛　C. 探　D. 貪

⑨ 藍天、白雲、綠水，________成了一幅美麗的圖畫。

A. 購　B. 構　C. 勾　D. 鈎

⑩ 他的作文寫得好，是因為他會用________喻、擬人等寫作手法。

A. 必　B. 筆　C. 此　D. 比

⑪ 你説的很有________理，做起來卻很難。

A. 道　B. 首　C. 到　D. 倒

選出與下列劃線詞語意思相同的選項。Choose the synonyms of the underlined words below.

⑫ 今天比賽的氣氛很愉快，看來大家都沒有壓力了。 □

A. 嚴肅　B. 緊張　C. 輕鬆　D. 張力

⑬ 他説的話很簡單、樸實，普通老百姓都聽得懂。 □

A. 老實　B. 接地氣　C. 高調　D. 普通

選擇正確的詞語填空。Fill in the blanks with the right words.

普及　宇宙　探索　廣闊　傳播者　主持人　解釋　高深　推動

⑭ 作者對環境的描寫____________了故事的發展。

⑮ 給小朋友上課時，不能直接用____________的理論來教他們。

⑯ 地球大氣以外的空間叫作____________。

⑰ 包老師是蒙古人，小時候經常在____________的草原上騎馬。

⑱ 倪老師是電視台的____________，普通話特別標準。

⑲ 每個人都有可能是新冠肺炎的____________，出門請一定要戴好口罩。

⑳ 何老師總能用簡單的一兩句話把一個複雜的問題____________得清清楚楚。

㉑ 科學家們積極____________人類的起源。

㉒ 隨着現代教育的____________，人們的平均文化水平有所提高。

填入正確的關聯詞。Fill in the blanks with appropriate correlative conjunctions.

㉓ 她太驕傲了，____________大家都不喜歡她。

㉔ ____________你已經知道錯了，那____________要改正。

㉕ ____________雨天路滑，她不小心摔倒了。

㉖ ____________路上堵車，____________我上學遲到了。

課堂活動 Class Activities

同音字遊戲 Homonym

老師將學生分成 A、B 兩組。每組學生按照 1-11 號編號。A、B 兩組的 1 號各到白板前寫出課文一生詞中的一個字。例如 A 組 1 號寫“解”，B 組 1 號寫“直”。A、B 兩組的 2 號到白板前寫出 1 號所寫的同音字。這些同音字不需要來自課文的生詞，聲調也可以不同。例如，A 組 2 號寫“姐”，B 組 2 號寫“知”。按號碼順序一直往下接，不能藉助字典或其他工具，但同組其他同學可以提示。五分鐘之內，哪一組寫得多，哪一組就獲勝。

The teacher divides students into Group A and Group B. Students in each group are numbered 1-11. Students of No.1 from each group choose one Chinese character from the vocabulary list of Text 1 and write it on the whiteboard. For example, one student writes " 解 " and another writes " 直 ". Students of No.2 from each group write the homophones of the Chinese character that No.1 student wrote. These homophones do not need to be from the vocabulary list of Text 1 and the tone could be different. For example, the student from Group A writes " 姐 " and the student from Group B writes " 知 ". Continue the game with these rules. Dictionaries or other tools are not allowed to use. But other students from the same group are allowed to prompt. Within 5 minutes, the group that comes with more correct Chinese characters wins.

口語訓練 Speaking Tasks

第一部分 **根據主題“科學技術”，選擇一種科技發明，做 2-3 分鐘的口頭表達。做口頭表達之前，先根據提示寫大綱。**

Choose a technological invention, make a 2-3 minutes oral presentation on the theme "science and technology". Before you start, use the form below to make an outline.

大綱 Outline	內容 Content
觀點 Perspectives	
事例 Examples	
名人名言 Famous quotes / 熟語 Idioms	
經歷 Experiences	
總結 Summary	

Tips

如何描述事物？How to describe an object?

通常我們在描述一個事物的時候，都會採用白描法，就是用簡單的詞彙進行直接簡練的描述，使用白描法雖然簡單直接、清楚明白，但是別人聽起來會比較沉悶。

The most common approach to describe an object is Direct Description which uses simple words to describe an object. This makes your description easy to be understood but also sounds depressing.

比如，"蘋果手錶是一種電子手錶，可以用來打電話、發短信，還可以連接車載電子設備、查看天氣、播放音樂、測量心跳、計步等，是一款全方位的健康和運動追蹤設備。"

For example, "The Apple watch is an electronic watch that can make calls, send text messages, connect to vehicle electronic devices, check the weathers, play music, measure heartbeats and count daily steps, etc. It is a comprehensive health and exercise tracking device."

其實，在對事物進行説明的時候，我們可以通過更加形象、生動、有趣的描寫手法，讓事物給人以具體的感受。比如，"蘋果手錶雖然只有積木大小，卻擁有和你身體器官一樣多功能的電子元件。你跑步的時候，它可以變成醫生，隨時注意你的心跳和步數；你要出門，它可以是交通警察，告訴你哪裏堵車，注意避開；它可以是氣象預報專家 , 在可能下雨時提醒你記得帶傘；你累的時候，它可以播放音樂，幫助你放鬆身心……"

In fact, we could make this description much more vivid by using another approach of descriptions. For example, "Apple watch is only the size of a children building block, but it has as many electronic components as your body organs. It is your doctor who monitors your heartbeats and steps when you are jogging. It is a policeman telling you where there is a traffic jam to avoid when you drive on the road. It is a weather forecast expert who reminds you to bring an umbrella when it's going to rain. And it plays music when you are tired to help you relax your body and mind..."

通過擬人手法，你説明的事物就變得更清晰、具體，也更有趣味，聽眾更容易明白蘋果手錶的特性。

By using anthropomorphic techniques, your description will be clearer, more specific and more interesting. It is easier for the audience to understand the features of the Apple watch.

第二部分 回答下面的問題。Answer the following questions.

① 你認為哪一項科學技術發明給人類帶來了好的影響？

② 你認為哪一項科學技術發明給人類帶來了糟糕的影響？

③ 你認為普及科學知識重要嗎？為什麼？

④ "科學" 在不同的文化中是否意味著不同的內容？

⑤ 如果讓你回到一個沒有任何現代科技的環境中，你會害怕嗎？為什麼？

2 課文 科技改變生活 14

——訪問沈康中局長

科技的發展給我們的衣、食、住、行都帶來了很大改變。智能手機、智能手錶、智能出行等為我們的生活增加了便利。但科技真的讓我們的生活變得越來越美好了嗎？今天，我們有幸採訪中國科技局局長沈康中。現在，有請沈局長和我們談談科技是如何改變我們的生活的。

記 沈局長好！我是《科技報》的記者，謝謝您接受我的採訪。隨著嫦娥五號的成功返回，人們對科技的熱情大大提高。您能和我們介紹一下，科技是如何改變我們的生活的嗎？

沈 首先，科技改變了我們的溝通方式。過去，我們只能通過寫信和他人聯繫，而且要好久才能收到信件。而現在，我們只要在社交媒體上發個消息或打個電話就可以了。其次，手機應用程序的發明，使人們的出行更加方便了，而且不用帶現金就可以走遍天下。不僅如此，隨著人工智能的發展，機器人已經可以幫助人們做家務了。

記 科技的發展讓我們對未來的生活充滿希望。您能和我們介紹一下未來的生活將是怎樣的嗎？

沈 未來人們如果想要控制周圍的東西，不需要自己親自動手；假如你想要認識所有的漢字，不需要辛苦背單詞，只要在大腦中放入中文詞彙芯片；如果身體哪個器官出了問題，醫生直接通過DNA克隆新的器官就可以解決問題；要是不幸被車撞了，也不用擔心，幾分鐘後你馬上就可以站起來了；即使不喜歡在地球上生活，也可以去太空，那

生詞短語

zhì néng
智能 smart

yǒu xìng
有幸 fortunate

cǎi fǎng
採訪 interview

kē jì jú
科技局 science and technology bureau

shè jiāo méi tǐ
社交媒體 social media

xiāo xi
消息 message

yìng yòng chéng xù
應用程序 app

chū xíng
出行 movement

rén gōng zhì néng
人工智能 artificial inelligence

jiā wù
家務 housework

xīn piàn
芯片 chip

kè lóng
克隆 clone

qì guān
器官 organ

tài kōng
太空 space

shì yìng
適應 adapt

jiàn kāng mǎ
健康碼 health code

yí dòng zhī fù
移動支付 mobile payment

sǎo mǎ
掃碼 scan code

shuā liǎn
刷臉 facial recognition

fán nǎo
煩惱 annoy

biàn jié
便捷 convenience

裏將是人類的新家。

記 科技發展得這麼快，每個人都能適應嗎？

沈 並不是每個人都能適應科技進步的社會。就拿智能手機來說，中國內地在新冠疫情期間要求每個乘車的人都出示健康碼，可是很多老人連手機都沒有，也不懂什麼是健康碼，因此很難出門。還有老人不懂如何上網買票，而是到火車站辛苦地排隊，還不一定買得到。高科技的時代，老人所熟悉的生活方式完全被改變了，世界正在迫使老人適應科技發展下的社會。所以，在普及先進的智能手機的同時，我們應該給不會使用智能手機的人提供幫助，讓他們不再為移動支付、掃碼、刷臉而煩惱。

記 是的，在追求速度的時代，從 2G 到 5G，當我們在享受便捷的同時，千萬不要忘了那些腳步慢的老人。我們應該幫助他們儘快融入新世界，讓老人與時代同行。

Culture Point

中國高鐵

China High-Speed Railway

中國高速鐵路，簡稱中國高鐵，是指中國境內建成使用的高速鐵路，為當代中國重要的一類交通基礎設施。至 2019 年底，中國高速鐵路運營總里程達到 35 萬千米，位居世界第一。中國高速鐵路經過多年發展，已經形成了獨具特色的交通體系。

China High-Speed Railway (CHSR) is the high-speed railways system built in China in recent years. It is one of the most important transportation infrastructures in contemporary China. By the end of 2019, China's total operating mileage of high-speed railways reached 35,000 kilometers which ranks the first in the world. After years of development, the high-speed railway has formed a special transportation system in China.

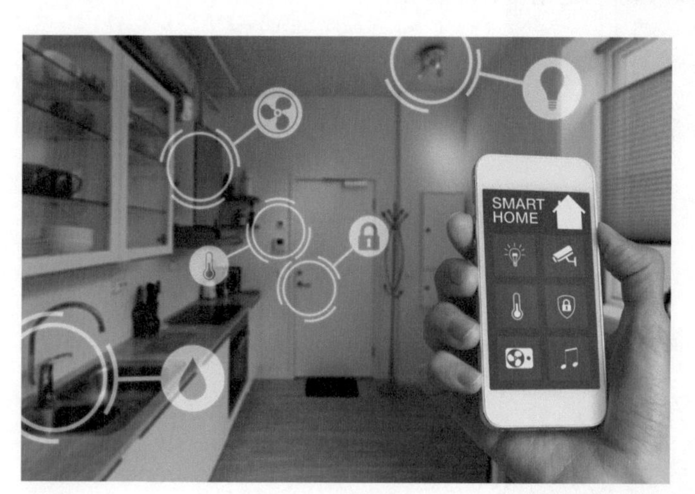

改編自：https://mp.weixin.qq.com/s/n_Oi1jBfXFHSBxPpn26EPw

語法重點 Key Points of Grammar

假設關係複句 Supposative Complex Sentence

由兩個假設關係的分句組成的複句，前一個分句假設存在或出現某種情況，後一個分句説明由這種假設的情況產生的結果。

It consists of two clauses with supposative relations. The former clause supposes the existence or occurrence of a certain situation, and the latter clause explains the outcome produced by this supposative situation.

常用關聯詞 Common Conjunctive Words

如果……就……；即使……也……；儘管……還是……；假如……就……；要是……就…… if...; even if...; although...; if...; so long as...

E.g.

- 如果你生病了，就去看醫生。
  If you are sick, please go to see a doctor.
- 即使明天下雨，我們也要去上學。
  Even if it rains tomorrow, we will go to school.
- 儘管失敗很多次，她還是堅持參加比賽。
  Despite many failures, she insisted on participating in the competition.
- 假如明天天氣好，我們就上室外體育課。
  If the weather is good tomorrow, we will have outdoor P.E. lesson.
- 要是你覺得身體不舒服，就待在家裏休息。
  If you are feeling unwell, rest at home.

課文理解 Reading Comprehensions

① 哪些科技發明給我們的生活帶來了便利？請舉一個例子。

② 傳統的溝通方式都有什麼？

③ 未來世界裏，如果我們的身體器官出了問題，可以怎麼解決？

④ 科技發展太快，使得不會使用智能手機的人都因為什麼事情而煩惱？

⑤ 科技進步的同時，我們應該幫助哪一群人跟上新時代？

概念與拓展理解 Concepts and Further Understanding

① 課文二的文體是什麼？ What is the text type of Text 2?

② 作者寫這篇文章的目的是什麼？ What is the writing purpose of Text 2?

③ 採訪對象不同，會改變文章的語氣嗎？ Will different interviewees change the tone of the article of interview?

④ 傳統的溝通方式一定不好嗎？ Is the traditional way of communication necessarily bad?

⑤ 現代科技一定能促進教育的發展嗎？ Will modern technology definitely promote the development of education?

語言練習 Language Exercises

把下面的詞語組成正確的詞組。

Connect the corresponding words below to form a correct phrase.

① 克隆	程序	② 人工	煩惱
應用	支付	社交	媒體
微信	器官	減少	智能

從生詞表裏找出與下列詞語意思相同或相近的詞。

Find words with the same or similar meanings as the following words in the vocabulary list.

③ 符合＿＿＿＿＿＿＿＿ ④ 好運＿＿＿＿＿＿＿＿ ⑤ 複製＿＿＿＿＿＿＿＿

從生詞表裏找出與下列詞語意思相反的詞。

Find words with the opposite meanings to the following words in the vocabulary list.

⑥ 複雜＿＿＿＿＿＿＿＿ ⑦ 地球＿＿＿＿＿＿＿＿ ⑧ 受訪＿＿＿＿＿＿＿＿

選擇正確的詞語填空。

Fill in the blanks with the right words.

智能　高鐵　科技局　採訪　短信　出行　家務　芯片　健康碼　掃碼　刷臉

⑨ 現在很多學校都通過＿＿＿＿＿來檢查學生是否準時上課。

⑩ 郵寄物品可以＿＿＿＿＿填寫收寄信息。

⑪ 這款手機擁有最好的＿＿＿＿＿，上網速度快，質量也很好。

⑫ 因疫情嚴重，在中國，進出地鐵都要展示＿＿＿＿＿。

⑬ 今年聖誕節，媽媽送給我一台＿＿＿＿＿手機，我高興壞了。

⑭ 中國＿＿＿＿＿四通八達，大家出行很方便。

⑮ 我偶爾回家也會幫媽媽做＿＿＿＿＿。

⑯ 你出門後給我發一條＿＿＿＿＿，我再出發。

⑰ 他雖然是名人，可是不喜歡接受記者的＿＿＿＿＿。

⑱ 早上下了一場大雨，我們的＿＿＿＿＿計劃泡湯了。

⑲ ＿＿＿＿＿的主要工作包括組織一些科技計劃，負責科技經費等。

填入正確的關聯詞。

Fill in the blanks with appropriate correlative conjunctions.

⑳ ＿＿＿＿＿心情不好，＿＿＿＿＿回家休息吧。

㉑ ＿＿＿＿＿人類沒有戰爭，世界將會和平。

㉒ ＿＿＿＿＿考試考得好，＿＿＿＿＿不能驕傲。

㉓ ＿＿＿＿＿老師一直提醒他要好好檢查試卷，他＿＿＿＿＿看錯了一道題。

課堂活動 Class Activities

幻想大比拼 Fantasy Competition

老師說一種科技發明，學生說出它的用途。一個學生只能講一次。這些用途不需要考慮可行性，想法越奇特越好。最後大家一起投票選出最受歡迎的發明。

The teacher talked about a technological invention and the students talked about its use. One student only speaks once. The uses of the invention do not need to be feasible. The more fantastic the idea, the better. Finally, students vote for the most popular invention.

口語訓練 Speaking Tasks

第一部分 **根據圖片，做 3-4 分鐘的口頭表達。做口頭表達之前，先根據提示寫大綱。**

Make a 3-4 minutes oral presentation based on the picture. Before you start, use the form below to make an outline.

大綱 Outline	內容 Content
圖片內容 Information of the picture	
圖片主題 + 文化 Theme of the picture and culture	
提出觀點 Make your points	
延伸個人經歷 Relate to personal experiences	
名人名言 Famous quotes / 熟語 Idioms	
總結 Summary	

第二部分 **回答下面的問題。Answer the following questions.**

① 網絡發明改變了人們的生活方式，也影響了人們溝通方式。互聯網對人們的社交、語言技能方面有哪些正面影響？

② 互聯網對人們的社交、語言技能方面有哪些負面影響？

③ 如果沒有互聯網，我們還能生存下去嗎？

④ 你平時如何通過互聯網進行學習？

⑤ 除了社交和學習，互聯網還給年輕人帶來了哪些好處？

技能訓練 Skill Tasks

閱讀訓練 Reading Tasks

文章 1 第六屆智能城市博覽會

仔細閱讀下面的短文，然後回答問題。

Read the passage carefully and answer the following questions.

科技的進步使得智能城市快速發展。為了方便大家交流，中國科技局決定在北京舉辦第六屆智能城市博覽會。

一、活動目的

為推動全球城市的智能化發展，為城市建設和科技進步提供展示平台，中國科技局特別舉辦第六屆智能城市博覽會。

二、活動對象

任何國家、地區和個人

三、活動詳情

日期：12 月 3 日至 12 月 6 日

地點：北京國際展覽館

四、活動安排

第一天：展區介紹。主要展示全球智能城市示範區、科技與城市生活區、綠色和可持續發展區、國際合作交流區等。

第二天：體驗智能城市生活。民眾可到智能生活區體驗 5G、AI 等技術在生活中的應用。比如，民眾一旦穿上智能衣服，它就可以根據人的身材自動改變尺寸，還可以搭配樣式和顏色。另外，智能衣服不用洗衣機清洗，它可以自動清潔，還可以根據天氣情況，自動調節衣服的溫度。

第三天：體驗變形汽車。民眾可以乘坐無人駕駛汽車，當遇到交通堵塞時，汽車將伸出兩翼升到空中飛行；當遇到河水時，汽車可以在水面航行；到達目的地後，汽車還會自動摺疊，解決停車困難的問題。

第四天：體驗智能運動。展覽區還有其他智能活動，目的是增加運動的趣味性和民眾的參與度。比如，你站在綠色展覽區的地磚上行走或奔跑，磚會自動將產生的能量轉化成電力，提供家庭用電。

五、注意事項

1. 出入展區，請展示健康碼。

2. 隨時隨地都要戴口罩。

3. 請不要在展區吃東西。

第六屆智能城市博覽會是在疫情之下舉行的，我們希望大家能克服困難，做好防護，積極參加博覽會。有興趣的國家、地區和個人請在 10 月 1 日前到 www.keji.cn 網站報名。如有問題，請聯繫微信公眾號：智能城市。

中國科技局

2021 年 9 月 1 日

改編自：http://www.chinasmartcityexpo.com/

Tips

尋讀法 Scanning

尋讀法主要用於從文章中找出某些重要信息，不需要閱讀全部文字。尋讀的目的是快速準確地找出資料和信息，應心中默記提示詞，避免無關的詞彙、思想的干擾。找到之後，就應仔細閱讀上下文了。

Scanning is mainly used to find key information from the text without reading all words. The purpose of searching is to quickly and accurately find out key information. You should keep those prompt words in mind and avoid interference from irrelevant words and thoughts. Once you find it, you should read the text intensively.

比如文章 1 的問題，只要抓住時間、地點、目的就可以在文章中找到答案，而不需要讀完全文。

For example, when read passage 1, you could answer the questions if you are able to catch the time, place, and purpose of the article but without reading the entire article.

為了節省時間，讀者必須熟知材料的排列順序。有些按字母排序，像詞典、索引之類；有的以邏輯排列，如節目表；而史料則以時間為序。

In order to save the reading time, readers must be familiar with the principle of the order of the materials. Some are sorted alphabetically, like dictionaries and indexes; some are sorted logically, such as program schedules. Historical materials normally arrange materials in order of time.

比如文章 1 的“活動安排”，是按照時間順序：第一天，第二天，第三天……

For example, passage 1 is in chronological order: the first day, the second day, the third day...

根據以上短文，回答下面的問題。

Based on the passage above, answer the following questions.

① 這次智能城市博覽會由誰舉辦？

② 博覽會已經舉辦過幾屆？

③ 舉辦博覽會的目的是什麼？

④ 博覽會總共舉辦幾天？

⑤ 博覽會在哪裏舉辦？

⑥ 如果要試穿智能衣服，應該去哪裏體驗？

⑦ 應該如何清洗智能衣服？

⑧ 變形汽車的哪個功能可以解決停車難的問題？

⑨ 想要體驗在地磚上奔跑發電，應該去哪個展覽區？

⑩ 如果對博覽會有疑問，怎麼辦？

文章 2 人類最糟糕的發明

愛分享博客

http://www.aifenxiang.blog.com

2021 年 5 月 1 日 星期六 18:08

人類最糟糕的發明

今天是五一勞動節，我們全家人決定到海邊散步。不走不知道，一走嚇一跳。海邊到處是五顏六色的塑料袋，這真讓人擔心，因為這些塑料正在污染地球環境，危害人類的身體健康。【–1–】塑料袋在地下兩百年也無法分解，大量的塑料袋埋在土裏，就會影響植物生長。【–2–】燃燒的話，會產生有害氣體，對空氣造成污染。塑料袋無處不在，土地、海洋、高山、河流等地方都能看到它們。

都說人類最糟糕的發明就是塑料袋，但我覺得除了塑料袋之外，【–3–】有很多糟糕的發明。

【–4–】是手機。手機的發明給社會帶來了很多便利，深受人們喜愛，然而它的危害也不得不引起重視。比如，不少車禍都是開車時接聽手機引起的。另外，手機的零件中含有許多有毒物質，使用不當的話會對人類造成危害。更糟糕的是，手機的輻射不但會讓人的記憶力變差，而且會增加得癌症的風險。

其次是電子遊戲。長期打電子遊戲不但嚴重危害健康，而且還會誤導青少年。電子遊戲是一種給人帶來刺激的娛樂方式，但也容易令人沉迷。

再次是電池。電池是人類的一項重要發明。但是，人們也不得不重視電池對環境造成的污染。人類也許能在兩百多年的時間裏享受電池帶來的好處，卻要用更長的時間承受其帶來的危害！一節電池爛在地裏，它可以毀壞一平方米的土壤，也可以使六百噸水受到污染——而六百噸水卻是一個人一生的飲水量。

最後是汽車。汽車的發明給出行帶來了便利，因此有很多人買汽車。然而也正是因為這樣，大量汽車出行不但製造了交通堵塞和交通事故，而且還會造成大氣污染。汽車問世的一百多年時間裏，已經有兩千五百多萬人因交通事故失去生命，還有更多的人死於跟汽車尾氣有關的空氣污染。

總之，人類的發明確實給我們的生活帶來了便利。但是，其中有一些發明同時也給我們帶來了痛苦和麻煩。我們理解科技都有兩面性，但也希望科學家在發明過程中能儘量避免給人類和自然帶來麻煩。

大家同意我的觀點嗎？如果你有其他看法，請給我留言！

閱讀（50）　評論（12）　轉載（3）　收藏（0）

改編自：https://zhidao.baidu.com/question/428847585.html

根據文章 2，選出相應的詞語，把答案寫在橫線上。

According to passage 2, choose the corresponding words and write the answers on the lines.

① [–1–] ______
② [–2–] ______
③ [–3–] ______
④ [–4–] ______

A. 首先
B. 原來
C. 再
D. 還
E. 由於
F. 卻
G. 如果
H. 無論

Tips

關鍵點的劃注 Circle and Underline the Keypoints

圈點劃線既可以對提出的問題邊讀邊想以加強閱讀效果，也能為再讀或日後溫習提供記憶線索。因為再讀時，受考試時間限制無法重讀全文，只需通過劃線部分就可記起內容的概略。

Circling and underlining could not only help readers thinking, but also provide memory clues for re-reading or future review. Due to the time limit of the test, you may not have time to reread the full text. In such case, the outline part of the content will remind you the main idea of the passage .

讀第一遍時，把握整體脈絡，用鉛筆劃出要點、難點、疑點。比如文章 2，直接劃出“手機”“電子遊戲”“汽車”“電池”四個要點，就可以把握這篇博客總體脈絡。

During the first time of reading, use a pencil to draw out the main points, difficulties and doubts. For example, in passage 2, you can easily draw the four main points which are mobile phones, video games, cars and batteries to help grasp the overall context of this blog.

注意：劃線在精不在多。如果滿篇全是線，非但沒有效果，反而遮蓋了要點。

Note: There is not much precision in drawing lines. Not only will it have no effect, it will obscure the main points if the passage is full of underlines.

劃線的詞語指的是誰 / 什麼？從文本中找出詞語答題。

To whom or to what do the underlined words refer? Use words in the passage to answer.

⑤ 這真讓人擔心……

____

⑥ 土地、海洋、高山、河流等地方都能看到它們……

____

⑦ 然而它的危害也不得不引起重視……

____

⑧ 它可以毀壞一平方米的土壤……

____

判斷對錯，在橫線上打勾（✓），並以文章內容說明理由。

Determine the following sentences are true or false with ticks (✓), and write your reason on the lines.

	對	錯
⑨ 大量車禍都是手機含有有毒物質引起的。 理由：______________________________	______	______
⑩ 手機的輻射使人喪失記憶力。 理由：______________________________	______	______
⑪ 沉迷打電子遊戲對青少年身體健康不好。 理由：______________________________	______	______
⑫ 死於空氣污染的人比因交通事故死亡的人多。 理由：______________________________	______	______

選出正確的答案。

Choose the correct answer.

⑬ 這是__________。

A. 一篇博客　　B. 一張海報　　C. 一封書信　　D. 一篇訪談稿

聽力訓練 Listening Tasks

一、《基因編輯》

你將聽到一位節目主持人向觀眾介紹基因編輯技術。你將聽到兩遍，請根據聽到的信息改正每句話裏劃線的詞語。

You will hear a host introducing gene editing technology. This audio clip will be played twice. Please correct the underlined words in each sentence based on the information you heard.

請先閱讀一下問題。Please read the questions first.

例：今天我想和大家談談基因藥物問題。

今天我想和大家談談基因編輯問題。

① 2020 年的諾貝爾化學獎頒發給法國兩位女科學家。

2020 年的諾貝爾化學獎頒發給______________兩位女科學家。

② 基因編輯就像寫文章，對文本進行重寫一樣。

基因編輯就像寫文章，對文本進行______________一樣。

③ 生命的真相可能就是這麼複雜的。

生命的真相可能就是這麼______________的。

④ 這項技術對生命科學產生了致命性的影響。

這項技術對生命科學產生了______________的影響。

Tips

如何猜詞語？How to guess the meanings of the words?

在做改錯題時，一定要關注劃線的關鍵詞語。在讀題時，劃出題目可能要考查的意圖和關鍵詞。關鍵詞就是捕捉答案關鍵信息所需要的信號詞句，分析句子中間所隱藏的信息結構關係和詞彙銜接關係，並對即將聽到的內容做相應的聯想和預測，大概知道要考查什麼成分，做到心中有數，有備而聽。

Tips on solving correction questions: Focus on the underlined words and draw the intent and key words in the question. Keywords are the signal words included in the sentences which help us to capture the answer. Analyze the information structure and vocabulary cohesion hidden in the sentence and make corresponding associations and predictions about the content to be heard. Then you may probably know what content may be tested and be well prepared during the listening.

改錯題一般是考和劃線詞語意思相反的詞語。所以考生在聽題的時候要有的放矢，根據信號詞集中精力找出要替代的詞語，不要試圖平分精力去聽懂每一個詞，也無需糾纏在個別詞句。

Correction questions are generally examining words that are opposite to the underlined words. Therefore, candidates should try to find the words to be replaced based on the signal words. Don't try to split the focus to understand each word and there is no need to entangle with each individual word and sentence.

Tips

如何讀題？
How to read questions?

做聽力考試題之前要抓緊時間讀題。讀題的時候要分析各個題目的側重點，了解說話人之間的關係及篇章所涉及的話題和場景。每道題目除了提示要注意的題號，一般還會簡述三個方面的問題：交代所聽內容的主題；告知誰是說話人或演講者；交代對話或演講發生的場所。所以，在讀題過程中要建立所聽篇章的信息框架。

Read the questions quickly before taking the listening test. Students should analyze the key words of each question and understand the relationship among the speakers as well as the topics and scenes involved in the text. In addition to prompting the number of the question to be paid attention to, each question will briefly describe 3 aspects which are the topics of what you are listening to, who the speaker is and the place where the dialogue or speech takes place. Therefore, student should learn to figure out the content structure of the passage after reading the questions.

⑤ 人類治療疾病有了類似的方法。
人類治療疾病有了＿＿＿＿＿＿＿＿的方法。

⑥ 這項發明為全球生物研究提高了大量成本。
這項發明為全球生物研究＿＿＿＿＿＿＿＿了大量成本。

⑦ 生物科學技術的發展離不開化學研究。
生物科學技術的發展離不開＿＿＿＿＿＿＿＿研究。

⑧ 人們意識到了基因改造的穩定性。
人們意識到了基因改造的＿＿＿＿＿＿＿＿性。

二、《對話鍾南山》

你即將聽到第二個聽力片段，在聽力片段二播放之前，你將有四分鐘的時間先閱讀題目。聽力片段將播放兩次，聽力片段結束後你將有兩分鐘的時間來檢查你的答案。請用中文回答問題。

You are going to hear the second audio clip. You have 4 minutes to read the questions before it starts. The audio clip will be played twice. After it ends, you have 2 minutes to check the answers. Please answer the questions in Chinese.

根據第二個聽力片段，回答問題 ①-⑨。

Answer questions ①-⑨ according to the second audio clip.

根據第二個聽力片段的內容，從 A，B，C 中，選出一個正確的答案，把答案寫在橫線上。

According to the second audio clip, choose the right answer for the questions. Write the answers on the lines.

① 鍾南山是＿＿＿＿＿。
A. 中醫醫生　B. 健康網絡專家　C. 工程院院士

② 新冠肺炎可能帶來的後遺症是＿＿＿＿＿。
A. 一直咳嗽　B. 心肺功能下降　C. 呼吸困難

③ 新冠肺炎的主要症狀不包括＿＿＿＿＿。
A. 咳嗽　B. 無力　C. 愛睡覺

填空題，每個空格最多填三個詞語。

Fill in the blanks, three words for each blank at maximum.

關於平時生活中的預防措施……

為了預防新冠肺炎，每個人要保證充足的【 -4- 】，合理作息有利於身體健康。老人如果想放鬆身心，增強心肺功能，可以打打【 -5- 】，促進血液循環。另外，得新冠肺炎死亡的人，大多是中老年人，因為他們很多人身體不好，同時還有【 -6- 】。這次疫情不但嚴重，而且傳播迅速，大家應該儘量保持身心健康，多休息，保持心情【 -7- 】。

④ [-4-]________________________________

⑤ [-5-]________________________________

⑥ [-6-]________________________________

⑦ [-7-]________________________________

回答下面的問題。Answer the following questions.

⑧ 對於恢復期的病人，可以採用中藥和哪些方法一起用，來促進病人快速康復？請舉出一例。

⑨ 此次疫情期間，人們可能會出現哪些心理問題？請舉出一例。

寫作訓練：評論 Writing Tasks: Review

熱身

- **根據課文一，討論評論的格式是什麼。**
  According to Text 1, discuss the format of a review.

- **如何寫好評論？How to write a review?**

> **Tips**
>
> **文體：評論**
> **Text Type: Review**
>
> 評論即讀後感、觀後感，是對一篇文章、一本書或一部電影發表自己讀後或看後的感想、評論等。
>
> Reviews record one's impressions after reading and viewing content, which may include reflections, criticisms, or comments on an article, a book or a movie.

格式 **參考課文一**

標題

——讀 / 觀《……》有感

作者

□□開頭：引出話題

□□正文：書 / 電影 / 新聞的主要內容 + 印象深刻的部分 + 看法感想

□□結語：總結全文

練習一

據《聯合早報》報道，新民中學將購買 10 台機器人幫忙打掃校園、保持教室衛生、收拾餐廳等等。很多學生認為學習任務繁重，讓機器人來幫忙打掃衛生是一件很有意義的事，在人工智能時代，我們應該學會放鬆身心。請寫一篇評論說說你對這篇新聞的看法。

以下是一些別人的觀點，你可以參考，也可以提出自己的意見。但必須明確表示傾向。字數：250–300 個漢字。

學生學習任務繁重，不應該再花時間去打掃教室、餐廳，保持校園環境。如果機器人能幫忙，那麼我們就有更多時間去學習和鍛煉身體。

打掃教室、保持學校環境是教育中的一環，能使學生學會基本的生存之道，懂得生活的艱辛，尊重他人的勞動。我們不應該讓機器人來代替自己打掃校園衛生。

練習二

今天你看了一場電影《通向未來 2045》，電影主要講述了隨著科技的高速發展，在未來世界里，人類不再需要面對死亡。因為人類不再有身體，也沒有任何器官，只有記憶和智慧，就像神仙一樣。請針對這部電影發表你的看法。選用合適的文本類型完成寫作。字數：300-480 个漢字。

新聞報道	演講稿	評論

Tips

如何寫好評論？How to write a review?

評論一般是針對事物進行主觀或客觀的自我印象闡述，包括新聞評論、文學評論、電影評論等。評論可以較快地表達自己的想法及感受，被大眾所廣泛使用。評論時要注意以下兩點：

Reviews are generally subjective or objective self-impression elaboration on something which include news reviews, literary reviews, movie reviews, etc. Reviews can express one's thoughts and feelings freely, so it is widely used by people. Pay attention to the following two points when writing a review:

1. 閱讀和了解對於評論來説是很重要的一環，要評論一部電影是否經典，一則新聞報道是否合理，首先就應該對所評論的東西有一個具體的認識。如果不了解，就千萬不要寫。否則肯定會離題，自己都不知道自己在寫什麼。

   Firstly, reading and understanding are very important for writing a review. To review whether a movie is classic or whether a news report is reasonable, we should have a specific understanding of what is being reviewed at the beginning. Please do not write what you don't understand. Otherwise your essay will definitely digress and you may even don't know what you are writing.

2. 寫評論文章，要有自己的觀點，而且這個觀點前後要一致。

   Secondly, you must have your own point of view which needs to be consistent when you are writing a review.

Lesson

5

Arts

藝術

導入 Introduction

藝術是生活不可或缺的一部分。它伴隨著人的成長，同時也是培養孩子想象力和審美能力的重要途徑。藝術包括視覺藝術、戲劇、舞蹈、音樂、電影和文學等。它是以生動的、可感覺的形象或聲音來反映現實或複製現實，並以此提高人們認識、把握美的能力。可以説，藝術建立的是美學。藝術的價值，不僅在於當代的審美觀念，更在於思考未來的價值所在。隨著互聯網時代的飛速發展，藝術的魅力也發生了變化。另外，我們還要思考藝術創作和欣賞要服從道德約束嗎？語言在藝術的傳承中扮演什麼樣的角色呢？

Art is an indispensable part of life. It accompanies the growth of people and is also an important way to cultivate children's imagination and aesthetic ability. Arts include visual arts, theater, dance, music, film, literature and so on. It uses vivid and sensible images or sounds to reflect reality or copy reality, and improve people's ability to recognize and percept beauty. It can be said that art establishes aesthetics. The value of art lies not only in contemporary aesthetic concepts, but also in thinking about the value of the future. With the booming of the Internet age, the charm of art has being changed. In addition, do we have to think about the moral constraints of artistic creation and appreciation? What role does language play in the inheritance of art?

學習目標 Learning Targets

閱讀 Reading

- 學會將抽象的語言文字具象化，深刻理解文章內容。
  Learn to turn abstract language into figurative pictures in your mind, and to understand the content of the article more deeply.

口語 Speaking

- 學會用欲揚先抑法，吸引考官的注意力。
  Learn to hold off before starting up to attract the examiner's attention.

聽力 Listening

- 學會應對填寫詞語的題型。
  Learn to cope with filling blanks.

寫作 Writing

- 學會確定辯論稿的立場。
  Learn to determine the position in a debate.

1 課文 學習音樂有利於學生發展 17

尊敬的主席、評委、對方辯友：

大家好！我是高一（8）班的學生張小力。今天辯論的主題是"學習音樂是否有利於學生發展"。作為正方，我方認為"學習音樂有利於學生發展"，以下是我方的理由。

首先，學習音樂可以提高智力和想象力。音樂是聲音的表現藝術。每一個音符都有不同的意義，這為學生的想象力和思維能力提供了無限的發展空間。學生可以根據自己的想象來詮釋心中的音樂。演奏樂器的時候，除了左右腦外，手、眼及身體各個部位的協調能力也能得到鍛煉。因此，學習音樂對開發大腦和提高智力有很大的幫助。

其次，學習音樂有助於增強記憶力。一場音樂會下來，每個人要表演多首樂曲，而一首樂曲就長達五到十分鐘。不用看樂譜就能把樂曲完美地演奏出來，這種鍛煉記憶力的效果是多麼驚人啊！

再次，在中國，很多小孩從小開始學習傳統樂器，如琵琶、二胡、古箏等。學習中國傳統樂器不僅是學習一門技術，更是對傳統文化的一種傳承。而且，加入民樂團學習民族音樂，也是了解中華文化的好機會。

最後，學習音樂能使人身心更健康。學生在休閒時可以用音樂來表達自己的喜悅或者宣泄自己的悲傷。很多性格內向的孩子通過學習音樂變得熱情大方了，也更懂得如何與人溝通了。研究顯示，音樂還對減輕身體疼痛有很大的幫助。

生詞短語

- zūn jìng 尊敬 distinguished
- zhèng fāng 正方 affirmative side
- lǐ yóu 理由 reason
- tí gāo 提高 raise
- zhì lì 智力 intelligence
- xiǎng xiàng lì 想象力 imagination
- biǎo xiàn 表現 expression
- yīn fú 音符 note
- kōng jiān 空間 space
- gēn jù 根據 according to
- quán shì 詮釋 interpret
- yuè qì 樂器 instrument
- xié tiáo 協調 coordinate
- duàn liàn 鍛煉 exercise
- zēng qiáng 增強 enhance
- jì yì lì 記憶力 memory
- yuè qǔ 樂曲 music composition
- yuè pǔ 樂譜 a musical score
- pí pá 琵琶 Pipa
- èr hú 二胡 Erhu
- gǔ zhēng 古箏 Guzheng
- mín yuè tuán 民樂團 Chinese folk orchestra

生詞短語

xuān xiè
宣 泄 release

nèi xiàng
內 向 inward

xiǎn shì
顯 示 show

zhèng shí
證 實 substantiate

shì shí
事 實 fact

nài xīn
耐 心 patient

fēn gōng hé zuò
分 工 合 作
work in cooperation

這是科學家已經證實的事實。

除此之外，學習音樂還能鍛煉我們的耐心，幫助我們理解分工合作的重要性。所以說，學習音樂好處很多。

綜上所述，我方再次強調“學習音樂有利於學生發展”。

謝謝各位！

改編自：hhttps://wenku.baidu.com/view/babfa927af45b307e87197db.html

Culture Point

中國民樂 Chinese Folk Music

中國民樂具有濃郁的民族特色，是中華文化的瑰寶。中國民族樂器有笛子、二胡、琵琶、古箏等。千百年來，中國音樂家創造了不少優秀的曲目，流傳至今的有《十面埋伏》《陽春白雪》《高山流水》等。在中國，幾乎每個地區都有民樂團。每到春節，這些民樂團就會被邀請到世界各地演出。中國民樂受到了世界各國人民的歡迎。

Chinese folk music, with strong nationalistic features, is a treasure of Chinese culture. As early as in the primitive times, Chinese people began to use musical instruments, like flute, Erhu, Pipa and Guzheng. For centuries, Chinese musicians have created numerous excellent songs and lyrics. The extant melodies include *The Ambush on All sides*, *Spring Snow*, *Lofty Mountains and Flowing Water*, etc. In China, almost every region has its own folk orchestra. Some of them have been invited to perform in different countries in the world during Chinese Spring Festival. The pleasant melodies not only impress the local audiences, but also win international popularity.

語法重點 Key Points of Grammar

介詞 Prepositions

介詞經常用在名詞、代詞等的前面，與這些詞組合起來，表示動作、行為、性狀的起止、方向、處所、時間、對象、方式、原因、目的、比較等。

Prepositions are often used in front of nouns and pronouns. Together with these words, they indicate the beginning and ending of actions, behaviors, traits, direction, location, time, object, method, reason, purpose, and comparison, etc.

① 表示時間 time：在 at/on/in/within、自從 since、從 from、當 when

E.g. ● 從去年到現在，我們都沒有出國旅行。
Since last year, we have never gone traveling overseas.

② 表示處所、方向 place, direction：從 / 朝 from、向 towards、在 at、沿著 / 順著 along

E.g. ● 沿著這條路直走，你就可以看到公車站。Down this road, you will see the bus stop.

③ 表示排除 exclusion：除 except for 、除了 in addition to/apart from

E.g. ● 老師每天除了上課，還要批改作業。
In addition to teaching, the teacher also corrects students' homework every day.

④ 表示對象、範圍 object, scope：對於 as for、和 / 跟 / 同 / 與 as well as、替 in place of、關於 about

E.g. ● 對於這個問題，我們下課後再討論。
As for this question, we will discuss it after class.

⑤ 表示方式、手段 manner：按照 / 依照 / 根據 according to 、以 by、憑 through

E.g. ● 根據新加坡的法律，你不可以破壞公物。
According to the laws of Singapore, vandalism is strictly not allowed.

課文理解 Reading Comprehensions

① 為什麼説學習音樂為學生的想象力提供了發展空間？

② 中國的傳統樂器有哪些？請舉兩個例子。

③ 如果要了解中華文化，可以加入什麼團體？

④ 性格內向的孩子學習音樂後會有什麼變化？

⑤ 學習音樂除了可以鍛煉耐心，還有什麼好處？

概念與拓展理解 Concepts and Further Understanding

① 你同意課文一正方的觀點嗎？ Do you agree with the point of view of the affirmative side in Text 1?

② 民樂團在香港和新加坡也稱作民樂團嗎？為什麼？
Is the folk orchestra also called the folk orchestra in Hong Kong and Singapore? Why?

③ 是否有“過時的”藝術？ Is there “outdated” art?

④ 我們個人的價值觀是否影響我們對藝術的理解？ Do our personal values affect our understanding of art?

⑤ 對藝術作品的文化和歷史背景的了解，會影響我們對作品本身的認知嗎？
Will our understanding of the cultural and historical background of an art work affect our perception of the work itself?

語言練習 Language Exercises

在方塊裏填字，使內框與外框的字組成詞語。

Fill in the outer boxes to make compound words with the word in the inner box.

①

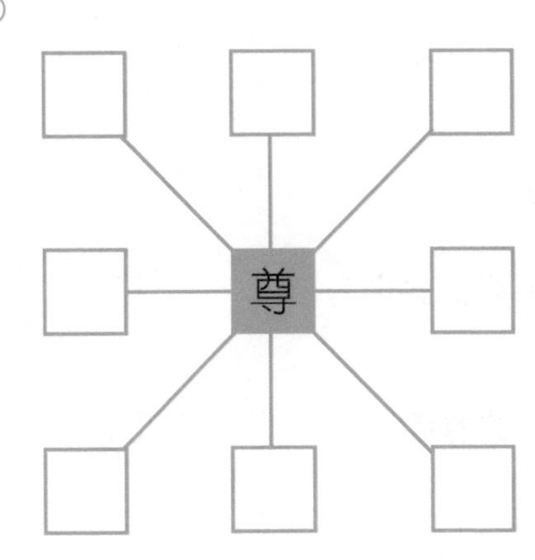

②

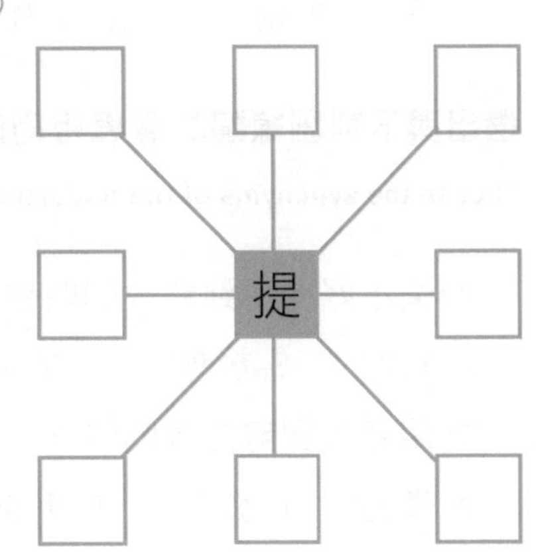

③

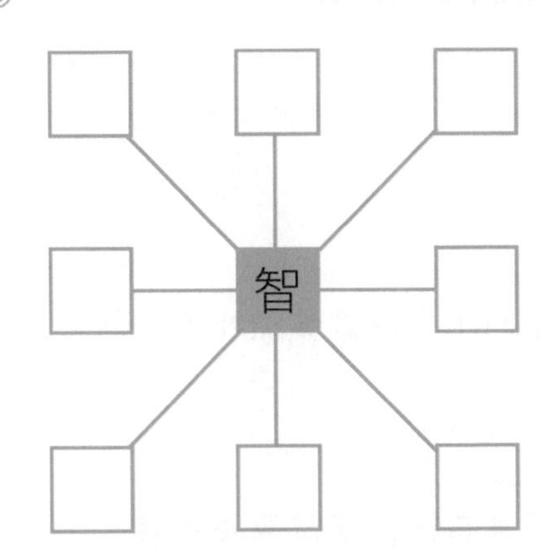

④

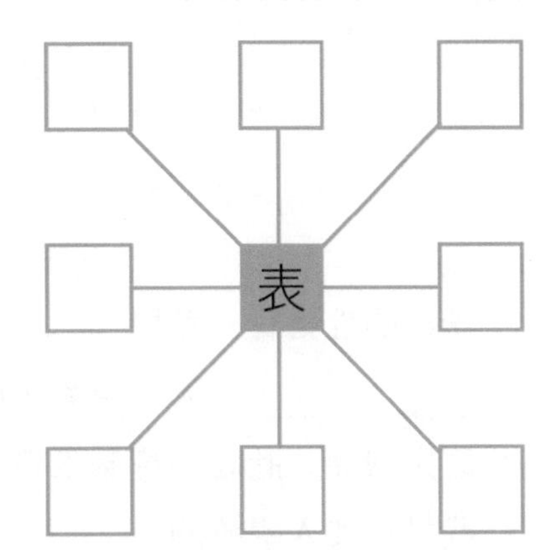

從所提供的選項中選出正確的答案。Choose the correct answer to the question.

⑤ 你會什麼樂________？

A. 哭　B. 品　C. 氣　D. 器

⑥ 沒有什麼________由的話，上課就不能遲到。

A. 里　B. 理　C. 哩　D. 鋰

⑦ 不看樂________，你能彈奏這首樂曲嗎？

A. 譜　B. 普　C. 鋪　D. 埔

⑧ 毛毛的________象力特別豐富。

A. 相　B. 想　C. 像　D. 湘

⑨ 你要經常鍛________，才能保證身體健康。

A. 連　B. 鏈　C. 練　D. 煉

⑩ 睡前多聽聽優美的樂________，有助於睡眠。

A. 曲　B. 取　C. 目　D. 由

⑪ 做事要有________心，不要著急。

A. 而　B. 耐　C. 奈　D. 寸

選出與下列劃線詞語意思相同的選項。

Choose the synonyms of the underlined words below.

⑫ 心情不好得不到釋放的時候，聽聽音樂可能會對你有幫助。 ☐

A. 宣泄　B. 放鬆　C. 放開　D. 宣導

⑬ 她用艱難卻努力奮鬥的一生，解釋了生命的意義。 ☐

A. 表達　B. 介紹　C. 解開　D. 詮釋

選擇正確的詞語填空。Fill in the blanks with the right words.

音符　空間　正方　根據　協調　增強　記憶力
民樂團　內向　顯示　證實　事實　分工合作

⑭ 李華的性格有一點兒________，平時不太喜歡參加社團活動。

⑮ ________天氣預報，明天會下雨。

⑯ 經過鍛煉，壯壯的身體素質________了。

⑰ 我打算加入學校的________，這樣才有機會學習傳統樂器。

⑱ 宇宙有無限的時間和________。

⑲ 雖然奶奶已經 90 歲了，但________還非常好。

⑳ 可可是藝術體操運動員，所以身體________能力很強。

㉑ 在辯論會上，________和反方爭得不分上下。

㉒ 你連________都看不懂，怎麼可能彈琴？

㉓ 數據________，大部分的同學喜歡選科學作為 IB 的主要科目之一。

㉔ 我們要________，才能完成老師交給我們的任務。

㉕ 人失去氧氣就無法生存，這是個不爭的________。

㉖ 網絡上的很多新聞最後都被________是假的。

填入正確的介詞。Fill in the blanks with appropriate prepositions.

㉗ ________這個説明書，我成功地做了一道西紅柿炒雞蛋。

㉘ ________這件事，我不想再多解釋了。

㉙ ________星期六去超市買菜，疫情期間媽媽從來不出門。

㉚ ________這條河一直往前走，就看到公園了。

㉛ ________學習彈琵琶後，她再不怕上台表演了。

課堂活動 Class Activities

“盲人”遊戲 Blind Game

將學生分成 A、B 兩組，圍成兩個圓圈。選一個學生扮演“盲人”，用布遮住眼睛。大家圍成圓圈開始走動，“盲人”説停，大家就停。“盲人”指向一個學生，請他猜詞語。“盲人”可以用手比動作，用中文解釋詞語，但解釋的句子中不能含有被猜測詞語中的任何一個字，也不可以用英文。詞語只限於課文一中的。如果被指的那個學生猜中詞語，那麼“盲人”還是繼續做“盲人”。如果猜不中，輪到這位學生做“盲人”，以此類推。

Divide students into Group A and Group B, and each group stands in a circle respectively. Choose a student to pretend to be blind. Cover his/her eyes with a cloth. The circle started to move. When the blind says to stop, everyone stops. The blind points to one student and let the student guess the words. The blind can use hand gestures to explain words in Chinese, but the sentence to be explained can neither contain any word of the guessed word, nor be in English. Students can only use the words in Text 1. If the pointed student can guess the word, then the blind man continues to be blind. If the student fails to get the answer, it will be the student's turn to be blind, and so on.

口語訓練 Speaking Tasks

第一部分 **根據主題“藝術”，選擇一種藝術形式，可以是繪畫、樂器、舞蹈、文學作品等，做 2-3 分鐘的口頭表達。做口頭表達之前，先根據提示寫大綱。**

Choose a lifestyle, make a 2-3 minutes oral presentation on the theme “arts”. Before you start, use the form below to make an outline.

大綱 Outline	內容 Content
觀點 Perspectives	
事例 Examples	
名人名言 Famous quotes / 熟語 Idioms	
經歷 Experiences	
總結 Summary	

第二部分 **回答下面的問題。Answer the following questions.**

① 你學習過藝術學科嗎？你為什麼要學習這門藝術？

② 許多中國家長都會讓孩子學習一門藝術，你怎麼看待這個現象？

③ 在世界著名音樂學院——美國柯蒂斯音樂學院的一個鋼琴班裏，二十個人中有十七個是來自中國的天才學生。於是有人説古典音樂的未來在中國，你同意這個觀點嗎？

④ 郎朗是聞名世界的中國鋼琴家，你會因為明星效應去學鋼琴嗎？

⑤ 有的孩子每天會寫八個小時的書法。你認為這是因為孩子比較自律，還是因為父母的逼迫？

欲揚先抑 Hold Off Before Starting Up

在口頭表達中，要想吸引考官的注意力，有時候可以採用“欲揚先抑”的方法，即先把你要介紹的事物不好的一面説出來，然後再從另一個角度去讚揚該事物。

In verbal expressions, you could try the approach of “hold off before starting up” to attract the examiner's attention. Firstly, you could address the negative side of the matter you are going to introduce and then shift your angle to praise it.

例如：“大家都知道，書法是瞬間表現的藝術，需要在很短的時間裏展現出‘台上一分鐘，台下十年功’的技術和意境。書法也是一種遺憾的藝術。一個筆畫沒寫好，書法的意境就會受到很大影響。書法的不可重複性決定了它的難度。所以，很多人都不喜歡學習書法。”

For example: “We all know that calligraphy is an art of instant performance. It needs to show the technique and artistic conception of ‘one minute on stage needs ten years practice off stage’ in a very short time. Calligraphy is also a regrettable art. If one stroke is not written well, the artistic conception of calligraphy will be greatly affected. The non-repeatability of calligraphy determines its difficulty level. Therefore, many people don't like learning calligraph.”

“可是，學習書法有助於加深孩子對中國傳統文化的了解，培養孩子的觀察、思考和表達能力。雖然學習書法很難，但是很多家長仍然喜歡讓孩子通過學習書法來磨練意志力，提高孩子的審美能力。”

“However, learning calligraphy helps to deepen children's understanding of traditional Chinese culture and cultivate children's ability to observe, think and express. Although it is difficult to learn calligraphy, many parents are still willing to let their children hone their willpower and improve their aesthetic ability through learning calligraphy.”

2 課文 京劇學習指南 (18)

京劇是什麼？學習京劇有什麼好處呢？如果想要學習京劇，又需要注意什麼呢？希望這篇京劇學習指南可以回答你的疑問。

一、什麼是京劇

京劇是中國的國粹，作為流行最廣的戲曲形式之一，它集合了文學、音樂、舞蹈、美術、武術等多種藝術形式，是一種綜合的表演藝術。

二、學習京劇的好處

1. 了解中華傳統文化，提升中文水平。

2. 通過背台詞、記動作，提高大腦思維能力，同時了解歷史人物。

3. 加強分工合作能力，讓孩子在合作中建立自信、學會相互欣賞。

4. 培養對美好事物的理解能力，豐富生活閱歷，成為一個心胸開闊的人。

三、學習京劇的注意事項

1. 京劇學習是很枯燥無味的，幾乎每天都要練習，比如武術、唱歌需要天天練五六個小時。“一天不練自己知道，兩天不練老師知道，三天不練觀眾知道”，所以一定要能吃苦。

2. 學習京劇不僅要吃得了苦，還要腦子聰明。一場戲演下來，光台詞就要背十幾頁，如果記憶力不好，就沒辦法表演。另外，老師在教動作的時候，只教兩遍，剩下的全靠自己理解

生詞短語

jīng jù 京劇 Peking Opera
guó cuì 國粹 quintessence
xíng shì 形式 form
wén xué 文學 literature
wǔ dǎo 舞蹈 dance
wǔ shù 武術 martial art
biǎo yǎn 表演 performance
tái cí 台詞 speech
xīn shǎng 欣賞 appreciate
lǐ jiě 理解 understand
yuè lì 閱歷 experience
xīn xiōng kāi kuò 心胸開闊 open-minded
kū zào wú wèi 枯燥無味 boring
chī kǔ 吃苦 suffer
jué sè bàn yǎn 角色扮演 role play
fā jué 發掘 discover
tiān fù 天賦 talent
guān niàn 觀念 perspective

和練習。

3.“唱”是京劇中最重要的表現形式，因此學好京劇台詞的咬字很重要。

學習京劇不僅可以讓孩子們在角色扮演中思考人與人、人與社會、人與自然的各種關係和問題，而且還能發掘孩子的表演天賦，幫助他們學會與人溝通交往，增強社會適應能力。

很多人認為傳統藝術沒有用，希望這篇京劇學習指南能讓大家改變固有觀念，讓孩子們通過學習京劇表演來激發創造力和想象力，從不同的角度思考問題。

新加坡南華京劇社

2022 年 6 月 1 日

改編自：https://www.sohu.com/a/224118607_775574

Culture Point

京劇 Peking Opera/Beijing Opera

京劇是中國流行最廣、影響最大的劇種，有近 200 年的歷史。

Peking Opera is the most popular and influential opera in China with a history of almost 200 years.

京劇演員分為生、旦、淨、丑四個行當。“生”是男性人物，“旦”是女性人物，“淨”是扮演性格豪爽的男性，“丑”則是扮演幽默機智或陰險狡猾的男性。

There are four main roles in Peking Opera: Sheng, Dan, Jing, and Chou. Sheng are the leading male actors. Dan are female roles. Jing are mostly male who represent warriors, heroes, statesmen, adventures and demons. Chou, most of the time, play roles of wit, alert and humor.

京劇作為中華民族戲曲的代表，在國內外都有很大的影響。許多外國人專門到中國來學習京劇。許多京劇表演藝術家也到世界各地訪問演出，受到各國人民的喜愛。

Peking Opera, as the national opera, enjoys a high reputation both at home and abroad. Many foreigners have come to China to learn Peking Opera, while many Peking Opera troupes and famous opera actors and actresses have frequently been invited to perform abroad and have been highly appreciated by audiences around the world.

語法重點 Key Points of Grammar

副詞 Adverbs

常用來修飾動詞、形容詞性詞語。Adverbs are often used to modify verbs or adjectives.

① 表示程度 degree：很 very、非常 really、十分 quite、最 extremely

E.g. ● 我非常喜歡《展望》這個課本。I really like this textbook Future.

② 表示範圍 scope：都 / 全 all、只 very few、僅僅 only、共 altogether

E.g. ● 我們班只有兩個男生，其餘都是女生。
There are only two boys in our class and the rest are all girls.

③ 表示時間 time：已經 already、剛剛 just now、就要 almost、馬上 / 立刻 immediately、往往 always、再 again

E.g. ● 我馬上就來，你們先出發吧！ I will come immediately. You all go first.

④ 表示處所 place：到處 everywhere

E.g. ● 新加坡是花園城市，到處都可以看到花。
Singapore is a garden city with flowers everywhere.

⑤ 表示可能、估計 estimation：大概 probably/might、一定 necessarily

E.g. ● 火車也許會遲到。The train might be late.
● 不一定是這個意思。It doesn't necessarily mean that.

課文理解 Reading Comprehensions

① 京劇集合了哪些藝術形式？

② 學習京劇有什麼好處？至少舉一個例子。

③ 為什麼學習京劇要能吃苦？

④ 為什麼説學習京劇有利於鍛煉記憶力？

⑤ 學好京劇台詞的咬字對學習京劇重要嗎？

概念與拓展理解 Concepts and Further Understanding

① 你會去報名學習京劇嗎？為什麼？
Will you sign up to learn Peking Opera? Why?

② 和書法、繪畫相比，學習京劇時感官感知是否起到非常不同的作用？
Does sensory perception play a very different role when learning Peking Opera rather than learning calligraphy or painting?

③ 為什麼很多人認為學習傳統藝術沒有用？
Why do many people think that learning traditional art is useless?

④ 京劇的某些知識是否只能通過體驗獲得？
Is some knowledge of Peking opera only available through experience?

⑤ 藝術作品能否具有連藝術家自己都沒有注意到的意義？
Can a work of art have a meaning that even the artist himself fails to notice?

語言練習 Language Exercises

把下面的詞語組成正確的詞組。Connect the corresponding words below to form a correct phrase.

① 表演	無味	② 心胸	扮演
豐富	閱歷	角色	亮點
枯燥	京劇	發掘	開闊

從生詞表裏找出與下列詞語意思相同或相近的詞。

Find words with the same or similar meanings as the following words in the vocabulary list.

③ 認識__________ ④ 體驗__________ ⑤ 平淡無奇__________

從生詞表裏找出與下列詞語意思相反的詞。

Find words with the opposite meanings to the following words in the vocabulary list.

⑥ 妒忌__________ ⑦ 氣量狹小__________ ⑧ 埋沒__________

選擇正確的詞語填空。Fill in the blanks with the right words.

舞蹈　形式　表演　台詞　吃苦　天賦　角色扮演　觀點

⑨ 佳佳從四歲就開始學習中國__________，還經常在中國新年的時候上台表演。

⑩ 在辯論會上，正、反雙方都陳述了自己的__________。

⑪ 現在的孩子喜歡玩兒多人在線的__________遊戲。

⑫ 菲菲從小就表現出很高的繪畫__________。

⑬ 歷史上很多傑出人物都具有不怕__________的精神。

⑭ 做演員，能背__________是很重要的。

⑮ 人們為他的精彩__________大聲喝彩。

⑯ 老師採取多種教學__________培養學生的動手和動腦能力。

填入正確的副詞。Fill in the blanks with appropriate adverbs.

⑰ 他__________忘了今天要上班，你提醒他一下。

⑱ 學生的視力問題__________應該引起注意了。

⑲ 他平時不説話，關鍵時刻__________一鳴驚人。

⑳ 上課時要注意聽講，不要＿＿＿＿＿亂看。
㉑ 聽說國家隊輸了足球比賽，他心情＿＿＿＿＿沉重。
㉒ 這條鐵路＿＿＿＿＿用了一年時間就修成了。

課堂活動 Class Activities

畫京劇臉譜 Painting the Facial Masks in Peking Opera

京劇臉譜是一種非常有特色的化妝方法。臉譜色彩豐富，每個人物都有一種譜式。主色一般象徵某個人物的品質性格。紅色代表忠貞、英勇的人物形象，多為正面角色。黑色代表大公無私、正直的人物形象。白色代表陰險狡猾的人物形象。紫色代表沉著、幹練的人物形象。黃色代表兇猛、彪悍的人物形象。綠色代表急躁、魯莽的人物形象。藍色代表有心計的人物形象。金色、銀色代表神仙、鬼怪的人物形象。

The painting of facial masks in Peking Opera is a unique and fascinating style of makeup. It has a wide selection of colors, and a specific pattern for each kind of character, and the base color symbolizes the most memorable quality of that character. Red stands for loyalty and brave, mostly portraying heroic characters. Black stands for righteousness and selflessness of the character. White is always used on a cunning and treacherous character. Purple stands for steadfastness and a character of composure. Yellow is used to present the ferocious and aggressive personality. Green is used to present characters that are reckless and quick-tempered. Blue is used on characters who are calculating. Gold and silver are used to paint faces of mythical characters.

發揮創意，選擇一個臉譜，塗上你喜歡的顏色。

Paint the facial masks with your favourite colors.

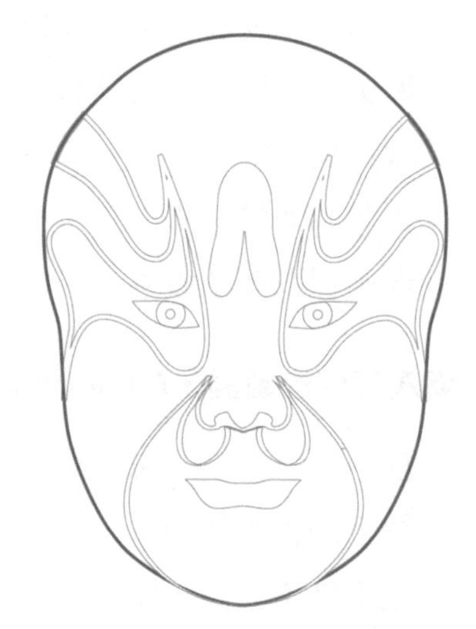

口語訓練 Speaking Tasks

第一部分 **根據圖片，做 3–4 分鐘的口頭表達。做口頭表達之前，先根據提示寫大綱。**

Make a 3-4 minutes oral presentation based on the picture. Before you start, use the form below to make an outline.

大綱 Outline	內容 Content
圖片內容 Information of the picture	
圖片主題 + 文化 Theme of the picture and culture	
提出觀點 Make your points	
延伸個人經歷 Relate to personal experiences	
名人名言 Famous quotes / 熟語 Idioms	
總結 Summary	

第二部分 **回答下面的問題。Answer the following questions.**

① 你學過跳舞嗎？你認為學跳舞有什麼好處？

② 中國的大媽平時都在跳廣場舞，你認為這會破壞藝術的美感嗎？

③ 你贊同孩子從三歲就開始學舞蹈嗎？

④ 很多學藝術的人，最後並沒有走上藝術的道路，你怎麼看待這種現象？

⑤ 藝術創作應該受道德約束嗎？

技能訓練 Skill Tasks

閱讀訓練 Reading Tasks

文章 1 新加坡藝術

仔細閱讀下面的短文，然後回答問題。

Read the passage carefully and answer the following questions.

TRAVEL 登錄

新加坡藝術 ▼ 搜索

A. 新加坡藝術館

點評 1 展覽內容以繪畫、書法、攝影和互動媒體等多種不同藝術形式呈現。除了當代藝術展覽之外，這裏還提供適合家庭與兒童參與的親子活動項目，名為“體驗互動藝術”，包括時空、自然、感官探索等不同主題。

點評 2 這裏不僅有充滿生命氣息的藝術空間，還經常展示新加坡年輕藝術家的作品。例如，“總統青年藝術家”展覽就包括了充滿創意的傑出人物和藝術組織的作品。

B. 新加坡國家美術館

點評 1 集中展示 19 世紀至今的新加坡及東南亞藝術，呈現新加坡和東南亞的社會、文化和歷史。除了看美術和藝術展覽外，還可以在這裏的餐廳品嚐特色食物。這裏提供的美食充分地反映了美術館獨特的視覺理念。

點評 2　年齡較小的孩子可以到美術教育中心享受獨特的藝術體驗。這是新加坡第一個美術教育中心，提供適合學生的美術教育活動。趣味性的學習體驗，讓各個年齡層的學生都能樂在其中。

C. 金沙藝術科學博物館

點評 1　這是世界上首個藝術與科學相結合的博物館，2011 年首次向公眾開放。整個建築造型就像一朵蓮花，目的是探索如何將藝術與科學結合在一起。

點評 2　在每年六月學校放假期間，這裏都會推出一系列的活動，今年的活動是“當數字遇上藝術”。在燈光照射下的美術作品，真是美得讓人驚奇！你也可以參與創作，並將你的藝術品作為展覽的一部分。

D. 濱海藝術中心

點評 1　它的外形看起來像榴蓮，是新加坡標誌性的建築之一。這裏不但有正式的音樂會演出，而且經常有一些免費的小型音樂會。在它的周邊，還可以欣賞到新加坡河畔的美景。

點評 2　這裏每天有大量的活動、表演和展覽，而且很多活動都免費。你可以在室內或者戶外觀看這些演出。晚上八點左右，這裏有燈光秀。劇院的芭蕾舞表演很精彩，但是前排的票價太貴了，二層或三層的位置比較便宜。

內容源自 https://tripadvisor.com

Tips

發揮想象力，理解句子的意思

Use your imagination to understand the sentences

豐富的想象可以帶你走進多姿多彩的閱讀世界。在閱讀時，如果能夠發揮豐富的想象力，將抽象的語言文字變成腦海中有趣的畫面，就能更深刻地理解文章內容，感受閱讀的樂趣。

Rich imagination can take you into the colorful world of reading. When reading, if you can use your rich imagination and turn abstract language into interesting pictures in your mind, you will understand the content of the article deeply and feel the joy of reading.

例如：在讀到“這裏提供的美食充分地反映了美術館獨特的視覺理念”時，我們彷彿看到用不同食材做成的藝術作品，比如花朵、樹木、山河等。難怪文章説是“獨特的視覺理念”。這就是用想象的方法加深對句子的理解。

For example: when we read "The food served here fully reflects the unique visual concept of the art museum", we seem to see the works of art made with different ingredients, such as flowers, trees, mountains and rivers. No wonder the article says it is a "unique visual concept." This is the way to use imagination to understand unintelligible sentences.

培養自己的想象力，通過發揮想象來理解句子的意思，最終可以提高理解文章內容的能力。

Cultivate your own imagination and use it to understand the meaning of sentences, and ultimately you can improve your ability to understand the content of the article.

根據以上短文，選擇正確的段落。在方格裏打勾（✓）。

According to the short passage above, tick (✓) in the correct boxes.

① 哪個展館將藝術與科學結合在一起？

A. ☐ B. ☐ C. ☐ D. ☐

② 哪個展館提供親子活動項目？

A. ☐ B. ☐ C. ☐ D. ☐

③ 哪個地方可以讓大家在展館裏吃東西？

A. ☐ B. ☐ C. ☐ D. ☐

④ 哪個地方可以讓你的藝術品參與展覽？

A. ☐ B. ☐ C. ☐ D. ☐

⑤ 哪個地方可以看芭蕾舞表演？

A. ☐ B. ☐ C. ☐ D. ☐

⑥ 哪個地方有免費的音樂會？

A. ☐ B. ☐ C. ☐ D. ☐

⑦ 哪個地方有書法展覽？

A. ☐ B. ☐ C. ☐ D. ☐

⑧ 哪個地方可以帶孩子去學美術？

A. ☐ B. ☐ C. ☐ D. ☐

⑨ 哪個地方可以看燈光秀？

A. ☐ B. ☐ C. ☐ D. ☐

⑩ 哪個地方可以看到新加坡青年藝術家的作品？

A. ☐ B. ☐ C. ☐ D. ☐

文章 2　在線少兒美術課程

每個父母都希望孩子擁有豐富的想象力和創造力。孩子的精彩人生從小就要開始。打開在線少兒美術課程，真人一對一在線互動上課。用孩子喜歡的方式，激發大腦的藝術潛能，並享受繪畫的樂趣，提高審美和創造力，陪伴孩子快樂、自信地成長。

通過一台電腦，就能連接全球優質藝術教育資源。在線少兒美術課程，擁有來自世界各地的眾多優秀老師。

繪畫階段	開發期	觀察期	成長期	寫實期	專業期
年齡	3-6 歲	6-8 歲	8-10 歲	11-12 歲	13-18 歲
知識內容	掌握基本的繪畫語言和色彩基礎知識。	學會通過觀察、想象將事物用多種繪畫形式表現出來。	培養全面的觀察能力，學會欣賞藝術作品。	學會繪畫寫實技巧並能表現出來。	系統學習繪畫技巧並提高表現力。
能力培養	培養獨立自主、勇敢自信的社交能力。	激發對生活的熱愛，培養長久學習美術的興趣。	建立藝術和傳統文化的聯繫，並培養獨立人格。	建立美術與其他學科的聯繫，能夠說明作品的創作思路。	能夠以多元化的文化視角，進行藝術創作，建立基本的藝術思路。

在線少兒美術課程，專注於解決 3-18 歲孩子在線學畫畫的問題，採用國際化課程體系，以豐富有趣的學習內容，全面提升孩子的想象力和創造力，培養孩子成為未來世界藝術小公民。

現在，可以免費領取價值 699 元的畫畫大禮包。

包含
- 1 節美術體驗課
- 12 節在線課程
- 1 套內含 18 件工具的畫畫工具箱

領取方式　添加微信"15201234567"，發送"領取資料"即可。

改編自：http://www.pinghuabao.com/

從選項中，選出最適合的敘述。Choose the appropriate from the list for each statement.

① 開發期 ______ A. 學會表達創作目的。
② 觀察期 ______ B. 開始獨立創作。
③ 成長期 ______ C. 能看懂藝術作品。
④ 寫實期 ______ D. 學會多種繪畫形式。
⑤ 專業期 ______ E. 掌握基本色彩知識。
F. 開始對美術感興趣。
G. 能根據當地文化進行創作。
H. 開始完全獨立。

根據文章 2，從選項中選出最接近下列詞語 / 詞組的意思。把答案寫在橫線上。

According to passage 2, choose the corresponding words and write the answers on the lines.

⑥ 希望 ______ A. 出色
⑦ 精彩 ______ B. 精華
⑧ 互動 ______ C. 互相
⑨ 在線 ______ D. 期盼
E. 網上
F. 上網
G. 交流

判斷對錯，在橫線上打勾（✓），並以文章內容說明理由。

Determine the following sentences are true or false with ticks (✓), and write your reason on the lines.

	對	錯
⑩ 在線少兒美術課程的招生對象是中學生。 理由：____________________	______	______
⑪ 在線少兒美術課程屬於中國當地課程。 理由：____________________	______	______
⑫ 畫畫大禮包不需要花錢就可以領取。 理由：____________________	______	______

回答下面的問題。Answer the following questions.

⑬ 如何領取畫畫大禮包？

____

⑭ 大禮包裏有什麼？至少列出兩個。

a. ____________________

b. ____________________

聽力訓練 Listening Tasks

一、《美的感受》

你將聽到台灣知名畫家、詩人與作家——蔣勳談“美的感受”。你將聽到兩遍，請聽錄音，然後回答問題。

You will hear a recording of "Feeling of Beauty" by the famous painter, poet and writer Jiang Xun from Taiwan district. The clip will be played twice. Please listen and answer the questions.

請先閱讀一下問題。Please read the questions first.

① 你每天都能____________到身邊美的東西嗎？
② 他今天和我們____________了他對美的看法。
③ 我們要學會____________吃一些對我們身體有益的食物，而不是隨便吃。
④ ____________是一個緩慢的過程，不是一口喝下去。
⑤ 關於穿衣，我們一定不要被____________帶著走，要學會做自己。
⑥ ____________就是選擇自己所要的，培養自己對美的一種感動。
⑦ 宋代山水畫裏的亭子就是告訴我們人生不一定是要____________的，要懂得停下來。
⑧ 只有苦後回甘才能讓你懂得什麼是____________。

Tips

如何應對填寫詞語的題型？How to cope with filling in word questions?

填寫詞語的考試題型要求學生先理解題目的要求，再根據聽力篇章，找出合適的詞語填入句子空格中。填寫詞語比聽力選擇題更強調語言綜合運用能力，要求考生不僅有良好的聽力水平，還應具有較強的書寫能力、理解能力和做筆記能力。

The test mode for filling in words asks students to understand the sentences for qustions firstly, and to find the appropriate words to fill in the blanks according to the recording. It emphasizes the comprehensive use of language skills more than the listening multiple choice questions, and requires candidates not only to have good listening skills, but also to have strong writing and note-taking skills.

應對這種題型，首次應該要邊聽邊做筆記，做筆記應簡潔明了，充分利用符號、簡寫字等進行快速記錄。然後，通過卷面文字捕捉信息，找出線索。這種題型的文章一般主題突出，條理分明，層次清楚，語言簡潔。

To deal with this type of question, candidates should take notes while listening for the first time. The notes should be concise and clear. Candidates should make full use of symbols, abbreviated writing, etc. for quick recording, then capture the information through the text to find clues. Articles of this genre generally have prominent themes, clear clues levels and concise language.

例如"④……是一個緩慢的過程，不是一口喝下去。"從題目中我們捕捉到一個重要的信息"緩慢"，而另一條重要線索跟"喝"有關係。再通過注意聽文章的內容，馬上就可以找出"品茶"這個答案，而不是"品味"。

For example, "④... is a slow process, not a sip." From the sentence, we can capture an important information, which is "slow", another important clue has something to do with "drinking". By listening to the content of the article, you can immediately find out the answer to which is "drinking tea" instead of "taste".

二、《藝術人生》 

你即將聽到第二個聽力片段，在聽力片段二播放之前，你將有四分鐘的時間先閱讀題目。聽力片段將播放兩次，聽力片段結束後，你將有兩分鐘的時間來檢查你的答案。請用中文回答問題。

You are going to hear the second audio clip. You have 4 minutes to read the questions before it starts. The audio clip will be played twice. After it ends, you have 2 minutes to check the answers. Please answer the questions in Chinese.

根據第二個聽力片段，回答問題 ①-⑥ 。

According to the second audio clip, answer questions ①-⑥.

根據第二個聽力片段的內容，從 A，B，C 中，選出一個正確的答案，把答案寫在橫線上。

According to the second audio clip, choose the right answer for the questions. Write the answers on the lines.

① 鍾玲是________。

A. 中國藝術體操代表人物　　B. 中國體操國家隊隊員　　C. 亞洲藝術女皇

② 藝術體操是________。

A. 力與藝術的結合　　B. 競技與藝術的結合　　C. 美與藝術的結合

③ 藝術體操不要求運動員有________。

A. 音樂修養　　B. 藝術表現力　　C. 漂亮的長相

④ 學習藝術體操有哪些好處？請選出五個正確的敘述。

______ A. 幫助孩子長高。

______ B. 培養孩子的音樂能力。

______ C. 讓孩子更自信。

______ D. 讓孩子更有氣質。

______ E. 幫助孩子獲得獎盃。

F. 養成吃苦的精神。

G. 可以參加世界比賽。

H. 有助於大腦發育。

回答下面的問題。Answering the following questions.

⑤ 藝術體操加入哪些形式來構成它的美？至少舉兩個例子。

a. ______

b. ______

⑥ 藝術體操的辛苦表現在哪裏？至少舉一個例子。

______

寫作訓練：辯論 Writing Tasks: Debate

熱身

- **根據課文一，討論辯論稿的格式是什麼。According to Text 1, discuss the format of the debate.**

- **如何寫好辯論稿？How to write a debate?**

Tips

文體：辯論

Text Type: Debate

辯論稿是在辯論中闡述代表方觀點的文體。

The debate is a style of writing that expounds the views of the representative in the debate.

格式 **參考課文一**

尊敬的主席、評委、對方辯友：

☐☐開頭：問候語 + 自我介紹 + 表明立場

☐☐正文：有條理地論證論點

☐☐結尾：總結觀點 + 重申論點 + 表達感謝

練習一

隨著智能科技的高速發展，科技進步對藝術的影響越來越大。你將參加學生會舉辦的辯論會，辯題是“科技進步是否有助於藝術的發展”。請寫一篇辯論稿，表達你的立場與看法。以下是一些別人的觀點，你可以參考，也可以提出自己的意見。但必須明確表示傾向。字數：250–300 個漢字。

現代科學技術使藝術變成商品，更加大眾化，導致人們的審美水平下降。藝術中運用了太多高科技，也使觀眾的感官被刺激得麻木了。

現代科學技術為藝術創造了前所未有的文化環境和傳播手段，為藝術提供了更廣闊的天地。

練習二

在你的班級裏，很多同學從小學習藝術，上中學後就放棄了，覺得學習藝術沒有用。不過，也有一部分同學上了中學後仍然學習藝術，他們認為堅持學習藝術好處多，不但可以緩解學習壓力，還能促進身心健康。請選擇一個觀點，說明你的立場。選用合適的文本類型完成寫作。字數：300–480 個漢字。

辯論稿	傳單	提案

Tips

如 何 確 定 立 場 ？ How to detemine the position?

寫辯論稿，最重要的是確定你的立場。所謂立場，就是你贊成題目的觀點或者反對題目的觀點。確定立場很重要，這是辯論稿的核心所在。一旦確定立場，就能根據這個核心來發揮，思路才會集中，寫出來的東西才不會東拉西扯、自相矛盾。

The most important thing to write a debate is to establish your position. The so-called position is your opinion for or against the topic. It is very important to establish a position, which is the focus of the debate draft. Once the position is determined, it can be used according to this key point, the thinking will be concentrated, and the written things will not be inconsistent or contradictory.

如何確定立場？首先要根據題目，設想一個有趣味、有價值的句子，確定它是這篇文章的核心，然後朝這個方面尋找例子、盡力表達，才會發揮文章感人的效果。

How to determine the position? First of all, according to the topic, imagine an interesting and valuable sentence, determine that it is the focus of this article, and then look for examples in this aspect and try your best to express it. Only then will the article have a touching effect.

例如“堅持學習藝術好處多”，先根據你的立場列出幾個好處：

1）提高人的修養；2）開闊眼界；3）培養毅力、注意力、想象力；4）身體健康；5）性格開朗

For example, "Keeping learning art has many benefits", first list a few benefits:

1) Improve people's accomplishment; 2) Broaden your horizons; 3) Cultivate perseverance, attention and imagination; 4) Good health; 5) Cheerful personality

以上哪幾個句子比較有意義、有價值，有豐富的材料可以用來表達呢？

1）2）3）都很好闡釋，但 4）和 5）的表達不太明確。4）改成“身心健康”就能包括很多的藝術形式在裏面。5）則很難包含大部分的藝術形式，而且寫不清楚，建議刪去。選出句子後，就可以作為文章發揮的核心，傾力寫作。那麼寫出來的辯論稿，就不會被人家説立場不明確了。

Among the above sentences, which ones are more meaningful, valuable, and rich in materials to express?

Sentences 1), 2), 3) are easy to illustrate, but sentences 4) and 5) are not very clear. Changing the fourth sentence to "healthy mind and body" can include a lot of art. 5) is also difficult to include most of the art, and it is difficult to illustrate. So it is suggested that sentence 5) should be deleted. After the sentence is selected, it can be used as the focus of the essay and devoted to writing. Then the composition will not be said to have no standpoint.

Lesson
6
Education and Future Career Plan
教育與未來職業規劃

導入 Introduction

教育的目的是培養有行動能力、思考能力和創造力的人。教育不只是傳授已有的東西，更要激發人的創造力，喚醒生命感、價值感。教育對人的職業發展起到什麼作用呢？是否要根據別人的看法來決定自己未來的職業？如何將個人目標與職業發展聯繫起來？在今天看來“非常火”的職業，幾年、幾十年後，仍然是這樣嗎？人工智能時代的到來給職業發展帶來了哪些影響？這些都是我們要考慮的因素。制定科學合理的職業發展計劃對每個中學生來説都很重要。如果能在中學時期對自己的未來有一個清楚的規劃，就能夠選擇合適的大學和專業。

Education is to cultivate people with the ability to act, think and be creative. The ultimate goal of education is not to teach what is already there but to induce people's creative power to awaken the sense of life and value. What roles does education play in people's professional development? Should we decide our future occupations based on others' opinions? How to link personal goals with professional development? Will those very popular careers nowadays still hot in the future? What does the artificial intelligence age impact on one's career development? These are all factors we have to consider. Making a scientific and reasonable career development plan is very important to every middle school student. If you have a clear plan for your future in middle school, you can choose the befitting university and major on the next stage.

學習目標 Learning Targets

閱讀 Reading

學會積累詞語和句子。
Learn to accumulate words and sentences in reading.

口語 Speaking

學會介紹職業規劃。
Learn to introduce career planning.

聽力 Listening

學會聽力時使用圈畫技巧。
Learn to use the circle to draw words that need to be listened to when reading the questions.

寫作 Writing

學會在個人陳述中説明自己的優缺點。
Learn to explain your strengths and weaknesses in your personal statement.

1 課文　申請大學獎學金 21

個人陳述

彭小紅

我是香港國際學校的學生。從小我就希望自己長大後能成為一名中文老師，傳播中國傳統文化。在讀高中期間，我一直嚴格要求自己，努力學習。同時，我也在社會實踐中利用中文特長，鍛煉自己，服務社會。北京師範大學"人人都能成才"的教育理念讓我很受鼓舞，因此，我想去北京師範大學學習並申請獎學金。

在學習上，為了更深入地了解中國傳統文化，我每個週末都會到中國文化中心學習中國歷史。另外，我還選修了IBDP中文A文學課程，通過學習中國四大名著等作品，我對中國文學有了更深刻的理解和認識。課餘時間，我還報名參加了中文教師培訓，在學習更多和中文教學相關知識的同時，也對未來職業發展有了一個好的規劃。今年，我已經通過了HSK六級考試，我會一步一個腳印來實現更大的目標。在過去的兩年裏，我學到了很多知識，在各方面都取得了巨大進步，通過努力，我IBDP每科預考成績都拿到了88分，總分也達到了滿分45。

在生活上，我是一個性格開朗、樂觀向上的人，喜歡尋找機會來鍛煉自己各方面的能力。我積極參加與中國文化相關的活動，比如"漢語橋"比賽、世界中學生中文演講比賽、辯論賽等，並且都取得了很好的成績。參加比賽，讓我認識了很多中國朋友，也加深了我對中國文化的理解，這些都有利於我今後的中文教學實踐。

生詞短語

- chén shù 陳述 statement
- yán gé 嚴格 strict
- shí jiàn 實踐 practice
- fú wù 服務 service
- lǐ niàn 理念 concept
- gǔ wǔ 鼓舞 encouragement
- shēn qǐng 申請 apply
- jiǎng xué jīn 獎學金 scholarship
- xuǎn xiū 選修 take as an elective course
- míng zhù 名著 masterpiece
- péi xùn 培訓 training
- jiào xué 教學 education
- guī huà 規劃 planning
- yù kǎo 預考 mock exam
- xìng gé 性格 character
- tǐ yàn 體驗 experience
- bǔ xí 補習 tutoring
- yīn cái shī jiào 因材施教 teach students in accordance of their aptitude
- tuán duì 團隊 team work

在教學實踐上，我在學校負責組織每週一次的“漢語角”活動，目的是讓更多的中文學習者和中國學生一起交流，練習口語。通過這個活動，很多學生的中文口語能力得到了不小的提升。放假期間，我們也會到老人院教老人普通話，和他們一起玩遊戲，讓他們在玩中學，體驗學習普通話的樂趣。除此之外，我還和朋友成立了中文補習班，利用週末時間幫助其他同學學習中文。我積極實踐中國古代著名教育家孔子“因材施教”的教學理念，取得了很好的教學效果。目前一共有 15 位同學加入了我們的團隊，我們所教的學生已經有 50 多人。我想要報考北京師範大學，學習更多優秀的中文教學方法，幫助我把教育事業做得更大、更好。

如果能進入北京師範大學學習，我將更加確定未來的職業發展計劃。未來我會更加努力，不斷充實自己，取得更大進步，請各位老師考慮我的獎學金申請。

改編自：http://www.gaosan.com/gaokao/220783.html

Culture Point

孔子（公元前 551－公元前 479） Confucious (551BC-479BC)

孔子是中國古代偉大的思想家和教育家。據說，他有三千多名學生，其中很多是貧苦家庭的孩子，改變了以往只有貴族子女才有資格上學的傳統。孔子的很多思想即使在今天看來也很有價值。比如，“三人行，必有我師焉”，意思是“別人的言行舉止，必定有值得我學習的地方”。孔子在教育上主張用啟發的方法促使學生獨立思考，在學習書本知識的同時還要有自己獨立的見解等。

Confucious was a great thinker and educator in China. He had instructed more than 3000 disciples, and a lot of them were from poor families. In this way, Confucius had gradually changed the tradition that nobody but nobilities had the right to receive education. Even in modern times many of Confucius' ideas are quite valuable. For example, " From any three people, I will find something to learn for sure." In terms of education, Confucius maintained that teachers should enlighten students to think independently, and students should formulate their own oipnions when acquiring knowledge from textbooks.

北京師範大學 Beijing Normal University

北京師範大學是中國歷史上第一所師範大學，是一所以教師教育為主要特色的著名大學。在中國，如果要成為老師，大多數人會先選擇考入師範大學接受專業培訓。

Beijing Normal University is the first normal university in Chinese history. It is a famous university with teacher education as its main feature. In China, if you want to become a teacher, you would probably choose to be admitted to a normal university.

中國四大名著 China's Four Major Masterpieces

中國四大名著，是指《水滸傳》《三國演義》《西遊記》《紅樓夢》。四大名著是中國文學的經典作品，是寶貴的世界文化遺產 。這四部巨著在中國文學史上的地位是難分高低的，都有著極高的文學水平和藝術成就，細緻的刻畫和所蘊含的深刻思想都為歷代讀者所稱道，其中的故事、場景、人物已經深深地影響了中國人的思想觀念、價值取向，可謂中國文學史上的四座偉大豐碑。

China's four major masterpieces refer to *Water Margin*, *Romance of the Three Kingdoms*, *Journey to the West* and *A Dream of Red Mansions*. The four major masterpieces are classics in the history of Chinese literature and are valuable cultural heritage in the world. The status of these four masterpieces in the history of Chinese literature is indistinguishable. They all have extremely high literary level and artistic achievements. The meticulous depiction and the profound thoughts contained in them are praised by readers of all generations. The stories, scenes, and characters in them have deeply affected the Chinese people's ideology and value orientation. It can be described as four great monuments in the history of Chinese literature.

語法重點 Key Points of Grammar

目的關係複句 Purposive Complex Sentence

由兩個具有目的關係的分句組成。一個分句表示實現某種目的或避免某種結果，一個分句表示為此而採取的行為。

The purposive complex sentence consists of two clauses with purpose related clauses. A clause means achieving a certain purpose or avoiding a certain result, and a clause means an action taken for this purpose.

常用關聯詞 Common Conjunctive Words

為了 / 為的是 in order to、免得 / 以免 lest、以便 so that

E.g.
- 你快讓他進去，免得他又不高興。Let him in lest he gets upset again.
- 父母每天辛苦工作，為的是讓孩子能上得起學。
  Parents work hard every day so that their children can afford to go to school.

課文理解 Reading Comprehensions

① 小紅長大後想要做什麼？

② 小紅學習怎麼樣？從哪裏可以看出來？

③ 小紅是如何找機會鍛煉自己的？

④ 小紅有哪些教學實踐經歷？

⑤ 小紅為什麼要報考北京師範大學？

概念與拓展理解 Concepts and Further Understanding

① 課文一的寫作目的是什麼？ What is the writing purpose of Text 1?

② 你認為申請獎學金，必須具備哪些條件？
What do you think is necessary to apply for a scholarship?

③ 如果你是北京師範大學的獎學金評定人，你會給小紅獎學金嗎？
If you were the scholarship assessor of Beijing Normal University, would you give Xiaohong a scholarship?

④ 你同意孔子“因材施教”的教育理念嗎？為什麼？
Do you agree with Confucius' educational philosophy of "teach students in accordance with their aptitude"? Why?

⑤ 你現在能確定你未來的職業發展規劃嗎？為什麼？
Can you determine your future career development plan now? Why?

語言練習 Language Exercises

選擇合適的詞語，填寫在橫線上。

Fill in the blanks with the appropriate words.

① 老師對我們要求很＿＿＿＿＿＿（嚴格 / 嚴肅），每天都要聽寫單詞。

② 今年學校參加 IBDP 中文考試的學生全部都拿了 7 分，這對明年考試的學生是很大的＿＿＿＿＿＿（鼓動 / 鼓舞）。

③ 學校開設了很多＿＿＿＿＿＿（選修 / 選擇）課程供我們選擇。

④ 他＿＿＿＿＿＿（性格 / 性別）不好，經常發脾氣。

⑤ 作家要懂得＿＿＿＿＿＿（體驗 / 體會）生活，才能寫出好的小說。

⑥ 所謂"十年樹木，百年樹人"，我們做事都要有長遠＿＿＿＿＿＿（規則 / 規劃）。

⑦ 我們希望有愛心的人能加入我們的義工＿＿＿＿＿＿（團結 / 團隊）。

⑧ 學校＿＿＿＿＿＿（領隊 / 領導）正在規劃蓋幾棟教學樓。

⑨ 多參加口語＿＿＿＿＿＿（培訓 / 培養）班，會讓你的口語能力很快提高。

⑩ 唐老師每天放學後都耐心地幫小芳＿＿＿＿＿＿（補習 / 補課）中文。

從所提供的選項中選出正確的答案。

Choose the correct answer from the following choices.

⑪ 你如果想報考南京大學，需要先提交個人陳＿＿＿＿。

A. 術　B. 木　C. 沭　D. 述

⑫ 年輕人要在社會實＿＿＿＿中鍛煉自己。

A. 踐　B. 淺　C. 戈　D. 見

⑬ 她工作熱情，＿＿＿＿務周到，大家都很喜歡她。

A. 福　B. 服　C. 報　D. 刖

⑭ "誠樸雄偉，勵學敦行"是南京大學的辦學理＿＿＿＿。

A. 戀　B. 練　C. 念　D. 今

⑮ 我向福建師範大學提交了入學＿＿＿＿請書。

A. 日　B. 申　C. 田　D. 伸

⑯ 他學習成績優異，每年都獲得＿＿＿＿學金。

A. 將　B. 漿　C. 獎　D. 講

⑰《西遊記》是中國四大名＿＿＿＿之一。

A. 主　B. 者　C. 注　D. 著

選出與下列劃線詞語意思相同的選項。

Choose the synonyms of the underlined words below.

⑱ 模擬考考得不好沒關係，期末考試要再認真一點兒。 ☐

A. 初考　B. 期中考　C. 正式考　D. 預考

⑲ 不同的學生學習能力有所差別，我們要對症下藥，不能用同樣的教學方法對待所有人。 ☐

A. 吃不同的藥　B. 公平對待　C. 因材施教　D. 同等對待

填入正確的關聯詞。

Fill in the blanks with appropriate correlative conjunctions.

⑳ 工人這麼辛苦地工作，________能讓公路早一天通車。

㉑ 鄰里之間有矛盾要趕緊處理，________影響鄰里關係。

㉒ 書店開設網上購書，________學生和家長購買課本。

㉓ ________備課，老師經常要上網查資料。

課堂活動 Class Activities

填字遊戲 Crossword

把適當的字填寫在空格裏。

Fill in the table with correct words.

教　理　獎　劃　考　鼓　習　領

補			狀		想	
	慣			學		念
		施		金		
	材		隊		舞	
因				導		勵
	計				預	
規				試		查

口語訓練 Speaking Tasks

第一部分 **根據主題"教育與職業規劃"，選擇一種職業，做 2-3 分鐘的口頭表達。做口頭表達之前，先根據提示寫大綱。**

Choose an occupation, make a 2-3 minutes oral presentation on the theme "education and career plan". Before you start, use the form below to make an outline.

大綱 Outline	內容 Content
觀點 Perspectives	
事例 Examples	
名人名言 Famous quotes / 熟語 Idioms	
經歷 Experiences	
總結 Summary	

第二部分 **回答下面的問題。Answer the following questions.**

① 你從什麼時候開始確定你未來的職業？

② 你認為必須具備哪些能力才能從事你喜歡的職業？

③ 人工智能時代，你覺得什麼職業最受歡迎？為什麼？

④ 你接受的教育會影響你對職業的選擇嗎？為什麼？

⑤ 你覺得是選擇你喜歡的職業好，還是選擇賺錢的職業好？為什麼？

Tips

如何介紹職業規劃？How to introduce your career plan?

介紹職業規劃的時候，一定要清楚自己將來要做什麼，過去做了哪些類似的工作。面試官看中的是現在的你，希望未來的你能有好的發展，而這個未來又基於你的歷史和現狀。所以介紹時，一定要按照"現在—將來—過去"的順序。

另外，面試官非常注重面試者對未來的規劃，回答的時候要具體、合理，並且符合你作為學生的身份。

When introducing career plan, you must be clear about what you will do in the future, and what similar work you have done in the past. What the interviewer cares about is your current situation, and hope that you can develop well in the future, and this future is based on your history and current situation. Therefore, when introducing your plan, remember to follow the present–future–past order.

In addition, the interviewer pays great attention to the interviewer's future design, and the answer should be specific, reasonable, and consistent with your identity as a student.

生詞短語

bō kè
播客 podcast
xīn yǐng
新穎 novel
shén qí
神奇 magic
qíng jǐng
情景 situation
wù lǐ
物理 physic
huà xué
化學 chemistry
qì tǐ
氣體 gas
chù diàn
觸電 electric shock
bào zhà
爆炸 bomb
huàn dēng piàn
幻燈片 slides
cān guān
參觀 visit
tú xiàng
圖像 image
chǎng jǐng
場景 scenario
mó nǐ
模擬 simulate
nán shòu
難受 sick
duō méi tǐ
多媒體 multi-media
chén jìn
沉浸 immerse
fù dān
負擔 burden
shì jué
視覺 visual
tīng jué
聽覺 hearing
chù jué
觸覺 touch
xū nǐ
虛擬 virtual
dìng yuè
訂閱 subscribe

2 課文 VR 教學體驗 22

南洋世界的播客

http://www.nanyangpodcast.com

2022 年 9 月 8 日　星期四　2 分 30 秒　12MB

大家好！歡迎各位收聽我的播客。前不久，我們學校開始進行 VR 教學，我一下子就被這種新穎的教學方式吸引住了。今天我就來和大家談談 VR 教學。

第一次戴上 VR 設備上課時，我真的嚇了一跳。真是太神奇了！因為我們可以在真實的情景中學習新知識，不像以前那樣只看課本，很多知識都沒聽懂。VR 還讓我們的學習環境變得更安全，比如它可以將普通教室變為生物實驗室、物理實驗室或者化學實驗室，那樣就不用擔心碰到有毒氣體、觸電或爆炸等危險。最讓我興奮的是歷史課，老師只花五分鐘的時間讓我們觀看幻燈片，剩下的時間就用 VR 讓我們"參觀"秦始皇陵兵馬俑，通過 360 度的視頻圖像來親身感受真實的場景。

另外，使用 VR 技術還能模擬"吸食毒品"的感受，向學生宣傳禁毒。體驗時，我感覺頭很暈，耳邊一直有人在叫，還會聽到有人要殺我，真是太可怕了！原來吸毒帶來的反應讓人如此難受。這樣利用 VR 技術還原真實的場景，就可以達到禁止吸毒的宣傳效果，真是不錯。

最近幾年，教育從面對面上課發展到了線上，從最初的依照書本到加入幻燈片、視頻等多媒體。就在線上教育還沒完全成熟的時候，VR 教學出現了，它比視頻教學更豐富，更能讓

學生沉浸在學習中。VR不但減輕了老師的教學負擔，同時也增加了教學的趣味性。比如，教外國人學中文，可以利用VR技術進行詞彙、語法教學，還可以開展遊戲、角色扮演，甚至對文化環境進行模擬。學生可以從視覺、聽覺、觸覺等方面體驗各種真實學習情景。這樣的"虛擬課堂"所具有的互動性對語言學習非常重要。不僅如此，VR教學還能幫助學生提高學習成績，增強記憶力。

你體驗過VR教學場景嗎？歡迎大家留言，和我分享你對VR教學的看法。

播放（53）　評論（10）　分享（30）　訂閱（45）

改編自：https://m.sohu.com/a/124932236_571550

Culture Point

秦始皇陵兵馬俑

Terracotta Warriors and Horses of Qinshihuang Mausoleum

秦始皇陵兵馬俑被稱為世界第八大奇跡。秦始皇是中國歷史上一位很有作為的帝王，他生前用了大量人力、物力為自己修建陵墓。秦陵兵馬俑就是為陪葬這位皇帝而製作的陶兵和陶馬。八千多個與真人真馬一般大小的陶俑，排列成整齊的方陣，再現了秦始皇統一中國時兵強馬壯的雄偉軍陣。

Terracotta Warriors and Horses of Qinshihuang Mausoleum is regarded as the eighth wonder of the world. The first emperor of the Qin Dynasty, known as Qinshihuang, made great achievements in Chinese history. While still alive, he mobilized huge manpower and used a great deal of materials to build this mausoleum. The terracotta warriors and horses were used as burial objects to accompany the emperor in the afterworld. Over 8000 lifelike soldiers and horses standing in formation, indicate the powerful military might of Qin when it united China.

語法重點 Key Points of Grammar

結果補語 The Complement of Result

結果補語是動作發生後的變化結果。
The complement of result is the result of the change after the action occurs.

Structure 動詞 + 表示結果的詞語　V.+words that indicate result

動作	補語	結果
看	見	看見
聽	懂	聽懂
洗	乾淨	洗乾淨
吃	完	吃完
修理	好	修理好
考慮	清楚	考慮清楚

注意 Notes

① 結果補語應該緊跟在動詞後面，賓語和動態助詞“了”都應該放在結果補語的後面。
The complement of the result must directly follow the verb. The object and the aspect particle “ 了 “ are placed after the complement of result.

② 否定形式

Structure 沒有 + 動詞 + 表示結果的詞語　沒有 +V.+words that indicate result
“沒有”要放在動詞之前。“沒有”should be placed before the verb.

E.g.
- 我學會了。→我沒有學會。
I have learnt. → I have not learnt.

課文理解 Reading Comprehensions

① 為什麼“我”覺得用 VR 上課很神奇？

② 為什麼 VR 可以讓學習環境變得更安全？

③ 為什麼"我"覺得"禁止吸毒"的宣傳效果很好？

④ 多媒體教學是什麼樣子的？

⑤ VR 除了能幫助教學外，還有什麼好處？

概念與拓展理解 Concepts and Further Understanding

① 課文二屬於什麼文體？和博客有什麼不同？
What is the text type of Text 2? How is it different from a blog?

② 課文二的寫作對象是誰？為什麼？
Who is the target audience of Text 2? Why?

③ 作者通過哪些方式來説服讀者認可他的觀點？
In what ways does the author convince readers that his point of view is correct?

④ VR 教學除了優點外，會有哪些弊端？
Besides the advantages of VR teaching, are there any disadvantages?

⑤ VR 教學方式的改變真的會影響學習效果嗎？
Will changes in teaching methods really affect learning effects?

語言練習 Language Exercises

將上下框的字組成詞語，填寫在橫線上。

Combine the characters in the upper and lower boxes into words and write the words on the line.

化	播	物	觸	圖	模	觸	情	新
景	擬	理	覺	電	像	穎	學	客

① ______

從左邊的方框裏選出適當的字，填寫在橫線上。

Select the appropriate character from the box on the left and write it on the line.

②	伸	神	______奇 / ______手
③	汽	氣	空______ / ______水
④	爆	瀑	______布 / ______炸
⑤	擬	似	相______ / 虛______
⑥	訂	盯	______著 / ______閱

重新排列詞語，組成完整的句子。Rearrange the words to form a complete sentence.

⑦ 多媒體　老師　教學　用　進行

______

⑧ 今天　了　給　小芳　介紹　我們　中國歷史

______

⑨ 很靈敏　雖然　小狗多力　仍然　聽覺　年紀大了　但是

______

從生詞表裏找出與下列詞語意思相同或相近的詞。

Find words with the same or similar meanings as the following words in the vocabulary list.

⑩ 陶醉__________ ⑪ 遊歷__________ ⑫ 新奇__________ ⑬ 眼力__________

從生詞表裏找出與下列詞語意思相反的詞。

Find words with the opposite meanings to the following words in the vocabulary list.

⑭ 享受__________ ⑮ 真實__________

判斷下面結果補語的使用是否準確，如果錯誤請訂正。

Determine whether the complement of result in the following sentences are used appropriately or not, and correct them if there is any mistake.

⑯ 阿姨洗衣服好了。

⑰ 我聽了懂老師講的內容。

⑱ 今天晚上飯菜太少，他可能不吃飽。

課堂活動 Class Activities

007 倒著說 Say 007 in Reverse Order

圍成一圈，老師指定一個人，這個人會先說“0”，然後立馬指另外一個人，這個人要馬上說出“0”，再指第三個人。第三個人要說“7”，然後用手指做成開槍的樣子指向第四個人。第四個人就是“中槍”的人。“中槍人”不說話不做任何動作，但“中槍人”左右兩邊的人要馬上舉起雙手投降，而且同時發出“啊”的聲音。做錯的人，則站到圈子中間。

In a circle, the teacher designates a student who will immediately say “0” and then immediately point to another student. This student will immediately say “0” and then point to the third person. This third person will say “7” and then point their fingers at the fourth person like shooting. This fourth person is the “shot” student is the one who is shot. The student who is shot does not speak or do any movement, but students around him should raise their hands and surrender immediately, and make an “ah” sound at the same time. Those who do it wrong will stand in the middle of the circle.

請說“7”的那個人說一句話，規定字數在四個字以內，而且至少有一個詞語來自課文二的生詞。例如：我聽覺差。圈中間的人必須在 5 秒之內把說“7”的人說的句子倒著說。例如：“我聽覺差”→“差覺聽我”。說不出的話，就算失敗。輸的人作為第二輪的第一個“0”，由此類推。如果玩得好，可以把字數限制提高到 8 個字以內。

Student who says "7" will complete a sentence. The sentence should contain at most four characters, and at least one character should come from the new word in Text 2. For example: I have poor hearing. The person who surrenders must say the sentence of the one who says "7" backwards within 5 seconds. For example: "I have poor hearing" → "hearing poor have I". If you can't say it, you lose. The loser is regarded as the first "0" in the second round, and so on. If you play well, you can increase the word count to less than 8 words.

口語訓練 Speaking Tasks

第一部分 **根據圖片，做 3–4 分鐘的口頭表達。做口頭表達之前，先根據提示寫大綱。**

Make a 3-4 minutes oral presentation based on the picture. Before you start, use the form below to make an outline.

大綱 Outline	內容 Content
圖片內容 Information of the picture	
圖片主題 + 文化 Theme of the picture and culture	
提出觀點 Make your points	
延伸個人經歷 Relate to personal experiences	
名人名言 Famous quotes / 熟語 Idioms	
總結 Summary	

第二部分 **回答下面的問題。Answer the following questions.**

① 臉書和蘋果的 CEO 都沒有讀完大學，卻創業成功了。你認為讀書有用嗎？

② 你認為教育的意義是什麼？

③ 教育改變了你對人生的看法嗎？

④ 很多人為了考入大學，下課後就去補習，而忽視了對其他能力的培養。你怎麼看待這種現象？

⑤ 有些人讀完大學仍然不知道自己要做什麼。你認為這是教育的失敗嗎？

技能訓練 Skill Tasks

閱讀訓練 Reading Tasks

文章 1 21 世紀的學生需要哪些能力？

仔細閱讀下面的短文，然後回答問題。

Read the passage carefully and answer the questions.

隨著全球化的加快，傳統的以知識為核心的人才素質結構已越來越難以滿足未來社會的發展需求。培養學生面向 21 世紀的核心技能是當今國際教育發展的重點。那麼面對複雜的未來，什麼樣的知識和技能才是最重要的呢？

A. 創新能力

創新性思維的關鍵，不僅在於提出自己的觀點和想法，還在於堅持不懈的嘗試。當你有了新想法時，要勇於嘗試。即使失敗了，也要學會將失敗作為新的起點，思考並總結其中的經驗和教訓。創新是一個漫長的過程，未來的學生必須要有開放的學習態度，學會接受和嘗試新的理念。

B. 批判性思維

批判性思維不僅是一種理解和分析的思維，還是一種判斷和決策的思維。學生要學會根據自己的知識和經驗判斷好壞。通過不斷提出問題、分析問題、解決問題來提升自己的問題解決與決策能力。在這個過程中，要學會平等地對待他人。

C. 溝通能力

溝通交流的前提是掌握良好的語言知識。在全球化時代，未來學生不但要掌握自己的母語，做到聽說讀寫流暢，而且至少要學會一門外語。掌握語言知識並不等同於具備良好的溝通能力。溝通首先要求學生能夠接受不同意見、傾聽不同觀點，並能做出適當的回應。學會如何真誠、自信、開放地與他人進行溝通將是未來學生面臨的一大挑戰。

D. 合作能力

團隊合作不僅要求學生尊重不同的文化、不同的觀點，還要學會以專業的態度向團隊陳述自己的觀點。同時，團隊合作也需要學生能根據團隊目標組織和計劃工作。學生要懂得如何激發團隊裏每個人的熱情，學會分享團隊成功的喜悅，同時還要積極承擔團隊失敗的後果。

改編自：https://www.sohu.com/a/203325798_808442

根據以上短文，選擇正確的答案，在方格裏打勾（✓）。

According to the passage above, tick (✓) in the correct boxes.

① 哪個能力需要懂得和別人一起承擔失敗的結果？

A. ☐ B. ☐ C. ☐ D. ☐

② 哪個能力要求自己能做出決定？

A. ☐ B. ☐ C. ☐ D. ☐

③ 哪個能力要求學會第二語言？

A. ☐ B. ☐ C. ☐ D. ☐

④ 哪個能力需要有嘗試精神？

A. ☐ B. ☐ C. ☐ D. ☐

⑤ 哪個能力需要懂得總結失敗？

A. ☐ B. ☐ C. ☐ D. ☐

⑥ 哪個能力需要有組織、有計劃地工作？

A. ☐ B. ☐ C. ☐ D. ☐

⑦ 哪個能力需要有真誠的態度？

A. ☐ B. ☐ C. ☐ D. ☐

⑧ 哪個能力需要學會平等地對待他人？

A. ☐ B. ☐ C. ☐ D. ☐

⑨ 哪個能力需要耐心地聽取他人的觀點？

A. ☐ B. ☐ C. ☐ D. ☐

⑩ 哪個能力需要學會分享？

A. ☐ B. ☐ C. ☐ D. ☐

Tips

積累詞語和句子
Accumulating Words and Sentences

學會在閱讀中積累詞語和句子非常重要。閱讀時把一些優美的詞語和生動的句子摘抄下來，並試著在生活中使用，或者在寫作中運用這些好詞好句，將會為你的對話和文章增添光彩。

Learning to accumulate words and sentences in reading is very important. Record some beautiful words and vivid sentences while reading, and try to use them in life, or use these good words and sentences in writing, which will make your conversations and articles brilliant.

文章 2 維護校園秩序指南

你在校園生活安全嗎？你知道如果沒有遵守校園秩序的話，將會引發觸電、爆炸或食物中毒等危險嗎？你知道如何保護自己嗎？希望本指南可以幫助大家增強自我防範意識，提高維護校園秩序的能力。

一、【–1–】

1. 不要到處亂跑。

2. 乘坐電梯要抓好扶手。

3. 人多的時候，要保持安全距離。

4. 參與集體活動要遵守秩序。

二、【–2–】

1. 不吃過期、腐爛食品。

2. 多吃綠色食物，少吃垃圾食品。

3. 購買食物請排隊。

4. 用餐後將餐具放回指定地點。

三、【–3–】

1. 上課期間有問題，怎麼辦？

可以舉手或者等下課後問老師；不可以在教室大聲講話，影響其他同學的學習。

2. 被老師批評怎麼辦？

要敢於自我反省，認真反思；多和老師溝通。

3. 與同學發生矛盾怎麼辦？

要冷靜，不要通過打架解決問題。

4. 覺得身體不舒服怎麼辦？

及時通知班主任和老師。

生命是美好的，生活是豐富多彩的，而擁有這一切的前提是安全。所以我們要增強安全意識，努力提高維護校園秩序的能力！

台灣高雄國際學校學生會

2022 年 10 月 10 日

改編自：http://www.safehoo.com/Files/Lesson/200909/30434.shtml

根據文本，從選項中選出適合的段落標題。

Choose an appropriate heading from the list that completes each gap in the passage.

① [–1–] ______ A. 就餐
② [–2–] ______ B. 乘坐電梯
③ [–3–] ______ C. 操場
D. 課間
E. 上課

根據文章 2，從選項中選出最接近下列詞語 / 詞組的意思。把答案寫在橫線上。

According to passage 2, choose the corresponding words and write the answers on the lines.

④ 遵守 ______ A. 維繫
⑤ 防範 ______ B. 尊敬
⑥ 保持 ______ C. 服從
⑦ 秩序 ______ D. 禁止
E. 紀律
F. 保證
G. 戒備

根據文章 2，選出最適合左邊句子的結尾。把答案寫在橫線上。

According to passage 2, choose the suitable endings of the sentence on the left side. Write the answers on the lines.

⑧ 乘坐電梯 ______ A. 要冷靜。
⑨ 吃完飯 ______ B. 要排隊。
⑩ 被老師批評 ______ C. 將碗筷放回指定地點。
⑪ 和同學鬧矛盾 ______ D. 要打架。
E. 抓好扶手。
F. 要通知老師。
G. 要反思。

聽力訓練 Listening Tasks

一、《混合式學習方式》 

你將聽到一所國際學校的校長談“混合式學習方式”。你將聽到兩遍，請聽錄音，然後回答問題。

You will hear a recording about “Blending Learning” by a principal of an international school. The clip will be played twice. Please listen and answer the questions.

請先閱讀一下問題。Please read the questions first.

① 數字化和____________將打開一個全新的教育局面。

② ____________將取代傳統的面對面課堂教學。

③ 2019 年新冠疫情打亂了很多國家的____________。

④ 這所國際學校的遠程教學主要是通過____________進行。

⑤ 在線教育能幫助中學生發展____________能力。

⑥ 實體學校不會被在線教育完全取代是因為教育是一個“____________”的過程。

⑦ 混合式學習方式就是____________與線上學習相結合的方式。

⑧ 我們以後可能會“感歎”是____________促成了混合式學習方式的開始。

Tips

圈畫關鍵詞 Circling the Key Words

在讀題的時候，可以圈畫出需要注意聽的詞，這樣做不僅可以讓你在考試時更加專注，還可以提高你的聽力成績。即使聽不懂整個篇章，也能寫出正確答案。

例如第一題，圈出“數字化”這個關鍵詞，你在聽聽力的時候，只要寫出“數字化”後面的“人工智能”這個詞語就可以，不一定需要聽懂所有的句子。

When reading the questions, you can use the circle to draw words that need to be listened to. This will not only make you more focused during the exam, but also improve your scores. Even if you don't understand the whole chapter, you can write the correct answer.

For example, in the first question, circle the keyword “digitalization”. When you are listening, you only need to write the word “artificial intelligence” after “digitization”. You don't need to understand all sentences.

二、《素養教育》 

你即將聽到第二個聽力片段，在聽力片段二播放之前，你將有四分鐘的時間先閱讀題目。聽力片段將播放兩次，聽力片段結束後你將有兩分鐘的時間來檢查你的答案。請用中文回答問題。

You will hear the second audio clip. You have 4 minutes to read the questions before it starts. The audio clip will be played twice. After it ends, you will have 2 minutes to check the answers. Please answer the questions in Chinese.

根據第二個聽力片段的內容，回答問題 ①-⑩ 。

Answer the questions ①-⑩ according to the second audio clip.

請在正確的選項裏打勾（✓）。Please tick (✓) in the correct option.

這是誰的觀點？	記者	葉丙成	家長
① 舊的教育制度培養了很有知識的學生。	______	______	______
② 替孩子裝備面對未知的素養是全球教育趨勢。	______	______	______
③ 喜歡原來的應試教育。	______	______	______
④ 世界變化速度很快。	______	______	______

根據第二個聽力片段的內容，從 A，B，C 中，選出一個正確的答案，把答案寫在橫線上。

According to the second audio clip, choose the right answer for the questions. Write the answers on the lines.

⑤ 台灣有__________大學生不喜歡做和大學專業相關的工作。

A. 58%　　B. 61%　　C. 6%

⑥ 台灣每年從大學退學的學生大概有__________。

A. 6 萬　　B. 17 萬　　C. 15 萬

⑦ 現在學生所處的時代不包括__________。

A. 人口多　　B. 氣候變化快　　C. 疫情嚴重

回答下面的問題。Answer the following questions.

⑧ 葉丙成教授每年都會在哪裏做新生講座？

____

⑨ 如果不喜歡大學所讀的專業，一般畢業後會做什麼工作？至少舉一個例子。

⑩ 什麼是素養教育？

寫作訓練：個人陳述 Writing Tasks: Personal Statement

熱身

- **根據課文一，討論個人陳述的格式是什麼。**

According to Text 1, discuss the format of a personal statement.

- **如何寫好個人陳述？**

How to write a personal statement?

Tips

文體：個人陳述
Text Type: Personal Statement

個人陳述是關於申請人過去背景、目前成就和未來目標的自我介紹性文章，通常用於申請大學或獎學金。

A personal statement is a self-introducing essay about the applicant's background, current achievements and future goals. It is usually used when applying for a university or scholarship.

格式 **參考課文一**

個人陳述

作者

□□開頭：問候語 + 自我介紹 + 申請意願

□□正文：自我介紹 + 申請理由 + 未來打算

□□結尾：申請意願

練習

你是音樂專業的學生，不但鋼琴彈得很好，而且會作曲，你的作品還經常獲獎。除此之外，你的學習成績也很優秀。你參加了中央音樂學院的開放日，覺得這所大學很符合你將來的職業規劃，你想報考這所大學。選用合適的文本類型完成寫作。字數：300–480 個漢字。

訪談	個人陳述	評論

Tips

如何在個人陳述中說明自己的優缺點？

How to explain your strengths and weaknesses in your personal statement？

在個人陳述中巧妙地説明自己的優缺點，才能讓對方接受你，這一點很重要。因為對方會根據你陳述的材料來判斷你是否真實地陳述了自己的優點，或者你所陳述的優點是不是符合這所大學的要求。

How to articulate your own strengths and weaknesses in your personal statement so that the other person can accept you is very important. Because the examiner will judge whether you have truly stated your strengths based on the materials you have stated, or whether the strengths you stated meet the requirements of this university.

關於優點 About the advantages

1. 陳述優點時一定要準備幾個真實的例子，一般是你學習、做義工的經歷和生活中的事情。
   When stating your strengths, you must prepare a few real examples to illustrate. Generally, it is your study, volunteer experience and things happened in your daily life.

2. 你陳述的優點要和你所申請的大學專業相關。
   Your strengths should be related to the major you are applying for.

3. 寫個人陳述之前，最好能了解一下這所大學的發展史和辦學理念。
   Before writing a personal statement, you should better understand the philosophy and development history of this university.

關於缺點 About the disadvantages

在個人陳述中稍微談一下你的缺點，會讓你的陳述顯得更真實。可以談一些高中生普遍存在的弱點，例如缺少實踐經驗、閱歷淺，或者是專業知識不足，還需加強學習等。

另外，你可以談談看似缺點、但可能也是優點的地方，比如過分追求完美、過於追求學習效率等。這些其實不完全算是缺點。在陳述個人缺點時，要説明自己正在克服和改進。

A little talk about your shortcomings in your personal statement will make your statement more authentic. You can talk about the common weaknesses of high school students. such as for lack of practical experience and professionalism, you need to improve you study, etc.

In addition, you can talk about some shortcomings which may be the advantages such as pursuit of perfection and learning efficiency too much, etc. These shortcomings are actually not really shortcomings. When mentioning your weaknesses, remember to clarify that you are overcoming and improving them.

The World Around Us
同一個世界

Unit

Lesson 7

Globalization
全球化

Lesson 8

The Environment
環境

Lesson 9

Recycling Resource and Renewable Energy
回收資源與可再生能源

Lesson
7 Globalization
全球化

導入 Introduction

隨著科技的發展，特別是網絡的普及，世界各國的交流越來越頻繁，全球化已經是大勢所趨。一方面，人們開始接受不同的生活方式和價值觀。比如，在日常生活中，咖啡、奶茶、中國手機、蘋果電腦等在全球流行。世界各地的人們也開始接受其他國家的傳統文化。比如，中國春節的慶祝活動，也在西方國家的節日慶典中出現。中國年輕一代，也熱衷於西方的聖誕節。世界變成了“我中有你，你中有我”的地球村。另一方面，在全球化時代，各個國家保持自己獨特的傳統文化，保護世界文化的多樣性變得更為重要。如何尊重各自的傳統文化，又能互相交流、共同發展，是我們青少年要關注的問題。此外，後疫情時代的新型全球化更需要人類共同價值觀的支撐。

With the development of science and technology, especially the popularization of the Internet, communications across countries has become more and more frequent. Globalization is already inevitable. On one hand, people have begun to accept different lifestyles and values. For example, coffee, milk tea, China branded mobile phones, Apple computers etc. have become popular in daily life all over the world. Some traditional cultures have also been accepted by people all over the world. For example, the celebration of Chinese Spring Festival also appears in the festival celebrations of western countries. Chinese young people are also enthusiastic about western Christmas. The world has become a global village which is also a community where everyone has a stake. On the other hand, how each country maintains its own unique traditional culture and protects the diversity of the world have become more important. It's important for our teenagers to learn to respect each other's traditional culture, communicate with each other and develop together. In addition, the new trend of globalization in the post-epidemic era needs the support of our common human values.

學習目標 Learning Targets

閱讀 Reading

學會提取信息。
Learn to extract information.

口語 Speaking

學會做口頭報告。
Learn to make an oral report.

聽力 Listening

學會搶讀預測。
Learn to read and predict.

寫作 Writing

學會寫口頭報告。
Learn to write an oral report.

生詞短語

kǒu tóu bào gào
口頭報告 oral report

quán qiú huà
全球化 globalization

nìng yuàn
寧願 would rather

mài dāng láo
麥當勞 McDonalds

miàn tiáo
麵條 noodle

kāi zhǎn
開展 conduct

wèn juàn
問卷 questionnaire

shèn zhì
甚至 even

rén shēng guān
人生觀 view of life

hǎo lái wù
好萊塢 Hollywood

dí shì ní
迪士尼 Disney

wēi xié
威脅 threat

kāi shè
開設 set up

dà dǎn
大膽 bold

huí guī
回歸 return

1 課文 全球化對傳統文化影響的口頭報告 25

尊敬的各位領導：

大家好！我是北京八中的學生會主席陶小樂。今天我的口頭報告的主題是"全球化對傳統文化的影響"。

一、調查目的

全球化在促進文化交流的同時，也對各國的傳統文化造成了嚴重的衝擊。現在的中學生寧願過聖誕節、吃麥當勞、講英文，也不願過春節、吃麵條、說中文。此次學生會開展調查的目的是通過調查學生對傳統文化的看法，了解全球化對中華傳統文化造成的影響，從而對如何保護傳統文化提出建議。

二、調查方法

我們通過電話採訪、電子郵件問卷等方式對全校兩千多名學生進行了調查。

三、調查結果

調查顯示：超過一半的學生喜歡西方文化，不喜歡中國傳統文化。其中三分之一的學生不認同自己的傳統文化，有五成的學生甚至認為不需要保護傳統文化，也不認為全球化已經對傳統文化造成了不好的影響。

四、調查分析

中學生通過互聯網獲取的信息越來越豐富，他們的世界觀、價值觀和人生觀也隨著全球化的發展而發生改變。好萊塢電影、迪士尼動畫、臉書、推特等流行文化大多數展現的是西方的價值觀和生活方式，對中國傳統文化的傳承造成了一定的威脅。

五、建議

為了保護中華傳統文化，改變中學生對傳統文化的看法，學生會建議首先在校園開設傳統藝術課程，讓中學生了解學習傳統藝術的重要性；接著鼓勵學生大膽創新，讓傳統藝術回歸到現實生活中；然後在學校慶祝傳統節日，通過舞台表演的形式向中學生展現傳統藝術；或者讓同學們走進社區，和居民一起慶祝傳統節日等等。

謝謝大家！

改編自：https://wenku.baidu.com/view/50ec5fa91be8b8f67c1cfad6195f312b3169ebfc.html

Culture Point

麵條，是一種中華民族的傳統美食，蘊藏著中華傳統文化，象徵著長長久久。比如，麵條長而不斷，被寄予了“長壽”的美好寓意。又如，在現代生活中，有些父母還沿襲著“出門餃子進門麵”的習俗，每次有出遠門歸來的孩子，回家的第一餐總是麵條，而離開家的最後一頓則是餃子。餃子與麵條一樣，被人們賦予了很多寓意，但它代表的更多是喜慶的節日和紀念日，而麵條則代表著家長里短的平常日子。

Noodle is a traditional Chinese cuisine which reflects Chinese traditional culture and symbolizes permanence. For example, noodles symbolizes longevity because they are long. In modern life, some families still keep the custom of eating dumplings when a member leaves home and eating noodles when she/he comes back home. Whenever child returns home from outside of the town, the first meal at home is always noodles while the last meal before leaving away is dumplings. Dumplings have been given too much meaning by the Chinese. Other than that, dumplings mainly represent important festivals and anniversaries while noodles represent the ordinary daily life.

語法重點 Key Points of Grammar

數詞 Numerals

指表示數目的詞。
Numerals are the words that indicates numbers.

基本的數詞：兩、半、一、百、千、萬、億
Basic numerals: pair, half, one, hundred, thousand, 10 thousand, 100 million

基本的數詞又叫基數詞，基數詞連用或者加上別的詞，可以表示序數、分數、倍數。
Basic numerals are also called cardinal numerals. Cardinal numbers can be used together or with other words to express ordinal numbers, fractions and multiples.

① 序數：第一、第二、三姐、四月、五樓
Ordinal: first, second, third sister, April, fifth floor

② 分數：三分之一、七成（70%）、八折（80%）、百分之八（8%）
Fraction: one third, seventy percent, eighty percent, eight percent

③ 倍數：兩倍、十倍
Multiple: double, ten times

課文理解 Reading Comprehensions

① 現在的中學生喜歡做什麼？

② 這個口頭報告中的調查是通過什麼方式進行的？

③ 大概有多少名學生認為不需要保護傳統文化？

④ 西方的價值觀和生活方式通過哪些方式得到宣傳？

⑤ 如何向中學生展現傳統藝術？

概念與拓展理解 Concepts and Further Understanding

① 我們的文化背景在何種程度上影響我們的觀點？
To what extent are our views affected by our specific cultural identity?

② 傳統藝術形式，如手工藝品，在分享知識的過程中起到什麼作用？
What role do traditional arts such as handicrafts play in sharing knowledge?

③ 在獲取和分享知識的過程中，民間傳説、儀式和歌曲起了什麼作用？
What role do folklore, rituals and songs play in acquiring and sharing knowledge?

④ 土著居民用什麼方法來幫助他們記錄、保存和保護自己的傳統文化知識？
What methods do indigenous people use to support them in recording, preserving and protecting their traditional knowledge?

⑤ 在全球化背景下，如何尊重與保留文化差異？
In the context of globalization, how can we respect and preserve cultural differences?

語言練習 Language Exercises

重新排列詞語，組成完整的句子。Rearrange the words to form a complete sentence.

① 對　造成了　傳統　嚴重　衝擊　全球化　文化　的

② 我　也　寧願　吃麵條　不願　去麥當勞　吃漢堡　去中國餐廳

③ 好萊塢　更喜歡　迪士尼　哪一個　和　電影　動畫　你

④ 必須　口頭報告　然後　他們　做好　先　問卷調查　為了　開展　進行分析

---

⑤ 威脅　傳統文化　開設　受到　為了　在學校　避免　我們　中華藝術課程　應該

選擇合適的詞語，填寫在橫線上。

Fill in the blanks with the appropriate words.

⑥ 現代人追求簡單生活，喜歡＿＿＿＿＿＿（回歸 / 歸還）自然。

⑦ 學生會建議學校多＿＿＿＿＿＿（展開 / 開展）健康有益的課外活動。

⑧ 老師注重培養學生獨立＿＿＿＿＿＿（解析 / 分析）問題的能力。

⑨ 廣告對我們美的＿＿＿＿＿＿（觀念 / 觀看）會產生一定的影響。

⑩ 森林不斷地減少，已經＿＿＿＿＿＿（威逼 / 威脅）到了動物們的生存。

選擇正確的答案。Choose the right answer.

⑪ 根據調查，全校 1200 名學生中，40% 的學生都近視。大概有＿＿＿＿＿名學生近視。

A. 480　　B. 720　　C. 400

⑫ 水果店到了晚上就會大減價，所有水果都打 6 折。原價 100 塊的水果，如果晚上去買，可以節省＿＿＿＿＿元錢。

A. 60　　B. 40　　C. 20

⑬ 圖書館裏有 1000 本中文書，其中四分之一是漫畫書。圖書館裏有＿＿＿＿＿本漫畫書。

A. 400　　B. 200　　C. 250

課堂活動 Class Activities

找句子 Find a Sentence

請一名學生背對全體同學站立。老師一方面將句子投影在白板上，另一方面將寫有句子的卡片藏在某個學生的桌子裏。請台上學生轉過身尋找這張卡片。同時，全班同學一起讀投影上的句子。尋找卡片的學生離藏卡片的桌子位置越近，其他同學的朗讀聲音要越大；離桌子越遠，朗讀聲音就越小，直到找到句子卡片。

Ask one student face away from all his classmates. Teacher projects a sentence on the whiteboard, while hiding the card with the sentence in one student's desk. Ask the student on the stage to turn around and look for this card. At the same time, the whole class read the sentence on the slide together. The closer the student looking for the card is to the table, the louder other students will read out; the further away from the table, the more other students will lower their voices, until he/she finds the sentence card.

口語訓練 Speaking Tasks

第一部分 **根據主題"全球化"，做 2–3 分鐘的口頭表達。做口頭表達之前，先根據提示寫大綱。**

Make a 2-3 minutes oral presentation on the theme "globalization". Before you start, use the form below to make an outline.

大綱 Outline	內容 Content
觀點 Perspectives	
事例 Examples	
名人名言 Famous quotes / 熟語 Idioms	
經歷 Experiences	
總結 Summary	

第二部分 **回答下面的問題。Answer the following questions.**

① 你認同全球化會對傳統文化造成不良影響嗎？

② 中學生不認同自己的傳統文化，主要原因是什麼？

③ 你認為家庭和社區會對中學生觀念的形成有決定性影響嗎？

④ 全球化除了體現在經濟方面以外，還體現在哪些方面？

⑤ 全球化除了對傳統文化造成影響以外，還有其他影響嗎？

Tips

如何做口頭報告？ How to make an oral report?

做報告，是一種訓練理解能力和答辯能力的方式。在陳述的時候，要明確說明你調查的問題、調查的結果和建議。要注意：

Making a report is a way of training the ability of understanding and oral defense. In the presentation, you should clearly state the questions you intend to investigate with the findings and suggestions. Please note:

1. 你的主張必須是準確且容易理解的。Your claim must be accurate and easy to understand.
2. 按點列出報告重點，根據調查目的進行論證。
   List the key points of the report and focus on the purpose of the investigation to demonstrate.
3. 舉例子可以幫助你說明你的觀點，也能說服考官。
   Using examples can help you illustrate your point of view and persuade the examiner.
4. 陳述時要使用正式語氣或專業術語。Use formal tone or technical terms when making statements.

生詞短語

wēi jī
危機 crisis
fáng fàn
防範 be on guard
kǒng bù xí jī
恐怖襲擊
terrorist attack
jǐn jí
緊急 urgent
qíng kuàng
情況 situation
bào lì
暴力 violence
rén yuán
人員 staff
shāng wáng
傷亡
injuries and deaths
xíng wéi
行為 behavior
jǐn zhāng
緊張 nervous
dōng zhāng xī wàng
東張西望
looking around
chuān zhuó
穿著 apparel
shāng chǎng
商場 shopping mall
kě yí
可疑 suspicious
zhù yì
注意 notice
bào jǐng
報警 call the police
pāi zhào
拍照 take a photo
fǎn kàng
反抗 resist
hū yù
呼籲 appeal

2 課文 防範恐怖襲擊指南 26

在生活中，我們可能會遇到各種傷害，如何在危機中保護自己呢？《防範恐怖襲擊指南》將告訴您，恐怖活動可能會對您及您的家人造成的危害，以及在緊急情況下如何應對恐怖襲擊，希望對大家有用。

一、什麼是恐怖襲擊

恐怖襲擊是指以危害公共安全為目的，採取暴力、破壞等手段，造成人員傷亡等嚴重危害社會的行為。

二、如何辨別恐怖襲擊者

進行恐怖襲擊的人一般會有一些行為可以提前引起我們的注意，例如：

1. 說話緊張、東張西望。

2. 穿著與普通人不同。

3. 一直在商場、醫院、車站等人多的地方走動。

三、發現可疑的人怎麼辦

1. 保持平靜，不要引起對方注意。

2. 及時報警，說明情況。

3. 在不被發現並保證自身安全的情況下，可以拍照。

四、遇到恐怖襲擊怎麼辦

1. 儘快遠離手拿危險物品的人。

2. 無法遠離就利用身邊的東西（衣服、傘等）進行反抗。

3. 一離開危險的地方，就及時報警，向警方說明時間、地點和恐怖襲擊者的特點。

4. 保護好身邊的老人和孩子，將他們送到安全的地方。

恐怖襲擊給世界帶來了巨大的危害。我們應該團結起來，一起呼籲和平，反對恐怖襲擊。希望本指南能夠幫助您了解一定的安全防範知識，在危險時刻能夠給您及您的家人提供幫助。

防範恐怖襲擊中心

2021 年 12 月 22 日

改編自：https://www.sohu.com/a/393048621_366845

Culture Point

尊老愛幼 Respect the Aged and Love the Young

尊老愛幼是中華民族的優良傳統。華人對後代的關懷愛護是愛中有教、慈中有嚴，包含強烈的道德責任感。在碰到困難或者危害時，老人和孩子是首要保護的對象。華人教育子女，要像尊敬自己的長輩一樣尊敬別人的長輩，要像愛護自己的孩子一樣愛護別人的孩子。尊老愛幼是中華民族一筆寶貴的道德財富，這種傳統在當代得以繼承和發揚，保證了家庭的和睦和社會的穩定。

Respecting the aged and loving the young is a traditional Chinese virtue. Chinese people take care of the next generation with love, education, kindness and strictness, embodying a strong sense of moral responsibility. When they face difficulties and threats, the aged and the young are the first ones to be protected. They educate their kids that one should respect the elderly relatives of other people as one's own and take good care of others' children as one's own. Respecting the aged and loving the young is precious tract on moral education, and this tradition has been carried forward in modern times. It ensures the harmony of the family and stabilization of society.

語法重點 Key Points of Grammar

承接關係複句 Successive Complex Sentence

由兩個或兩個以上的分句組成，一個接著一個地敘述連續發生的動作，或者接連發生的幾件事情。分句之間有先後順序。

It consists of two or more clauses which describe successive actions or several things that happen one after another. There is prioritization of certain clauses.

常見關聯詞 Common Conjunctive Words

一……就……；起先……後來…… as soon as...; at first...later...

首先……然後……；……接著…… first...then...; then...

……就……；……於是…… at once...; ...then...

……才……；...just...

……便…… ...thus...

E.g.
- 他昨天一寫完作業，就去玩兒電腦遊戲。
  As soon as he finished his homework yesterday, he went to play computer games.
- 我從香港出差回來後，就去拜訪大學英語老師。
  After I came back on a business trip from Hong Kong, I went to visit my college English teacher.

課文理解 Reading Comprehensions

① 《防範恐怖襲擊指南》的主要內容是什麼？

② 什麼是恐怖襲擊？

③ 恐怖襲擊者一般有什麼特點？

④ 什麼時候可以對恐怖襲擊者進行拍照？

⑤ 報警的時候要向警方說明什麼？

概念與拓展理解 Concepts and Further Understanding

① 導致恐怖襲擊發生的原因是什麼？
What cause terrorist attacks?

② 社交媒體對防範恐怖襲擊起到什麼作用？
What roles do social medias play in preventing terrorist attacks?

③ 恐怖襲擊組織如何利用情緒化的語言來說服和操控恐怖襲擊人員？
How do terrorist organizations use emotional language to persuade and manipulate terrorist attackers?

④ 如何說服青少年不要加入恐怖襲擊組織？
How can we convince young people against joining terrorist organizations?

⑤ 遭遇恐怖襲擊時，你贊同先保護老人和孩子，而不是自己嗎？
Do you agree that when you encounter a terrorist attack, you should protect elderly and children first before you protect yourselves?

語言練習 Language Exercises

將上下框的字組成詞語，填寫在橫線上。

Combine the characters in the upper and lower boxes into words and write the words on the line.

恐	警	暴	商	照	意	抗	為	亡

拍	報	場	識	力	行	反	傷	怖

① ______________________________

從左邊的方框裏選出適當的字，填寫在橫線上。

Select the appropriate character from the box on the left and write is on the line.

②	防	仿	________真 / ________範
③	清	情	________楚 / ________況
④	暴	瀑	________布 / ________力
⑤	凝	疑	懷________ / ________視
⑥	拍	怕	害________ / ________手

重新排列詞語，組成完整的句子。

Rearrange the words to form a complete sentence.

⑦ 恐怖　跑開　要　襲擊　遇到　儘快

____

⑧ 看到　在　報警　人員　要　商場　及時　可疑

____

⑨ 緊急　冷靜　要　先　緊張　碰到　情況　不要

---

⑩ 意識　人員　危機　注意　穿著　要有　那些　奇怪的

從生詞表裏找出與下列詞語意思相同或相近的詞。

Find words with the same or similar meanings as the following words in the vocabulary list.

⑪ 回擊________　⑫ 奇怪________　⑬ 著急________

從生詞表裏找出與下列詞語意思相反的詞。

Find words with the opposite meanings to the following words in the vocabulary list.

⑭ 生存________　⑮ 目不轉睛________　⑯ 平安________　⑰ 放鬆________

填入正確的關聯詞。Fill in the blanks with appropriate correlative conjunctions.

⑱ 孩子找到媽媽後________大聲哭起來。

⑲ 小狗________聽到主人的聲音________開始搖尾巴。

⑳ 如果要自助遊，________要確定旅遊城市，________確定出行路線，最後再定酒店。

㉑ 路上一直堵車，________我上學遲到了。

課堂活動 Class Activities

砰！！！BANG!!!

將學生分成四個小組。每個小組圍成一圈。每組選出一位同學做槍手。這位同學用手比作手槍，開始原地轉圈，然後突然停下。手槍指向的那位同學必須蹲下。蹲下的同學旁邊的兩位同學必須互相射擊對方。更慢舉起手槍射擊對方的人，就輸了。輸的同學將被要求朗讀課文中的任意一段，或者回答槍手的問題。

Divide students into four groups. Each group forms a circle. Each group chooses a classmate to be the shooter. This classmate uses his hand as a pistol, circles around, and stops circling instantly. Anyone pointed by the pistol must squat down. The two students next to the one who is pointed must shoot at each other. The person who raises the pistol and shoots the opponent slower loses.Students who lose the game will be asked to either read any one paragraph of the text aloud or answer questions from the shooter.

口語訓練 Speaking Tasks

第一部分 **根據圖片，做 3-4 分鐘的口頭表達。做口頭表達之前，先根據提示寫大綱。**

Make a 3-4 minutes oral presentation based on the picture. Before you start, use the form below to make an outline.

大綱 Outline	內容 Content
圖片內容 Information of the picture	
圖片主題 + 文化 Theme of the picture and culture	
提出觀點 Make your points	
延伸個人經歷 Relate to personal experiences	
名人名言 Famous quotes / 熟語 Idioms	
總結 Summary	

第二部分 **回答下面的問題。Answer the following questions.**

① 什麼是全球化？你能舉一些例子嗎？

② 全球化的好處是什麼？全球化給人類帶來了哪些不好的影響？

③ 你喜歡吃華人的傳統食物嗎？為什麼？

④ 你對在中國的麥當勞賣豆漿和油條有什麼看法？

⑤ 你如何看待現在的年輕人越來越喜歡吃西餐這一現象？

技能訓練 Skill Tasks

閱讀訓練 Reading Tasks

文章 1 舌尖上的世界

仔細閱讀下面的短文，然後回答問題。

Read the passage carefully and answer the following questions.

2022 年 9 月 15 日　　程小芳報道

今天，香港哈羅國際學校舉行了“第十八屆國際美食嘉年華”活動。這次活動由學生會主辦，致力於展示世界各地的優秀文化，吸引了一千多名老師和學生，還邀請了來自世界各地不同國家的家長一起慶祝這個美食活動。

日本壽司、意大利麵包、美國漢堡、中國火鍋……香港哈羅校園成了“舌尖上的世界”。全校師生不僅品嚐到了中國各地的美食，還對世界各地的飲食文化有了更加直觀的體驗。而且，很多料理結合了中西做法，給人眼前一亮的感覺。隨著全球化的加速，飲食也成為了全球化的一種文化表現形式。

“每一年，同學們參加‘美食嘉年華’都非常興奮。通過美食節，大家可以將自己國家的美食和傳統文化與來自世界各地的朋友分享。因為飲食的背後蘊藏著文化，所以在某種程度上也促進了各國人民的交流，促進了全球化的發展。”校長說道。

學生會會長說：“互聯網的發展也是美食全球化的原因。網絡使信息的交流更加便捷，人們頻繁使用微博、臉書、抖音等網絡平台分享美食體驗，青少年也更容易通過這樣的方式了解美食。因此，不同的飲食文化迅速在世界各地傳播，這也是我們的美食節這麼受大家歡迎的原因。”

來自英國的凱瑞說：“這是我第一次參加‘美食嘉年華’。我非常喜歡中國的食物，今天我見到了很多以前沒吃過的東西，中國的同學們還向我講解了很多中國飲食文化。”

這次的“舌尖上的世界”國際美食嘉年華活動受到大家的一致好評。美食節活動現場，還有一群志願者幫助大家準備食物。他們認為：“這是一次很好的學習機會，不但可以結交來自世界各國的朋友，而且可以提高自己的英語能力和動手能力。跟來自不同國家的同學一起做美食的體驗非常特別，可以深入地了解到他們的飲食文化和風俗習慣。”

改編自：http://www.shxwcb.com/264262.html

根據以上短文，選擇四個正確的答案，在方格裏打勾（✓）。

Choose four correct answers by ticking (✓) in the boxes.

① A. 參加“美食嘉年華”的人主要是老師和學生。 ☐
B.“美食嘉年華”由學生會主辦。 ☐
C. 同學們可以直接品嚐美食。 ☐
D. 飲食促進了全球化的發展。 ☐
E. 青少年不喜歡通過抖音了解美食。 ☐
F. 志願者也幫忙準備了嘉年華活動。 ☐
G. 做志願者可以提高漢語能力和動手能力。 ☐

根據短文填空。Fill in the blanks based on the short passage.

例：香港哈羅國際學校舉行 了 第 十八屆 國際 美食嘉年華活動。

（第　舉行　國際　十八屆　推行）

② ______飲食的背後______蘊藏著傳統文化，反過來______促進了全球化的______。

（也　都　發展　由於　雖然）

③ 互聯網的______ ______是美食______的______。

（也　全球化　結果　發展　原因）

④ 今天我見到了______沒吃過的東西，他們______向我______了很多中國飲食文化。

（解釋　講解　還　很多）

⑤ 做志願者，______可以結交______世界各國的朋友，______可以提高學習能力。

（另外　而且　來自　不但）

Tips

簡單提取信息 Extract Information Simply

人工智能的出現，就是因為我們掌握了大量的信息數據，使用各種代碼進行編程，提高了信息的有序度和完整度，讓機器人有了“意識”。換句話説，機器人之所以有智能，就是具有提取信息、加工信息的能力。所以只要提取信息的能力增強了，閱讀速度就會進一步提升。比如在一開始閱讀題目的時候，就要懂得找出有用信息、干擾信息和隱含條件。

The emergence of artificial intelligence is because we have mastered a large amount of information and data and have used various codes for programming to improve the order and completeness of information, which enables the robots to have awareness. In other words, the reason why robots became intelligent is because of their ability to extract and process information. Therefore, a person's reading speed will be further improved once his/her ability to extract information is enhanced. For example, when you start reading a question, you need to find useful information, irrelevant information and implicit conditions at the same time.

例如：

______飲食的背後都蘊藏著某些傳統文化，所以在有些情況下______促進了各國人民的交流，促進了全球化的______。

（也　發展　由於　雖然　還）

隱含條件：“所以”。就去掉選項“雖然”，因為連詞“雖然……但是……”。

Implied condition: " 所以 ". Just remove the option " 雖然 " because of the conjunction " 雖然……但是……".

有用信息：“促進”，後面可以選擇“發展”，因為其他詞都是連詞。

Useful information: " 促進 ", you can choose " 發展 " because other words are conjunctions.

干擾信息：“還”和“也”是干擾信息，題目中出現“都”，表示所有飲食都有文化這個條件，所以表示文化“也”同時促進了全球化的發展。而不是更進一步，所以不能選擇“還”。

Interference information: " 還 " and " 也 " are interference information. " 都 " in the sentence indicates that all food has the condition of culture. So it means that culture also promotes the development of globalization. You can't choose " 還 " as there is no meaning at going further.

文章 2　關於疫情全球化的思考

大海

美篇號 5858660

被訪問 1314　收穫讚 2　被收藏 1

文章：8　收藏：1　關注：2　粉絲：6

大海 / 2020-04-08 閱讀 1088

大海　樓主　2020-04-08　17:48

全球疫情爆發，世界上沒有一個地方可以完全阻斷病毒進入。那麼，在國際疫情形勢日益嚴峻的當下，大家對全球化又有什麼新的看法呢？

舉報 / 分享 / 樓主 / 讚（10）

過去四十年，中國人和美國人增進了交流。美國人希望送孩子到中國接受教育，到中國旅遊等；中國人希望與美國人合作，送孩子到美國接受教育等。事實上，兩國之間的關係正是全球化發展的基礎。但是疫情一爆發，美國禁止出口口罩和疫苗，讓全球化進程往相反的方向發展。

作者：可可　1 樓 / 回覆 / 評論 / 讚（11）

2020 年 3 至 10 月，中國增加了五百多次飛行任務，在全球範圍內運送了超過 18 億隻口罩。然而有的國家卻在這時候反對全球化，他們開始禁止出口大米和疫苗。

作者：毛毛　2 樓 / 回覆 / 評論 / 讚（80）

有人說全球化就是疫情擴散的主要原因，我不同意這樣的觀點。在歐洲還是靠走路出行的時代，2500萬歐洲人死於鼠疫，佔當時人口的三分之一。一百多年前，一場大流感也是在一年之內就傳遍全球。這就是說即使是在一百年前，人們也無法阻止疫情的傳播。

作者：動動　3樓 / 回覆 / 評論（11）/ 讚（36）

病毒面前，人人平等。不管你來自哪個國家、哪個種族、哪個階級，你都有可能得新冠肺炎。在全球化的今天，沒有一個國家或一個人能夠自己關起門來，解決疫情問題。現在大家應該共同合作，才有可能盡早擁抱美好健康的未來。

作者：小狗　4樓 / 回覆 / 評論 / 讚（40）

改編自：https://www.meipian.cn/c/5853110

根據文章 2，選出最適合左邊的觀點。把答案寫在橫線上。

According to passage 2, choose the corresponding opinion on the left side. Write the answers on the lines.

① 樓主 ______	A. 美國人和中國人都想送孩子去對方的國家留學。
② 可可 ______	B. 有些國家禁止出口大米。
③ 毛毛 ______	C. 全球化就是疫情擴散的主要原因。
④ 動動 ______	D. 沒有人可以阻擋病毒進入自己的國家。
⑤ 小狗 ______	E. 100 多年前，全球也發生過一場大流感。
	F. 大家應該一起努力解決疫情問題。

根據文章 2，從選項中選出最接近下列詞語 / 詞組的意思。把答案寫在橫線上。

According to passage 2, choose the corresponding words and write the answers on the lines.

⑥ 爆發 ______ A. 病菌

⑦ 病毒 ______ B. 爆炸

⑧ 禁止 ______ C. 產生

⑨ 傳播 ______ D. 阻擋

⑩ 擁抱 ______ E. 歡迎

F. 散開

G. 停止

聽力訓練 Listening Tasks

一、《全球化》 27

你將聽到六段錄音，每段錄音播放兩遍。請在相應的橫線上回答問題 ①-⑥。回答應簡短扼要。每段錄音後會有停頓，請在停頓期間閱讀問題。

You will hear 6 recordings and each audio will be played twice. Answer the questions ①-⑥ with short answers. There will be a pause after each recording is played. Please read the questions during the pause.

請先閱讀一下問題。Please read the questions first.

① 韓國的麥當勞會賣什麼？

______

② 民族語言逐漸消失的原因是什麼？至少舉一個例子。

______

③ 什麼全球化問題需要全球共同應對？

______

④ 全球化有什麼好處？請舉一個例子。

______

⑤ 全球化的代價有哪些？請舉一個例子。

______

⑥ 科技全球化對疫苗開發有什麼影響？

______

二、《全球化是世界衝突的根源》 

你即將聽到第二個聽力片段，在聽力片段二播放之前，你將有四分鐘的時間先閱讀題目。聽力片段將播放兩次，聽力片段結束後你將有兩分鐘的時間來檢查你的答案。請用中文回答問題。

You are going to hear the second audio clip. You have 4 minutes to read the questions before it starts. The audio clip will be played twice. After it ends, you have 2 minutes to check the answers. Please answer the questions in Chinese.

填空 • Fill in the blanks.

活動名稱：	世界和平論壇		主辦單位：	【–1–】	
時間：	【–2–】		演講題目：	全球化是世界衝突根源	
演講者：	張小酉	學校：	【–3–】	職位：	【–4–】
全球化造成的不好影響： • 對環境、文化、經濟的發展造成不好影響。 • 對【–5–】造成不同程度影響。			全球化在社會發展中的作用： • 鼓勵各種新技術的研究和開發。 • 推動了新產品的生產和消費。 • 促進了【–6–】的發展。		

①[–1–]__________ ②[–2–]__________ ③[–3–]__________

④[–4–]__________ ⑤[–5–]__________ ⑥[–6–]__________

Tips

搶讀預測 Read and Predict

聽力考試時，“搶讀預測”是積極主動做好聽力問題的關鍵技能之一。“搶讀預測”就是利用播放聽力錄音之前的 4 分鐘，提前閱讀選項，預測出題方向，等錄音內容開始播放後就可以有目的地記下所需信息。然後，在播放聽力錄音的時候，邊聽，邊理解，邊複述（適用於單句、短對話和數據方面的內容），邊做筆記，邊猜測（推斷）。這種能力的培養，需要學生平時多做練習，以幫助強化記憶，記錄答題要點。

Learning to read and predict is an important listening skill. "Read and Predict" is use of making the 4 minutes silent time to read the questions in advance, so that when the recording starts, you can purposefully write down the useful information. When the listening audios are played, follow the steps of listening, understanding, repeating (applicable to single sentences, short conversations and data), making notes and guessing (making inferences). The cultivation of this skill requires students to do more exercises to help strengthen their memory and write down the useful information.

寫作訓練：口頭報告 Writing Tasks: Oral Report

熱身

- **根據課文一，討論口頭報告的格式是什麼。**

According to Text 1, discuss the format of an oral report.

格式 **參考課文一**

XXX 口頭報告

尊敬的 XXX：

□□開頭：問候語 + 自我介紹 + 介紹報告

一、調查目的
二、調查方法
三、調查結果
四、調查分析
五、建議

□□結尾：表達感謝

Tips

文體：口頭報告
Text Type: Oral Report

口頭報告是向機構或組織以口頭陳述的形式匯報調查結果、分析、建議等。

Oral reports utilise oral statements to report investigation results, analysis, suggestions, etc. to institutions or organizations.

練習

為了不影響學生的學習，學校規定學生一到學校後，就要把手機交給班主任保管，放學的時候才能拿回去。假如你是學生會會長，你組織學生會對這個規定是否能幫助學生專心學習進行了一次調查。請將這次調查的目的、方式和結果向學校領導匯報，並向校方提出你的建議。選用合適的文本類型完成寫作。字數：300–480 個漢字。

訪談	個人陳述	口頭報告

Tips

怎樣寫好口頭報告？How to write an oral report?

要使口頭報告寫得好聽、耐聽，達到更直接、更方便、更傳神的效果，需要注意一些方式、方法。

To write an oral reports that is more attractive, direct, convenient and vivid, you need to pay attention to certain methods and approaches.

1. 要開門見山、直奔主題，儘量做到直接把事情説清楚，為領導提供有效信息，讓他人在最短的時間內聽明白你所要表達的意思。
   Be straightforward. Go straight to the point and clarify your opinions. Provide effective information for others to let them understand your opinions in the shortest possible time.
2. 先説明你的調查結果，簡要地把結果和最新鮮、最有吸引力、最能反映事情本質的部分講出來。這樣既節省時間，提高效率，又給他人留下判斷、回想的空間。
   Present the results of your investigation and briefly state the results and the newest, most attractive and most reflective part of the matter. This will save time and improve efficiency, and also leaves room for others to judge and reflect.
3. 注意調查的數據要準確、客觀，不可以含糊。應多擺事實，將基本情況説清楚，不可以主觀地發表自己的觀點。
   The survey data should be accurate, objective and clear. More facts should be presented and the basic situation should be clarified. Personal opinions should not be presented in the report.

Lesson 8

The Environment
環境

導入 Introduction

人類生存的空間，以及其中可以直接或間接影響人類生活和發展的各種因素，稱為環境。環境分為自然環境和人文環境。其中，自然環境包括大氣、水、土壤和生物等，是人類賴以生存和發展的物質基礎。隨著經濟的快速發展，人類正面臨全球性的三大危機：資源短缺、環境污染、生態破壞。為了保護環境、促進全球環保意識，各國政府都在採取行動提高民眾對環境問題的關注，比如舉行“世界環境日”等活動，提醒大家注意地球狀況和人類活動對環境的影響，強調保護和改善環境的重要性。

Environment is the space of human being's existence and includes various natural factors that directly or indirectly affect people's life and development. Environment is identified as the natural environment and the humanistic environment. The natural environment includes the atmosphere, water, soil and living beings. The natural environment is the material basis for human survival and development. With the rapid economic development, human beings are facing three major global crises: resource shortage, environmental pollution and ecological destruction. In order to protect the environment and promote global environmental awareness, governments of countries around the world are raising the public's attention to environmental issues. They hold "World Environment Day" and other activities to remind people to pay attention to the status of the earth and the influences of human beings' activities to the environment so as to emphasize the importance of improving the environment.

學習目標 Learning Targets

閱讀 Reading

- 學會在閱讀説明文中準確獲取信息。
  Learn to obain information accurately in reading expository essay.

口語 Speaking

- 學會回答體驗類的問題。
  Learn to answer experiential questions.

聽力 Listening

- 學會邊聽邊做筆記。
  Learn to take notes while listening.

寫作 Writing

- 學會寫小冊子 / 宣傳冊 / 傳單。
  Learn to write a pamphlet / brochure / leaflet.

1 課文 保護地球 從我做起 29

2022年4月22日，是第52個"世界地球日"。碧山社區決定舉辦"世界地球日"宣傳活動，增強居民的環保意識，鼓勵大家多參加環保活動，改善社區的整體環境。

一、活動目的

豐富社區居民的生活，增強環保意識，保護環境，關愛地球。

二、活動對象

碧山社區居民

三、活動詳情

日期：4月22日

地點：碧山社區廣場

四、活動安排

- 8:00–9:30：親子閱讀

家長和小朋友一起閱讀關於環保的繪本，從小培養他們關愛地球、愛護環境的意識。

- 9:30–11:00：變廢為寶

教居民如何重複利用廢舊物品，變廢為寶，並且一起來動手改造。

- 11:00–12:30：製作環保手冊

製作有趣的環保手冊，宣傳環保行動。用自己的行動呼籲身邊的每一個人保護環境。從身邊的小事做起，如節約水電、不亂扔垃圾。

生詞短語

- jǔ bàn 舉辦 hold
- jū mín 居民 resident
- gǎi shàn 改善 improve
- guān ài 關愛 care
- duì xiàng 對象 object / target
- xiáng qíng 詳情 detail
- huì běn 繪本 picture book
- chóng fù 重複 repeat
- lì yòng 利用 make use of
- fèi jiù 廢舊 waste
- wù pǐn 物品 materials
- biàn fèi wéi bǎo 變廢為寶 change waste into treasure
- gǎi zào 改造 reform
- shǒu cè 手冊 handbook
- xíng dòng 行動 action
- hū yù 呼籲 call on
- jié yuē 節約 sove
- lā jī 垃圾 rubbish
- jù lí 距離 distance
- zūn zhòng 尊重 respect

五、注意事項

1. 由於疫情，請大家在活動中保持至少一米的安全距離。

2. 請大家各自準備一個垃圾袋，不亂扔垃圾。

3. 活動結束後，請在微信群分享活動照片。

有興趣參加的居民，請在3月30日之前到社區居委會報名。

人類只有一個地球，尊重地球就是尊重生命。親愛的居民們，讓我們一起積極行動起來，從小養成良好的行為習慣和保護環境的意識，一起建設綠色家園！

碧山社區居委會

2022年3月10日

改編自：https://www.meipian.cn/2w0luii2

Culture Point

勤儉節約 Diligence and Thrift

勤儉節約不僅是一種生活習慣，而且是一個人道德修養的體現。在中國人長久以來的價值觀裏，儉樸不但是一種行為方式，還是一種大的德行，是培養良好道德的基礎。提倡節約，不僅是要倡導一種健康、適度的生活方式，更是要讓人們在節約中展現素養，擁抱更美好的生活。面對資源相對不足而且生態環境脆弱的世界，我們都需要養成勤儉節約的習慣。

然而在現實中，一些人缺乏節約意識，有意無意地浪費糧食；一些人愛面子，不同程度地過度消費，造成浪費，這些都是不文明的行為。我們應該了解“一粒米，千滴汗”的辛勞，進而感恩大自然的饋贈和勞動者的付出；懂得“取之有度，用之有節”的道理，因此盡己所能減少浪費，以節約資源、保護環境。

Diligence and thrift are not only a living style but also a way to reflect a person's moral cultivation. In Chinese values, frugality represents not only a person's behavior but also a great virtue. It is the basis for cultivating good morals. Advocating conservation is not only to promote a healthy and moderate lifestyle but also to encourage people to show their accomplishments in conservation to embrace a better life. We are facing a world with insufficient resources and a fragile ecological environment. Therefore we must develop a diligence and thrift living style.

In reality, some people are lack of the awareness of saving.They waste food intentionally or unintentionally. People also overconsume and cause waste. These are all uncivilized behaviors. We should understand that "there are thousands drops of perspiration behind a grain of rice" and be grateful for the gifts of nature and the efforts of the peasants. We should also understand the principle of "appropriateness and restraint" so that we could try our best to reduce waste,save resources and protect the environment.

語法重點 Key Points of Grammar

讓步關係複句 Concession Complex Sentence

讓步主要指接下來提及的信息是一種期待之外的結果。表示讓步關係的句子，在語言運用中有一個共同點，都帶有連詞“儘管”和“即使”，與它們一起搭配的常有“也、還、總、仍然、但是、卻”等詞。

Concession mainly means that the information mentioned next in the sentence is an unexpected result. Concession complex sentences have one thing in common which is they always carry the conjunctions “儘管” and “即使”. These words are often followed by other words like “也、還、總、仍然、但是、卻”.

E.g.
- 即使下雨也不會太大。
  Even if it rains, it won't be too heavy.
- 這輛車子即使能修好，我也不敢開了。
  Even if the car can be repaired, I dare not drive it.
- 儘管放假出國旅遊，他仍然不停止工作。
  Although he travels abroad on holiday, he never stops working.

課文理解 Reading Comprehensions

① “世界地球日”活動在哪裏舉辦？

② 為什麼要舉辦“世界地球日”宣傳活動？

③ “變廢為寶”是什麼意思？

④ “世界地球日”活動結束後，居民還需要做什麼嗎？

⑤ 如何報名參加“世界地球日”宣傳活動？

概念與拓展理解 Concepts and Further Understanding

① 課文一的寫作對象是誰？
Who is the target audience of Text 1?

② 如果把課文一的對象改成幼兒園的小朋友，宣傳單應該做哪些改變？
If the target audience of Text 1 is changed to kindergarten children, what changes should be made to this leaflet?

③ 除了課文一的宣傳活動外，你認為還可以做哪些活動來鼓勵大家進行環保？
In addition to the publicity activities in Text 1, what other activities do you think can be done to encourage everyone to protect the environment?

④ 在宣傳環保活動這件事情上，語言發揮著什麼作用？
What role does language play in promoting environmental protection activities?

⑤ 不同的語言在宣傳環保活動時，會有不同的效果嗎？
Will the impact be different when promoting environmental protection activities in different languages?

語言練習 Language Exercises

重新排列詞語，組成完整的句子。

Rearrange the words to form a complete sentence.

① 醫院　決定　收入　舉辦　把　他們　音樂會　一次　捐給

② 很重要　終於　回收　是　環保行為　廢舊物品　我　意識到　的

③ 變廢為寶　重複利用　應該呼籲　改造物品　我們　和　大家行動起來　將它們

④ 垃圾分類　社區　為了教　介紹詳情　環保手冊　如何進行　居民　將製作

⑤ 尊重對方　為了　互相關愛　我們　鄰里關係　改善　應該

根據句子的意思，選出合適的詞語，填寫在橫線上。

Choose the correct answer from the following choices.

⑥ 我們應該＿＿＿＿＿＿（節約 / 節省）用水，隨手關閉水龍頭。

⑦ 這個城市＿＿＿＿＿＿（遠離 / 距離）杭州很遠，最好坐飛機去。

⑧ 這本＿＿＿＿＿＿（繪畫 / 繪本）比小説更好看，故事內容更簡單，小孩子容易看懂。

⑨ 這次競爭＿＿＿＿＿＿（對象 / 對手）很厲害，我們還是要多加努力。

填入正確的關聯詞。

Fill in the blanks with appropriate correlative conjunctions.

⑩ 即使孩子做錯什麼事，做父母的＿＿＿＿＿＿會原諒他們。

⑪ 儘管他的口試考得很好，他的 IB 總分＿＿＿＿＿＿是不能拿到 7 分。

⑫ 即使明天天氣好，我們＿＿＿＿＿＿不會出去玩兒。

⑬ 儘管他考試作弊被抓住，他＿＿＿＿＿＿不承認。

課堂活動 Class Activities

接力賽 Board Games

將學生分成兩組，每個小組給一支彩色的馬克筆。如果班級人數多，可以分成 3-4 組。在白板中間劃一條線，將白板分成兩塊，每一塊區域上方寫上“環境”兩個字。學生排隊按順序到本組的白板區域寫上與“環境”相關的詞語，一人寫一個詞語。每對一個詞語得一分，書寫錯誤或者與主題無關的詞語將不得分。

Divide the students into two teams and give each team a colored marker. Divide the students into 3 or 4 teams if the class size is big. Draw a line down the middle of the board and write a topic "environment" at the top of each area. Each student from both teams writes one word related to the topic in the two areas of white board. Each team wins one point for each correct word. Any words that are unreadable or misspelled are not counted.

口語訓練 Speaking Tasks

第一部分 **根據主題"環境"，做 2-3 分鐘的口頭表達。做口頭表達之前，先根據提示寫大綱。**

Make a 2-3 minutes oral presentation on the theme "environment". Before you start, use the form below to make an outline.

大綱 Outline	內容 Content
觀點 Perspectives	
事例 Examples	
名人名言 Famous quotes / 熟語 Idioms	
經歷 Experiences	
總結 Summary	

第二部分 **回答下面的問題。Answer the following questions.**

① 你喜歡大自然嗎？為什麼？

② 你的國家有環境問題嗎？

③ 你和家人為保護環境做過哪些努力？談談你的體驗和感受。

④ 你的學校如何鼓勵大家環保？談談你的體驗和感受。

⑤ 你的社區如何鼓勵居民環保？談談你的體驗和感受。

Tips

如何回答體驗類的問題？How to answer experiential questions?

考生在回答老師提出的關於體驗類的問題之前，應該先在心裏組織一下要說的內容，使表達條理分明，結構完整。分享體驗類的問題可以先回應老師的問題，說明時間、地點、人物和事件，最後再總結自己的感受和看法。

Before you answer the teacher's questions about your personal experience, you should organize what you want to say in your mind clearly and sort the information in good structure. For questions about sharing experiences, you can respond to the teacher's questions by addressing the time, place, people and events first. Thereafter summarize your reflections and opinions.

例如問題 4：你的學校如何鼓勵大家環保？談談你的體驗和感受。

① 回應問題	我們學校會組織很多活動鼓勵學生環保。
② 內容： ● 時間 ● 地點 ● 人物 ● 事件	一、在班裏 1. 在班會上，老師讓我們分組做關於"如何做環保活動"的 PPT 簡報。 2. 成立環保小組，保持教室清潔，防止亂扔垃圾。 3. 在班級進行垃圾分類。 4. 邀請專家做"如何環保"的講座，和同學們一起討論如何保持環境清潔、廢物利用等。 二、在校園裏 1. 在校園裏舉辦"廢物再利用"活動，將可回收物品放進環保回收箱裏再循環利用。 2. 在校園舉辦"廢物再利用"宣傳活動。在校園張貼宣傳環保的海報。 3. 舉辦有關環保的演講比賽或"廢物再利用"設計比賽。
③ 總結： ● 感受 ● 看法	我特別喜歡學校舉辦的"廢物再利用"設計比賽。不但能環保，而且能發揮我們的想象力。我曾經收集了很多小玻璃瓶子，粘貼起來，做成了一個漂亮的台燈，還獲得了一等獎。那是一次非常難忘的體驗，讓我很自豪。勤儉節約是中華民族的傳統美德，我們應該多鼓勵大家參與環保活動。

生詞短語

yí cì xìng
一次性 disposable

bào dào
報道 report

hǎi yáng shēng wù
海洋生物 marine life

fēn jiě
分解 resolve

xiāo huà
消化 digest

tòng kǔ
痛苦 painful

shēng tài huán jìng
生態環境 ecosystem

pò huài
破壞 damage

duì fu
對付 cope

gōng jù
工具 tool

suí biàn
隨便 randomly

diū qì
丟棄 throw away

zǔ wū
組屋 HDB flat

gōng dé xīn
公德心 civism

kōng huà
空話 overtalk

2 課文 一次性口罩對生態環境的影響 30

包小亮

今天我在網上看到一篇關於一次性口罩對生態環境影響的報道。報道講述了在新加坡海邊的樹林裏，隨處可見丟在地上的一次性口罩；還有很多口罩被直接扔進海裏，對海洋生物造成了很大的威脅；有些海洋生物誤將口罩當作食物吞下，導致肚子裏都是垃圾。口罩被分解大約需要五百年的時間，大量的海洋生物因為無法消化這些口罩而痛苦地死去。另外，口罩流入海洋會對海水造成污染，導致海洋生態環境被破壞。人類吃了海洋生物後，身體健康也會受到影響。更可怕的是，海水蒸發後會以雨水的形式落到地面，對土壤環境也造成嚴重污染。

口罩本是人類對付病毒的工具。但如果隨便丟棄，受傷害的卻是自然界的動物們。在新加坡的武吉知馬山上，由於疫情，遊客減少，猴子吃的食物也減少了。當它們看見藍色的口罩就會撿起來吃，但這樣可能會要了它們的命。

“天哪！我真的沒有想到在新加坡也會有人亂扔口罩。所以當我看到這篇報道時覺得很驚訝！”一位居民說，“自從新冠疫情在新加坡發生後，有些口罩就被人隨手扔在組屋樓下，或者掛在樹上。”許多居民認為這種行為是沒有公德心的表現。因為隨意丟棄用過的口罩，可能還會造成病毒的傳播！

除了新加坡，世界上其他許多地方也出現了口罩廢棄的現象。我認為這些口罩已經給全球帶來了重大污染！大量使用過的口罩被隨便扔掉，對人類和動植物都造成了嚴重的影響！保護環境不是一句空話，我們需要從自身做起，從身邊的小事做起，不要隨意亂扔口罩，應該為保護生態環境做出自己的努力。

改編自：https://mp.weixin.qq.com/s/86JvN4OSFFzP1F7QEt6MGQ

Culture Point

公德心，是一個民族在社會實踐活動中積澱下來的公共道德準則、文化觀念和思想傳統。在社會生活中，個人的生存發展離不開社會和與他人的交往，因此要求人們要有社會公德心。比如，坐公車要學會讓座，不要亂扔垃圾，不插隊，不大聲説話影響別人的生活，外出旅遊不亂塗亂畫，等等。只有這樣，我們的生活才會更美好。

Civism is the public moral code, cultural concept and ideological tradition that a nation has accumulated in its social practices. In social life, the survival and development of an individual is inseparable from the social interaction with others. People are required to abide by the civism. For example, you must learn to give up your seat to those people in need when taking a public transport, not to throw rubbish, not to jump the queue, not to speak loudly to affect other people's lives and not to scribble when you travel. This is the way to make our lives better.

語法重點 Key Points of Grammar

感歎句 Exclamatory Sentences

漢語中的感歎句，是帶有濃厚感情的句子。它表示快樂、驚訝、悲哀、厭惡、恐懼等情感，句末都用歎號“！”表示。感歎句一般由歎詞構成。有的歎詞所代表的感情，我們一聽就知道，如“哦”表示醒悟，“呸”表示鄙視、厭惡；但有的歎詞要結合前後的語境才能確切知道。還有些感歎句不包含歎詞。

Exclamatory sentences are sentences with strong emotions. They express strong feelings such as happiness, surprise, sorrow, disgust, fear etc. An exclamation mark "!" is used at the end of the sentence. Exclamatory sentences generally consist of interjections. Some interjections show the feelings they represent. For example, "Oh" means awakening and "Bah" means contempt and disgust. But some interjections can only be known by looking at the context. And some exclamatory sentences don't have interjections.

E.g.
- 今天天氣真好呀！ How nice the weather is today!
- 那該有多好啊！ That would be great!
- 你今天太漂亮啦！ How beautiful you are today!

課文理解 Reading Comprehensions

① 口罩大約需要多久才能被分解？

② 海洋生物為什麼會因為廢棄口罩而死亡？

③ 廢棄口罩除了破壞海洋生態環境以外，還有哪些害處？

④ 為什麼説亂丟口罩沒有公德心？

⑤ “保護環境不是一句空話”是什麼意思？

概念與拓展理解 Concepts and Further Understanding

① 課文二是什麼文體？What is the text type of Text 2?

② 課文二的寫作目的是什麼？What is the writing purpose of Text 2?

③ 如果把課文二改成新聞報道，語言和語氣應該做什麼改變？
If Text 2 is rewritten to a news report, what changes should be made to the language and tone?

④ 課文二為什麼用“我”來講述，而不是“你”或者“他”？
Why does Text 2 use "I" to state instead of "you" or "he"?

⑤ 課文二中哪些句子是感歎句？感歎句在文章中起到什麼作用？
Which sentences in Text 2 are exclamatory sentences? What role do exclamatory sentences play in the article?

語言練習 Language Exercises

將上下框的字組成詞語，填寫在橫線上。

Combine the characters in the upper and write the words on the line.

報 分 對 苦 環 破 工 隨 丟 組 空

話 棄 壞 痛 便 解 屋 具 境 道 付

① ______

從左邊的方框裏選出適當的字，填寫在橫線上。

Select the appropriate character from the box on the left and fill in the blank on the right.

② 哨 | 消　口______ / ______化　③ 破 | 坡　山______ / ______壞

④ 咐 | 付　吩______ / ______出　⑤ 組 | 且　而______ / ______織

⑥ 控 | 空　管______ / ______話

重新排列詞語，組成完整的句子。

Rearrange the words to form a complete sentence.

⑦ 垃圾　組屋區　隨便　居民　丟棄　社區　不要　要求　在

____

⑧ 公德　都要　遵守　社會　每個居民

____

⑨ 對　分解　塑料垃圾　容易　很難被　生態環境　造成破壞

____

⑩ 很痛苦　吞下　據報道　要是　一次性口罩　海洋生物　會活得

____

從生詞表裏找出與下列詞語意思相同或相近的詞。

Find words with the same or similar meanings as the following words in the vocabulary list.

⑪ 發表____________ ⑫ 應對____________ ⑬ 器材____________ ⑭ 謊言____________

從生詞表裏找出與下列詞語意思相反的詞。

Find words with the opposite meanings to the following words in the vocabulary list.

⑮ 快樂____________ ⑯ 愛護____________ ⑰ 認真____________ ⑱ 保存____________

課堂活動 Class Activities

找真相 Call My Bluff

學生有 5 分鐘準備時間，寫出三個關於環保的句子，其中兩個是錯的，只有一個句子是對的。學生可以上網查找內容。讓一位學生把他寫的句子都說出來，其他學生可以對他所說的句子進行提問，然後判斷哪個句子是對的。

第二輪可以讓學生兩人一組，其中一個學生寫兩個正確的句子，再寫一個錯誤的句子，另一個學生判斷哪個句子是錯的。然後兩個學生角色互換。

Give students 5 minutes to prepare 3 statements about environmental protection, two of which should be fault and one should be true. Ask one student to speak out three statements. Allow other students to ask questions about each statement and then judge which statement is true.

Ask students to play games in pairs in the second round. One student writes two true statements and one fault statement and the other student judge which statement is fault. Then the two students rotate roles.

口語訓練 Speaking Tasks

第一部分 **根據圖片，做 3-4 分鐘的口頭表達。做口頭表達之前，先根據提示寫大綱。**

Make a 3-4 minutes oral presentation based on the picture. Before you start, use the form below to make an outline.

大綱 Outline	內容 Content
圖片內容 Information of the picture	
圖片主題 + 文化 Theme of the picture and culture	
提出觀點 Make your points	
延伸個人經歷 Relate to personal experiences	
名人名言 Famous quotes / 熟語 Idioms	
總結 Summary	

第二部分 **回答下面的問題。Answer the following questions.**

① 為什麼垃圾分類很重要？

② 你認為人類應該採取哪些行動來保護環境？

③ 你認為地球遇到的最大的環境問題是什麼？

④ 你的學校如何鼓勵學生進行環保？

⑤ 日常生活中，你採取了哪些措施來保護環境？

技能訓練 Skill Tasks

閱讀訓練 Reading Tasks

文章 1　地球遭到破壞的四大現象

仔細閱讀下面的短文，然後回答問題。

Read the passage carefully and answer the following questions.

A. 空氣污染

在一定範圍的空氣中，出現了原來沒有的物質，並可能對人或生物造成危害的現象就屬於空氣污染。造成空氣污染的主要原因是工業氣體、垃圾燃燒、汽車尾氣等。隨著人類活動和生產的迅速發展，人們將大量的有害氣體排入空氣中，嚴重影響了空氣質量。空氣污染對氣候的影響很大，比如，可能引發"溫室效應"，使地球氣溫上升。另外，空氣被污染後，也會對人體呼吸系統造成危害。

B. 水污染

人類在社會活動過程中將大量的工業、農業和生活垃圾排入水中，使水受到污染，導致水質變差，進而危害人體健康，破壞生態環境的現象被稱為水污染。人們將污水、垃圾、汽油和化學物品倒進大海，有害物質便進入海洋生物環境中。另外，人口增長以及洗潔精等的使用也會使人類的生活用水受到污染。生態環境變得惡劣，魚類因此大量死亡，吃魚的鳥兒也會受此影響，最終，人類自身的健康也會受到危害。

C. 垃圾大量堆放

現代社會中，人類活動的每一環節都會產生各種垃圾。垃圾正成為困擾人類社會的一個大問題。全世界每年產生超過10億噸的垃圾，大量的生活和工業垃圾因無人處理而大量堆放。垃圾堆放在一起不但很臭，而且會產生大量的病毒。這些有毒物質會污染地下水，嚴重危害人類的健康。同時垃圾還會滋生出很多蚊子和蒼蠅，如果不及時處理，人類將面臨更多的疾病。

D. 生物多樣性減少

生物是多種多樣的，在不同環境中會產生不同的生物。隨著工業文明的發展，人類社會逐步擴張，改變了廣大地區的生物環境，嚴重影響了生物的生存。許多生物正在迅速地從地球上消失。據估計，全世界每年有上千種生物滅絕。對全球植物和動物的威脅主要是生態環境的破壞。而大部分生物無法離開它早已適應的環境。比如，世界生物種類最豐富的地方是熱帶雨林，但是現在人類正在加速破壞它。根據世界自然保護基金會估計，全球的森林正以每年2%的速度消失，按照這個速度，50年後人們將看不到天然森林了。

總的來說，地球遭到破壞是人類活動的結果。

Tips

從說明文中準確獲取信息

Obtain information accurately from expository essay

說明文是以"說明"為主要表達方式，用來介紹事物的一種實用文體。說明文主要考查考生從文中準確獲取信息的能力。閱讀技巧上，要先讀原文，了解大概意思，再讀題做標記，在原文中找出要考查的範圍，最後比較考題的選項有什麼不同。讀題很重要，要給重要詞語做上標記，並找出答題範圍。

Expository essays is a text type introduces things mainly by using the writing approach of "explanation". An expository essay normally examines candidates' ability to accurately obtain information from the text. Students should read the original text and understand the general meaning first, then read the questions and mark the answer in the text to understand the content to be tested. Finally, compare the options of the questions to find out the testing point of each question. Reading the questions is very important and the key words should be highlighted.

例如第一題：先讀題，就可以在"燒東西"上做好標記。找出考查的範圍，是和氣體有關係。再比較其他選項"B. 水污染 C. 垃圾無人處理 D. 生物多樣性減少"都和"燒東西"沒有關係，所以確定答案是"A. 空氣污染"。

Take the first question as an example. You should read the question first and then highlight the key word "燒東西". Make it clear that the testing point of the questions will be related to air pollution. Comparing with 3 other options: B-water pollution, C-garbage, D-organisms, which are irrelevent to "燒東西". So the answer is A.

根據以上短文，選擇正確的答案，在方格裏打勾（✓）。

According to the passage above, tick (✓) in the correct boxes.

① 哪種現象和燒東西有關係？

A. ☐ B. ☐ C. ☐ D. ☐

② 哪種現象是因為生態環境被破壞造成的？

A. ☐ B. ☐ C. ☐ D. ☐

③ 哪種現象和垃圾無人處理有關係？

A. ☐ B. ☐ C. ☐ D. ☐

④ 哪種現象會導致地球溫度上升？

A. ☐ B. ☐ C. ☐ D. ☐

⑤ 哪種現象是因為人口增長導致的？

A. ☐ B. ☐ C. ☐ D. ☐

⑥ 哪種現象會產生病毒？

A. ☐ B. ☐ C. ☐ D. ☐

⑦ 哪種現象是由於人類逐步擴張造成的？

A. ☐ B. ☐ C. ☐ D. ☐

⑧ 哪種現象會導致更多疾病的產生？

A. ☐ B. ☐ C. ☐ D. ☐

⑨ 哪種現象會影響鳥類捕食？

A. ☐ B. ☐ C. ☐ D. ☐

⑩ 哪種現象會對人類呼吸造成危害？

A. ☐ B. ☐ C. ☐ D. ☐

文章 2　全球變暖的十大危害

環保論壇

全球變暖的十大危害

2022 年 10 月 10 日　　10:10

在近 100 年裏，全球平均氣溫大約【–1–】了 0.8 度。氣候變化會造成很多影響，我查看了一些關於全球變暖的資料，總結出以下幾個方面。

一、海平面上升。氣溫過高造成冰山融化，【–2–】海平面上升。目前世界上有很多像新加坡、印尼這樣的國家都面臨著海平面上升帶來的威脅。

二、冰川融化。冰川是河水的主要來源。河水為人類【–3–】飲用水，可是過多的冰川融水會引發河水氾濫。

三、高溫。2003 年，歐洲的高溫【–4–】了約 3.5 萬人。高溫會導致火災發生的機率增加，還會引發相關疾病。

四、暴風雨。在短短 30 年裏，四級到五級強烈暴風雨出現的次數【–5–】以前增加了一倍。

五、乾旱。因為乾旱，所以沒有足夠的水來種田，進而導致全球的糧食生產減少，人們受飢餓威脅的【–6–】越來越大。

六、疾病。高溫天氣給病毒創造了很好的生長環境。蚊子、蒼蠅、老鼠等帶著疾病亂飛亂跑，會導致病毒【–7–】得更快。

七、經濟問題。嚴重的風暴和洪水造成的經濟【–8–】多達數十億美元。食品價格不斷上升，人們卻沒有錢購買。

八、衝突和戰爭。糧食、水和土地的減少，會引起衝突和戰爭，從而威脅全球各地方的【–9–】。

九、生物多樣性減少。全球氣溫的上升導致沙漠化、森林消失、海水變暖，很多生物因為無法【–10–】氣候變化而死亡。

十、破壞生態系統。氣候變化污染了水和空氣的清潔，也影響了糧食和藥品的生產。這意味著世界上任何變化都與土地、水和生物生態的變化密切【–11–】。

我認為我們關注這些變化對地球造成的影響，不是為了預言未來，而是為了幫助人類減少可能引起氣候變化的行為。大家認為全球暖化的危害還有哪些呢？請給我留言。

閱讀（36）　評論（12）　轉載（9）　收藏（20）

改編自：https://tech.huanqiu.com/article/9CaKrnJxO8o

根據文章 2，從下面提供的詞彙中，選出合適的詞填空。

According to passage 2, choose the suitable words in the box to fill in the blanks.

比　適應　相關　上升　傳播　導致　安全　提供　害死　可能性　損失

① [–1–]__________ ② [–2–]__________ ③ [–3–]__________ ④ [–4–]__________

⑤ [–5–]__________ ⑥ [–6–]__________ ⑦ [–7–]__________ ⑧ [–8–]__________

⑨ [–9–]__________ ⑩ [–10–]__________ ⑪ [–11–]__________

根據文章 2，選出最適合左邊句子的結尾。把答案寫在橫線上。

According to passage 2, choose the suitable endings of the sentence on the left side. Write the answers on the lines.

⑫ 海平面上升 ______　A. 是乾旱造成的。

⑬ 糧食生產減少 ______　B. 是因為海水變暖、森林消失。

⑭ 衝突和戰爭 ______　C. 是因為人類沒有錢。

⑮ 生物多樣性減少 ______　D. 是冰山融化的結果。

E. 是因為糧食、水和土地減少。

F. 是因為蚊子、蒼蠅亂飛。

G. 是因為火災發生太多。

聽力訓練 Listening Tasks

一、《後天》

你將聽到一篇影片《後天》的觀後感。你將聽到兩遍，請根據聽到的信息改正每句話裏劃線的詞語。

You will hear a recording of a movie review *The Day After Tomorrow*. The audio will be played twice. Please correct the underlined words in each sentence based on the information you heard.

請先閱讀一下問題。Please read the questions first.

① 《後天》是一部關於地球遭受海水襲擊的影片。
《後天》是一部關於地球遭受＿＿＿＿＿＿＿＿＿＿襲擊的影片。

② 冰川融化導致海平面快速上升，海水向海中央流去。
冰川融化導致海平面快速上升，海水向＿＿＿＿＿＿＿＿＿＿流去。

③ 不論是建築物還是生命都在十秒之內消失了。
不論是建築物還是生命都在＿＿＿＿＿＿＿＿＿＿消失了。

④ 人們不得不躲到房間裏想辦法對付寒冷的天氣。
人們不得不躲到＿＿＿＿＿＿＿＿＿＿想辦法對付寒冷的天氣。

⑤ 這些行為都讓動植物失去了賴以生存的森林。
這些行為都讓動植物失去了賴以生存的＿＿＿＿＿＿＿＿＿＿。

⑥ 海平面上升就是大自然對我們人類做出的懲罰。
＿＿＿＿＿＿＿＿＿＿就是大自然對我們人類做出的懲罰。

⑦ 見識到大自然一旦報復起來，人類是多麼的傷心。
見識到大自然一旦報復起來，人類是多麼的＿＿＿＿＿＿＿＿＿＿。

⑧ 動物們卻能開始驚恐萬分地在街道上走動。
動物們卻能開始＿＿＿＿＿＿＿＿＿＿地在街道上走動。

二、《光污染》

你即將聽到第二個聽力片段，在聽力片段二播放之前，你將有四分鐘的時間先閱讀題目。聽力片段將播放兩次，聽力片段結束後你將有兩分鐘的時間來檢查你的答案。請用中文回答問題。

You are going to hear the second audio clip. You have 4 minutes to read the questions before it starts. The audio clip will be played twice. After it ends, you have 2 minutes to check the answers. Please answer the questions in Chinese.

填空。Fill in the blanks.

<table>
<tr><td>節目名稱</td><td>【-1-】</td><td>醫生</td><td>吳華麗</td></tr>
<tr><td>醫生來自</td><td>【-2-】</td><td>討論問題</td><td>光污染</td></tr>
<tr><td>發明電燈的年份</td><td>【-3-】</td><td>全球生活在光污染中的人數比例</td><td>【-4-】</td></tr>
<tr><td colspan="4">過度的燈光對人體帶來的危害：
• 光污染是造成孩子【-5-】高發的重要因素。 • 燈光會使人【-6-】而無法睡覺。
避免光污染的方法有：
• 在書房、客廳、廚房採用冷色燈光，如【-7-】。
• 在臥室、衛生間、陽台等採用暖色燈光，如【-8-】。
• 可以買一些【-9-】來調節室內光環境。</td></tr>
</table>

① [-1-] ________________ ② [-2-] ________________ ③ [-3-] ________________

④ [-4-] ________________ ⑤ [-5-] ________________ ⑥ [-6-] ________________

⑦ [-7-] ________________ ⑧ [-8-] ________________ ⑨ [-9-] ________________

Tips

學會做筆記 Learn to Take Notes

做筆記能幫助我們理解聽力材料，提高區分有用信息和無用信息的能力。更重要的一點還在於它能幫我們減輕大腦的負擔，完整而準確地把握所聽材料的主要內容。記筆記的方式可因人而異。你可以在選項旁邊儘可能記下文中所提及的人名、地名、各種數據、事實和理由等重要的信息。好的筆記應是對所聽內容作出的簡要提綱，可以用關鍵詞，也可以用短語或句子來表示，關鍵是要簡潔、明白。例如：在看表格中的空格時，如果能邊聽邊對空格加以記錄，便可以寫出正確答案。

Taking notes can help us understand the listening text and improve the skill of distinguishing between useful and useless information. It helps us reduce the burden on our brains and accurately catch the main content of the text. The way of taking notes can vary from person to person. You can write down the information that is important as much as possible, such as the names of people, place names, various data, facts, reasons, etc. The good notes should be a brief outline of what you are listening to, which can be keywords, phrases or sentences. The key is to be brief and clear. For example: for the question of filling blanks in the table, you could write the correct answer if you record the blanks while listening.

比如，你可以從空格中預測本篇的九個空格屬於客觀性（或細節性）問題，即：

For example, you can predict from the blanks that the nine blanks in this article are objectivity (or detail) issues, namely:

① 什麼 What...? ② 來自 Where...?

③ 時間 When...? ④ 數字比例 What is the number...?

⑤ 燈光危害 Light Damage... ? ⑥ 方法 Methods... ?

寫作訓練：小冊子 / 宣傳冊 / 傳單 Writing Tasks: Pamphlet/Brochure/Leaflet

熱身

- **根據課文一，討論小冊子 / 宣傳冊 / 傳單的格式是什麼。**

According to Text 1, discuss the format of a pamphlet/brochure/leaflet.

- **寫出小冊子 / 宣傳冊 / 傳單與指南的相同點和不同點。**

Compare the similarities and differences between a pamphlet/brochure/leaflet and a guide.

文體	小冊子 / 宣傳冊 / 傳單	指南
相同點		
不同點		

Tips

文體：小冊子／宣傳冊／傳單

Text Type: Pamplet / Brochure / Leaflet

小冊子／宣傳冊／傳單是主辦者告知公眾舉行活動的一種文體。

Pamphlets / brochures / leaflets are a style of writing used by organizers to inform the public about an event's details.

格式 參考課文一

標題

□□開頭：活動簡介

一、活動目的

二、活動對象

三、活動詳情

四、活動安排

五、注意事項

□□結尾：報名方式 + 呼籲報名

XX

X 年 X 月 X 日

練習

學校學生會決定在世界環境日當天舉辦宣傳活動，呼籲同學們為環保活動盡一份力。請介紹這次環保活動的詳細安排，並號召大家積極參與。選用合適的文本類型完成寫作。字數：300–480 個漢字。

訪談	小冊子	口頭報告

Lesson

9

Recycling Resource and Renewable Energy

回收資源與可再生能源

導入 Introduction

自然界存在的一切物質中，能被人類加以利用並為人類帶來好處的，就稱為資源。資源不都是一次性的，有些資源是可以被重複利用的。人類在生產和消費過程中會將產生的廢物作為資源加以回收利用。回收資源可以大量節約自然資源並降低生產成本，還可以減少環境污染。同時，許多資源不可再生，所以資源回收利用具有不可估量的價值。生活中，常見的可回收資源有廢金屬、塑料、紙張等。而可再生能源是指風能、太陽能、水能、地熱能等清潔能源。可再生能源是綠色低碳能源，對於改善能源結構、保護生態環境、應對氣候變化、實現經濟社會可持續發展具有重要意義。

All the substances in nature are called resources when they are used by human beings and bring benefits to us. Some resources are not disposable and can be reused. Human beings also recycle the waste generated in the process of production and consumption as resources. Recycling resources can help us to save natural resources and reduce the production costs as well as environmental pollution. Meanwhile, some resources are non-renewable and it makes recycling of renewable resources an immeasurable value. Some common recycling examples in our daily life are recycling of metal, plastic, paper, etc. Renewable energy refers to energy such as wind energy, solar energy, hydropower, geothermal energy, etc. These energy resources are green and low-carbon and have great significance for improving the energy structure, protecting the ecological environment, coping with climate change, achieving sustainable economic and social development.

學習目標 Learning Targets

閱讀 Reading

學會找近義詞。
Learn to find synonyms.

口語 Speaking

學會回答觀點類的問題。
Learn to answer questions about opinions.

聽力 Listening

培養即時複述的習慣。
Develop the habit of retelling immediately.

寫作 Writing

學會寫提案。
Learn to write a proposal.

生詞短語

chuàng jiàn
創 建 found

huí shōu
回 收 recycle

tí àn
提 案 proposal

dǎ bāo
打 包 wrap up

cān jù
餐 具 dinner set

sù liào
塑 料 plastic

zhǐ zhāng
紙 張 paper

fèi yong
費 用 cost

xiāo hào
消 耗 consume

zǔ zhǐ
阻 止 prevent

bān huì
班 會 class meeting

ài hù
愛 護 care

jiǎng zuò
講 座 lecture

zhāng tiē
張 貼 paste

kōng tiáo
空 調 aircon

hé xié
和 諧 harmonious

1 課文 創建綠色校園 33

尊敬的校長：

您好！我是高一（5）班的一名IB學生。此次寫信的目的是向您提出“創建綠色校園”的建議，請求您多關注校園資源回收問題，為環保盡一份力。希望我的提案能引起您的重視。

最近，受疫情影響，學校不允許學生中午外出吃飯，於是很多學生選擇打包。但有些人處理不當，造成很多一次性餐具、塑料瓶、紙張等被隨意扔在校園的各個角落。對此，我感到很傷心，因為這嚴重影響了學生的學習和生活環境。

我認為以上問題如果不儘快解決的話，將給我們的校園乃至生態環境造成污染。很多學生不知道他們每天扔掉的垃圾是需要送到垃圾場處理的，而處理垃圾的費用非常高。可是人們還是在大量消耗資源，同時也在大量製造垃圾。我認為作為學生，我們應該站起來阻止這種破壞環境的行為，呼籲大家一起努力，為回收資源、保護環境做出自己的努力。

基於以上原因，我建議學校應該“創建綠色校園”，鼓勵大家進行垃圾分類。建議如下：

一、舉行主題班會，讓學生懂得愛護環境的重要性。引導學生關心人類生存環境的變化，養成良好的衛生習慣。

二、鼓勵學生每人自備一個垃圾袋，養成不隨手扔垃圾的習慣。在校園各處設置兩個垃圾桶，教會學生如何進行垃圾分類，懂得回收資源的重要性。

三、邀請專家到學校開辦講座，並開展環保活動，建立綠色班級。

四、在校園內張貼海報，呼籲大家減少使用一次性用品，儘量減少產生垃圾，節約資源。

五、要求班級只在中午天氣熱的時候使用空調，節約用電。

聽說您一向認同中華文化中“天人合一”的理念，注重人與自然的和諧。希望您也能關注一下校園資源回收問題。為了保證學生擁有良好的學習環境，請接受我的提案！

此致

敬禮！

學生

羅小平敬上

2021 年 10 月 9 日

改編自：https://wenku.baidu.com/view/25728f341b2e453610661ed9ad51f01dc281573a.html

Culture Point

天人合一 Harmony of Man and Nature

“天人合一”是中國人最基本的哲學思想之一，具體表現在人與自然的關係上，是中國文化的核心和基本精神所在。“天人合一”主要是指人與自然，天道與人道，自然與人文的融合貫通，集中體現了中國人對宇宙真理和人生真諦的信仰。

Harmony of Man and Nature is one of the most basic Chinese philosophical ideas. It is embodied in the relationship between nature and man. Harmony of Man and Nature is the core and basic spirit of Chinese culture. It mainly refers to the integration of mankind and nature, heaven and humanity,and, nature and humanity. It embodies the Chinese people's belief in the truth of the universe and the truth of life.

語法重點 Key Points of Grammar

祈使句 Imperative Sentences

祈使句一般用於請求、要求、建議、勸告別人做或不做某件事。句末一般用感歎號。結尾通常是“吧”“嗎”等。祈使句通常沒有主語，而直接用動詞作為開頭。

Imperative sentences are usually used to ask for advice, to advise someone to do or not to do something. An exclamation mark is usually used at the end of a sentence. The ending is usually “ 吧 ”, “ 嗎 ” and so on. Imperative sentences usually have no subject but directly begin with a verb.

表示命令的句式 Imperative sentences: Command

E.g. ● 保持安靜！不要講話！ Keep quiet! Don't talk!

表示請求的句式 Imperative sentences: Request

E.g. ● 請等我一下。Please wait for me.

表示禁止的句式 Imperative sentences: Forbidden

E.g. ● 此處不准停車！此處禁止吸煙！ No parking here! No smoking here!

課文理解 Reading Comprehensions

① 學生為什麼不能出校園吃飯？

② 羅小平為什麼感到傷心？

③ 問題如果不解決的話，會有什麼後果？

④ 為什麼要在校園內張貼廣告？

⑤ 為什麼要到中午天氣熱時班級才能開空調？

概念與拓展理解 Concepts and Further Understanding

① 課文一的寫作目的是什麼？
What is the writing purpose of Text 1?

② "空調" 這個詞語一般在哪個地方使用？中國內地、中國香港、中國台灣還是新加坡？
In which part of the world is the term " 空調 " used? China's Mainland, Hong Kong, Taiwan or Singapore?

③ 你認為校長會接受羅小平關於 "創建綠色校園" 的提案嗎？為什麼？
Do you think the principal will accept Luo Xiaoping's proposal on "creating a green campus"? Why?

④ 課文一的提案所使用的語言有什麼特點？
What are the language features used in the proposal of Text 1?

⑤ 如果羅小平用英文寫這個提案，你覺得在文體、語言、語氣等方面會有什麼不同？
If Luo Xiaoping wrote this proposal in English, do you think there will be any difference in text type, language, tone, etc?

語言練習 Language Exercises

重新排列詞語，組成完整的句子。Rearrange the words to form a complete sentence.

① 買外賣　打包　儘量　或者　塑料盒　一次性餐具　不要用

② 講座海報　在校園裏　關於如何　的　回收資源　張貼　學生會　了

③ 比如　一切過度　行為　我們　消耗資源　一直開空調　的　應該阻止

④ 如何　的　紙張　關於　在班會上　讓我們　設計一個　老師　減少浪費　提案

---

⑤ 幫忙　回收　來　生活費用　廢舊物品　我們可以　創建網站　越來越高

選擇合適的詞語，填寫在橫線上。

Fill in the blanks with the appropriate words.

⑥ ____________（創建 / 創造）一個新學校需要很多費用。

⑦ ____________（回答 / 回收）廢舊物品，可以節約很多資源。

⑧ 我每天訓練四個小時，____________（消費 / 消耗）了很多精力。

⑨ 要____________（阻止 / 阻擋）戰爭的爆發，就要先解決糧食危機問題。

⑩ 不可以隨意在街道____________（補貼 / 張貼）廣告。

課堂活動 Class Activities

畫一畫 Draw a Leaflet

全班分成幾個小組，每組根據課文一製作一份海報或一個公益廣告，呼籲大家減少使用一次性用品，儘量減少產生垃圾，節約資源。

Divide the class into several groups. Each group makes a poster or a public service advertisement according to Text 1, to call on everyone to reduce the use of disposable products, minimize the generation of garbage, and save resources.

口語訓練 Speaking Tasks

第一部分 **根據主題“回收資源”，做 2-3 分鐘的口頭表達。做口頭表達之前，先根據提示寫大綱。Make a 2-3 minutes oral presentation on the theme “recycling resource”. Before you start, use the form below to make an outline.**

大綱 Outline	內容 Content
觀點 Perspectives	
事例 Examples	

大綱 Outline	內容 Content
名人名言 Famous quotes / 熟語 Idioms	
經歷 Experiences	
總結 Summary	

第二部分 **回答下面的問題 • Answer the following questions.**

① 你有資源回收的經歷嗎？

② 你對資源回收在生活中並沒有被廣泛實行有什麼看法？

③ 有些人不喜歡回收資源，覺得很麻煩，你會怎麼勸導？

④ 你的學校是如何鼓勵大家進行資源回收的？談談你的體驗和感受。

⑤ 你所在的社區是如何鼓勵居民進行資源回收的？談談你的體驗和感受。

Tips

如何回答觀點類的問題？ How to answer questions about opinions?

考生在回答老師提出的關於觀點類的問題前，應該先在心裏組織一下要説的內容，使表達條理分明，結構完整。回答時可以先回應老師的問題，説明觀點，給出例子，進行解釋，最後再總結自己的感受和看法。

Before you answer the teacher's questions about your points of view, you should organize what they want to say in their minds, so that the expression will be clear and structured. For questions about sharing opinions, you can respond to the teacher's questions by explaining your opinions, giving examples, then summarize your feelings and opinions.

例如問題 2：你對資源回收在生活中並沒有被廣泛實行有什麼看法？

① 回應問題	我覺得在現實生活中，資源回收沒有被廣泛實行是很可惜的。
② 説明觀點，給出例子，進行解釋	首先，資源回收可以對紙張、玻璃、廢金屬、塑料等資源進行回收利用，這不但有利於處理有毒有害物質（如廢電池等），還有利於充分利用資源（如有機垃圾可製成肥料），而且能避免對環境造成污染。如果不對資源再回收利用，會產生很多危害，最重要的是我們生活環境的質量會降低。我們不僅浪費了大量資源，也間接危害了身體健康，還佔用了大量的土地空間堆放廢品。
③ 總結： • 感受 • 看法	另外，資源回收沒有被廣泛實行，也可能是因為我們沒有積極向民眾進行宣傳。學校和社區可以多舉辦一些活動來鼓勵大家一起為環保做貢獻。勤儉節約是中華民族的傳統美德，我們應該多鼓勵大家一起對廢舊物品進行回收再利用。

2 課文 開發可再生能源 34

尊敬的主席、評委，對方辯友：

大家好！我是來自高一（5）班的林小鬆。今天辯論的主題是"是否有必要開發可再生能源"。作為正方，我方認為"有必要開發可再生能源"，以下是我方的理由。

首先，在中國古代，人們搬不動木頭，就利用水來運木頭；磨不動大米，就發明了用水作動力的水磨。但現在，人們卻大量使用石油和煤等不可再生能源，從而引發了氣候暖化問題。氣候變化威脅著地球上生物的生存，威脅著我們的生態環境和生物多樣性。氣候變化的主要原因是燃燒不可再生能源。為了控制氣候變化，我們必須減少使用不可再生能源，轉向開發可再生能源。

生詞短語

- bì yào 必要 essential
- kāi fā 開發 explore
- kě zài shēng néng yuán 可再生能源 renewable energy
- shí yóu 石油 petrol
- méi 煤 coal
- bù kě zài shēng néng yuán 不可再生能源 non-renewable energy
- qì hòu 氣候 climate
- nuǎn huà 暖化 warming
- shēng cún 生存 survive
- rán shāo 燃燒 burn
- qīng jié 清潔 clean
- huǎn jiě 緩解 reduce
- wēn shì qì tǐ 溫室氣體 greenhouse gases
- rè liàng 熱量 heat
- sàn fā 散發 radiate/give out
- diàn chí 電池 battery

其次，可再生能源如風能、太陽能、水能等是清潔能源。它不會像不可再生能源那樣燃燒，也不會將污染氣體排放到空氣中，可以減少對當地空氣的污染，從而給人類提供更清潔、更健康的生活環境。這對保護生態環境、應對氣候變化具有重要意義。

最後，開發可再生能源有利於緩解全球變暖。燃燒不可再生能源產生的溫室氣體會阻止熱量從地球散發至太空，從而導致全球變暖，進而使得冰川融化、海平面上升。但是，開發利用可再生能源不會產生溫室氣體，有助於保持地球的溫度穩定。所以，對於氣候變化帶來的威脅，開發可再生能源絕對是解決問題的最好辦法。

當然，可再生能源也有局限性。比如白天有太陽能，晚上就沒有了；風大的時候可以發電，但是風小的情況下就不行。不過，也有相應的解決辦法，那就是把白天和風大的時候產生的電儲存在巨大的"電池"中，這樣一來，在夜晚或者風小的時候也有電可用了。

當今，能源的發展及其與環境的關係，是全世界共同關心的問題。石油和煤作為重要的能源，是不可再生能源，總有一天會用完，因此，開發可再生能源就變得越來越重要。綜上所述，我方再次強調，有必要開發可再生能源。

謝謝各位！

改編自：https://www.sohu.com/a/339304608_694489

Culture Point

木材水運 Water Transportation for Timber

千百年來，在與大自然的相處中，人類學會了利用大自然的優勢為自己服務。例如，古代交通不發達，也沒有汽車，如果在森林中砍倒一棵大樹，用普通的馬車是運輸不了的，所以就只能利用水流進行運送。在長江一帶，生活在這裏的人們會把上游砍伐好的木頭放在江水裏，木材順著江水漂流到下游地區。中國古代建造宮殿、廟宇和房屋等所用的木材大多就是用水運這種方式運送的。木材水運的基本建設投資小，耗能少，運輸成本低，短期內運送量大。因此，在河流密佈、水源充足的林區或流域多採用這種運輸方式。但水運時木材損耗較大，還常受水位和氣溫的影響。

Since thousands years ago, human beings have learned using the advantages of nature to serve ourselves. For example, in ancient times, the traffic was not well-developed and there were no vehicles. If a big tree was cut down in the forest, it could not be transported by ordinary carriages but only be transported by water. In the Long River area, people living there cut the wood from the upper reaches and put it in the river. The logs will be drifted to the downstream area. In ancient China, most of the timber used to build palaces, temples and houses was transported by water. The basic construction investment of water ways for timber transportation is small and the energy consumption is low. Transportation cost is low and the amount of timber transported in a short period of time is large. Therefore, this method of transportation is often used in forest areas or watersheds with dense rivers and sufficient water sources. However, the loss of wood during water transportation is large and it is often affected by water level and temperature.

水磨 Water Mill

水磨是中國古代勞動人民智慧的結晶。磨是把米、豆等糧食加工成粉的一種工具。最開始時是靠人和動物推動運轉。後來，中國人發明了用水作動力的水磨。水磨的原理是利用流水沖打水輪帶動磨轉動。

The water mill is the crystallization of the wisdom of the Chinese people in ancient China. Mill is a machine that processes grains such as rice and beans into flour. At the beginning, it used manpower and animals to run. Later, China invented the water mill powered by water. The water mill uses running water to impulse the water wheel to drive the mill to rotate.

語法重點 Key Points of Grammar

可能補語 The Complement of Potentiality

用在謂語後面，補充說明動作能否達到某種結果或情況的詞或詞組叫可能補語。

The complement of potentiality is used after the verb in the sentence. It indicates the possibility of the procedure or the realization of an action.

Structure V+ 得 / 不 + 可能補語　V.+ 得 / 不 + the complement of potentiality

E.g.

- 老師：（網課上，對著麥克風）同學們，你們聽得見老師說話嗎？
  Teacher: (During the online class, face the microphone) Hi class, can you hear me?
  學生：聽得見。
  Student: Yes. We can hear you.
  老師：同學們，你們聽得懂老師講的內容嗎？
  Teacher: Class, do you understand what I taught?
  學生：聽不懂。
  Student: Don't understand.

上面的例句中，"聽" 是動詞，"見" "懂" 分別為 "聽" 的結果，是補語。

In the above example sentences, " 聽 " is a verb, and " 見 " and " 懂 " are the potential results of " 聽 " respectively, which are called complements.

課文理解 Reading Comprehensions

① 不可再生能源有哪些？

② 燃燒不可再生能源有什麼後果？

③ 可再生能源有哪些？

④ 開發可再生能源可以給人類帶來哪些好處？

⑤ 可再生能源的局限性有哪些？

概念與拓展理解 Concepts and Further Understanding

① 技術的發展在何種程度上使可再生能源得以大量開發和使用？
To what extent has the development of technology led to the massive development and use of renewable energy?

② 那些開發不可再生能源的人是否應該對環境污染負責？
Should those who develop non-renewable energy be responsible for environmental pollution?

③ 關於風能和水能的開發利用，從古至今，是靠語言來傳承經驗的嗎？
From ancient to the present, does the inheritance of the technique of using wind and water power depend on language?

④ 可再生能源技術的開發如何擴展人類對能源的認知？
How does the development of renewable energy technologies expand our knowledge of energy?

⑤ 在某種情況下，無知或者缺乏對可再生能源的認識是否可以成為不道德行為（比如污染環境）的借口？
Under certain circumstances, can ignorance or lack of awareness of renewable energy be an excuse for unethical behavior such as environmental pollution?

語言練習 Language Exercises

將上下框的字組成詞語，填寫在橫線上。

Combine the characters in the upper and lower boxes into words and write the words on the line.

必 石 減 開 威 生 清 熱 電

脅 存 潔 油 要 池 緩 量 發

① ____________________

____

從左邊的方框裏選出適當的字，填寫在橫線上。

Select the appropriate character from the box on the left and fill in the blank on the right.

② | 脅 | 協 | 威______ / ______會

③ | 燒 | 澆 | 燃______ / ______花

④ | 清 | 請 | 邀______ / ______潔

⑤ | 暖 | 緩 | 減______ / ______和

⑥ | 執 | 熱 | 炎______ / ______著

重新排列詞語，組成完整的句子。Rearrange the words to form a complete sentence.

⑦ 不可再生能源　可再生能源　污染嚴重　所以　由於　開發　環境　對　是必要的

____

⑧ 等　氣候暖化　燃燒　石油　如　不可再生能源　煤　排放溫室氣體　使　會

____

⑨ 清潔能源　威脅　的　作為　生存環境　風力　不會　人類

____

⑩ 環境污染　有毒物質　減緩　散發出　廢棄電池　大量　不利於

____

從生詞表裏找出與下列詞語意思相同或相近的詞。

Find words with the same or similar meanings as the following words in the vocabulary list.

⑪ 開採 ____________　⑫ 活著 ____________　⑬ 乾淨 ____________　⑭ 需求 ____________

從生詞表裏找出與下列詞語意思相反的詞。

Find words with the opposite meanings to the following words in the vocabulary list.

⑮ 凍結 ____________　⑯ 滅火 ____________　⑰ 加快 ____________　⑱ 收集 ____________

課堂活動 Class Activities

我的問題是什麼？What is my question?

老師在每張貼紙上寫一個關於可再生能源的問題，並在每個學生的後背貼一張貼紙。每個學生要去問別人有哪些辦法可以解決後背貼紙上的問題。學生根據其他同學給的建議猜出

老師貼在她 / 他背後的問題並寫出來。問題越複雜越好玩。學生寫完問題後，再核對老師貼在她 / 他後背的問題。

The teacher writes questions related to renewable energy on the post-it notes and sticks one note on every student's back. Students will ask others to seek the answers to the question at their backs. Students will figure out the question based on the advice they got from other classmates and write down the question. Use more complicated or obscure questions to make the game more interesting. Students check the answer after writing down the questions.

口語訓練 Speaking Tasks

第一部分 **根據圖片，做 3-4 分鐘的口頭表達。做口頭表達之前，先根據提示寫大綱。**

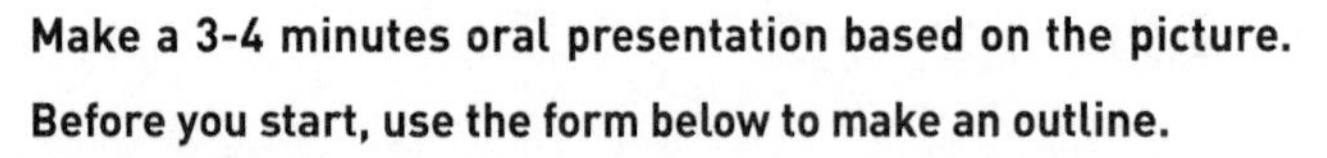

Make a 3-4 minutes oral presentation based on the picture. Before you start, use the form below to make an outline.

大綱 Outline	內容 Content
圖片內容 Information of the picture	
圖片主題 + 文化 Theme of the picture and culture	
提出觀點 Make your points	
延伸個人經歷 Relate to personal experiences	
名人名言 Famous quotes / 熟語 Idioms	
總結 Summary	

第二部分 **回答下面的問題。Answer the following questions.**

① 你的國家是否開發可再生能源？請舉例說明。

② 如果讓你說服當地政府使用可再生能源，你會如何建議？

③ 你日常生活中用過可再生能源嗎？是什麼能源？

④ 可再生能源有哪些優點和缺點？

⑤ 為了綠色用電，你會建議父母在家裏裝太陽能嗎？

技能訓練 Skill Tasks

閱讀訓練 Reading Tasks

文章 1 各國節水方法

仔細閱讀下面的短文，然後回答問題。

Read the passage carefully and answer the following questions.

A. 中國

中國是一個嚴重缺水的國家，缺水程度世界排名第四位，僅次於巴西、俄羅斯和加拿大，是全球人均水資源最少的國家之一。嚴重的水污染也威脅到居民的用水安全和身體健康。中國專家認為，全球現有 12 億人面臨嚴重的缺水壓力，80 個國家水源不足，20 億人的用水得不到保障。在未來的五年內"水將像石油一樣在全世界運轉"。

B. 以色列

水是最重要的可再生能源之一。以色列把水作為重要再生資源進行嚴格的控制和管理，國家制定了法令《水利法》。以色列非常注重污水再利用，他們將廢水用於農業，還將海水轉變為可利用水。這既節約了水資源，也有利於環境保護。以色列人平時過日子也懂得節水，比如推出節水馬桶，上廁所的時候，小便用小水、大便用大水。此外，政府為了增強全民的節水意識，通過報刊、電視等宣傳"節約每一滴水"的理念。廣告也教市民如何在洗碗時節約用水，推廣節水馬桶，提醒人們不用水時關緊水龍頭等等。

C. 英國

在英國，雖然水資源基本能滿足居民生活需求，但是考慮到民眾的用水需求一直增長，政府近些年來非常注重教育民眾如何節約用水和減少水污染。他們通過電視、報紙和社交媒體告訴民眾保護水資源不僅僅是政府的責任，也需要公眾的關注和支持。另外，政府還儘可能多地建立污水處理廠，城市的污水處理率目前已達到95%以上。為進一步治理水污染，英國政府對污水治理不好的地區，持續增加水源管理費，基本解決了全國的水污染問題。

D. 德國

德國雖然不缺水，但許多德國家庭往往將煮完麵的水用來洗碗，將洗衣服的水拿來拖地。作為世界上雨水利用最先進的國家之一，德國的雨水用途很廣泛。除了用來改善環境外，雨水還被廣泛用於洗廁所、洗衣服、澆花園、清潔道路等等。此外，在德國的城市，人們經常看到有水沿著街道兩側的水溝，從高處流向低處。這是雨水利用的又一成功例子。城市街道建水溝，既沖洗了街道，又收集了雨水，一舉兩得。收集到的雨水進入到水池進行再處理後，就可以用來洗廁所、澆草地等。

改編自：https://zhidao.baidu.com/question/244490401 html?fr=iks&word=%CA%C0%BD%E7%B8%F7%B5%D8%C8%E7%BA%CE%BD%DA%D4%BC%D3%C3%CB%AE&ie=gbk

根據以上短文，選擇正確的答案。在方格裏打勾（✓）。

According to the passage above, tick (✓) in the correct boxes.

① 哪個國家是雨水利用最好的國家？

A. ☐ B. ☐ C. ☐ D. ☐

② 哪個國家的水污染問題已經基本得到解決？

A. ☐ B. ☐ C. ☐ D. ☐

③ 哪個國家推出節水馬桶？

A. ☐ B. ☐ C. ☐ D. ☐

④ 哪個國家的人認為以後水會像石油一樣缺乏？

A. ☐ B. ☐ C. ☐ D. ☐

⑤ 哪個國家將海水轉變為生活用水？

A. ☐ B. ☐ C. ☐ D. ☐

⑥ 哪個國家非常注重教育民眾重視水資源問題？

A. ☐ B. ☐ C. ☐ D. ☐

⑦ 哪個國家制定了《水利法》？

A. ☐ B. ☐ C. ☐ D. ☐

⑧ 哪個國家缺水最嚴重？

A. ☐ B. ☐ C. ☐ D. ☐

文章 2 快時尚破壞生態環境

環保論壇

快時尚破壞生態環境

2022 年 10 月 10 日 10:10

快時尚行業，通過迎合年輕人追逐流行的心理，每個季節都會採取較低的價格、賣出當年流行的時裝。據《時尚代價》報道，全球每年生產約 800 億件衣服，是 20 年前的 4 倍。過去服裝只有春夏、秋冬兩個時裝季，而快時尚的流行則以週計算。比如西班牙某個快時尚品牌每年可發佈超過 20 個產品；瑞典某個快時尚品牌每年則可發佈 16 個產品。

大家都知道，人們在製造衣服的過程中大量使用棉花。而種植棉花需要大量使用水與農藥。處理不當的話，不僅污染水土，還會造成乾旱。而且，扔掉的舊衣需要再作處理。每年約有 1050 萬噸的舊衣被送往垃圾處理場。衣服上的色彩雖然讓衣服顯得很好看，但所含有的有毒物質危害卻很大。快時尚加快了生產衣服的速度，嚴重污染了土地、水和空氣，同時產生了大量浪費，從而威脅我們的生態環境。我們必須行動起來，保護環境。

首先，為減少快時尚對生態環境的破壞，我認為購買衣服的人可以做點事來幫助環保。我們要通過廣告引導他們選購採用優質棉花製成的衣服，因為好的棉花使用較少的農藥，比較環保。另外，也可以引導大家購買有利於環保的其他衣服，當然這些衣服價格都比較高。

其次，人們可以通過回收舊衣服來保護環境。在英國，儘管回收舊衣服的商店很多，但仍有 75% 的英國人選擇直接扔掉舊衣，所以舊衣回收還有很大發展空間。而在德國，舊衣回收箱分佈在每個城市的街頭，有 75% 的德國人會將舊衣放進回收箱裏。過去，不少回收的舊衣會被運往一些亞洲和非洲國家。不過，2015 年起，很多亞洲國家已經禁止舊衣進口；2018 年 1 月，中國正式禁止舊衣等物品進入國內。

聯合國環境部表示，讓年輕人支持環保的最好方式是將使用衣服的時間延長。根據綠色和平組織 2017 年發佈的《國際時尚調查報告》，在對約 5800 名年輕人的調查中，超過 50% 有過度購買衣服的行為。

希望在未來，年輕人不要一味追求快時尚，購買新衣時不要買太多。應該鼓勵我們年輕人多參加和快時尚相關的環保活動，這樣他們也會設計出更多環保衣服給大家選擇。

閱讀（36）　評論（12）　轉載（9）　收藏（20）

改編自：http://www.xinhuanet.com/globe/2018-05/17/c_137177960.htm

根據文章 2，選出最適合左邊的描述。把答案寫在橫線上。

According to passage 2, choose the corresponding description on the left side. Write the answers on the lines.

① 西班牙 ______
② 英國 ______
③ 德國 ______
④ 中國 ______
⑤ 聯合國 ______

A. 建議年輕人延長使用衣服的時間。
B. 大部分的人直接扔掉不用的衣服。
C. 大部分年輕人喜歡過度購買衣服。
D. 大部分的人會將舊衣服進行回收。
E. 禁止進口舊衣服。
F. 有一個品牌每年設計出 20 多種服裝。

根據文章 2，從選項中選出最接近下列詞語 / 詞組的意思。把答案寫在橫線上。

According to passage 2, choose the corresponding words and write the answers on the lines.

⑥ 流行 ______
⑦ 污染 ______
⑧ 環保 ______
⑨ 回收 ______
⑩ 調查 ______

A. 渾濁
B. 環境
C. 時尚
D. 接收
E. 考察
F. 流動
G. 污名
H. 節能

Tips

如何找近義詞？How to find synonyms?

近義詞是指意思相近的詞。快速找出近義詞主要有兩種方法：

Synonyms refer to words with similar meanings. There are two ways to quickly find synonyms:

1. 從有共同詞素的詞語中去找。Look for words with common morphemes.

   許多近義詞都有一個共同的特點，那就是它們中間往往有一個相同的詞素。如：回收、接收、回籠。

   這些共同的詞素，決定了它們的基本意義是相近的。因此，在找一個詞的近義詞時，可以抓住這個詞中表示基本意義的詞素，並用它來組詞，然後找出近義詞。比如找“回收”的近義詞，可抓住詞素“收”來組詞：接收，這個詞就是“回收”的近義詞。

   Many synonyms have a common feature, that is, they contain the same morpheme (Chinese character). For example: recycling(回收), receiving(接收), returning(回籠).

The common morphemes in these synonyms determine that their basic meanings are consistent. Therefore, when looking for synonyms of a word, you can grasp the morpheme that represents the basic meaning of the word and use it to make new words then find the synonyms. For example: to find a synonym for 回收 , you can use the morpheme "收" to form word "接收" . The word "接收" is a synonym for "回收" .

2. 從詞的意義上去找。Find in the meaning of the words.

即先弄清這個詞的意思，然後想一想和它意思相同或相近的詞。如找"流行"的近義詞，先弄清"流行"是"時興、時髦"的意思；然後找一下選項中有哪個詞與"時興、時髦"相近。那麼這個詞就是"流行"的近義詞。另外，還要小心有共同詞素的詞語，像"流動"這個選項就是干擾項。

Firstly, figure out the meaning of the word then think about other words which have the same or similar meanings. If you are looking for a synonym of "流行", firstly you should know that 流行 means fashionable. And then you need to look through the options and find out the word that has the closed meaning of "時尚". So this word is a synonym of "流行". The answer "流動" is just a distractor. Please be careful of words that have common morphemes.

掌握了找近義詞的方法，還要注意積累詞語，詞語積累多了，找近義詞也就比較容易了。

After mastering the methods of finding synonyms, you should also enhance your vocabulary to make finding synonyms easier.

聽力訓練 Listening Tasks

一、《為地球發聲》 

你將聽到六段錄音，每段錄音播放兩遍。請在相應的橫線上回答問題 ①-⑥。回答應簡短扼要。每段錄音後會有停頓，請在停頓期間閱讀問題。

You will hear 6 recordings and each audio will be played twice. Answer the question ①-⑥ with short answers. There will be a pause after each recording. Please read the questions during the pause.

請先閱讀一下問題。Please read the questions first.

① "地球一小時" 環保活動在什麼時候舉行？

____

② 我們應該如何實現城市的可持續發展？

____

③ 一台太陽能熱水器最長可以使用多久？

____

④ 清潔電能有哪些？

⑤ 可再生能源的缺點是什麼？至少舉一個例子。

⑥ 為什麼要進行垃圾分類？至少舉一個例子。

二、《新加坡垃圾島》

你即將聽到第二個聽力片段，在聽力片段二播放之前，你將有四分鐘的時間先閱讀題目。聽力片段將播放兩次，聽力片段結束後你將有兩分鐘的時間來檢查你的答案。請用中文回答問題。

You are going to hear the second audio clip. You have 4 minutes to read the questions before it starts. The audio clip will be played twice. After it ends, 2 minutes will be given to you to check the answers. Please answer the questions in Chinese.

填空 • Fill in the blanks.

報社：	海峽時報	垃圾島填滿時間：	【-1-】
改革方式：	【-2-】和回收	遊客登島時間：	週一到【-3-】
理念：	建設【-4-】生態環境	學校活動：	組織學生去島上接受環保教育

海平面上升情況：
- 新加坡四十年來海平面上升了【-5-】。
- 到 2100 年，海平面上升也許會超過【-6-】。

如何應對海平面上升：
- 新加坡政府未來 100 年將花費至少【-7-】。
- 興建第二個水泵房，加強【-8-】能力。
- 建立新的【-9-】防洪。

① [-1-] ______ ② [-2-] ______ ③ [-3-] ______
④ [-4-] ______ ⑤ [-5-] ______ ⑥ [-6-] ______
⑦ [-7-] ______ ⑧ [-8-] ______ ⑨ [-9-] ______

Tips

培養即時複述的習慣 Develop the Habit of Retelling Immediately

很多同學覺得考聽力的時候自己都聽懂了，可等到要寫答案的時候，卻記不清了。這是因為我們在聽的時候，大部分注意力放在理解方面，如果沒有及時對所提細節做筆記，自然就會聽了後面忘了前面，而聽力測試的重點往往就在細節的辨識上。因此，考生不僅要聽懂錄音中的語言信息，還應通過一些有效途徑在短時內強記重要信息，如年代、人物、事件、地點、數字、折扣價、門牌號等。一個人即使記憶力再好，要記清如此多的細節也不容易，那麼只有靠筆記幫忙。

Many students felt that they understood the listening text, but when they were about to answer the questions, they couldn't remember what they heard. This is because we pay more attention on understanding the text and if we do not take notes on the details in time, we will naturally forget the details we heard. The focus of the listening test is often on the identification of details. Therefore, candidates should not only understand the text but also memorize the important information such as age, person, event, location, number, discounted price, house number, etc. in a short time. No matter how good a person's memory is, it is not easy to memorize so many details. In this case, taking notes will help.

記筆記是有訣竅的。在聽單句時，由於句子完全孤立，沒有任何語境，又只唸一遍，聽者只能靠一遍的理解和記憶。因此，準確捕捉所給信息是解答問題的關鍵。這時必須藉助"即時複述"這一有效手段，即：在聽錄音時以僅落後 1-2 秒的時間立即複述原句，以幫助強化記憶，做出正確選擇。在平時訓練中很有必要加強複述練習，它一方面可以幫助你加深對聽懂部分的印象，另一方面也有助於重新咀嚼、理解未聽懂部分，從而有效捕捉並記錄重要信息點，提高準確率。

There is a skill for taking notes. A single clause is often completely isolated without any context and only be read once. The listener can only understand and remember it once also. Therefore, accurately capturing the information given is the key to answer the questions. At this situation, the skill of "retelling immediately" must be used which candidates can repeat the original sentence immediately after only 1-2 seconds when listening to the recording. This will help the candidate strengthen the memory and to choose the correct answer. It is necessary to strengthen retelling exercises in daily training. On one hand, it can help you deepen the impression of the comprehensible part. On the other hand, it can help you review the understood part and capture the information in the ununderstood part so as to effectively capture and take notes of the important points and improve accuracy.

寫作訓練：提案 Writing Tasks: Proposal

熱身

● **根據課文一，討論提案的格式是什麼。According to Text 1, discuss the format of a proposal.**

格式 **參考課文一**

標題

尊敬的 XX：

□□開頭：問候語 + 自我介紹 + 提案目的

□□正文：事件背景
提案理由
提案內容

□□結束語：希望 + 期待回覆

□□此致
敬禮！

（身份）
XXX 敬上
X 年 X 月 X 日

Tips

文體：提案

Text Type: Proposal

提案是指提請會議討論或處理的方案或建議。

A proposal is a plan or suggestion submitted to the meeting for discussion or processing.

練習

你所在的社區雖然實行垃圾分類，可是回收效果很差。大多數居民不知道如何對垃圾進行分類。社區也沒有對居民進行宣傳教育，居民環保意識不強。垃圾也沒有及時處理，導致社區環境髒、亂、差，嚴重影響居民生活。請向社區居委會提出你對垃圾分類問題的看法和建議。選用合適的文本類型完成寫作。字數：300–480 個漢字。

訪談	提案	博客

第一課

聽力一

今天讓我們來聆聽一位義工如何幫助社區居民的故事。她叫周小麗，今年 45 歲，是香港國際學校的中文老師。她每週工作五天，每天至少工作十個小時。下班後到社區做義工，每天至少三個小時。她還用吃飯節省下來的錢資助社區貧困的學生上學。每個得到過她幫助的人，都對她的行為讚歎不已。

很多人一下班就去看電影或者找朋友聊天，然而周小麗堅持每週到社區為那些沒錢請家教的學生補習。她認為將知識教給別人是幫助社區的最有效的方法。周小麗通常會在社區裏教那些讀寫能力較差的小孩和成人學習中文，或者跟他們一起運動，比如在週末的時候組織社區的小孩一起踢足球、跑步等等。除此之外，周小麗也會組織社區的居民打掃衛生，幫忙給貧困鄰居發放食物。周小麗也會參與組織籌款活動，比如在新冠肺炎疫情期間，她就幫忙籌集到兩萬元現金，購買了口罩和其他醫療用品，送到武漢。周小麗認為，在社區做義工不僅給社區帶來了正面影響，也加強了她和其他社區成員的聯繫，這讓她覺得很欣慰。此外，她還會組織社區成員一起積極改善社區，比如舉辦一些文化慶祝活動、健康運動等，努力讓社區變得更好，同時也可以吸引更多的年輕人來參加義工活動。

周小麗説，隨著春節臨近，最近的社區活動主要是美化社區公共空間。她認為，如果社區空間變漂亮了，居民就會喜歡出門，不會一個人待在家裏，生活質量也會得到改善。對於如何美化社區空間，她打算先去公園除掉雜草，多種綠樹和鮮花，並建立社區菜園，讓每個家庭都有一塊小空地，自由地種菜，還能擴大老人活動空間等。

周小麗的建議得到了社區管理者的肯定，在她的帶動下，她所在的社區被評為香港最漂亮的社區，也吸引了很多遊客來參觀。

聽力二

觀眾朋友，大家好，歡迎收看我們的節目。我們現在都知道很多人會為孤獨老人送便當，但我們並不知道這件事已經持續了很長一段時間。今天是大年初一，我們特別向大家介紹一部紀錄片，叫《慈濟如常》，它講述的是台灣鄉村貧困家庭的小孩和無人照顧的孤苦老人的故事。

每個人都會有突如其來的苦難，紀錄片提出一個關鍵問題：到底怎樣能“如常”走過苦難呢？《慈濟如常》的開頭講述了志工陳瑞凰如何照顧獨居老人阿嬤的故事，她的愛包容無私，細緻入微。

陳瑞凰：我是志工陳瑞凰。你看到各式各樣的案例，就會知道他們到底有多苦。如果你沒有親身經歷或者親眼看到，你根本無法體會什麼叫苦難。

老人：很寂寞，沒有辦法，要忍耐呀！

陳瑞凰：沒關係，有空我會來陪你聊天。你的腳怎麼了？

老人：我昨天在這裏跌倒了。

陳瑞凰：你要打電話告訴我，我帶你去看醫生。

老人：好。昨天沒人來，我爬不起來，又是禮拜天，就沒去找醫生，現在痛得要命。

陳瑞凰：家裏東西這麼多，當然容易被絆倒。晚上我多帶一些志工來，把亂七八糟的東西都清一清，客廳寬敞了，你走路就不會摔倒。

老人：我心臟不好，有時候話也説不出來，沒有力氣，要翻身要吃飯，都需要人幫忙。我一直看著照顧我的志工，心裏很過意不去。為什麼一個小女孩要被我這樣拖累，她也不是我的親人。我這個身體狀況是隨時都會走的，我一直覺得我最多活到六十歲，結果我現在已經六十七歲了。能夠多活一天，我就多做一件事，給我的都是賺到的，我自己也很感激志工對我的幫助。我要趁我還活著，把志工的精神傳承下去。

71 分鐘的紀錄片《慈濟如常》，是對好幾位資深的慈濟志工整整一年半的隨身紀錄。有些老人其實等不到紀錄片問世的那一天就不在了。今天我們選取了其中非常感人的部分，謝謝這些志工們！謝謝各位的收看！

第二課

聽力一

錄音一

M：同學，你好！請問你知道中國的教師節是幾月幾號嗎？

F：9 月 10 號。

M：為什麼要設立教師節呢？

F：中國有句老話叫“一日為師，終身為父”。設立教師節，是為了表達對教師職業的尊重。

錄音二

M：一香，聽説中國有“九九重陽節”這個傳統節日？

F：是的，重陽節也叫“敬老節”，因為尊老愛幼是中華民族的傳統美德。人們在這一天登高望遠，表達對老人健康長壽的祝福。

錄音三

M：毛毛，你媽媽怎麼給你取這麼難聽的名字？

F：毛毛是我的小名兒。中國人通常會給小孩取一個小名兒，希望孩子能健康成長。

M：那叫你毛毛是因為你身上長很多毛嗎？

F：哈哈，不是！毛毛在中國是指剛出生的嬰兒，跟“毛”沒有關係。你要多了解中國的文化觀念，不然會鬧笑話的。

M：哦，原來是這樣！好像還有一個歌星叫毛阿敏？

F：那是姓，不是小名兒。唉，你還是要多學習一些中國的文化知識。

錄音四

自古以來，中國民間有一個傳統習俗，人一出生，就用一種動物作他的屬相。中國人用十二種動物作為屬相，也叫“十二生肖”。十二生肖是悠久的民俗文化符號，民間流傳著很多描寫生肖的詩歌、春聯、繪畫和書畫等作品。除了中國之外，還有很多國家會在春節期間發行生肖郵票，以此來表達對中國新年的祝福。

錄音五

聽眾朋友們，晚上好！今天向大家介紹一個有趣的中國傳統民俗——“抓週兒”。“抓週兒”就是在小孩兒滿一週歲那天，大人們擺好書本、錢、筆、算盤、食物、玩具等日常用品，讓小孩兒任意挑選。由此來推測孩子將來可能從事的職業。

錄音六

M：歡迎到中國來遊玩！今天晚上我請你吃晚餐。中國的四大菜系，你想吃哪一種？

F：我知道中國飲食文化博大精深而且花樣繁多，四大菜系是指哪些呢？

M：四大菜系就是山東菜、四川菜、廣東菜還有……淮揚菜。

F：可以介紹幾個有名的菜嗎？

M：山東菜最有名的是糖醋鯉魚，廣東菜有烤乳豬，四川菜有水煮魚，淮揚菜有獅子頭。

F：太可怕了！還有獅子頭？

M：你誤會了，獅子頭不是真的獅子……

聽力二

M：朋友們好！歡迎大家收看《感受中國》節目！今天我們邀請到了中國最年輕的 90 後茶藝師陳曉珍，和我們談談她與茶的故事。曉珍，你好！歡迎你來到我們的演播室！你能先和我們簡單介紹一下茶的來歷嗎？

F：中國人喝茶最早要從神農時代説起了。古時候有一個叫神農的人在野外煮開水喝，一片葉子不小心落入水中，白開水便煮出了香味，他喝了之後覺得人很精神。於是人們就在日常飲用水中加入茶葉來改進水的味道，這就是茶的來歷之一。直到今天，雖然有了咖啡、可樂等飲料，但中國人喝茶的習慣還是傳承了下來。

M：中國茶文化有著上千年的歷史，然而年輕人卻好像不怎麼了解茶。現在的年輕人比較喜歡喝飲料，對茶文化的了解也很少。你怎麼看待這個現象？

F：確實如此。現在的學生更喜歡喝奶茶，平均每人每天約喝半杯。他們覺得泡一壺茶很麻煩，可是點一杯奶茶卻很快。另外，年輕人喜歡吃甜的，他們覺得喝茶太苦，也體會不到苦後的甘甜。其實，茶有深厚的歷史知識，又有豐富的表現形式，我們需要引導年輕人親近茶文化，讓他們看到茶葉有趣、不同的一面。所以我在上海開了一間茶館，向年輕人傳達茶葉背後有趣的故事，希望能打破年輕人對茶古板的印象，讓更多年輕人喜歡上茶、愛上茶。

M：你怎麼看待傳統文化的傳承？

F：關於傳統文化的傳承，我認為應該以年輕人的方式去表達歷史，這樣才能吸引年輕人關注傳統文化。年輕人也應該多了解自己的傳統文化，進而改變一些觀念。比如，喝茶並不是要求年輕人必須馬上靜心。現代生活節奏如此快，大多數的年輕人根本不會選擇喝茶，那我們怎麼能要求他們在喝茶的一瞬間就喜歡上茶呢？所以，我們要讓年輕人知道，喝茶並不只是對身體有好處。茶在中國人的生活裏，不僅有利於社交，還有利於修養身心。茶文化的傳承，還是要靠我們年輕人的努力。

M：你怎麼看待傳統茶和現代奶茶？

F：大部分的年輕人都喜歡喝奶茶，不喜歡品嚐傳統茶。而有的人則認為一些現代茶飲店對茶的表達形式不傳統，這種茶並不重視茶葉本身的滋味。但我並不這麼認為，我覺得茶葉的表達形式本來就是豐富多樣的。我們一方面是要教會年輕人如何欣賞純茶的滋味，另一方面是讓茶發展出更多不同的呈現形式。不管是夏天在賣的冷泡茶，還是奶茶、茶與酒的結合等，它們的核心都是茶。喝茶的人在被茶的味道吸引之後，才會慢慢去探尋茶本身有趣的地方，從而傳承茶文化。

第三課

聽力一

錄音一

M：2020 年真是不尋常的一年，因為疫情，我們的生活方式被迫改變很多。

F：對呀，我們每天只能待在家裏，哪裏也去不了。

M：最明顯的改變是每個人出門都要戴口罩，我覺得即使新冠疫情以後結束了，我們還會繼續戴口罩。

F：是的，口罩是 2020 年每個人出門都會戴的防護用具。這種生活方式既是保護自己，也是保護他人。

錄音二

M：老闆，來一份水煮魚，一盤青菜，一份猴腦，六碗飯。今天我要和朋友一起慶祝生日。

F：你好，我們這裏沒有猴腦等野味，國家也規定不能吃野生動物。我給你們做其他的菜，做好後會幫你們分成六份，大家分開吃，一樣能慶祝。這也是為了你們的健康著想。

錄音三

M：開播了！開播了！今天主播帶你來看看各地出產的水果。

F： 歡迎剛剛進入直播間的朋友們。今天給大家帶來的是紅蘋果。

M：新進來的寶寶們，大家都來瞧一瞧，看一看啦！咱這個蘋果個頭大，顏色鮮紅。全部都是純天然的，沒有打農藥。大家可以放心吃，又脆又甜。保證全網最低價。

M：大家如果喜歡，請趕緊下訂單。

F： 也可以在屏幕下方為我們點讚，開啟小鈴鐺。

錄音四

各位網友，因為疫情，大家都不能外出旅行，所以今天我們要介紹一種新型旅行方式，叫“雲旅遊”。雲旅遊通過 5G、VR 等技術，讓大家從圖文語言到虛擬現實再到視頻直播，從單向的圖文欣賞到多人的直播互動，實現立體旅遊。雲旅遊一定會給你帶來耳目一新的視聽體驗，你也來試試吧！

錄音五

聽眾朋友們，晚上好！今天我跟大家聊聊在家上網課的問題。很多人都覺得上網課好，可以隨時隨地上課。可是，他們忘了學生都還是孩子，沒辦法好好自我管理。很多同學的手機和電腦擺在一起，上課根本不專心，同學之間還互傳短信息、聊天，注意力沒辦法集中。以前我一有問題，可以直接問老師；現在要等很久，老師才能回覆我，那個時候我早就忘了什麼問題了。另外，我在家學習，隨時想要睡覺、吃東西，很難進入學習狀態。你們都和我一樣嗎？

錄音六

M：今晚去看電影吧！

F： 不行，我要回家做健身操。

M：健身館不是開放了嗎，你為什麼還在家裏運動？

F： 在家裏舒服，跟著網上教練跳，也不怕別人笑話我動作做不好。

M：不過，這次新冠疫情倒是讓很多人意識到健康的重要性了。

F： 是呀，堅持運動是一種積極的生活方式，是追求自律、完善自我、積極生活的體現。

M：這麼說來，我也要趕緊去報一個運動班。

聽力二

記： 各位網友，歡迎收聽 958 中文頻道，今晚的主題是“如何養成健康的網絡生活方式”。為此，我們專門請到網絡健康專家王小燕博士來為我們回答問題。王博士，謝謝你專門到我們直播間來幫忙解答中學生的上網問題。我們先來接聽第一個問題。

學生 1：王博士好！我喜歡熬夜打遊戲，有時候怕媽媽發現，我就關著燈打。結果現在視力變壞了，第二天上課也沒精神，學習效率很低。有什麼辦法能擺脱網癮嗎？

王： 在現代的網絡化社會裏，不玩遊戲是不可能的，但打得太多也不好。不過，你已經意識到自己的問題，這就是很大的進步。我覺得你現在要做的是多參加學校的一些課外活動，也可以和家人、朋友做戶外運動。這樣可以轉移你的興趣，不用天天在家對著電腦。

學生 2：王博士，我媽媽一直不給我買電腦。別的同學都有電腦，只有我沒有，我覺得很沒有面子。大家聊網上的事情，我都不知道，我覺得我被孤立了。我該如何和媽媽溝通呢？

王： 沒有個人電腦沒關係，你可以在圖書館使用公共電腦，也可以試著和你媽媽說說上網的好處。比如，利用網絡獲取更新的知識和參考資料，還可以利用網絡購買各種學習工具和生活用品，省時省力，又比較省錢。

學生 3：王博士，我媽媽雖然讓我上網學習，可是她會限制我在電腦裝聊天工具比如微信、臉書、推特等。這限制了我交朋友的權利，我真的很生氣，每天都跟她吵架。

王：你媽媽的擔心是對的。現在網上騙子很多，作為中學生，心智還未完全成熟，很容易上當受騙。網絡詐騙形形色色，如兼職詐騙、中獎詐騙、交友詐騙等，令人防不勝防。特別是網絡交友，一定要慎重對待！如果只是和自己認識的朋友聊天，那還比較安全。你可以和你的媽媽再好好溝通一下。

記：好的，我們今天時間有限，先聊這麼多。感謝同學們提出的問題，也感謝王博士的耐心指導。相信王博士的建議會幫助大家保持健康的網絡生活方式。那我們下期再見！

第四課

聽力一

觀眾朋友們，大家好！歡迎收看今天的《文倩世界週報》，我是陳文倩。今天我想和大家談談“基因編輯”這個話題。2020 年的諾貝爾化學獎頒發給了法國女科學家埃瑪紐埃勒·卡彭蒂耶和美國女科學家珍妮弗·安妮·道德納，因為她們開發了基因編輯技術。

那麼，什麼是基因編輯呢？所謂基因編輯就是對基因進行編輯，實現加入或刪除 DNA 片段的功能，最終改變目的基因序列的技術。舉個形象的例子：基因編輯就像寫文章要對文本進行修改一樣，首先要把錯誤或想要修改的地方找出來，然後使用工具，按照修改的意圖，插入、刪除部分詞句或者改寫一段文字。

基因編輯技術相當於是一個工具，主要進行剪切、複製、粘貼等操作。生命的真相可能就是這麼的簡單。這項技術對生命科學產生了革命性的影響。根據這項發明，人類不但可以識別病毒，而且能識別任意的 DNA 片段，還能在識別後對其進行修改。也就是說，以後科學家們幾乎能對各種動物、植物和微生物的基因進行編輯。換句話説，從此以後，人類治療疾病就有了全新的方法，而過去無法治療的遺傳性疾病可能會被治好。這項發明為全球生物研究節省了大量成本。未來隨著基因編輯藥物試驗的快速進行，以後會有越來越多的基因編輯藥物面世。

生物科學技術的發展離不開基因研究。基因編輯技術的發明，為科學家打開了一個新世界。至於這個新世界帶給人類的結果是好是壞，目前還不知道。即便基因編輯技術上完全可以保證其安全性，但有誰知道潘多拉魔盒一旦打開，會不會關不上呢！現在這項技術在世界上引起了一片反對聲，其實就是人們意識到了基因改造的不確定性。就像蒸汽、電、炸藥、核能剛出現時一樣，我們還不知道這項新技術帶給人類的將是快樂還是悲傷。

聽力二

2020 年，新冠肺炎疫情突如其來，是人類的一場大災難。世界疫情如此嚴重，應如何看待中醫在新冠肺炎疫情防控中的作用呢？針對這個問題，我們獨家邀請到中國工程院院士——鍾南山來一一解答。

記：有些人説得了新冠肺炎，即使治好了，也會有後遺症，您認為呢？

鍾：我不認為會有明顯的後遺症。雖然一部分病人的心肺功能有所下降，但我相信隨著治療和時間的推移，會慢慢恢復。

記：中醫作為傳統醫學，在本次疫情中提供了很多藥方和治療方案。在您看來，傳統醫學在此次新冠疫情防控中起到了什麼作用？

鍾：新冠肺炎的主要症狀有咳嗽、發燒、無力等。中醫對這些症狀的治療往往是有效的。對於重症肺炎，如果中西醫結合的話，病死率就會減少，所以初步來看，中醫在治療新冠肺炎上是有效的。不過，治療新冠肺炎，不能只靠中醫，要中西結合。有中醫做預防，再用現代醫學做支持，效果會很好。總的來説，就是對於輕型和普通型病人，第一時間使用中藥；對於重型病人，中醫和西醫結合治療。對於恢復期的病人，可以採用中藥和針灸、按摩等方法一起用，促進病人快速康復。

記：平時生活中，我們還可以採取哪些預防措施呢？

鍾：首先要有合理作息，保證睡眠充足，並注意保持室內空氣流通、陽光充足。晚上十一點前入睡，早上六點起床，有利於身體健康。老人可以打打太極拳，活動全身關節，調節精神緊張，增強心肺功能，促進血液循環，科學養生。其次，新冠肺炎病死患者有一個共同特點：大多為中老年人，他們體質較差，還可能有其他慢性病。所以，科學合理安排三餐很重要，生、熟食要分開煮，確保無病毒傳播。當然，此次疫情傳播迅速，嚴重影響人們的身心健康，難免會引起恐慌、焦慮、抑鬱等心理問題。大家應該保持心情舒暢，情緒穩定，避免過度勞累。

記：是的，中醫在治療上的副作用相對於西醫較小，對病人傷害小。西醫雖然直觀看來恢復快，但副作用也很大。中醫見效慢卻能全面調節免疫系統，讓身體自癒。感謝鍾南山院士接受我們的採訪！希望他的建議，對大家有益！

（改編自：http：//www.ce.cn/xwzx/gnsz/gdxw/202004/15/t20200415_34691126.shtml）

第五課

聽力一

今天，有很多年輕人來聽我的演講。看來大家都很關心美。什麼是美呢？充實就是美，美就是無目的的快樂。現代社會的每一個人都忙到沒有時間去感受身邊的事物。“忙”這個漢字就是告訴我們，忙是心靈的死亡，是心亡。如果心靈死亡，他對身邊的事物是沒有感覺的。所以，我希望通過一些簡單的方式，把“天地有大美”的觀念跟大家一起分享。

首先是食物之美。在城市忙碌，有的人每天隨便吃三餐，有的人天天吃大餐。他們都忘了食物跟我們的身體有關，也跟“美”有關。我們應該懂得任何時候都要選擇對我們身體有益的食物。也就是説，我要充分地知道我要什麼，這就是品味。口渴的時候一口把茶喝下去，那不是品。真正的品茶，是一個非常緩慢的過程，好像在品味自己生命裏面一個非常美好的一個記憶。

其次是穿衣之美。我們常常説這個人穿衣服很有品位，因為他有他自己的選擇。這個人完全可以樸素地做自己。從食物的美學轉到穿衣服的美學，我們會發現衣服跟某一種生命情調有關。美其實就是做自己，而不是被流行帶著走。所以説，品位就是選擇自己所要的，這個是從生活裏培養自己對美的一種感動。

最後是出行之美。如果人的一生都在趕路，急急忙忙地走，就像剛才提到的“忙”這個字是心靈的死亡，那他到底能夠看到什麼，能夠感覺到什麼？在宋代的山水畫裏，我們看到亭子的位置，大抵都在風景最美的地方。在那裏，人可以看到最美的風景。這就是在告訴你，你的人生不一定是要拚命趕路的。只有懂得停下來，你才能夠感覺到周邊的東西，所以“停”跟“忙”剛好變成了一個互動。

美是一種生活方式。我們都不喜歡吃藥，因為藥太苦，可是人生當中有一部分就是要學會吃苦的。歐洲最好的咖啡和中國最好的茶都強調苦後回甘。你只有在吃到苦味之後再回來體會的那個甜，它才是真正的甜。它告訴我們，人生到底應該怎麼去看。所以，我常常會反省自己，我是不是太忙了？我有必要這麼忙嗎？還是應該留出一些時間給我自己，去感受我生活周邊的東西？我想，在食衣住行的部分，我們應該回到傳統。懂得生活就是一種藝術，是美。謝謝大家！

（改編自：https：//www.sohu.com/a/309370553_161835）

聽力二

記：觀眾朋友們，歡迎收看《藝術人生》。今天來到我們演播室的是中國藝術體操的代表人物——鍾玲。鍾玲，你好！謝謝你來參加我們的訪談。你能先跟我們介紹一下什麼是藝術體操嗎？

鍾：簡單來説，藝術體操是一項在音樂伴奏下，以自然性動作為基礎的，帶有較強藝術性的女子體操項目。藝術體操的種類主要包括繩、棒、球、圈和帶等。藝術體操是力與美、競技與藝術的結合。藝術體操還會融入芭蕾舞、民族舞、體操、武術、雜技、戲劇等形式，從而構成它的美。

記：鍾玲，你是中國藝術體操國家隊隊員，還是“亞洲藝術體操女皇”，你認為學習藝術體操有什麼好處呢？

鍾：學習體操不只是為了參加比賽，獲得獎盃。學習藝術體操不僅有助於幫助孩子發育、長高，也會讓孩子變得更自信，更有氣質。學習藝術體操是一個漫長的過程，孩子必須學會吃苦。在這個過程中，孩子要學會讓身體能夠協調，這樣對孩子大腦的發育也會有促進作用。

記：我們注意到每個運動員選的音樂都不一樣，音樂在藝術體操中起到什麼樣的作用？

鍾：藝術體操是一項體育與藝術相結合的運動項目。它要求運動員需有一定的音樂修養和藝術表現力。藝術體操的音樂和一般音樂不同。在訓練時，音樂能起到控制動作節奏和速度、調整運動員心情的作用。在藝術體操中，音樂和動作是緊密結合的，沒有了音樂，就會削弱動作的藝術表現力。

記：大家都説練藝術體操很辛苦，你能和我們分享一下你的經歷嗎？

鍾：和每一個運動項目一樣，練藝術體操也是很辛苦的。每天需要有七八個小時的基本功訓練。一個動作沒有做好，就要至少再重複二十多遍，這是多麼地枯燥無味。但是艱辛的日子總會過去的，日復一日的訓練，會讓動作越來越漂亮。所謂“台上一分鐘，台下十年功”講的就是這個道理。只要能堅持下來，就會有收穫。

（改編自：http：//www.ce.cn/xwzx/gnsz/gdxw/202004/15/t20200415_34691126.shtml）

第六課

聽力一

在新冠疫情發生之前，很多教育學家一直預言，數字化和人工智能將打開一個全新的教育局面。傳統模式下的面對面課堂教學將會被在線教學取代。這個預言終於在疫情期間部分成真了。

新型冠狀病毒的嚴重性遠遠超出了所有人的想象，大家都不知道怎麼應對。而且疫情時好時壞，學校經常要在疫情嚴重的時候停課，這打亂了中國和全球其他許多國家的教育秩序。也許就是因為不知道疫情什麼時候能夠結束，一場安靜的變革正在每個學校展開。大家都想盡辦法，通過網絡進行遠程上課。

我們學校主要通過網絡平台進行遠程教學，老師也會通過網絡分享教學和視頻資料，學生根據自己的時間進行遠程學習和提問。目前，我們的學生已逐漸適應了這種混合式學習方式，即在家中甚至海外進入線上教學空間，完成學習任務。

當然，線上教學有利也有弊。對中學生來說，在線教育能夠幫助他們發展自我管理能力。對小學生來說，面對面教學更容易集中注意力。我認為無論科技如何發展，教育是一個"以人為本"的過程，在線教育在未來依然不能完全取代實體學校。年輕人的成長需要互動。也許課程可以很容易地移到線上，網絡世界也能在一定程度上滿足人們的社交需求，但學生的品格教育不能只依靠網絡，更需要的是老師面對面地進行交流、培養。

新冠肺炎疫情爆發帶來的影響或許需要更長時間去觀察，但可以肯定的是，這場疫情將加速發展混合式學習方式——即課堂學習與線上學習相結合、靈活安排的方式。

或許，十年之後，當我們再回顧這段日子時，可能會"感歎"是病毒促成了這個改變的開始。

（改編自：https：//baijiahao.baidu.com/s?id=1665379369440923670&wfr=spider&for=pc）

聽力二

記：觀眾朋友們，歡迎收看《天下雜誌》，今天來到我們演播室的是台灣大學教授葉丙成。葉教授，您好！謝謝您接受我們的訪談。我們知道台灣正在進行 108 課改計劃，也就是素養教育計劃。您能先跟我們談談為什麼台灣的教育需要進行改革嗎？

葉：我每年在台灣大學完成新生講座後，總是很難過。因為總會有學生哭著跟我說："老師，我讀的專業和我想象中的根本不一樣，我讀得很痛苦，請問我應該怎麼辦？"我就說："那你重考呀！"然後這個學生說："即使我重考，我也不知道自己該選擇什麼專業。"說完一直哭，旁邊很多學生也跟著一起哭。這說明什麼？根據調查，全台灣有將近六成的人不喜歡做和他大學專業相關的工作。很多家長花了很多心力，讓孩子參加各種補習，想將孩子送進大學讀熱門的專業，但到最後，這些孩子都不會選擇這些熱門專業的相關行業，因為他們根本就沒有熱情或者不喜歡做這個行業。這樣的情況在台灣每個大學都有，將近七成的學生後悔讀自己現在所選的專業。最終這些學生畢業後，都不得不去做司機、酒店打掃人員等服務工作。而這些工作，根本不需要讀大學就可以做。他們白白浪費了四年的高等教育資源。過去，台灣的教育只注重知識，考試也只是考知識而已，沒有考察學生解決實際問題的能力。這樣教育出來的結果是我們培養了很有知識的大學生，但這些學生不會運用知識來解決真實世界的問題，這就是台灣為什麼迫切需要改革的原因。

記：世界變化的速度，已經快到令人難以想象，替孩子裝備面對未知的素養而非過時的知識，已是全球教育趨勢。那麼您能跟我們介紹一下，什麼是素養教育嗎？

葉：素養教育就是要培養學生學會運用知識解決真實世

界問題的能力。素養教育會減少很多必修課，讓學生有更多的時間去探索自己今後學習的方向和興趣。

記：很多家長都喜歡原來的應試教育，他們對素養教育很不適應，也有很多疑問。您能跟我們談一談為什麼素養教育是未來人才很重要的部分，而不是用考試分數來看一個人的能力嗎？

葉：台灣的家長們真的需要反思一下，灌輸知識為主的教育模式已經過時了。每年有不少於 16 萬的學生從大學退學，這是為什麼呢？千萬不要只相信分數和名校，卻不關心孩子的興趣。全球化的今天，世界變化速度很快，每天發生的事情都是難以預料的，比如 2020 年新冠疫情大爆發，根本無法從應試知識上找到答案。現在學生所處的時代，全球化程度之高，人口之多，氣候變化之快，這些都是人類歷史上從來沒有發生過的，如果只知道死背知識，我們怎麼指望他們來解決人類未來所要面對的問題呢？

（改編自：https：//www.youtube.com/watch?v=dY6SNFPHefs&feature=youtu.be）

第七課

聽力一

錄音一

M：我要吃地瓜稀飯，我妹妹要吃漢堡包。真不知道去哪裏吃早餐。

F：去麥當勞呀！那裏就有漢堡包和中國的地瓜稀飯。現在都全球化了，麥當勞在世界各地也會提供符合當地口味的食物。

M：這真是一個好主意，沒想到麥當勞也這麼本土化。

F：是的，比如日本的麥當勞也賣日本壽司，韓國的麥當勞也賣韓國泡菜。

錄音二

M：受全球化和互聯網的影響，英文逐漸被很多國家的民眾接受並使用。很多民族語言正在逐漸消失。於是，一些機構和組織都在積極搶救這些民族語言。為什麼要搶救這些民族語言呢？

F：因為保護民族語言，有利於人類文明的傳承和發展，也有利於民族團結、社會安定。

錄音三

M：全球化促生了很多跨國公司，比如耐克、星巴克、麥當勞等。人們在自己的國家也能買到世界各地的商品。

F：但是疫情在全球爆發後，人們開始反對經濟全球化。

M：事實上，控制疫情還是需要全球化，比如疫苗的研發就需要全球科學家的合作。

F：疫情不僅奪去數百萬人的生命，還使得窮人更窮、富人更富。很多生活在較窮的國家的人民，就沒辦法打疫苗。

M：不管怎麼樣，很多全球性問題，比如氣候變化等，還是需要全球共同應對。

錄音四

M：各位網友，因為疫情，大家開始反對全球化。但是，今天我想來講講全球化的好處。首先，全球化降低了商品的價格，每個人都可以買到來自世界各地的商品。其次，有些國家缺乏特殊的人才，可以從其他國家引進。例如新加坡缺乏護士，可以從中國招聘護士來幫忙照顧病人。

錄音五

F：聽眾朋友們，晚上好！今天跟大家聊聊全球化的代價。全球化加速全球氣候變暖，環境污染問題更加嚴重。另外，全球化導致文化多樣性逐漸消失，很多人更喜歡外國文化，而不重視本國文化。全球化使外來的大型跨國公司受益，但犧牲了本土公司的發展。

錄音六

M：為什麼現在需要全球科技合作？

F：因為整個地球需要共同面對氣候變暖、能源危機、生物多樣性喪失的挑戰。除此之外，還要共同面對重大疾病、糧食短缺、人口變化的煩惱。越來越多全球性的重大問題正在給人類的生存發展帶來威脅。而解決這些困難的辦法就是要實現科技全球化，大家一起合作。

M：科技全球化會給大家帶來哪些好處呢？

F：每個國家都可以在科技合作中學到先進國家的科學技術成果，節約創新成本。通過合作，科學技術人才可以得到更多學習的機會。

M：您能舉個例子來說明科技全球化的重要性嗎？

F：比如疫苗的研發，如果大家一起合作，就會縮短疫苗研發的時間。任何國家都可以享受科技成果，人類必須擁抱科技全球化。

聽力二

尊敬的主席、各位來賓：

大家好！我是台灣國際學校的學生會主席張小酉。非常感謝校長邀請我參與這次由上海國際學校主辦的 2022 年世界和平學生論壇，這是一個具有歷史意義的、充滿智慧的論壇。今天我演講的題目是“全球化是世界衝突根源”。

在演講之前，請允許我向在世界各地遭受恐怖襲擊的受害者及家人表示慰問。我們的世界充斥著各種紛爭，從地區不穩定性和大國的衝突中都能看出全球化是造成衝突的根源。

那麼，什麼是全球化呢？全球化是不同國家的人民之間互動和整合的過程。全球化是一把雙刃劍，在社會發展中具有正反兩方面的作用。從正面來看，它可以鼓勵各種新技術的研究和開發，從而推動新產品的生產和消費，全球化在全球範圍內促進了人類文明的發展。

但正如大家現在看到的一樣，全球化對環境、文化、經濟的發展及人類身體健康也會造成不同程度的負面影響：世界各國財富分配上的不平等，加大了貧國與富國之間的差距；西方的價值觀、文化觀、人權觀被強行輸入到落後國家，迫使當地人民接受西方文化和價值觀。

其次，全球化雖然使各國在政治、經濟和文化上相互依存，推動了合作，但是也傳播了恐懼和暴力。在這個方面，全球化不僅沒有加強各地的聯繫和對話，反而帶來了新的衝突。有些落後國家無法適應全球化，就採用恐怖主義的方式取得利益。

此外，全球化也導致環境污染、資源減少等生態問題。移民、難民、恐怖襲擊等問題，都日益成為困擾人類發展的全球性重大問題。因此，全球化是世界衝突根源。

謝謝！

第八課

聽力一

今天我們來談一部關於地球遭受極端氣候襲擊的影片。這部影片叫做《後天》，講述的是全球氣候變暖、北極冰川融化。海水溫度突然升高，冰川融化導致海平面快速上升，海水向四面八方流去。在人們還來不及做出反應的時候，災難發生了，不論是建築物還是生命都在一瞬間消失了。那個場景真是令人感到害怕，讓人不敢想象。然而災難並沒有就此結束。大水過後，接下來是不停地下大雪，有的地方還下起冰雹，來不及躲起來的人就被冰雹打中而死去。更慘的是，龍捲風也來了，捲走了路上的車輛和行人。人們不得不躲到地底下想辦法對付極寒的天氣，有的人想出去找吃的，但很快就被凍死了。

影片在最後指出，人類只有在這一刻，才開始意識到導致災難發生的原因是人類一直以來都在破壞自然。為了自己的生存，人類砍伐樹木，將污水排入河流，還過量排放二氧化碳，導致氣候變暖，這些行為都讓動植物失去了賴以生存的環境。不僅如此，人類甚至還到處獵殺老虎、大象等野生動物，所以大自然要報復。災難就是大自然對我們人類做出的懲罰。

通過觀看這部影片，我深深地感受到破壞自然的後果的嚴重性，也見識到大自然一旦報復起來，人類是多麼的無力。想到新冠疫情發生後，人們被迫待在家裏，無法出門，動物們卻能自由自在地在街道上走動，海裏的生物也多了起來。我想，不管是這部電影還是新冠病毒都是在警告我們，要關注自然，要反省我們的行為。如果我們人類再這樣浪費資源、破壞環境，氣候危機將不僅僅出現在電影裏，而且會出現在現實生活中，出現在我們身邊。

聽力二

記：觀眾朋友，大家好！歡迎收看今晚的《健康》節目，今天我們請到了新加坡國立醫院的吳華麗醫生來和我們談談現代生活中的光污染問題。吳醫生好，您能先跟觀眾們談談什麼是光污染問題嗎？

吳：1879 年 10 月 21 日，愛迪生發明了有實用價值的電燈。他或許沒有想到，電燈給大家帶來了光明，卻也因此帶來了新的環境災難——光污染。現代化技術讓人們的生活越來越明亮，就連晚上也如同白天一樣，但其實過度的燈光會對人的健康造成嚴重的影響。這就是光污染問題。

記：一份調查報告顯示：全球約有三分之二的人生活在光污染中。而且，人為光造成的污染逐年增加。有人說“燈光是一種毒品。濫用燈光，就是危害健康”。吳醫生，請您跟觀眾朋友們講講過度的燈光會給人體帶來哪些危害。

吳：首先，光污染是造成孩子近視高發的重要因素。長時間在光亮的環境下工作和生活，眼睛的功能將受影響。其次，燈光會使人心煩而無法睡覺。人睡覺的時候，眼睛雖然是閉著的，但亮光依然會影響睡眠。一旦失眠，人體得不到充分休息，又將引發其他健康問題，比如流鼻血、掉牙齒等。彩色光源不但對眼睛不利，而且會讓人出現惡心、嘔吐、失眠、注意力不集中等症狀。

記：那我們應該如何避免光污染呢？

吳：從房間的用途來看，書房、客廳、廚房等宜採用冷色燈光，如白色；而臥室、衛生間、陽台等宜採用暖色燈光，如黃色。這樣既可以保護視力，也能提高工作和學習效率。還可以買一些植物來改善環境。將大自然引入室內，不僅能調節室內光環境，也能讓人心情變好。

（改編自：https：//zhuanlan.zhihu.com/p/21834949）

第九課

聽力一

錄音一

M：為什麼家裏都不開燈？

F：現在是晚上八點半，全球都要參加"地球一小時"環保活動，為地球發聲。

M：對哦，這是為了應對全球氣候變化提出的節能環保活動。

F：是的，每年三月的最後一個星期六，大家都要為地球熄燈一小時，表示對節能環保的支持。

錄音二

M：為了面對、適應、解決氣候和污染問題，我們應該如何實現城市的可持續發展？

F：我認為減少碳排放、開發綠色建築才能讓城市發展更具可持續性，也能減少城市發展對氣候的惡劣影響，治理污染問題。

錄音三

M：聽説你家新裝了太陽能熱水器，效果怎麼樣？

F：效果很好啊！太陽能不但節能省錢，而且在使用時不會對環境造成污染。太陽能熱水器還可以用很久，使用壽命最長可達十五年。只要水箱中有熱水，就不會出現先熱後冷的現象。

M：那沒有太陽的時候，就沒有熱水了嗎？

F：下雨天，可以用電加熱。其實太陽能熱水器在下雨天仍舊在工作，只是加熱的熱水溫度達不到用戶洗澡的需要，但是水箱中的水是溫的，比普通的自來水溫度高，因此，就算是陰雨天使用，它也比普通電熱水器省電。

M：不錯不錯，我讓我媽媽也去買一台。

錄音四

M：各位好，今天給大家介紹電是如何發出來的。最普遍的方法是火力發電，就是通過燃燒煤炭或者某些材料進行發電，但這個方法容易污染環境。現在很多國家也會利用水力發電，把水往低處流的能量轉化成電能；還會利用風力發電，在田野、沙漠和海面上，裝上大風車，把風能轉化為電能。水力發電和風力發電都屬於清潔電能，是可再生能源，有利於環境保護。

錄音五

F：聽眾朋友們，晚上好！今天跟大家聊聊可再生能源的缺點。首先，可再生能源需要的技術或設備比較貴。其次，可再生能源不穩定，不能一整天持續地提供能量。比如太陽能，到晚上能量就會不足；如果乾旱，不下雨，水能源就會減少。而燃燒煤炭等不可再生能源就可以在任何時候發電。

錄音六

M：什麼是垃圾分類？

F：我們生活中產生的大量垃圾，正在嚴重影響我們的生存環境，危害我們的健康，垃圾分類就是按照要求將垃圾分類處理。

M：為什麼要垃圾分類？

F：垃圾分類收集後，便於對其進行分別處置。生活垃圾分類處理可以減少佔地，去掉能回收的部分就可以減少 50% 以上的生活垃圾。垃圾分類還可以減少環境污染。比如廢棄的電池含有毒物質，會對人體產生嚴重的危害；土壤中的塑料會導致農作物減產，因此回收和再利用可以減少危害。最後，垃圾分類還可以變廢為寶。回收 1500 噸廢紙，可以少砍伐用於生產 1200 噸紙的林木。因此，垃圾分類既環保，又節約資源。

聽力二

記：王部長，您好！謝謝你接受《海峽時報》的採訪。您能告訴我們新加坡是如何處理垃圾的嗎？

王：新加坡的所有垃圾經過分類處理後，會被送到垃圾島上。它是新加坡唯一的海上垃圾填埋場，由於填埋的垃圾已經過燃燒處理，所以不會發出臭味。

記：按照現在每天接收 2100 噸垃圾的運送速度，大約到 2045 年這個垃圾島就填滿了，無法再接收新的垃圾。新加坡政府將如何解決這個問題呢？

王：是的。為了延長垃圾島的使用壽命，我們希望每天運送的垃圾量可以減少約三分之一。要實現這一目標，需要改革垃圾處理方式，對個人、企業進行"減少、再用和回收垃圾"的宣傳教育。

記：垃圾島除了填埋垃圾，還有其他什麼作用嗎？

王：新加坡垃圾島是唯一一個鼓勵公眾參訪的垃圾填埋場，通過生態還原向遊客開放，遊客可以在星期一至星期五登島遊覽。這一切都源於新加坡政府建設和諧生態環境的理念。許多學校還會組織學生去島上接受環保教育，向下一代傳播最先進的環保理念。

記：隨著全球溫室效應越來越顯著，全球海平面持續上升。據報道，新加坡周圍的海平面 40 年來上升了 14 厘米。我們應該如何應對海平面上升呢？

王：如果人類不控制溫室氣體排放量，海平面將加速上升，到了 2100 年可能上升超過 1 米或更多。未來 100 年新加坡政府將投入至少 1000 億元，應對海平面上升造成的威脅。我們將興建第二個水泵房，加強排水能力；也會探討以填海的方式在東部海岸外填海造島，形成新的蓄水池來防洪。

（改編自：https：//www.shicheng.news/show/935667.amp）

責任編輯　郭　楊
書籍設計　吳丹娜
排　　版　陳先英　楊　錄

FUTURE

Coursebook 2

掃描二維碼或登錄網站 www.jpchinese.org/future2 聆聽錄音、下載參考答案。

Scan the QR code or log in to listen to the recording, and download the reference answer.

書　　名　展望 —— IGCSE 0523 & IBDP 中文 B SL（課本二）（繁體版）
Future - IGCSE 0523 & IBDP Chinese B SL (Coursebook 2) (Traditional Character Version)

編　　著　吳星華

出　　版　三聯書店（香港）有限公司
香港北角英皇道 499 號北角工業大廈 20 樓
Joint Publishing (H.K.) Co., Ltd.
20/F., North Point Industrial Building,
499 King's Road, North Point, Hong Kong

香港發行　香港聯合書刊物流有限公司
香港新界荃灣德士古道 220-248 號 16 樓

印　　刷　中華商務彩色印刷有限公司
香港新界大埔汀麗路 36 號 14 字樓

版　　次　2024 年 6 月香港第一版第一次印刷

規　　格　大 16 開（215 × 278 mm）248 面

國際書號　ISBN 978-962-04-5460-8